IN BLOOD & ICE

A VAMPIRE ICE AGE NOVEL, BOOK 1

SUSAN PERSON

PERSON
PUBLISHING

For my mother, my biggest cheerleader.

IN BLOOD & ICE

CHAPTER 1

JOSEPHINE

Blood. The only currency valuable enough to trade, whether vampire or human. Worth more than water or diamonds in a world covered with ice. And, unlike the ice, the deposits of red gold had diminished.

My role in these dire times waited for me a few feet away. The excitement of the mission, a chance of adventure, built inside me. I stood straight, making myself taller, and rapped my knuckles on the solid wood door. Determination pushed any nerves away. Permission not needed, I entered my father's office.

"Josephine." He smiled from behind the large oak desk. The massive desk should dwarf someone so lean and tall, but it only seemed to create a frame around him. He motioned me forward. Friendly but formal. His tone normal, but his brows pinched together. A hint of fresh blood drifted off his breath.

I stood across from him and ignored the hollow emptiness formed around my heart. The love he gave harsh compared to my mother's gentle touch. "Hello, Father. You've made a decision?"

"So eager," He said, his face grave. "You will be the first expedition team we have sent in thirty years. The last one never came back. Still want the job?"

As his heir, he expected me to lead, but the risk taking of traveling outside the immediate area delighted me. My prepared list on my mini-tablet in my pocket, I reached in for it. "Yes, I already have a list of team members--"

"The team members have been chosen. I'm asking you to the lead them."

My fingers loosened around the mini, and I left it snug in the pouch. Profanities formed. I clamped my teeth down on the inside of my jaw. The obscenities remained safe in my throat, which tightened from the restraint. "May I see the names?" I dropped into the padded chair across from the ostentatious desk he so loved.

His shoulders relaxed a small fraction. "Of course." He slid his larger tablet across the desk to me.

I cleared my throat. A knot remained solid, as if grasped by a vampire's hand ready to rip it free. "Vincent Cavanaugh is on the list?" My gut twisted in an awkward dance similar to how bitter wine mixed with old blood tasted. A little anticipation and a lot of pain. The last person I would have chosen for my team. I wouldn't trust him as a poison tester, much less on a life or death mission.

"Yes, he's the best tracker. You'll need him."

"What about the tracker on Captain Scott's team? He's more than adequate."

"He's not gifted like Vincent." My father's eyes shift slightly out of focus. An action only a vampire would see. "No one is as gifted as him."

The tablet clanked against his desk where I dropped it.

Father's eyes focused back on me. "Knowing what is out

there as early as possible is going to help you. Whether or not you admit it, you need him."

"Need? He's part of the former military. They aren't the most loyal to the vampire world."

"His allegiance is with us."

"How sure are you?"

His eyes darkened, and his voice lowered. "I'll tolerate you questioning me in private, but it will not happen in public again. Are we clear?"

"Yes, we're clear." A good soldier would follow without question. My hands, clasped tight enough to cause a twinge of pain, rested in my lap. The discomfort kept me in the present. "Now, how sure are you?"

"It's been a hundred years, Josephine. A hundred years since he pledged his allegiance to me. What more evidence do you need?"

I couldn't argue the point. He'd never given us one reason to doubt his allegiance to the Emperor, my father. His betrayal was personal to me and to me alone. I pursed my lips against the ache in my gut.

"The blood stores have been increased in anticipation of the journey. You'll be allowed to take as much as you need."

"That's dangerous."

The blood stores furnished food for our entire territory. Our devoted vampires depended on what we provided. Fewer and fewer donors could be found to replace those lost as their lifespan grew shorter. Blood prized above all else, the price increased each day. With vast stores, our house lived without the hunger many faced in the territory, but it created a delicate cycle between humans and vampires. If the cycle tipped one way or the other, it could mean extinction.

"We can't afford to increase the extraction. It's too risky. We can ration and make do," I said.

He turned his head away, and his voice was a low rumble. "No, it is important you complete this mission. Our future depends on it."

"If you lose your donors, it won't matter if we come back."

"We're losing them anyway." He leaned his head into his hand. Fingertips rubbed his temple.

I slid a hand across the table and stopped short in front of him. He had never been affectionate like Mother. "Then we'll find new donors. We will."

He stood from behind his desk and walked around to the front. His back stiff. *Had he sparred this evening?* Unusual for his body language to be so rigid when we spoke alone. A hand rested on my shoulder. Fingers a little tighter than normal.

I assessed his grip. His affection doled in small doses, unlike Mother. My gaze turned to his face. I studied it but did not find answers. Maybe the urgency of the mission put him on edge.

"You will succeed, or we will all die."

Every muscle in my body tightened. The death he spoke of, anything but a gentle passing, ended in madness and brutal bloodlust. Rogues. My stomach rolled at the thought. Bile rose and hung in my throat. *The worst of vampire kind.*

The weight of the vampire world on my leadership sat heavy on my chest. Skilled and experienced vampires failed before me, but my practice sessions and missions increased in preparation. I can do this. I will do this. My peers called me the most skilled fighter seen in decades. Second only to my friend, Killian, but I'd surpassed him with my agility, as many of the elders had told me. The biggest compliment I could receive.

I stood and hugged my father. A human gesture, but one we observed.

His arms wrapped around me to return the gentle embrace.

The action caught me off guard. Father was never accused of being soft with his touch.

"You remind me so much of your mother at times like this." Strange comparison, considering she spent most of her time in the garden. I inherited her build, dark wavy hair, and blue eyes, but I'd never possess the same kindness as her. Her compassion was legendary to those who knew her. I couldn't entertain the thought I was anything close to the incredible force she radiated.

He put his hands on either side of my face. "I chose you as my successor, so you must return." To most, he was the Emperor, to a few he was Ezra, but he was my father.

As Ezra's biological daughter, I'd been the obvious choice for successor but not guaranteed until his announcement a few days ago. Satisfied to lead missions, I hoped it would be a long time before I'd be called on to rule. My exploration days would end when I succeeded Ezra, and I would mourn the loss.

"I will return. I promise." A vow made to be kept. My honor demanded it.

Not to look back was our way. The door closed with a soft thud, and I headed for my room.

The click of my shoes on the marble floor reminded me it might be months before I'd wear heels again. No complaints there. I'd also be in tight quarters with Vin for possibly months. The door to my room in sight, I rushed to the safety it offered, my only sanctuary away from prying eyes and gossip. The toe of my shoe caught on a crack and pitched me forward. My hands planted against the wall to steady me. Thank the gods no one saw that. Clumsy vampires weren't allowed and damn sure didn't lead important missions. A vision flashed of Vin pressing me into a wall on a night when thundersnow drowned out the sounds of our first night together. I clamped my eyes shut and counted backwards from ten.

My fingers wrapped around the door handle until my nails dug into my palm. The desire to lean against the door until the memory disappeared tried to derail me. I depressed the brass lever with my thumb and slipped inside. No time for personal drama. I pulled the snow boots out of my closet. Our bodies were impervious to the cold, so we didn't really need them. But the humans did, and we needed to look as human as possible. The appearance of being human allowed us to get closer.

Excitement crept up my spine. We would use my childhood home as the base of operations while we explored. The last place I saw my mother alive. The last trace of decency in our society died there. My elation dwindled. Life for everyone changed in a matter of days. Since then, nothing mattered but blood.

A soft knock and the door opened. I didn't need to look up to know it was her. "Hello, Agata. I can pack for myself, but thank you." I faced her.

"Yes, Miss. I understand, but it's my job." Her hair piled on top of her head in the usual bun. It made her look taller than me, but we stood the same height. She wore the casual grey uniform with no adornments today. The dressier uniforms reserved for when visitors were on site, but those had been fewer as the years passed.

"Very well." I smiled at her. She'd anticipated my every

need in the decades since she joined our household. Father hired her in an attempt to replace the goodness we lost when Mother died. Agata's kind demeanor never gave away any resistance to the terrible system.

She poured a glass of crimson liquid from the carafe on the table and handed it to me.

I took a long, slow sip. We never hungered in the mansion unlike those in other parts of the compound, but Agata refused to drink with me. It violated one of the many unwritten rules between us. A rule my mother hadn't allowed at our old home and one I would change when my time to rule came to be.

In my absence for the mission, she would be required to serve others, and I worried how she would be treated. Some openings in other areas requiring more skill held some promise.

"Agata, you are smart. Why do you not do something more? You could work in the computer lab. I've seen how well you navigate them."

"The payment is better here than anywhere else. I provide the blood for my family."

"You mean the one who created you, and by the pay is better here, you mean they prefer to hire born vampires in the lab." Bitterness filled me at the divide between born and created and how it expanded after the ice covered so much of the world.

Her eyes focused on the floor. "I have many siblings."

Selfish of the vampires to sire so many with the knowledge of how the others treated them. The created vampires always treated as lesser than the born. "So, your wage covers the blood for all of them? None of them work?"

"They do, but it's not enough to sustain them."

"You're the bloodwinner." She didn't volunteer any of her life details without me asking. Why hadn't I asked about her more often? Because exploration called me with a constant nag, and I paid little attention to anything else. *I'd do better on my return.*

"You are good to me. Better than others treat us."

While I was thankful for the kind words, it didn't make up for the ignorance of others. "Even as demanding as I am? Even better than being at home?"

She paused for a long time and nodded. "You are far from demanding, Miss." A soft smile formed.

"I've insisted you call me Josie since we met, but you still call me Miss."

"It's better to follow protocol." She turned back to the suitcase.

And there it was. The separation between us made by those born to vampirism and those created by others. It had always been so, from what my mother told me. She never believed it should be that way. She died near the start of the new age, and Father insisted I conform into this life of better treatment than those created. Much like my mother, I never understood the division. To me, either you made blood, or you drank it, and all vampires drank it. There should be no difference. Yet, the created ones, considered inferior, weren't born into it and needed more blood to sustain them. *Except Vin... He'd always been different.*

Vincent Cavanaugh judged as the exception, created but existed on little blood. A phenomenon among us my father found intriguing. Vin claimed no memories of his creator, which sparked rumors around the compound. No doubt it made him even more interesting to my father. He intrigued

IN BLOOD & ICE

most everyone, but my feelings were more. *Much more.* I'd have to bury them to make it through the trip.

Solitude to think about the mission beckoned me. "Thank you, Agata."

I left her to pack and walked to the armory in search of a few quiet moments to clear my head. The crude weapons secured there kept more for the humans to help fight when needed. *From a time when there were more humans.* We'd take some with us for appearances. I'd always been partial to the swords, but the sunshine sticks proved more effective on Rogues, brutal and mad creatures. Their sensitivity to sun was extreme compared to even the created vampires. A peak of sun through the clouds ignited them like kindling. A sunshine stick accomplished the same task when clouds provided cover for them.

Distinct steps echoed through the passageway. A faint fragrance of woods and vampire announced his arrival. My mind drifted to a time when his scent brought me joy. My chest ached.

He made a special trip to get those boots he had altered for him. His lucky boots. It was a ritual for him before every battle or excursion. They'd been repaired a dozen times, at least. Probably not even an original part left on them.

I slid a sword out of the slot on the wall. " Hi, Vincent." I didn't look up or turn around. I didn't need to see the dark hair my fingers had been through.

"Josie, I wouldn't have expected to see you here."

Warmth exploded in me at my pet name on his lips, like an unwelcome bomb he left behind. "I trained with them, too."

"You don't believe in using them."

"But you do, because you cling to your human life." I glanced over my shoulder, willing the words to sting with the fierceness of fangs in a savage battle. His blue eyes resembled the ice that covered the empire. The only ice in this world that melted and looked back at me.

"I enjoy the challenge and skill of each one."

"That could be said for many of your interests." I tightened my grasp on the sword, hoping it would give me some resolve, and faced him.

His voice softened. "Josie." He twisted some loose hair and tucked it behind my ear. Strong fingers rested in a caress on my cheek. "If you would just listen to me."

My mouth went dry with a strong urge to soothe it with venom. His touch chipped open a part of me I'd closed off. I wanted to reach out and run my hand over the stubble of a beard, dark like his hair. Instead, I closed my eyes against him. My unneeded heart pounded in my chest. "No one calls me Josie." The proximity smothered me even though I didn't breathe. I shuffled back away from him.

His hand dropped to his side.

I studied his agonized face.

"Why don't you believe me?"

Because I can't. My heart pounded faster. The inside of my throat closed. I cleared it. "If we're going to be on the same team, we need to set some rules."

He nodded. His eyes crinkled at the corner.

A tingle sparked in my chest. I tamped it back down. "This is my team. I am the leader, and I expect my commands to be followed without question."

"Like your father," he said under his breath.

"Our personal relationship no longer exists. It is strictly an expedition. You will not speak of our previous time together to me or anyone else on the team."

"Fine, Josie." His voice flat and low.

The world slowed down each time he used my nickname. The constant reminder interfered with my judgement. Formality needed to be in place. "And you will address me by my name. Josephine."

Crestfallen, he relented. "You'll always be my Josie, but I will respect your wishes from here on out. When do we leave?"

I clamped down on the inside of my cheek to keep myself grounded in the moment. So many times, I wished I could be his Josie.

"Tomorrow at dusk. Father ordered additional stores for us that should be ready by then," I said.

"Is that safe?"

I couldn't blame him for questioning Father's choice when I questioned it myself.

"No, but we are at a critical point where it is only delaying the inevitable. We need to find new resources."

"Do you think this is the next step in evolution?"

"Don't be silly, Vincent." I slid the sword back into the sheath on the wall. He liked to listen to the human stories and the theories that we were on the verge of a major evolutionary change brought on by the ice age.

"I'm being serious. Humans nearly died at the start of the ice age. The way to survive was to become vampire. With so many of us, maybe this is the next natural--"

"The world changed because humans had no regard for the resources of the planet. They caused the earth to transform from ten percent to ninety percent ice. Vampires do not need to consume the same natural resources to survive."

His face tightened. "You are looking at it like a vampire."

"I am a vampire." I studied his face. His dark hair cut in an edgy style the younger vamps liked. Those crystal-like eyes were unusual in a vamp or a human. His good looks probably the reason he was turned. "And so are you."

He sneered. "I'm an outsider. A lowly created one. Never good enough for the born ones."

"You know I don't believe in that split. I've felt like an outsider my entire existence, and I was born to it." I looked away and ran my tongue across the point of one of my fangs. The sharp slice leaked blood and venom. A wake up call to settle the sting of memories.

"But you're not only a vampire or a born one. There's a destiny for you. You'll be a great leader when Ezra relinquishes his time. You don't understand the life of a created one."

"He'll never relinquish. It will be a true death when he does. We know war is likely. Vampires are eating vampires in other regions. It will not matter who is born and who is created if we can't feed the territory." The blood and venom I'd swallowed rose back up. The horrible cost of a vamp-eat-vamp world would be annihilation of our kind. All of us. Born and created.

"We eliminated some on our recent mission. Not me specifically, but it was done." He held up a fist to the wall, but he didn't punch it. "There has to be another way. Vampires, born and created, are starving. Humans are so scarce. They can't control their thirst to maintain the supply."

"Yes, they will not last long this way." *Neither will we.*

"The vampires or the humans?"

"Both. Which is why our mission must succeed. Are you able to meet my conditions, Vincent?" *If he doesn't agree, do I have the strength to kick him off the team? Would Father even allow it?*

"Of course, Jos..." He coughed. "Josephine."

His lack of argument surprised me. "Be packed and ready. We leave as soon as our rations are loaded."

I brushed past him into the hallway. Weapons clanked together from behind the closed door. My back flattened against the wall.

Months with him. Closed up in tight quarters. My only choice to channel the pain into the mission.

CHAPTER 2

JOSIE

Helicopters, snowmobiles, and the multipurpose tundra vehicles took up the majority of the space in the hangar. The tundras were designed to be snow tanks capable of carrying humans, but they were more like a luxury ship with holding areas. The snow tires could be retracted into a continuous track depending on the surface. Vampires had used them to gather donors. Four soldiers would be in the second tundra. Two others planned to join Killian, Vincent, and me in the lead vehicle. The gear for the team stood near a large track of the latter, along with the blood. *Excessive. Way more than we should need.*

"We can travel faster on foot than the tundra vehicles," Vincent said.

Ezra clasped Vincent's shoulder. "Humans will know you are vampires if you do not take them. It makes you somewhat more approachable."

"Few humans can afford transportation capable of traversing the ice and snow."

"The wealthy do," Ezra replied before I could. "The infrastructure we maintained has helped."

Wealthy humans traded in blood just like wealthy vampires. Although humans found a harder time holding on to it. The business became more lucrative as more donors died off. A lot of outlying areas lost all their donors. Vampire skills were better at detecting the purest of blood, and the wealthy humans would employ created ones to find blood for a portion of the recovery. The traders sold it for a premium to those areas. More and more human traders ended up as donors instead of dealers. The ice age broke the cycle and made it an ever-tightening circle. Ezra shut down attempts to question it. I hated what the frozen world had done to our world.

"We'll take the tundra vehicles," I said. The instruments on board would be helpful if we encountered white out conditions. "Everyone load up."

Vincent grabbed my elbow and pulled me aside. "You're bringing Killian?"

I jerked my elbow free. My body reacted to the smallest touch from him, and I didn't need that distraction. "Yes." Not divulging Father had assembled the team.

"Killer Killian's personality isn't exactly inviting."

"No, but he's strong." I ignored the reference to the nickname from the younger vampires. Other vampires referred to Killian as the tall blonde powerhouse. His good looks and strength won him much favor in our community, including with my father.

"And he has made it no secret he wants you."

"None of your business, Vincent." Killian had been a loyal friend to me in some of the worst days of my existence.

"As you wish." He bowed and spun towards the ramp. His

normally quiet steps pounded the metal.

Jealous? He had no right if he was. How in the hell am I going to deal with this for months?

The last inside, we secured the vehicle. The final step sealed the compartment airtight. Our scent concealed, for the most part, to prevent outsiders finding us.

Large hangar doors parted to expose the sparse green surroundings, and the clock started on our mission. I glanced at Vin. Venom leaked into my mouth. *No. Don't even think it.* I faced ahead at the terrain in front of us.

The small amount of vegetation around the compound expanded only a short distance over decades. It took mere minutes before we were in the permafrost. Our patrols covered this distance easily, but we were headed past the regular limits. The vehicles jostled us around so hard there were no naps. Not that we needed them, but the time passed slower without one. I trained my eyes out the window. The ice and snow already deep only a few hours into the journey. A drastic change from the green fields we left.

"What's the temperature here?"

"Still hovering around freezing but barely," Vincent said. "It's already dropping. Are you going to tell us our precise destination?"

"North," I said, eyes still on the frozen ground.

"That's not exactly what I meant, Princess."

"I'm not a princess. I'm the daughter of the Emperor."

"That's kind of a princess," Vincent said.

"Not really. He's not a king."

"But he is a ruler."

"Why do you have to challenge everything? Just let it go." I spun the seat and narrowed my eyes on him.

"I thought we were talking." He smirked.

"I don't feel like idle chatter." My hand found the lever and spun the chair to face the instrument room. I walked over to the radar panels and leaned on Killian's chair. "Anything out there?"

He kept his eyes on the monitors and his voice low, so the others couldn't hear. "No, nothing yet. Are we headed where I think we are?"

I lowered my voice to match his. "If we can get that far. Father insisted we use it as our base." The green we enjoyed at the Southern Compound contrasted in a harsh extreme to the deep levels of ice and snow we encountered here. Some animals survived, some died off, and some moved south when we did. Some vampires turned to animal blood to survive. Father refused to do so. The land covered with small trees, but otherwise as baron as the born vampires had become.

"Do any of the others know?"

"No, and let's keep it that way." The Northern Compound lived in the memories of most as a time of an unlimited food source. I didn't want to get their hopes up tit would be anything like we left, especially given none of the earlier missions made it back to the Southern Compound.

"Of course," he paused. "You shouldn't torture him." Killian inclined his head in Vin's direction.

It wasn't torture. Was it? I swatted his arm. "Out of everyone, I thought you'd be on my side."

"I love you, Josephine. We've known each other our entire existence. If you loved me, I'd fight for you."

My heart nor my head could return the love the way he wanted, but I did care for him. "I do love you, my friend."

"In a vampire family sort of way," Killian said.

"I will never live those words down. Will I?" I gave him a half smile. Friends from our youth, Killian and I dated during our early twenties. My father's strong desire for us to be together caused me to push away. We both moved on to other relationships. By the time he made his feelings known years later, I had grown past our puppy love. We became the closest confidants, and he took the position of the head of my personal guard. When Vin showed up, things changed. Our friendship was strained for a while, but we got past it. He even tried to take the blame for Vin's betrayal.

He laughed the warm Killian laugh others rarely heard. "No, never." He cleared his throat. "All young vampires make mistakes. I'm sure it's very overwhelming turning from a human to one of us."

Mistakes, yes, but we have consequences for those mistakes too. "I don't understand why everyone is so supportive of him. Even Father, who would have never been for me marrying a created, wants me to forgive him."

"Ezra wants you to be happy. Something that was denied him twice."

"I'm not sure that second one counts. My mother was the love of his life." They had the love story we all wanted. The kind that never relented and never wavered. That wasn't Vincent and me. "I don't know what makes him think I'd be happy with someone who can't be faithful." A pit formed in my abdomen. *Gut punch, saying it aloud. Damn. Every time.*

"You should at least let him explain."

"Careful, Killian. The others might find out how sensitive you are." My heart couldn't take an explanation. It broke every time I was in the same room with him.

"I can ruin that impression easily."

"I have no doubts." I laughed and patted his shoulder.

The monitors turned red and flashed in front of us. My stomach tightened.

"Go buckle up. We might need to run," Killian said.

My hands shook as I buckled the crisscrossed straps. "Vincent, do you see anything?"

"Not yet." His chair now faced forward to the direction the alarms warned us to.

Killian stood between the driver and Vincent.

Two figures formed in front of us. *Our first encounter already.* My muscles tightened. "Are they?"

"I'm not sure," Vincent said. He stood. Hands on the dash, he leaned in close to the window.

I wrestled to unbuckle the straps and stood next to him. "Children? There haven't been any born vampires in close to a century." *What if they are?*

"I don't think they were born. Look at their eyes."

"It's forbidden to turn human children." I grabbed my stomach. "They endanger their kind." Bile rose to the top of my throat. I didn't dare swallow; afraid it would come right back.

"My kind, you mean." Vincent glanced at me for only a second. "They're starving. Look at how hollow their faces are."

"They've fed on other vampires. See how their eyes glow. They aren't just red. The illumination is like a light on our instrument panel." They'd become my worst nightmare, mindless, out of control, and lost in their thirst. My heart beat fast in my chest. Each thump pounded painfully against my chest cavity.

"Stop here. We need to release them," Killian said.

The crunched ice noise from the tread ceased. The tundra vehicle stopped to a short distance away. I jostled forward with the motion.

"You mean end them." Vincent stiffened.

"Yes, they will never grow and will always want vampire

blood now."

"I can't kill a child," Vincent said.

"They are no longer children."

"I can't." Vincent's head dropped.

It wasn't in me to ask him to do it, but it needed to be done. "Killian, radio the other vehicles. We need someone to eliminate them."

"I'll do it," Killian said.

"I know you can, but take some of the others with you for my peace of mind. The Rogues might not be alone."

"Done."

Killian took three of the soldiers from the second tundra with him. The two female created cannibals cocked their heads to the side.

"I can't watch them murder two young girls," Vincent said. He turned his back and moved to the rear of the vehicle.

"They are not humans any longer, nor are they young girls." Even as I said the words I knew to be true, I knew he was right, too. These creatures didn't ask to become this, but the people they once were no longer existed. My eyes stung as I fought to keep the liquid from spilling out the corners, but I knew nothing would save them at this point, either.

"So you said. I still see kids."

"Because you were human, and you see human first." My thoughts clouded.

His voice grew louder. "And you're a vampire and only ever see vampire."

I stepped backwards. Father raised me to view everything through a vampire lens. *Was I too jaded to see all sides? How could I see it from a human view when all I'd ever known was vampire? Vincent might be right.* "It's incredibly sad, Vin, but they haven't been human in a very long time. There is no saving them. No turning back to human. They will never have a thought other than of vampire blood." The idea of ending them was hard to swallow for me too, but I couldn't say that to him. A leader shouldn't acknowledge weakness.

A flash of light illuminated the tundra and drew my attention. The bodies burst into flames.

"It's wrong, Josie." His hands covered his face. "It's callous and wrong."

"No, it's survival, and more importantly, it's a release for them from the pain. We will likely need to end more Rogues on this mission. Are you sure you are up for it?" Although, I wouldn't say it out loud. I wanted him here, but I wouldn't force him to stay.

"I—" A shuffle outside the tundra interrupted Vin.

Killian opened the door. His clothes soiled with the dark blood of a vampire who'd fed on others for quite some time.

"Was there a fight?"

"No more than usual," Killian said. "We didn't use sunshine sticks, because I noticed something interesting."

"Did they give you any information?" Any knowledge from their crazed minds would need scrutiny, but we might glean something useful.

"They'd lost their minds long ago. Probably years. They had these marks on them. Do you know what it is?" Killian held up a piece of flesh.

I looked at Vin. My stomach tightened.

"It's a military tattoo," Vincent said.

I met his eyes. His eyes held concern. I'd seen the tattoo before, and it always raised questions with few answers.

He slipped his jacket off and pulled his sleeve up. His mark a little lighter, but the same stamp.

I gripped the chair. "Vampires can't get tattoos. We heal--"

"Too quickly. Which means they got them before they became vampire," Killian said.

My chest tightened. Only a monster would brand children. "They were too young. The military was disbanded." I looked to Vincent for confirmation.

"Maybe they turned a long time ago." Vincent shrugged.

"A hundred years?"

"Definitely not." Killian said.

"Someone branded them and left them here using the military brand?" I reached my hand up to my throat. Someone, likely a vampire, branded and turned children under the guise of a military unit that no longer existed.

"Why is the question." Vincent moved to the front and examined the pieces of flesh. "My guess would be they were used for watch dogs. Tell me they covered the seals on the vehicles. The last thing we need is an attack for the high value target on board."

"We're supposed to look human from a distance. Can't very well do that if we have the Emperor's seal announcing who we are." Killian slid into the driver's seat and sent the soldier to the back.

"We need to get out of here." Vincent sat on the edge of the co-pilot seat and stared out at the ice.

"Something else out there?" I asked.

Vin rolled his shoulder. "It doesn't feel right."

"Do it." I nodded to Killian. When I tracker focused and became intense, you trusted their instincts. "Get us out of here."

"Killian, can we go helio?" Vin asked.

"No, the temperature has dropped too low for it to fly," Killian said.

"Fuck. I don't like this." Vin grabbed his shoulder and

shook his arm.

I whipped my head around to look at Vincent. The shock of a profanity from his mouth caught me off guard. "Are you sensing something?"

His tracking skills more powerful than any tracker in Ezra's empire. My senses went on alert.

"I don't know." He scratched at his arm. Nails dug at the mark on his shoulder. Red beads formed. "I feel ill."

"Killian, we need to get out of here." Vin's skills weren't the cause of this. I'd seen this happen before in many created ones, and the more distance from the source, the better. I rejected the outcome I'd seen most often. *Ending. This will not be his ending.*

I hoisted Vincent up out of the seat.

His nails scraped deep against the tattoo. Blood covered the sleeve. His steps froze two away from the chair at the back of the vehicle.

Vincent's body stiffened in my arms. His full weight now in my control. Small twitches led to a full seizure.

I held back a sob and eased him down to the ground. My throat tightened. His symptoms progressed faster than I'd witnessed with others. My heart broke into a thousand pieces, and I turned to the gods Vin believed in. *Please.*

He coughed up blood. His last meal. *Not good. A later stage reaction. Damn. Damn. Damn.*

My fingers wrapped around his hand while I slipped his head into my lap. "You're going to be all right. Focus on my voice."

His body thrashed. The force lifted his shoulders off the ground and crimson erupted from his lips. It bubbled up and over his mouth like a fountain. A terrible red geyser. The eruption grew in strength and shot the length of his body.

My voice echoed off the walls of the tundra. "Killian, get us as far away from here as you can. Now." *If he dies in my arms... No. He's going to live.*

"We can't leave the others. They are cleaning up outside."

"It's an order."

I stroked Vin's forehead and leaned in close so my lips touched his ear. "You have to live. This existence isn't done with you. I haven't had a chance to forgive you yet."

His eyes rolled back. Blood streamed from the corners. Arms and legs thrashed in a painful dance. He coughed and gagged red fluid.

I held him as still as possible, which didn't help. Even with my vision blurred, I realized it pooled around us. *Too much blood. Way too much.*

I closed my eyes. *Pure hell. This is Hell.* I focused on what I knew. *Distance helped break the bond.* Each second took us further away, but this bond didn't relent.

Vin's eyes remained closed. Blood stopped pouring out of him. His body stilled.

Too still.

My forehead pressed against his, I whispered. "Don't die." A stupid thing to say. We didn't die. Not like humans. Our kind simply ceased to exist. *This can't be happening. Not now.*

Awareness came to me. The tundra wasn't moving. "Killian? Why have we stopped?"

"The others will not be able to catch up if we go further." He knelt beside me. "Gods, that's a lot of blood."

I closed my eyes tight against the tears. "I know."

"Most do not survive the call," Killian said. "What can we do?" Killian squeezed my shoulders.

I wiped at the blood on his face and made a smeared mess. "Wait. It's up to him now."

CHAPTER 3

VIN

M y hand found my throat. The inside burned like I'd eaten fresh coals from a kiln. "Thirsty," I croaked.

A blood bag. In my hand. I ripped it open with my teeth and sucked the contents down. "More." A delicate blood covered hand passed me another one. *Josie.* I slurped the second back deep into my mouth. It coated my throat and slid down to my gut. The burn reduced to an irritation.

She handed me another bag.

I downed it in three quick gulps. Conscious of our limited stores, I declined another one despite the ache for it.

My hunger under control, I sat up and my back protested. My neck stiff and tight, I rubbed my throat. "What happened?"

Josie's forehead wrinkled. Her voice soft. "Your creator called you."

"Now? After a hundred years?" *What an asshole. Who the fuck does that?* I'd witnessed it a few times, but the created vampires couldn't resist it. Some never returned. It looked different from the other side, and I thought it would feel different. More of a draw. It was pain. Sharp twisted pain. I ran a hand through my hair, and it came back wet. *Red. Blood.*

"My thoughts too." Her hands and clothes streaked with crimson stains. Her cheeks, blotted with dried vampire tears, chipped a piece off my heart.

"Gods. You're covered in blood. Is it mine or yours or..."

"All yours. You power puked it on me." Her forehead creased.

How will I get that memory of me out of her head? I contemplated my chances of fitting into the storage compartment for the remainder of the trip. "What better way to let someone know you care?" I shrugged.

She smiled and wiped at her eyes. Pink smeared across her pale skin.

She's upset. She does care. I can't have her worrying about me on this mission, but maybe this will open a door between us. "Hey. I'm ok." I touched her face with my own blood coated hand.

She covered it with her own. *Her mouth opened and closed. Maybe she will talk to me now. And if my creator calls again, I might not survive. I have to try.*

"So you're ready to listen to what I have to say?" I leaned closer to her.

Her smile faded. "Get cleaned up. Humans won't come near you with all that blood, and you smell like death." She slumped against the chair right outside the small bathroom.

"You could come shower with me. Cleaning you up is the least I could do." I wagged my eyebrows at her. I recognized the straight-faced look. *She'd already closed the door on the moment.*

A shadow lurked behind her. *Killian. Always there. Always in the way.*

She arched a perfect eyebrow. "I'll take care of myself."

"Are you going to wait here for me?"

"I don't have anything better to do."

"You could wash my back."

The corners of her mouth curved up, but she smashed her lips together. "Go wash that blood off, or I'm going to tell them to take off while you're still in there." *She smiled. Maybe the door isn't completely closed. Or maybe she just thought it was funny.*

"No way am I going to fit in that." I stared at the hobbit sized shower.

"Killian has gone weeks in these rovers. You'll fit."

I shut the door and muttered. "Killian doesn't shower, obviously."

Josie's laughter bubbled through the door. Vampirism. No privacy as usual. I missed that laugh, though. I missed the softness of her dark hair flowing through my fingers. I missed the way her perfect ass fit in my hand when she relinquished control.

Damn it. Let her go Cavanaugh. She's never going to believe you anyway.

That was a straight up pecker punch.

I looked at myself in the mirror. Red crust formed around my mouth from the dried blood. My reflection resembled a murder victim more than a killer. I hadn't taken a human life, that I knew of anyway, but I didn't turn down the supplies provided by Ezra either. Humans died in servitude to him, so I couldn't deny my own culpability. I wanted to hate this life, but even one night with Josie was worth it. *Even almost facing my ending like a created vampire with an asshole of a creator.*

Water steamed in the sink. I pulled the bloodied shirt up over my head and threw it in the corner. Josie was right. I stunk like death. *Nothing like the rotted flesh odor of vampire puke as a reminder I am undead.* The waterlogged washcloth dissolved the blood from my face, neck, and chest. The heat reminded me of humanity. I dunked my head into the sink. *Not going to work.*

I sighed and turned the shower on full blast. Steam filled the small closet of a room. Pealed the rest of my clothes off and stepped in. I hunched over so my head would fit under the showerhead.

Most of my memories from the brief time I lived were unrecognizable. So vague they could be any created vampire's from a time before ice covered most of the Earth. Before becoming vampire was the only option for survival. Before blood became a commodity more valuable than diamonds or platinum. My creator, whoever that was, had jumbled my brain up like scrambled eggs before they dumped me in Dallas. There had to be a reason for calling me now. My gut twisted tight like barbed wire around tender flesh. Whatever the reason, it couldn't be a coincidence it happened on this mission. I'd fight it to protect the team. To protect Josie.

"Is pretty boy getting beautiful for you?" Killian's voice travelled through the door.

"Evidently, I don't look human covered in blood, jackass," I said in my normal voice.

"Whatever. We can't stay here much longer. Put your junk in your pants already."

I swung the door open with the towel hung around my hips.

Josephine's eyes settled on my chest. Her tongue passed across her lips. Eyes traveled down.

I dropped the towel into a lower a drape . A feeble attempt to cover my reaction. "Where did they put our packs? I need a clean shirt."

"And pants." Josephine shook her head slightly and turned to one of bins on the wall. "You still wear a large, right?" She handed me a black t-shirt and jeans.

All in my size. "Whose stuff is this?"

"They are just some basics kept in case we need them for humans. Like the bottles of water in the other rover. Our stuff is in the storage compartment." She turned her back to me and walked to the front.

I tugged on the pants and pulled on the shirt. My boots had blood on them. First time it was mine. The floor cleaned to the point in almost sparkled while I was in the shower.

"Buckle up bitches," Killian said. "And Josephine." He took the driver's seat.

Josie sat in the instrument room.

I settled in the co-pilot seat. "We have a lot of ground to make up."

"Thanks to your blood vomit," he said. "You're not a very good vampire."

"Tell me something I don't already know, fucker."

"You owe me for having to clean up your buckets of guts off the floor." Killian flipped me the bird.

"How about you both shut up?" Josephine's authority did the job.

I glanced around. "Where is the rest of our crew?"

"You're upchucking scared them off." Killian chuckled.

"Dickhead," I said.

Josie's voice louder and harsher. "For gods' sake, children! I sent them to the other tundra. It seemed like it should be a private moment. Next time, we will all make barf jokes when someone nearly dies."

Killian and I exchanged side eye and smirks, but we shut our damn mouths.

I searched the white abyss in front of us. Trees blackened as if they had been burned, but others survived the permanent freeze. They stood lush and green among the remnants. The beauty once here long dead like us. *Except for Josie. Her beauty never changed.*

"We'll be in Dallas by the morning," I said. The path confirmed my suspicions.

"They don't call it that anymore," Josephine said.

I smiled. "So that is where we're headed. It will always be Dallas to me." I glanced over my shoulder at the instrument room.

She smiled back for a moment. She focused down on her shoes, and I saw blood spatters. A reminder of my near ending. The words she'd said while I was vulnerable came back to me. *Good enough for now.*

Oblivious to the rough ride, she headed towards the rear of the vehicle. I followed her actions. She tossed my bloody clothes from the bathroom. The door shut. Water sounds bounced through the air. Her balance had always been good, especially in bed. I tried not to think about the wetness flowing over her bare breasts. *Get it together, Cavanaugh.*

I needed her forgiveness, but not for what she thought I'd done. I needed her forgiveness for letting her go without a fight. It'd been too long. Too much time had passed for me to expect it. But she'd said she hadn't had a chance to do it. She said it when she thought my existence was ending. But maybe if I could get some time alone with her...

She and Killian were a better match. Both born to vampirism. He understood the lifestyle in a way I never would. The women on the compound followed him. His girl-friends had to like rough play, or so the rumors went, and I'd never be okay with anyone inflicting pain on Josephine.

"Hey, tracker ass," Killian said. "Aren't you supposed to be tracking instead of drooling over your future Empress?"

I shook my head and faced front. *How long had I been checked out?* I looked over my shoulder to find Josie back in the seat.

Her hair still damp. She drummed her fingers across her lips, but her smile showed through. "Vampires don't drool. It's a waste of venom."

"Maybe we could start a new business with your boyfriend." Killian smirked.

"He's not my boyfriend." Josie spun the chair around.

She could shut it all off in the time a human took a breath. A born vampire trait. Created vampires carried their emotions forward. *Hell, I took breaths as if I still needed them.* Her chest never made the rise and fall except to taste the air. The subtle differences a reminder of our origins.

No, I wasn't her boyfriend, and it was best for her. It didn't matter how long I existed. I'd never be able to change how I became vampire, and she'd never believe I'd been faithful no matter if I had proof or not.

My stomach hardened into a knot. "Ugghhh."

"Please tell me you're not going to blood vomit again," Killian said.

"I'd swear a knife stabbed my gut." I rubbed the spot.

Josie appeared at my side. "He's checking to see if you are still there."

"She," I said. "She's wondering if she killed me."

"She?" Josie's eyes widened. "I thought you didn't know who created you."

"I don't." I paused. Somehow, I knew my creator was a woman. It wasn't a memory but more of a confirmation. "But I do."

Josie and Killian exchanged a look. It must be more than a stomachache by those looks. They knew what it meant.

"Tell me already."

"Your creator is a born vampire," Josephine said. She stared at me like she waited for the answer to click. "Your creator can communicate with you."

"But didn't for all these years. Why would a born reach out to a created one after this long?" *When I'd seen it happen before, the vampires were in close proximity, and usually a created vampire had called another created. Born didn't usually call their discarded, created children, but the ones they kept close had a stronger connection.* "The connection had strength to it. How is that possible?"

"There's a reason she is now. She wants something from you," Killian said.

I could go if she summoned me again, but I'd sensed danger. "If I don't respond and she keeps summoning me, it will kill me."

"You're already dead, dumbass," Killian said.

"Yes, for all intents and purposes, it will kill you." Josie sank back into the seat and stared into the open space of the tundra. "This born vampire is strong. That's why your connection was powerful."

"So what can I do? What are my options?"

"Nothing," Josephine said. She gazed out at the frozen scene outside the window.

I faced Killian.

His jaw set. "Answer the summons, die, or kill the creator."

"Killing a born vampire is against our laws," Josie said. "You'd face judgement, with a certain sentence of ending."

"I'm screwed."

"Answer the call," Josie said. "It's the only option."

"It's his choice." Killian shrugged.

I sunk down into the seat. *Fucking hell.*

Maybe he hoped I wouldn't go, so I'd die, and he'd have Josie for himself. Not that I had her now.

Stay or leave the mission? No question. I'd stay if for no other reason than Josie.

CHAPTER 4

JOSIE

I'd never considered Vincent's creator could be a born vampire. Definitely not one as powerful as this one must be. My assumption had always been it was a created one who didn't know what they were doing. I'd assumed he'd been left at the compound gates out of desperation. A hundred years my assumption had been wrong. He'd been left for a purpose.

"Are we going to the old compound first?" Killian jarred me from my thoughts.

"Yes, to try to get the network back up," I said. "If the servers are still functional and the generators have power, we can establish communication."

"They pinged them before we left," Killian said.

"I see lights." Vincent's eyes glued to the horizon. "The sun will be up soon." I was the only one in our vehicle who couldn't be in the daylight.

Could one of the previous missions have made it? Could they have the compound up and running?

"Doesn't matter to me," Killian said." I'm not going to turn to ash."

"Don't be an ass, Killian." I slapped his shoulder. "Get to the compound."

He laughed. "We don't know what's waiting there for us. No one has been there in decades."

"Then they're probably not there now," I said. A small part of me hoped we would find some of them there, but with no contact, it wasn't likely.

Killian snorted.

Vincent sat still, like he was entranced. *Not another call.*

I rubbed his forearm. "Are you okay?"

He blinked rapidly. An unnecessary action for vampires. "Something doesn't feel right."

"Open the window and take a whiff, tracker ass," Killian said.

Vincent narrowed his eyes on Killian. His hand came up between them with one finger held up. He smiled at Killian and turned back to the glass.

I stifled my amusement. Their banter bonded them, whether or not they saw it.

His finger jammed against the button to propel the window outward. He inhaled deeply, more humanlike than vampire. "Nothing. No blood. No death."

"Are you sure?" I stood behind him and sniffed. "Nothing close?" *Nothing.*

Vincent took the air in again. "Something faint in the distance. The scent wasn't there at first. I can't tell if it's human. It's still too far away."

I sniffed again, but all I could smell was the scent of Vincent. My eyes closed as it washed over me. Familiar and heady. The trust we had vacated my heart when he lied to me. I opened my eyes and let the past drift back to memories where it belonged.

"Rosewater."

"What?"

"You always smell like rosewater."

I laughed to cover the warmth building in me. "Not for much longer. I left that little luxury at home."

"If you two are done smelling each other, the compound should be a couple of blocks away. Provided it's still standing," Killian said.

Home. Memories came to me of life before the ice age. "We consistently pinged the servers, but no one could access the data," I said. "It could help us if things are working."

"Something works there. We just don't know what." Killian punched the gas in that direction.

I reached for the back of the chair to steady myself, but missed and grabbed Vin's shoulder instead.

His hand covered mine. "Did Ezra think about staying here after the ice age? I was so confused about who and what I was for the short time before we left."

"That's right. You were still new and disoriented then." I slipped my hand out from under his. He hadn't aged. His face unchanged, but the light in his eyes had. It showed an age beyond his youthful looks. "This was his home. He didn't want to leave. It became apparent quickly our food source would be scarce. He'd long owned the lands we live on now, so it was the obvious choice."

"Who knew then an old palace in Mexico would become our refuge..." Vincent's voice trailed off, but his eyes fixed on the road.

"Ezra did," Killian said. "He never wanted to be Emperor, but he wanted a place for us to survive. And why do you insist on calling them by their old names?"

"What would you rather me say? Ezra's Empire?"

I covered my mouth with my hand to muffle my snicker.

"Western International Nation," Killian said.

Vincent stiffened. "There it is," he said. "I recognize the gate." He scanned the area and sniffed the air through the open window. "We're clear. Whatever was in the air earlier is gone."

My unneeded heart fluttered at the sight. I wanted to rush out of the tundra. Light gray stone walls rose up ten feet high with little ice on them. The facade looked much like the fortification used for castles in medieval times. It was enclosure built to keep nosey humans out before we lived in the open. The ice age brought us out of shadows and secrets.

"Stay here with Josephine while I open the gate." Killian threw the door open.

My laughter spilled out. "You know I'm a better fighter than him."

"But you're the Emperor's daughter. It is his duty to give his life to protect you." Killian climbed out and slammed the door shut behind him.

Pain stabbed my chest so hard I looked down to make sure there wasn't something lodged there. I'd never let Vincent die for me. *Never.* My eyes traveled up to Vincent's face and followed his gaze. His eyes on the surroundings.

Killian's fingers traced along the gate to the power box. His hand covered it.

"There's electricity," Vincent said.

"That's not even possible. The backups were set to only keep the servers alive."

"We saw lights on in the city. Someone has kept the power on. Maybe the expeditions that came before us."

"Father did say the infrastructure was maintained at a certain level." I didn't expect things to be quite so normal here. The last expedition never came back, and they were presumed dead. If they betrayed Father and stayed here, we'd have to report them. I wouldn't have to ask the punishment. Father always sentenced those who betrayed him to death.

He opened his door and stepped out. "Killian, the power is on."

Even enough power for the gates. After all this time?

Killian gave a thumbs up. He opened the power box, but his body concealed what his fingers did.

The gate creaked and groaned open. Killian jogged back to the rover and hopped into the driver's seat.

I controlled my urge to fidget, unable to stop the flood of images of my mother coming back to me. *Mother in her garden. Her happiest place.*

Vincent pulled himself back inside. We inched forward slowly through the open gates. The second tundra pulled up beside us.

"How did you know about the electricity?" Killian glanced at Vincent.

"We saw lights on in the city."

"None over here though."

Vincent stared out the window. "I heard the hum and felt the vibration."

I leaned forward. My senses hadn't picked up on it. A created vampire shouldn't have those kinds of sensitivities, but Father noted before anyone else how special Vin was. Well, anyone except me.

"I felt it too," Killian said. "After I touched the metal."

"He's a tracker, Killian. He's trained for it." I knew it was abnormal, but it would be useful for the mission.

"Such skills are not for the created." He cut his eyes towards Vin.

"He's always been gifted," I said. "Born or created shouldn't matter."

"He is in the same vehicle with you two. You might remember that." Vincent waved at us.

I smashed my lips together to hide a grin.

"You might remember that you address the Emperor's daughter," Killian said.

"Can you drop the formality, Killian? We're all friends here." I peered out the windshield, ready to explore my former home. And weren't you the one telling us to stop sniffing each other?"

"We are not friends alone on a trip, Josephine. We are on a mission of the nation, and there are others traveling with us.

"I hear you, Kilian. They're in the other tundra, though. If they are gifted enough to hear, then so be it." The urge to smack Killian in the back of the head itched at my hand, but something put his sense on edge. It was the only thing that made sense with the sudden seriousness he portrayed.

"He might travel among high borns, but he is not." Killian scowled.

"Enough," I said. "We'll not talk like that. As the Emperor's daughter, I say we can speak as friends here."

Killian's hands tightened around the steering wheel. His new tension more likely from our situation on land now foreign to us than our verbal exchanges. Warrior vampires, especially the elite like him, were trained to go on alert at things out of place. The power at the gate was unexpected.

Vincent raised an eyebrow and gave me a sideways smirk.

I shook my head at him. He enjoyed Killian's discomfort way more than Killian would forgive.

"Stay with her while I take the others to assess the building," Killian said.

My home. Not a building. A home.

"I'm the tracker. I will go," Vin said.

"You are out of your element."

"We'll all go." I hit the button to open the cargo door. If anyone was here, we probably scared them off with the tundras... unless it is Rogues. *Rogues couldn't keep electricity running.*

They both looked at me with narrowed eyes.

"I'm a better fighter than both of you, so you can wipe that shit off your faces. We take half the blood bags. Everyone carries some, and we lock the tundras down so no one but us can access them." Over their battle of wits, I welcomed a stranger at this point, but I wasn't an idiot. If there were desperate vampires, we could take them or trade the blood.

"Your father--" Killian started.

"Is at the one of the southernmost points of Mexico. This is my decision." I slammed my hand on the button to deploy the spikes and locked the tundra in its spot.

"You mean the southern end of WIN?" The corner of Vin's mouth drew up.

"Alright, funny guy. Be sharp. I don't want you to end up as a puddle of goo."

"I've fought many battles."

Over the debate, I took brisk steps ahead of them, and they both jogged past me. *That worked. They both shut up.* Killian barked orders to the rest of the team. They moved at a clipped pace to complete the tasks. I took each step up to the door with care. Flashes of my old life bounced around me. My chest warmed to the memories.

The team flanked us, and we moved like cats up to the front entrance. No snow to clear. *Who has kept the compound so clean?*

49

"Clear!" one guard yelled for confirmation in each room. I slipped into the mansion like a ghost. Each of the rooms cleared one by one in the center section. The preservation was good. Too good for my taste. A hundred years in freezing temperatures shouldn't have been so kind. Sections should have collapsed and crumbled from the weight of the ice. Especially from when the temperatures dipped into subzero for years. Yet, everything looked pretty much the way we left it. Nothing was coated in a frosty ice sheet as if the mansion had been heated the entire time.

"The heat is on here," I said. "It looks like it was never off for long."

Vin and Killian nodded at me.

"We'll need to find them," Killian said.

"It could be the former expeditions," I said, hopeful it was.

"Not likely," Vin said. He met my eyes. "But maybe."

We settled in the study on the first floor. It looked like nothing had been moved since the day we left. The team unpacked and placed maps on the tables.

I studied the maps and reacquainted myself with the floor plan and surrounding areas. *Not that I'd forgotten.*

Vin inhaled deep. He'd done it several times since we walked into the room.

"Is someone here besides us?"

"No, not undead. It's a fresh smell. I think it's your rosewater."

Doubtful, but it gave me hope. Could it be there? Surely not. "I'll be back."

"Take a guard with you," Killian said as I brushed past him.

I yelled over my shoulder. "I don't report to you, Killian. Besides, we've smelled nothing inside."

Would it be as intact as the other rooms? I hurried down the hall to the end. My feet moved faster the closer I got.

I closed my eyes and imagined what it looked like the day we left. I drew in the scents around me. *It can't be.* A silent prayer said to the gods, if they listened to us, in hopes it still stood. The frosted glass shielded the view, but floral scents swirled in the air. My hand shook, but I wrapped it around the brass door handle and opened it. I stepped inside to a noticeable temperature change. *Warm. Warmer even than the rest of the house.* Butterflies dance in my belly.

I opened one eye and then the other. Blooms to match the scents filled the room. Swatches of bright vivid blues to soft pastel peach portrayed a broad band of color. *It's still here. It survived.* I blinked back tears.

The sublime stained glass windows Mother had installed to catch the sunrise still covered the far wall. The depiction of a vampire kneeling to a human done in vibrant colors. Her nod to the desire to reverse vampirism. My gaze traveled upwards. Every one of the skylights in place. Not a chip. Not a crack. Beams and columns added for support, but the glass was clear of ice. *Preservation.*

The hair follicles on the back of my neck stood up one after another. "I know you're there."

"Someone's been here. A lot." Vincent's voice came from behind.

"Yes, they've cared for it." Tears burned my eyes. *Tears. Twice in one day. Blooms, the colors of rainbows bring death, life, and hope was what she'd said of the many plants.* "This was my mother's garden. She tended it until she surrendered to the ultimate death."

He stopped with his body so close behind me.. His hands rubbed my arms and shoulders. "Who would be caring for it?"

The contact settled the unsteadiness in me. After seeing him close to death earlier, I gave into my longing and leaned back against him. "I don't know. She had supporters of her own. I'm sure it was someone loyal to her."

"Loyal to her?"

"Yes, she wanted to find a cure for vampirism. A way to turn those who had been created against their will back to their human self. My father wasn't so keen on the idea. It would have been treason by anyone else, but he would never deny her any whim. Then he forbid her name to be spoken after she died."

"Yet, he left the garden?"

"She died about the time you showed up on the doorstep." I turned in his arms. pained

His face pained with his forehead wrinkled in bunches. "I filled a void for both you and your father, it sounds like." His hand caressed my face.

"No, you filled the place that was yours." I tilted my head up to look into his eyes. My heart pounded in my chest like it had when Killian and I found him by the gate a hundred years ago.

His head leaned down toward mine. He licked his lips.

The thought of his near death still fresh on my mind. I allowed myself to surrender a moment. My eyes fluttered closed. Lush lips melded with mine. Heat built between us.

His hands in my hair pulled me close. Our tongues winded until they found their way.

"Huh humm."

Jarred from my fantasy, I pulled back to see Killian in the doorway. My hand covered Vincent's and removed it from my hair. I smoothed my hair down and straitened my clothes.

"Did you need something, Killian?" Vincent turned to face him.

"Only to ensure the safety of Josephine." Killian brooded by the door.

"As you can see, I am well." *Embarrassed, but well.*

"Yes," he paused. "How is this possible?" He extended his arms out to the side.

Vincent glared at Killian. "It shouldn't be a shock--"

I interrupted him. "You mean the garden, I presume."

"Yes. How is it here? I mean, someone obviously tended it, but who." Killian peered at the massive indoor garden.

"Someone who held my mother dear."

"I suppose you're right. You should return to the group. They would not be happy to find invaders here."

"This is our home. We are not invaders." I appreciated the care given to Mother's garden, but it remained hers. *Possibly the last thing of hers not wiped away.*

"He's right, Josephine. We haven't lived here in a hundred years. The caretaker obviously has."

It stung to hear him use my formal name after a tender moment, but he was doing as I asked. I blurred the line. *Damn it.* "I never thought the day would come when you two would agree on anything." I studied each of their faces. They were concerned, but I want this moment in the garden. "You may both go. I wish to stay in my mother's garden."

"I'll stay with her, Killian."

I glanced at Vincent. The moment early was wonderful, but it couldn't happen again.

"As you wish." The door closed softly behind Killian.

I walked down the aisles inhaling the soft aromas of each flower. My hand cupped a flesh-colored rose. Mother's touch reflected back at me in everything in this space.

"Your mother was fond of roses."

"Among others," I said. "This is a Night-blooming Cereus." My fingers grazed the long, narrow white petals.

"And this one?" He bent to take a whiff.

"A Stinking Corpse Lily." I pressed my lips tightly together to keep from laughing.

"Indeed." His brows furrowed together. He made a gagging noise. "It smells like death. True to its name." His hand passed over the next one in the row.

A giggle escaped my lips. "That is Bloodroot. See how it cocoons the flower before it blooms. And how the stalk of the mature one is red. The roots contain a red liquid that can dye the skin."

He looked up and leaned forward.

"It can be quite toxic in a large enough dose for human or vampire by irritating the mucous membrane. More for the humans, but a created vampire could overdose on it pretty easily. It can even be deadly in a born vampire if they consume a large amount in a short time."

"Why would a vampire use it?"

"One of the benefits is it stimulates respiratory functions. It's like a human simulation for a vampire."

Vin's eyebrows bunched together.

"It forces them to take breaths. Too much and a created vampire will expel all the blood in his body through ruptured blood vessels in the lungs. They can't heal fast enough to stop it. A born vampire would have to consume enough to explode the heart."

"Interesting how something so small could do so much damage."

"Yes, it is." I nodded. "She chose it, because it is endangered. Little did she know a lot more would be endangered." I winced at the memory of her in the garden as she explained different plants to me.

"Do you think whoever is caring for the garden is carrying on your mother's work?"

Mother had her followers. At times, they appeared to outnumber my father's own. *Would someone risk his wrath to maintain a garden?* "It's possible. Father forbid it when we moved south, but many of her followers had dispersed to the outlying areas by then. He wasn't as tolerant without Mother around to champion it."

"Losing love can make you want to shut out everything about that person." His fingers came close to a poisonous and euphoric plant.

I slapped his hand away. "Don't touch that one. It's deadly. To me, it's like he wanted to forget she existed. That's not how you honor someone you love. Tending their garden after they die. Now, that is how you honor them."

"Josephine, can we talk about--"

My name on his lips slapped each time, and it was a punishment of my own doing. "When we get back from the mission. Neither of us can afford to be distracted right now."

His chest raised and lowered. The motion of a human sigh. A puff of air from his nostrils made a little breeze. After a century, it appeared he still hadn't learned the patience of a vampire.

I squeezed his upper arm. "I'm not saying it won't ever happen. Now is not the time." Each touch we shared made it harder to let go.

He took my hand in his. His lips pressed against my fingers. "I'll wait."

The room closed in on me. The vast garden shrunk. I

stepped around him. "I don't want you to wait. I never want you to wait for what you want in life."

"We're immortal. A few decades is a blink of an eye."

Thoughts stopped forming. Too much road on this mission for this kind of distraction. My senses couldn't afford to be dulled by the rosy haze of love. *Love? Was it still love?* "I can't do this, Vin." *Quiet. I need a quiet place to think.*

"Then let's talk about the conditions for the donors."

The space around me expanded. My anxiety quelled. My irritation increased. "They are well compensated." The words I despised, but had to say as a representative of my father.

"Bullshit. They are prisoners on the compound." Vin crossed his arms over his chest.

"It's not like that. The contract they sign says they must stay within the walls for their protection and to fulfill their obligation. They are not forced to sign." Mother would have argued against the clause in the contract too, and I knew it.

"Contract or not. It's a prison for them. No way out except death."

"I'd be lying if I said I didn't have an issue with it, but I can't challenge Ezra publicly." *Exile is not something I desire.*

"This might be the opportunity for change."

"He would have you brought to your end for that talk. That's treason in his eyes." My heart quickened at the thought of Father executing Vin. *I'm not sure he would listen to me even as much as he likes Vin.*

"Lucky for me, you don't think like he does. It's time for change. One of the created has been brewing a synthetic blood, but it tastes terrible. If a scientist with a lab were to work on a similar formula, we could end our dependency on humans. "

"I can't make any promises." Conflict spread through me.

Conflict in my heart and conflict in the loyalty I had for my father.

"Just follow where your heart leads."

I nodded. It was the best I could give in the moment and not a promise I could make.

CHAPTER 5

JOSIE - VIN

"Damn it." My foot made contact with the chair on casters and sent it flying across the room. It banged hard against the metal case around the computer equipment. The door dented, and it ricocheted off. "Stupid ancient equipment."

"Whoa. I'm not the enemy." Vin held up his hands like a robbery victim and stopped the chair with his foot.

"Sorry." My fingers gripped the counter. "The servers are such old technology." Chemistry and plants. That made sense. How did we ever run models on these machines, much less communicate?

"Let me have a look."

"Why not?" I held my hands out.

"I worked on some of these when I was human, I think." He squatted down to look inside.

"Another memory? And I seem to recall you interned in the computer room at the Southern Compound before Father promoted you."

"Mmm hmm. Of sorts."

He interned right before Father promoted. Like a matter of weeks. "You were a hacker."

He smiled. "Yes."

"Were you a hacker when we ..." I trailed off, not able to say it out loud.

"No, Ezra thought I should learn the trade to become part of his security team. Turns out I had an aptitude for it. I helped crack into the systems of some of the other nations."

I turned my back and tinkered with one of the machines behind me to hide my surprise and embarrassment that I didn't know something so important. Father didn't tell me assignments of everyone he promoted me, but I knew most of his spies. "You could have mentioned that earlier." I peered over my shoulder.

He focused on the equipment. "You could have asked for help."

Or I could have looked in his file, which I didn't like an idiot. I hadn't looked at his or Killian's files before the mission. Father could have mentioned it too. I moved to the equipment box. "What can I do?"

"Give me another chance." He smiled but didn't look up.

"I was referring to--"

"The servers. I understood." He reached for the toolkit at his side. "Is there a screwdriver anywhere?"

"Here." I held the instrument out in the palm of my hand.

His fingers grazed along my palm and tickled all the way down.

Venom spilled into my mouth, and I swallowed hard. It warmed my insides. *No, Josie. No.*

His eyes followed the line from our hands up my arm until our eyes met.

More venom filled my mouth. I suspect his did too from the way he swallowed. He opened his mouth.

"Don't." I placed a finger across his lips. "Remember our agreement."

The rise and fall of his chest so human.

Mine did the same to take in his scent.

"Josephine." His lips brushed against my finger.

"No," I said. "Fix the servers."

I backed out of the door with my hand in the air like he was a wild animal. My back rested against the wall just around the corner. *I want him.* Nothing new. I'd wanted him since we met. The desire hard to fight. A primal instinct in vampires. I needed some space away from him, but we were running out of time to get the servers up for the check in.

My body betrayed me like a stupid girl. No doubt he smelled the pheromones. *We are vampires. This happens to all vampires.*

My lungs expanded and contracted to grab one last whiff of him. The air in them wasted. I cut off the aroma and ducked back into the room.

"Let's get these servers going. We're not done with our mission." I stood tall and held his gaze. The urge to look away gnawed at me. "We are here for humans."

"Willing humans, you mean," Vincent said.

"Any humans."

"We can't take them if they do not wish to go." He scowled.

"They need to produce, and this environment is not helping them. We'll provide safe passage to warmer climates." The words came out in a practiced manner.

"You mean take them prisoner and force them from their homes to do your will."

"No, I..." I couldn't finish the lie. No matter if I wanted to believe what I was trained to say, it was still a lie. We'd stopped turning humans to vampires. There were too few to feed the present vampire population.

"It's wrong, Josie," Vincent said. "You know it. When was the last time you gave someone the choice to become vampire or remain human?"

"I've never turned a human." I sided with my mother's belief in that we shouldn't turn humans, and the ice age hadn't changed that decision.

"You may have had someone else carry out the act, but you used to grant the humans the choice."

"Ezra decreed the population was at the maximum sustainability to keep a delicate balance of survival. No one turns a human to a vampire without Father's approval."

"So he makes the decisions about population control for vampires and humans?" He remained sullen.

"No..." I paused. *Did he?* "Yes..." I looked him in the eye and resisted the temptation to look away. "Why are you questioning Ezra's way? You certainly didn't question when he saved your life."

"I've always questioned it. He's known and accepted it. You just noticed." He dropped the screwdriver in the box. "Try it now."

I engaged the master switch on the wall, and the room came to life. Hundred plus year old servers were doing their job. My fingers worked the buttons from memory.

Vincent entered commands on the keyboard. "I pinged the satellite. We should be operational."

"Can we get a sat-line to Ezra?"

"Should be able to if the connection is stable," he punched on the keys. "Put on that headset."

A ring resonated in my ear. I stared at the screen in front of me, not really seeing it.

"Yes?" Ezra's voice echoed. The connection wasn't great.

"Father? It's me. Josephine. We made it."

"I knew you would. You've done well. Any humans?" His voice higher than normal, like he forced lightness.

"No." I hesitated. "A couple of young vampires. Nothing else."

"I hope we're not too late." His voice quiet. "The team here will tap into the servers now that they are online. Do some reconnaissance. We've lost several since you left that need to be replaced."

What if we made a mistake coming here? No, we will succeed. "The tasks of my mission are at the forefront of my thoughts." Static cut through the call. "Father? Ezra?" The static silenced. The line dead. I removed the headset and placed it on the counter.

"Can we get him back?" I asked Vin. "Several donors have been lost since we left."

Vin averted his eyes. "Not right now. I need to rewire here." He pointed to the different colored wires. "They were already at capacity when we tapped them."

"It seemed easy enough the first time." I leaned against the desk. "You just plugged us in."

"These servers have been in use recently. The garden wasn't the only thing they maintained."

"I think Father would have told me if they had been." *If it wasn't the previous expedition, then we had more to worry about. Someone had being using my home as a base.* I cringed inside.

"He may not have known. Whoever did it was pretty skilled."

"What do you mean?" I leaned down like the secrets would be divulged to me from the wires.

"Their tracks would have been hidden to most."

"It takes a hacker to know a hacker?"

He smiled. "Something like that. There are certain notes hackers leave for each other."

"It's almost sunset. We'll be able to move forward with the other part of our mission. The most important part. We'll need our tracker at his best."

"It's not like I need sleep."

"Just be ready." I patted him on the shoulder and headed to the garden.

HER FACE when our hands touched told me she felt something too. She'd agreed to talk after the mission. *Patience, Cavanaugh. Focus on the mission like she is.*

The activity on the computers left a carefully concealed trail. With so little mobility in this area and so few humans, why would someone go to so much trouble? *A hacker must hack.* I cracked my knuckles. An old habit from the all-nighters I used to pull on the network. *A memory.* I had so few of them they never seemed real. The little snapshots were never enough to put together.

A name kept showing up over, and over as I combed through the files. *Calidora. Whoever it was must be pretty important.* Calidora knew the ice age was coming long before it happened. Her name appeared on all the top level communications. She must have been a leader at the time.

Some of the files mentioned Ezra. He was one of those in the know. *I'm not surprised. Not at all.* I read some lines over a couple of times to make sure I hadn't misread. *Fuck. This is going to crush.* She'd never forgive me if I kept this kind of secret. *Better to hear it from me than find it on her own.*

I tapped the button on my jacket to connect to the group. "Mission Leader, can you return to the server room?"

"Copy that, Vincent. I'm on my way," Josie said. Vampire speed had her at the door in seconds. "What did you find?"

"The ice age was planned among leaders, including you father. I think you should see for yourself."

She crossed the room and stood beside me. Her eyes focused on the screen in front of us. She shifted weight from one foot to the other. Not a sign of fatigue. A nervous habit when something made her uncomfortable. I'd picked up on it when I first met her.

"This cannot be true." Her gaze on me. The confusion on her face written in the lines on her creased forehead. "How did you find it?"

"It was encrypted, but it was a weak one. Like someone put it here for us to find." The files were real. The timestamps couldn't be faked on this dated technology. I suspected the ones responsible for caring for the mansion wanted this information to be found.

"No doubt a ploy."

"Who is Calidora?"

"She's an old and powerful vampire." She paused. Her brows pulled together. "She's also responsible for my mother's death."

My gods, what it must be like to relive it. I reached for her hand, but she pulled away. "I thought your mother was a casualty of the ice age."

"My father has perpetuated it rather than the truth. It was easy to do with the timing."

"And he didn't seek revenge?"

"Calidora had my mother killed in retaliation for my father's movement against her. He knew we were relocating soon and opted to choose other battles. Plus, he had mercenaries on the payroll to handle under the radar activities."

"Where is she now? Could she be the one keeping all of this going?"

"No one really knows. Some thought father had her meet her finale. He would have if he'd found her, but he didn't, as far as I know. I would have if I'd found her. She disappeared though."

Josie answered in a methodical and practiced motion, so different from how she was when we were together. She guarded her memories of her mother. *Compartmentalized. That must be how she dealt with it.*

"Don't you want to track her down?"

"Every day. I promised Father I would let go of my need for revenge. That keeps me on track."

"What if they did know the ice age was coming? There would have been fights for territories."

"And humans? Is that where you're going with it?" She scrolled through the files on the screen.

"Yes, they could have evacuated more people. Saved lives. Instead, they buried the information except between themselves." Millions of humans died, and many vampires died or turned Rogue. *Because Ezra and his elitist vampire leaders thought they knew better.* I tamped down the anger before I chunked a chair.

"We don't know that is true. How do you know this wasn't planted after it all started?"

"The files have a date and timestamp. I think it's true, Josephine."

"Even if it is, it was a hundred years ago, and it doesn't change anything about today.

"Doesn't it? Don't you think the remaining vampires and humans born to this frozen abyss deserve to know the truth?"

She stared at me. Studied me. I could almost see the wheels turning in her head. Something had happened here. Something her father had his hand on. Something that caused her mother's death.

"It's not true. We don't have any proof it's true." She pushed her chair away from the desk.

She wasn't ready to hear it. Couldn't admit her father was more of a criminal than the savior many thought.

If what remained of the world population knew the truth, maybe someone was smart enough to fix the mess Ezra made of the world. My decision could drive a further wedge between us, but I owed it to my former race and my current one to find the truth.

CHAPTER 6

VIN

I stared at the area maps alone in the office. The room temperature varied a few degrees higher here. It reminded me of warm days in Dallas. Not that I remembered them in my scrambled head, but somewhere they peaked through like a ray of sun. My genuine memories begin with Josie and the blizzard early in the beginning of the change.

"Time to do your job, Vincent." Killian cast a shadow on the room.

I rolled my shoulders back and faced him. "Have you smelled any humans? I haven't."

"No, but we have our orders." He squared off in front of me. "And it is your job."

"Life is more than orders." Tracking made me valuable. I regretted it each time I succeeded in finding the prey.

"Not for us."

"Not for me, because I'm just a created vampire." I pushed past him.

He grabbed my elbow. His fingers tightened on it.

I raised an eyebrow.

His hand dropped to his side. "If you want others to see you differently, you need to see yourself differently."

"That's pretty deep for you, Killian. Easy to say when you're in the accepted circle."

"I wasn't always. Ezra saw your gifts from the beginning. Maybe it's time for you to see them as well."

"You'd almost think we're friends. Let's just finish this mission. Where's Josephine?"

"She's in the office. There's a laptop in there, and she took one of the tablets with her. She was trying to reach Ezra."

We walked down the hall. Our boots made annoying squeaks against the floor. *If these weren't my lucky boots, I take one off and beat Killian over the head.* I glanced down. The remnants of my blood barf still coated mine. Killian's were pristine and black as coal. *I should take one off and whack him.*

"You think I'm the enemy, but I'm not. She loves you. You just have to earn her back."

"From a rumor you started, that never really happened. That makes you the enemy."

"I wanted her. Can you blame me? She will never see me as anything other than a friend, and I want her to be happy," he said. "Even if that is with a dickhead created one."

I feigned shock. "Dickhead? Look in the mirror, asshole."

"I told her I started the rumor, but she didn't believe me."

I cut my eyes over to him, unsure if I believed him. There was one thing I was sure of. "Lies destroy people."

"We have the same goal. We both love her and want her to be happy. She loves you. You need to do what it takes to make her happy."

I nodded. He clearly had not heard the conversation Josie and I had earlier. He was here in Dallas when the ice age set in and might recognize some of the names from the files.

"What do you know about an old vampire called Calidora?" I asked.

He shrugged. "She and Ezra made a lot of power plays against each other."

Calidora doesn't seem to be a secret. Maybe it's grief that keeps them from talking about her. Grief and time. "And it cost Josephine's mother's life."

His shoulders drooped a fraction. "Yes, a dark day for all who serve Ezra. Although most do not know the truth. It almost killed Josephine, but you showed up. It gave her purpose. I cannot say why I didn't see it back then."

Purpose isn't exactly what I want to be. "How long before I arrived did she die?"

"Not long, if I recall correctly. I don't think it was even three full months."

Our feet crunched on the fresh ice and snow. A set of tracks led to the tundra. Josie sat in the instrument room chair. Killian took the pilot's seat, and I moved toward the navigator chair.

"Where have you two been?" Josie asked.

"On our way here." I smiled. "I thought you were in the office. How long have you been here?"

She didn't return it. "Long enough. You are lacking a sense of urgency." Her face stoic. She gazed out the window. "Let's do our job."

"Is there something we need to know?" Killian braved the question.

Her eyes narrowed on him. "You need to know your mission here. We do have a purpose." Her choice of words similar to Killian's on the walk here. The same brainwashing we all received to ensure our allegiance to Ezra.

I glanced over my shoulder. Josie worked the instrument

panel with grace. Her beauty magnificent even with the array of colors reflected off the board in front of her.

She turned her gaze on me. Her blue eyes like electric fire. Bright and painful.

"Helio?" I turned to Killian.

He studied the gauges. "We're good. Let's do it."

I radioed the other tundra and inputted the coordinates we'd decided on earlier.

"Beta team, Alpha team is going helio to the designated location. Copy?"

"Copy helio. See you in the blue."

"Copy. Alpha out." I disengaged the spikes to free the tundra.

The rotor blades extended out, and the ends came into view. A flip of the switch, and they whipped the air around us. White powered stirred. The craft lifted up over the compound. Our first aerial view of the area stunned me into silence. No one uttered a word.

The rooftop had been cleared of most of the ice and snow. It confirmed our suspicions someone was taking care of this property. The expanse of the compound, larger than I imagined, stood intact, outlined by the large stone wall. It looked more like a guarded castle than a mansion.

The tower had some repairs the human eye wouldn't have detected. I could see them, though. Along with the giant iron 'C' on the side of it. *Marked. Definitely not for Ezra.*

"Was that always there?" I angled my head toward the tower.

"No," Killian said. "It was not."

Josephine stood over my shoulder to get a better look. "Shit. Calidora. That's all it could mean."

"Did Ezra know?" Killian asked.

"He didn't mention it if he did." Josephine settled back in her seat. "That explains a lot. But where is she? I can't believe she would let us walk in and stay the day without confronting us."

"Or ending our existence," Killian said. "What kind of game is this?"

"She needs something from us," I said. "I wonder if she's been squatting there the whole time."

"She's powerful in her own right." Killian shook his head.

"But she's been in the frozen landscape for a hundred years while we escaped to an oasis," I said.

"He's right, Killian. There's no way she would have let us walk in so easily. We walked right into the spider's web," Josie said. "She's just waiting to strike."

"Do we abort the mission?" He asked.

"No, we need resources," Josie said.

"Maybe that's what she needs too," I said.

"Make us do the work would be her style. She should have her own force," Josie said. "Alert the other team. We need to stay aware of our surroundings."

"Beta team, eyes open. Repeat, eyes open," I called through the radio.

"Copy Alpha team."

"Think she would make a deal?" Killian asked.

I looked at Josephine. Her father didn't deal he dominated, and she had been taught by him and his advisors.

"The only commodity we have to trade of value is blood. We have extra, but not enough to make a worthwhile trade unless we find additional resources." Josephine fidgeted with the buckle on her seat.

"And you," I said.

Josephine pressed her lips together and gave me a brief nod.

The daughter of the WIN Emperor would be of more value than the blood we carried. A trophy. A bargaining chip. We'd have to be careful. *Did they know we were coming?*

A twinge in my stomach drew me back to the task in front of me. *Tracking.* I popped open the window. Took a whiff and inhaled the cold air into my lungs. Each of the little alveoli sacs in my lungs accepted the gift and left a sense of euphoria on departure.

"Human," I said, my eyes closed. My lids lifted slowly. Hunger dug a deep well in my gut.

The anticipation of the instinctual hunt grew like a tidal wave. Thirst scratched at the back of my throat. The desire to dine tough to battle, but my practice proved perfect for my record of not taking a human life. *So far.* I'd been thirstier since the blood vomit episode, and no other humans crossed our path.

"There." I pointed to the shadow under the evergreen foliage.

"We can't land there," Killian said.

"Vincent and I can jump with some of the guards," Josie said.

"You should stay in the helio," Killian said.

I headed to the back to prepare for the dive.

"I'm jumping," Josie stood.

"Talk some sense into her Cavanaugh."

"Her life is her own." I held up my hands. "It would be wiser to let us go while you stay."

She responded by zipping up the winter suit.

I pulled on my own and slammed my hand against the

button for the door. It slid open with ease. A fresh rush of cold air filled the compartment.

"There's more than one human." The scratch in my throat turned to a slow burn.

"Are you okay?" Josie asked.

"I'll be fine." I rubbed my hand on my throat.

"Together." Josie held out her hand. Her head over her shoulder, she looked Killian's way. "Let them know we go on one and give the count down for Beta after we clear."

My hand slipped into hers. The helio descended to a lower altitude.

"Three." Pause. "Two." Pause. "One."

Our feet left the ledge. *Freedom.* I dropped toward the white earth bathed in moonlight, my hand firmly in Josie's grasp. Pure exhilaration tingled through my body. Not from the fall, but from the contact with Josie.

Her hand released mine. We somersaulted in the air away from each other and landed in similar crouched positions. A smile crept across her face. Her beauty great but more so when she smiled.

The sound of blades grew loud around us. *I staggered back.* Snow blew up from the ground. *We need cover.* The second helio bared down on us sideways. My stomach leapt into my throat. *Josie.*

A blade broke off and barreled at us. I threw my arm around Josie and vaulted us away. The ground shuttered with a rumble. Flames heated the space around us. My body covered hers. Ice and snow liquified and puddled under my hands. Snow slid from branches onto my back.

I slapped the comm button on my suit. "Killian, what the Hell just happened?"

Josie pushed against me, and I rolled back off of her.

Killian yelled. "Beta team confirmed the jump but never did. Then descended below the safe zone."

"We'll check for survivors," I said. The chances slim in an explosion this hot, but I hoped they escaped before.

"Get Josephine out of there, and we can set up a safe rendezvous point. Whatever happened--"

"She's the target." Shock wore off. This Calidora or someone that worked for her, was after Josie. "We're exposed, Josephine. We need to go."

She was already on her feet and marched to the flames. "We're not leaving them on my watch."

"Josie, they didn't make it, or we'd hear them."

"And we're already dead, anyway?" She raised an eyebrow at me. "I'm aware of how you feel about our existence."

"Now is not the time." Precious seconds ticked away. Every second could bring a vampire, or worse, a vampire army too close for us to find a way out.

Bullets whizzed by. I ducked and pulled Josie down with me. Not at us, but straight at the helio Killian piloted. They tinked against the metal. The gunfire forced us backwards.

"Killian, go to a safe distance. And stay in radio range," I said.

"Heading North seems to be the option. I'll do some maneuvers to lead them away."

"Got it. North," I said. "Let's go, Josie."

"Have you both forgotten who is leading--"

The ground around us shook from a second explosion. A pillar of fire shot upward. I followed it up high in the sky. Hot wind carried a force that knocked me back to the ground. The fresh snow cushioned my fall. Josie landed on top of me. My arms wrapped securely around her, I rolled over, cradling her underneath me. Debris landed around us in thud after thud.

Killian's voice came through my comm. *What?* I lifted my head. The sounds muffled and blended together.

My hands on Josie to make sure she was whole. She pushed against me. Her struggle shook the fog from my mind.

"Killian?" I called on the comm. "Killian?" He might be out of range now.

I stood and held my hand out to her, but she didn't take it. Her gaze on the severed head at our feet. Venom oozed into my mouth to drive home my anger.

"We need to get to safety. You can't help them. They're already gone." I couldn't afford to mourn them now. I'd honor their sacrifice when Josie was safe. Her survival the most important thing right now.

She brushed past me and headed north at supernatural speed. She was fast. Faster than most. The best I could do was keep her in sight. I scented the air on repeat to taste for potential danger.

The snow and ice so deep here it had long buried the homes and strip malls that once filled the area. A cabin came into view in what was once a suburb. Josie stopped several yards away, and I caught up to her. The wooden structure built with great attention to detail. Strong joints faceted together without nails. A door carved with an intricate detail of moon phases. Waxing. Waning. Crescent. New. Full. They were all there. Few people paid homage to the moon.

Josie shot me a side glance. "How does it smell?"

"Nothing recent. Faded scents of human and vampire." The aroma familiar like it almost made a memory.

"How long?"

"It's been some time. A month at least. Probably an old safe house." Structures built for refuge, especially for the created like me, dotted the landscape to the north. Some very rudimentary while others built elaborate self-sustaining structures.

She nodded and stepped up onto the porch.

I held my arm out in front of her. "I'll go first." The door didn't squeak as it opened. Silence, a sign of the craftsmanship. I used my speed to investigate the area. "It's clear," I called over my shoulder. I relaxed for the first time since we left the crash site.

"Obviously," Josie said. She'd slipped into the small cabin. Her finger traced along the back of the couch. "It looks pretty well taken care of to me. Little dust and not frozen."

So stubborn. I loved the trait about her, but it infuriated me too. "Damn it. Listening every once in a while wouldn't kill you. Not listening might." I crossed the room and closed the door.

CHAPTER 7

I opened the cabinets and rummaged through for anything useful. *Blood would be good.* Each shelf emptied of contents. "Killian?" He paused. "Killian?" No response came over our earpieces. My chest grew tighter with each call he made on the comm. Vin tried for at least ten minutes.

Killian was strong. He was a warrior. I wouldn't lose him too. "Shouldn't he be in range by now?'

Vin didn't answer. He saved me. I should thank him. I wanted to thank him. My thoughts scattered between Killian, the crew, and if we were actually safe. The words wouldn't come. Answers are what I needed now. *Who attacked us?* The mission had to be a success. Ezra entrusted me to lead it. *There would not be failure. The nation can't afford failure. Our people need this mission.*

The familiar metallic smell hit me. Stronger now than before. "I smell blood."

"It's old. There's not any here." His voice sharp cut into me. "It's your thirst."

79

"I'm not thirsty," I whispered. My eyes focused on his. "But you are. You're getting irritated, and it shows. "

He needed more than I did. The stress strengthened his cravings. It was so with all created. He hadn't really had enough blood to recover from the vomit induced call either.

"How much do we have with us?" His hand rubbed his throat

"Two bags. One in each of the emergency packs from the jump." I patted the pack on his back.

"You take them." Vin slipped the pack off and held it toward me.

Even with his thirst high, he would sacrifice for me. Venom leaked into my mouth and swallowed hard against it. "You'll need them should we come to a battle." I pushed the pack back toward him. "And your thirst is now."

"Your survival is more important," he said.

I stepped back. "No, it's not."

He closed the space, his expression fierce. "You are the Emperor's daughter, and you must live."

"Drink the blood, Vincent." I rest a hand on his chest.

He stared me in the eyes. His breath quickened. Small ragged puffs brushed my face.

Only one thing came to mind to calm him. I leaned in, my lips brushed against his.

Strong hands pulled me against his firm chest. His tongue found mine. Venom mixed with venom. My moans mixed with his echoed in the air. He shoved me hard against the table. My heart quickened its unneeded beat. A dust cloud enveloped us. I ran my fingers over his lips. He kissed the tips.

My teeth bit against his skin, careful not to pierce it.

He lifted me up on the table and stood between my legs.

His lips forced mine apart. The bulge in his pants pressed against my inner thigh.

My body trembled. I ground against him. Harder and harder. My hands on his ass pulled him toward me.

He slid my shirt up over my head and tossed it aside. I wanted his skin against mine.

I yanked his shirt up and dropped it on my own. My hands ran across the lean muscles of his chest.

His head tilted up, neck exposed. A vampire submission move.

I pressed my lips against the bare skin.

His back stiffened. "I know what this place is. My mother was one."

My eyes blinked away the haze to focus on what he saw. I swallowed the venom pooling in my mouth and cleared my throat. "Is that what I think it is?" I slid off the table to his side.

"Yes, it is." He picked up our shirts and handed mine to me. "Those symbols are ancient."

"Wait. Your human mother practiced witchcraft?"

He looked in my eyes like he'd find the answer there. "I don't know how I know, Jos...Josephine."

I studied the ceiling. The intricate detail of the celestial bodies carved with meticulous precision. A double birth chart to the side of it. I'd studied some of the occult before the ice age hit, but there were stories of ancient magic practitioners.

Vincent's chest covered by his shirt.

My breasts exposed. I jerked mine on, too. "What was your human birthday?" It had been on the single piece of identification he had with him when he wandered up to the gate.

He stared at the birth chart. "It's not me."

"That is your vampire creation date as far as we know." My voice wavered. "What is your human birthday?"

"They are both represented there." His face grim.

"And you think it's coincidence?"

"No." He shook his head. "I don't know."

"Someone wanted us to find this place, and they attacked us to drive us North." My body shook. "I will not be a pawn in someone's game."

"You think I had something to do with this?"

His human birth and creation date were carved into the ceiling. It seemed this place was meant to represent him. "Did you?"

"Are you fucking kidding me, Josephine?" He put his hands on my shoulders and stared into my eyes. "I've never been anything but loyal to you and your family." He dropped his hands to his sides.

It was the truth. He'd been loyal to our family and still managed to live in his own moral code. I regretted asking. "I trust you."

"Then trust me when I say we need to get away from this place."

This opportunity might not come again. I wasn't sure the mission was salvageable, and he deserved answers. "What if the answers you've sought for the last hundred years are here? Would you still want to walk away if the answers to your past are this close?"

"My first duty is your safety." His eyes on the ceiling, studying every inch like he tried to memorize it. "Above all else on this mission."

"The mission went out the window when half of our team died," I said. "Maybe before then." I expected roadblocks, but this mission had been off since we saw the two Rogues. At least one tundra was lost, and maybe both. Killian still hadn't responded. Resolution for Vincent seemed like the only thing that made sense right now.

His eyes locked on mine. "We need to find somewhere else." He bit down on his lip.

"We will not be safe out there either, so we might as well stay put to see if Killian responds." I paused. "Besides, the sun will be up in an hour."

He exhaled and regarded the ceiling. "We'll stay here today. See what we can figure out while we're here. But we'll leave as soon as night falls."

I hated playing the sun card, but it was a valid argument in this case. I hated how it made him feel inferior to me. I hated the way he distanced himself every time it came up. Literally.

"I'll start over here." I pulled books off the shelf and flipped through them for anything to do with the symbols or Vincent. Desire thrummed through my body from our earlier. I gazed up at him.

Vincent opened drawers on the small desk. He slammed them shut with unnecessary force. One drawer made a hollow sound when it closed. We shared a glance. He opened it again and discarded a pile of papers on the floor.

"Pull it out all the way."

He looked at me. "It is." His hands maneuvered it until the drawer came free of the track. He retrieved a wooden box from behind the drawer. It matched the wood of the desk.

"Looks like a gift. Are you going to open it or stare at it?"

"It's a puzzle box," he said. "A complicated one." He rotated the box in his hand and passed it over to me. "Look."

The box sat heavy in my hands. Meticulous care used to piece it together, similar to the construction of the cabin itself. "The birth charts are entwined on this end." I glanced up. "Like the ceiling." These clues were meant for Vin. Someone wanted to leave a message for him.

"Yes. This is more your area. I've never had the patience for these games."

"There's a cradle on the top for a thumbprint." The box designed to open for one person.

Vin's lip curled up on one side in a snarl. "With a needle to prick."

"It takes blood to open it." I handed it back to him. "Someone wanted to make sure you were the only one who could get to the contents."

"I'm a vampire. My blood will not be the same."

"That could be why your birth date and created date are there. Whoever made it knew you were a created vampire." I didn't like the way the words tasted on my lips. A pit formed deep inside me. "The person who left this had your blood to set the locks."

Vin paced. "The one who created me?"

"That would be my guess."

He slid into a chair at the table. "I don't know what most of these symbols are. Like this one is obviously the sun, and this means day. I don't think it's a good idea to open it until I know it's not got to burn us up."

I nodded. Most of the symbols didn't register with me, either. "Agreed. Let's figure this bitch out."

He laughed. "Can you find a pen so we can write the ciphers down?"

"On it." I returned to the desk to scavenge our supplies. The scent of blood stronger. Old blood shouldn't get stronger in scent. "Did you notice the smell here?" I glanced over my shoulder.

"Yes." He grabbed his throat. Thirst in a created often came on quick. Stress exacerbated it. Even borns felt that kind of thirst in stressful times.

"Drink the blood, Vincent. At least one bag of it."

"Damn it," hissed from his lips. He jerked the bag out of the pack and sucked it down.

"Better?"

"Yes." A flush covered his cheeks. One of the more human traits we all had. "I hate how much I need it. It's like a drug. A drug that kills the donor but sustains us."

"I wish I could understand that intensity." My own cravings never more than an irritation, even less than most born vampires.

"No, you don't." His eyes locked on mine.

I'd seen what it drove some to do. They'd act like animals and had to be put down. If that was ever Vin... My stomach wrenched. It could never be him. Period.

"You're right." I leaned in next to him and rested my shoulder against his.

He inched a slight distance away. "I don't recognize much other than the birth charts."

"Let me see. We studied this practice in my youth. The symbols and old language look familiar."

"I'm surprised vampires would have any use for witches."

"We don't. Real ones don't really exist. There are some humans who possess greater strength than others. This can allow them to tap into things they really don't understand."

"What happens if one of them is made into vampire?" He asked, his voice serious.

"Most of them do not desire to be vampire. The only ones I know of lost their gifts when they turned, and it didn't end well."

He nodded, his eyes wide. "Do you recognize any of the symbols?"

I recognized some and dug deep in my memory to think of the meanings. "You're right about the sun and day. These two plus this one actually mean to walk in the sun." It can't be suggesting a created could walk in the sun. That would be suicide.

His brows scrunched together. "What else?"

"I've never seen the next sequence, but this shape is similar to transform or transformation." Each marking appeared deliberate, as if it told a story. A story neither of us knew how to read, and it made me want to chunk the damn box.

Vincent's voice rose with excitement. "You think it is saying I will be transformed to stand the sun again?"

"I don't know," I said. Someone with knowledge of old magic made the symbols, but I couldn't know how skilled or accurate they were.

"Only one way to know for sure." He moved his thumb in position to pierce it on the needle.

Worst case is… he dies. I blocked his hand from the box. "We need more answers. You don't know what will happen."

"If there is a chance I can feel the sun on my face again, I'll take the risk." His fingers brushed along my cheek. "To watch a sunrise or sunset with you would be worth it even if I only got one day."

Venom percolated through my body. My heart sped up. Fear gripped my heart. "I'm not willing to risk losing you."

"I'm not a servant, Josephine. It's my risk."

Anger flared in me at the ease of his decision. "No, you're not, but you don't have to be a stupid, impatient ass."

He sighed. "Fine. Do you recognize any of the others?"

"This one means first." My gut twinged. The box seemed

to claim Vin would be the first created to walk in the sun. "I think this is a box of false promises."

"It's meant for me." He scooted the box until it was centered in front of him.

I placed my hand on his arm. "Please wait until we know what all the symbols mean. Or at least until Killian meets up with us." He could restrain Vin if needed. *Gods hurry up Killian.*

"We don't have time. We need to figure it out and get moving." he said. "I love you, Jos-"

I put my finger over his lips. If it were me, my decision would be the same, and I was out of arguments. "Save it and tell me after."

He closed his eyes and poised his thumb over the thumb size indention coated in metal. The sharp point extended up high enough to pierce the skin but not higher than the top of the box.

I dropped my hand to the table and dug my nails into the wood. *Gods protect him.*

His eyes locked on mine. He pressed his thumb into the slot. A soft gasp escaped his lips. He lifted his hand. Blood already pooled in the groove.

The box came to life and shifted on its own. Sections slid out and into different positions. Light, bright like the sun, radiated from it. The shape changed from a rectangle to a square. A square to a pillar and back to a rectangle. Bigger than it started. At least five times larger. It finally stopped. The light retreated, and the box opened. A soft floral scent drifted out. *Peony.*

Vincent and I exchanged a quick glance of wonder. His hand moved more at a human pace than vampire. The urge to stop him built inside me, but this was a journey meant for him. His hand plunged down into the box. Deeper than it appeared. He swirled his hand around inside.

I peered over the edge but only saw darkness. Vin stopped moving. Panic froze my thoughts. I shook his free arm. "Vincent?" I waved my hand in front of him. His eyes glazed and unfocused. The lids softened slightly but didn't close. I ran my hand across his cheek. Tears blurred my vision.

"Vincent? Wake up," I said. "Please."

His expression reminded me of a coma patient we had in the infirmary. The patient's eyes remained open regardless of what we did. This wasn't a coma, though. Vin could be stuck somewhere else. *Could there have been a coma inducing poison on the needle?* Plants and flowers from Mother's garden raced through my mind. Three stood out immediately, but they took all muscle control. Vin stayed in a seated position. Could it be magic? Vampire training didn't include magic assaults. *Magic doesn't exist anymore. It died with the original vampire lines. Could it have survived somehow?*

CHAPTER 8

JOSIE

The sun shone high in the sky. Hours had passed, and Vincent hadn't moved. My stomach churned. I couldn't keep still. My mind raced through options to block out the sun. A couple of hours stood between us before the sun from the windows reached Vincent. I shook his shoulders several times to wake him up, but he returned to his frozen position. Some old threadbare blankets covered the bed. They wouldn't be enough. *Damn it. How am I going to get him out of here?*

"Killian? Are you there?" I tried the comm on my jacket. *Stupid, stubborn men. Both of them.* I regretted the thought. It might be true, but our situation suggested they both needed me. My feelings for Vin clouded my thoughts. I avoided him most days, because of it. I needed my mind clear to save him and shoved everything else down inside.

I paced the length of the cabin. Poison couldn't be ruled out. There were plenty of paralytics. I'd never seen one act that fast on a vampire. It didn't take long to establish a path in the single room. Not many options. A loose board squeaked. I walked the line I'd established, and the board squeaked again. Unusual for the quality, perfection really, in the cabin. *Definitely unusual.* I jumped back to the board and ripped it from the floor.

Darkness. Even my expert vision couldn't cut through it. I ripped another board off the flooring and crouched down low. A draft blew up. The scent of blood stronger. I inhaled the odor deep in my lungs. *Vampires had been here.* Old blood the most pronounced. Fresher blood mixed in, but it was a good distance away. The space below us went quite a distance by the judge of it. *Maybe the ones who wanted Vin to find this place were down there. If they didn't fix what they did, I'd rip them apart. I might do it anyway.*

Wood scraped against wood. The box had moved, but he still looked the same. "Vincent?" I got up to check on him. *Damn it. Come out of this.* Waved my hand in front of his face. I ran my fingers across his cheek.

He blinked. "Josie?" His voice hoarse, like after the creator's call. *Please don't let him get called again.*

"Yes." I squeezed his shoulder and rummaged through the pack for the other bag of blood. "Here."

He winced. "I think I'm good."

"Really? You've been in a trancelike state for quite some time."

"Yes," he said. "For now." He pushed my hand with the blood bag away.

Thirst should have been the first thing a created acknowledged, but he didn't seem to feel it. "What happened to you?"

"It's hard to explain." His forehead wrinkled and brows drawn together.

I rubbed his back. "Take your time."

"My head aches. It's still a little foggy. Have you been tearing the place apart?" His eyes fell on the hole in the floor.

"That's our next adventure or at least where you are going to avoid the sun." I didn't like the option, but there wasn't another choice.

"You want to crawl into a dark hole in the ground?" He shook his head.

"Well, I was going to use a flashlight." I grinned and flashed the light on and off a couple of times. The darkness of this hole was different. I couldn't let Vin die though, and this was the only real chance.

He chuckled. "It's really dark, huh?"

"Too dark for vampire vision, and the blood scent is strong. Varying ages of decay." Whatever was down there was meant to be hidden, and the blood odor came through fresh, so it was still there.

He nodded. "I'm not thirsty."

"You just refused a bag of blood. Don't be a hero. It will be overwhelming down there."

"I'm not. It's the first time since I became vampire I don't feel the thirst burning in my throat."

A created vampire should crave hard with the aroma flowing up from the hole. No illusions existed for me. The hole used to be or might still be the lair of a vampire, and I prepared myself to inflict ultimate death if necessary.

"So how long was I checked out?"

"Long enough for me to try to radio Killian and contemplate ultimate death for whoever set this… trap up. You were like a coma patient. You were there but not."

He rolled his head around and rubbed his neck. "That's kind of how it was. I was here, but I was somewhere else too."

"So you were aware of it?"

"Yes, and no." He ran his hands across his face.

I dropped into the seat next to him.

"Some random images," he said. "Memories returning, I think. It rolled by like a movie in fast forward. I saw my mother."

I held his hand between mine. "She died not long after the ice age hit, right?"

"I thought so," he said. "She seemed real."

"You saw her die, though. One of the few memories you had?" I said, trying to give him a grounded path to reality. *Did he remember that still?*

"I'm not sure."

"You want her to be alive. I understand." My grief knocked at my heart. Grief reared its head in ugly ways, especially for those of us who lost a loved one at the onset of the ice age.

"No, Josie. I saw her alive in this century. In this time."

"Humans don't live that long." My eyes filled with tears for him. The loss renewed for him.

"No, they don't." His eyes hard against mine.

"You think she became vampire?"

"No. She was..." He stared at the window and wiped his hands on his pants. His gaze turned back to me. "I don't know what she was."

"You're conflicted." I thought I saw my mother in every room of the mansion after she died. It was like being haunted at times. When I stopped seeing her, it was like she died again.

"No, I'm confused. It was like..." He paused. "Never mind."

"You can tell me." I scooted the chair back and stepped around behind him. My arms wrapped loosely around his shoulders.

He leaned back, head against my stomach. His hands

rested over mine. "I want to, Josie. I can't articulate it. Not yet."

"Maybe a trip in a dark hole will help put things in perspective." I smiled down at him. "Or give you some answers. This place. This message. It was obviously meant for you.

His lips curled up, but it didn't reach the rest of his face. "Let's go see what you found."

FLASHLIGHTS IN HAND and enough boards pulled up we could get through. The lights revealed the hole was deep. I couldn't see the bottom, but Vin and I dropped broken boards to judge the distance.

"There's no ladder," I said.

"Josie, since when do we use ladders?" A smirk formed on his face.

"Feeling a bit daring today?" It wasn't too far to jump, but we didn't know what the bottom looked like.

"Every day." He held a hand out for me. "Together?"

"Together." I slid my hand into his. *Gods, don't let the floor be covered in spikes.*

We leapt off the edge and fell towards the ground. The temperature cooled around us, and the fall seemed endless. We passed the upper layer, where remnants of human lives remained. The darkness held a pale blue glow from the walls in the next layer. Our feet met the ground with a thud and a scraping noise.

Vin rolled on the ground. "Fuck."

The pain in his voice hard to bear. "What happened?" I knelt beside him.

"I hurt my ankle. Landed on a rock that slid on this slick shit."

No way should a vampire, born or created, be hurt in that drop. "That was only 50, maybe 75 feet. You should be fine."

"Well, it's not." He sat up. "It's not broken, but I felt a sharp pain."

"Something's not right here." I took in a deep breath and looked around us. The blood scent much stronger than from cabin level. Lots of fresh blood in the air.

"I haven't had hurt like that since being vampire."

"Exactly. A vampire shouldn't hurt from such a short jump." Someone didn't want visitors.

"I've jumped from higher." He agreed.

I slid my arm around him to support his weight. We took a few steps together.

He distanced himself from me, bearing the weight himself. "I've got it. It's already healing. It will be fine in a couple of minutes."

The sting hit straight in my heart that he didn't want my help, but the Emperor's daughter smiled through it like I had been trained. "Of course you do."

"I've never seen any minerals shine like this." He ran his hand over the wall. "Yet, we couldn't see them from above."

"It's like they came to life when we jumped."

"Yeah." He studied it. "Almost like a hidden universe."

I turned to him. "It does kind of look like a night sky."

We moved forward in slow motion. The only direction the tunnel went. No need to duck. The ceiling extended well beyond our heads. The path smooth and well kept. Our lights reflected against the blue specks in the walls.

"I didn't dream it would go back this far," I said.

"Me either." His hands smoothing along the rock as we walked.

"Maybe we should turn back," I said.

"No, we need to see the end." His confidence returned in support of the adventure.

"What if it just ends?"

"Then it just ends," he said. "But it won't."

It gnawed at me how confident he was. He couldn't or wouldn't share with me his experience upstairs, but he seemed comfortable down here. All my senses were on full alert. Every smell, taste, sound, visual clue, even the touch of the wall brought a piece of knowledge to me.

"Have you noticed anything else down here?" The scent of blood had grown stronger the further down the path.

"Like what?"

"Nothing. Just curious." Vincent's thirst didn't seem affected by it.

It's like his vampirism turned down or turned off. Impossible, of course. Especially for a created vampire. He wasn't himself. No denying that.

"You seem different." I glanced at him.

His stance appeared more relaxed than me. "I feel different."

"Smell that?" I sucked in the air and tasted it.

"The blood? Yes, for a while," Vin said. *So he wasn't oblivious to it.*

"And the other scent. It's not just human." I reached for my hip where I normally kept a sunshine stick, but it had fallen off after we jumped from the tundra.

"No." He looked around. "Other vampires."

The scent hit me like a wave of a million distinct droplets. "Lots of them. Can you tell?"

"Both born and created. I don't think they've been eating each other." He paused. His eyes closed, and he inhaled so deep. "Definitely not feeding on each other.

Fear snaked up my spine. "That should make me feel better, but it doesn't."

"Me either." His hands brushed over his forearms. Goosebumps formed.

"Your human is showing," I said.

His chuckle bounced off the wall. "Shit. That just gave us away."

"They knew we were here long before a laugh echoed. Have you noticed how easily the sound carries? I'm sure they knew there were new vampires in their midst the moment we landed."

"I suspect you're right, my dear."

Light erupted from the end of the tunnel. I leapt in front of Vincent to shield him.

"Josie, it's not sun."

"Of course." Embarrassed, I smoothed down my clothes and stepped to the side.

Eyes peered back from the end of our sight. I searched for any that glowed with insanity, but none were to be found. My gut twisted into knots, and if I'd been human, my hands would have sweated.

"Come forward so we may see our visitors." The voice came from the mass of eyes, but I could not determine which one.

Vincent reached for my hand and wound his fingers through mine. "We can go back."

We were outnumbered, not by one or two, but a large clan of vampires stood ahead. I gripped Vin's hand. "No, I don't think we can."

He squeezed my hand, and cautious steps carried us forward.

"Ezra's daughter and my son together. I would have never expected it." The female voice boomed around us. My vision clouded with rage. I reached for the absent sunshine stick.

Vincent stiffened. His grip on my hand tightened. Could this be his creator? *What a sick joke to use someone's dead parent like a weapon. I will kill this bitch and enjoy it.*

I rolled my shoulder back. "And you are?"

"Calidora."

I snarled. *Death will come here today.*

She stepped forward. My father's worst enemy in front of me. My mother's killer. Here. *Yes, I would enjoy inflicting revenge in a way only a vampire can.*

Her look statuesque like my father. Hair dark like mine and Vincent's. Eyes the same translucent blue as Vincent's. She could be his birth mother instead of creator. Her garments strange for this time. A throwback to the Roman Empire my father was so fond of. The bold red and gold-colored fabric draped over one shoulder and bound with a gold obi belt just above the waist. She looked like a Roman Empress.

"My mother is dead." Vincent growled.

"I don't think Ezra speaks of his oldest friends often, so the confusion is understandable," she said.

Vincent clenched and unclenched my hand. Pain radiated each time.

"You called me your son. Do you mean you are my creator?"

"No, I mean you are my son."

Born. A born vampire. It would explain much, but Calidora's son? My stomach turned at the thought.

"I know my mother, and you are not her."

"No, you know the human woman I entrusted to raise you. You are indeed my son, and you have returned to me."

Vincent shuddered, his hand a vice around mine. "What proof do you have?"

"Come." She waved her hand to motion him forward. "A drop of my blood will show you."

His grip loosened.

Consuming another vampire's blood for a created was a Rogue sentence. I tugged back on his hand. "Vincent, if you are a created vampire, the damage could be irreversible from even one drop."

"And if I'm not? If I am a born vampire?" His eyebrows arched.

"It will be a rush of memories. The history of our ancestors is passed this way."

"How have I never heard of this?"

"Because..." The words knotted in my throat. Something so sacred we didn't share it with vampires who were not born. It showcased our separation in a way I tried to deny over and over again.

"Because I'm a created one."

"Yes."

His hand slipped from mine, and he strode to stand in front of Calidora. "If you are lying, you will be my first victim."

The smile grew on her face. "My existence is safe."

My stomach hurt. I ground my teeth together to keep from speaking. There was no good in her. Instincts warned every inch of my body. She was evil. *If her destructive ways taint Vin, I will make her suffer.* My nails dug deep into my palm.

Calidora gouged into her wrist with a sharp fingernail

until blood beaded. She held it out over Vin. The droplet fell into his mouth.

He stumbled back several steps. His knees buckled.

I ran to his side to see his eyes glaze over like they did with the box upstairs. He swayed a few times but remained upright. A created vampire would have immediately wanted more. He was a born vampire.

CHAPTER 9

JOSIE - VIN

The information flood weakened Vin. Vampire brains crunch information faster, but blood memories can overload even the most capable. I caught him, and we slid to the floor together.

"She's my mother. She is the one that has been reaching out to me," Vin said, his head heavy in my lap.

I leaned down low enough my lips brushed his ear. My whisper came out soft. "A born vampire cannot summon another born vampire."

"She's not lying, Josie." He sat up next to me, and his forehead rested against the palm of his hand.

Time varied by vampire when it came to blood memories. Sometimes it took hours and sometimes it took days. A vampire could share everything, or only those memories that involved the recipient. The trainers only taught born vampires the skill on how to navigate them. The skills reduced the confusion. Vin, as a created, never got training.

"I know you want to believe you have found your mother, but I've never heard of a born who can control another born."

"Unless they are old. Ancient even." Calidora squatted down next to me and looked at her nails. "Ask your father." Her lips curled up in a phony smile. She wore a fabricated personality like a mask. My first desire to shove the palm of my hand into her nose tempered by the number of vampires surrounding us.

"My father isn't here, and I'm not a child. I've studied and seen how it works." *My father would have struck you down already.*

"Oh, but you are a child in vampire terms." Her condescending tone grated like being scolded by my father.

Whatever, bitch. "A hundred and thirty years might be young to you, but it is certainly enough time to determine another vampire's intention."

She wrapped her fingers around my chin. Her pointy nails dug into my flesh. "And what do you think my intentions are, Josephine?"

Pain radiated from the punctures to my skin. The scent of fresh blood drew my attention. *Pain. She is old.* Her grip loosened, and she shoved me backward slightly. I stared her down.

Vin's fingers made indentions on her wrist. "You will not harm or threaten Josie."

The hard expression on Calidora's face softened. "Of course not. I would never hurt her, my son." Her hand caressed Vin's face like a mother.

Fake. Bitch. "I'm fine, Vincent."

His eyes met mine, and he released Calidora's wrist. He stared at me. My gut said he wanted reassurance from me, and I couldn't give it. The lesson I learned from my exchange with Calidora was that she liked to hurt people, and people in love were the easiest to hurt. Vin and I were the perfect pawns.

"You two are our guests. Let us have a feast to celebrate your homecoming, Vincent." She stood and moved forward toward a door.

Vin up righted himself and pulled me to my feet.

I didn't want to follow her, but I wouldn't leave Vin alone with her either.

"Josie, I want to stay, but I will make sure you are safe first." The strength of conviction in his voice worried me. *Once prey enters the spider's web, it seldom finds freedom again.*

"The team. What about the remainder of our team?." I shot a glare towards Calidora, her back to us.

"You have to understand, Josie. If your mother was alive, you'd want to spend time with her."

No denying that. "I would, but this is different." Fear twisted around my heart and squeezed.

"Trust me."

He asked me to trust him with the vampire who killed my mother. I bit down on my tongue and nodded. *Trust him, yes. Trust her no.*

CALIDORA TURNED. I laced my fingers through Josie's and made eye contact with Calidora. "I'll return once I have Josie on her way." Calidora's disdain for Josie would have been enough for me to want to send Josie away, but we had uncovered the history between Calidora and Ezra. This place would not be safe for the Emperor's daughter, and that wasn't acceptable.

Her body language betrayed the tension in the slightest way. She tried to portray calm and relaxed, but her fingers curled not quite in a fist. She tried to hide it by grabbing the fabric of her dress. Her eyes narrowed in the smallest fraction. Only a tracker picked up on those types of movements.

"We can't allow that," Calidora said. "Guards, close the entrance." She waved two fingers towards the hallway we entered through.

The hair on the back of my neck stood up. Josie's hand tightened on mine.

Guards surrounded us, and a small group moved to the doorway. I watched their actions. It took the strength of ten vampires to slide the enormous blocks of stone in front of the opening. No way we'd be able to open it to get out of here on our own.

My head rested temple to temple against Josie's. "I'm sorry for getting us into this. I will get you to safety."

"I wanted to explore the tunnel," she said. "We survived a helio exploding around us. We will survive this."

My hand firm around Josie's, I pivoted to face my mother. She didn't seem much like a mother. *My mother was a human. This is just the person who gave birth to me.* "What do you want, Calidora?"

"You tasted my blood. Tell me from the memories."

"There were too many." *Death.* It hurt to sift through her memories marred with so much of it. I shook my head. The memories passed so fast it was like a collage of random pieces.

"Sort through them to the time just before the Ice Age."

Images sped past my mind's eye. *Slow down.* The command heard. Pictures moved in a slow, notable pattern, more like changing channels on a TV. The mental video paused at the time before the world was buried in blood and ice.

Temperatures were unseasonably cool. Snow fell in areas where people had never seen it. Still, the humans argued it was a rare weather pattern. My humanity intact. *No, I only thought it was.*

Calidora and I stood in front of a group of vampires. The other vampires fuzzed in the memory, so I couldn't make out faces. "Awaken, my son. Our time is near." She slit the neck of a female with her nail and shoved my face into the neck. I drank the woman dry. *A life. I'd taken a life. Gods.*

I broke the internal movie feed and ground my palms into my eyes as if that wiped the memories away. "I can't watch this." *If only I could erase it again. No, I don't want to forget.*

"Oh, your awakening." Calidora smiled. "A special night. The others will come in time as you learn to control it."

"Awakening?" Josie whispered to me. She grabbed my forearm.

"You've heard of it?" I whispered back. *Will she still love me?*

"Of course she has," Calidora said. "She is the daughter of an ancient one."

"Only stories. We weren't allowed to study the practice. An early generation of vampires would withhold blood from their children. They would essentially grow up in human society until they tasted the blood of a human."

I fought back a gag. "That's what she did to me. She sacrificed a human, and I killed." I rubbed my chest as if I could rub the pain and anger away.

"The blood lust would have been overwhelming for a first feeding in an awakening," Josie said. "You couldn't have controlled it."

"Don't." I pulled my arm away from Josie. My hands rubbed over my eyes. The snapshots stuck like glue to the back of my lids. "I don't know who I am." *The one thing I thought I hadn't done as a vampire wasn't even true.*

"You are the same person you were yesterday and a hundred years ago when we met." Josie placed a hand on my cheek with a gentle touch to guide me to her gaze.

"Am I? I didn't know who I was then." I searched her eyes.

She looked at me the same way. "You are good, Vincent. Challenge what you don't trust. There's a reason for it."

"Even if part of what I don't trust is your father's motives?" *Shit. I'm an asshole.*

She held my gaze. Her body rigid and forehead wrinkled. "Yes."

One word, but it must have been hard to say. She'd been raised to support the Emperor's rule without fail. Her love for him important, but her need to fulfill the goal just as meaningful. *Yep. I'm an asshole for making her say it.*

"Enough of this drivel. The ice age was me. I did it." Calidora held her arms out wide. "And Ezra knew," Calidora said.

"Why would you kill off our food source?" Josie asked.

"Food source? How about humans that died? Humans that had lives?" *Like my mother. The one who raised me.* My voice boomed out of control. Rage threatened to spill. Josie flinched. The guards around us took a step closer, shrinking the perimeter.

"Calm down, my son." Calidora strode forward. "I'll tell you all in due time."

"I hope you are questioning her more than Ezra," Josie whispered out the side of her mouth.

"You should question Ezra at length." Calidora looked Josie up and down. "If you get the chance."

A feral growl erupted from me. "She is off limits if you want anything from me." Panic, led by anger, threatened on the edge.

"For now," Calidora said.

"Forever." My nose a mere inch from hers.

"We'll see," she said. Her voice too chipper for my liking. Fake or confident? I couldn't tell. "Come with me." She looked over her shoulder. "Both of you."

She led us down a long narrow corridor more sterile with low light fluorescents than the majestic glow of the tunnel. The guards flanked us. One turn to the right. One back to the left. Second door on the right. I memorized each turn for when our break at freedom came.

Her hand pressed against a light blue pad by the door. A quick click came from the panel. Not a hand scanner. The door swung opened. Her blood the key, similar to the puzzle box.

"Please," she motioned for us to enter.

I peeked inside to see beakers, microscopes, and other equipment. "Why did you bring us here?" I looked around at the laboratory for anything to use as a weapon. Josie stepped close to me.

"To help you understand what I am doing. There are only two surviving children of the ancient ones. Only two ancient ones left. One ancient and two children stand in this room." She stood silent like she gave us time to process it.

"Only one line will continue," she said. "Mine." Her gaze focused on me.

The uncontrollable growl erupted from me again, and I leapt to stand in front of my birth mother. "Stay away from her." My voice rumbled.

"If you do not wish her dead, we will sterilize her." I felt my face twist in confusion.

The calmness with which she spoke pissed me off. There hadn't been any born vampires in decades. *Why even make that threat? She didn't have a need to or plan to sterilize Josie, and I'd rip her throat out if she tried.*

"You will not touch her."

"There are many born vampires and leaders. What makes us so special?" Josephine crossed her arms.

"Your parents. Your mother and father were both old, and one was an ancient. Vincent's mother and father were both ancients."

"And this matters to us why? I said.

"The ancients had special strengths lost as the others bred." Calidora flipped pages on a journal.

"You want to be a god among your people," I said. *Greed... Insanity... What was her motive?*

She looked up and smiled. "Among all people."

"What do you need us for?" Josephine stiffened.

"I don't need you." Calidora waved a dismissive hand at Josie. "I want my son by my side. To help me rule this new world we have created."

"Created?" It seemed unrealistic that the ice covered world would be a new world for vampires, ancient or not.

"Yes, we engineered this new world for our purpose, and you were always meant to be a part of it." Her hand rested on my shoulder.

I shrugged it off.

"It took you a hundred years to find your son?" Josie asked.

"A hundred years for enough humans and vampires to die off. A little longer than we planned, but I am patient to an extent." She narrowed her eyes at Josie. "Your father made things difficult by keeping Vincent occupied."

"I am a gifted tracker. What is it you are gifted with?" I feared the answer as the words left my mouth, but it could help me figure out how to defeat her.

"You will find out soon enough, but you need to rest first."

"We don't require any rest," Josie said.

"You don't?" Calidora smirked.

She raised her hand and waved it in front of our faces. The edges of my vision darkened. *Josie. I couldn't see her.* I fought against the darkness in vain. The room went pitch black.

CHAPTER 10

JOSIE

I came to in a bedroom chamber similar to my own at the palace. The bedspread rough under my hands, I scrambled to my feet. *No Vincent.* Calidora separated us to proceed with the corruption of him.

The only way out a single door. This room didn't look like the prison it was. Not the modern flare I had chosen, but a more Romanesque style. A little too much for me.

"Josie?" Vincent's faint voice called my name. I spun around to face the door.

Was it really him? You know his voice, Josie. I'm an idiot.

"Yes." My voice a bit gravel like. I crossed the room and opened the door.

Two guards stood on either side of him. "We're not allowed to be alone in the room." His verbal agitation matched my insides.

"What are we teenagers?"

"We'll get more leniency if we cooperate." *Not like him to comply with anything.*

"As the Emperor's daughter, I can't bow down to her," I

said. "Even if I could, I'm not sure I would." I tempered my response for the guards. *No way would I. I'd rip her neck out before I ever bowed down to her.*

"The experience will be better if we do as is expected." Vincent's head tilted to the side and his eyes followed. *Was he drugged?*

Oh! He was trying to give me a signal. This was all for the guards' benefit. If they thought we obeyed, they would report it back to Calidora. Leniency would be ours.

"My trust is yours. What are the expectations?"

"We're never to be alone or interact on an intimate level. The rules of the compound are to be followed at all times. The premises cannot be left without approval of Calidora and a proper escort."

"Sounds a little familiar," I said under my breath. Not that different from Ezra's rules at the Southern Compound. "Understood. I will comply."

"And after my wedding, you'll be released to return to Ezra."

My hand clenched the fabric over my stomach. *Bloody fucking hell.* My entire insides shook while my outside remained composed. "I see. To return to my father is my desire."

His head nodded in the smallest movement. "Then I'll see you at the gathering this evening."

I nodded.

The door closed. A scrape grated against it. The click of a bolt echoed in my ears.

No chance of me interacting with Vincent if I'm locked in the room.

Wedding. His wedding. And I have to watch it. We will escape before that happens. We have to.

Nausea built in me like none I'd ever experienced. My own feet betrayed me. I sank to the bed. Dampness ran down my cheeks. I wiped it away. *Not pink. Red tears.* I'd never had them before, but I'd seen them mark other vampire's faces from internal and external wounds.

Was I wounded? The one place I guarded harder than our survival. Vincent had carved his path into it. My eyes closed, and I surrendered to the thought. *My heart. He doesn't know how deep he'd made it in. He couldn't.*

I rolled onto my side and curled into a ball. *If I had told him, would we even be here now? If I had just told him I love him.* My useless heart beat in a rhythm in time with the repetitive thoughts in my head.

As much of a release as the tears brought, they didn't help me with a plan. My focus shifted to the quiet meditation practice from training. The pictures slowed in my mind until only darkness remained. I sat up in the position we were taught. Legs crossed. Hands relaxed on my knees. The conversation played back through my mind. My heart hopeful for a clue to how to free us both.

He'd given me nothing to go on. Only a smidgen of hope with nods and carefully chosen words. I'd play my part at the gathering tonight if only to get information.

I will not give up. I will not give up on him. I will not give up on us.

My worries quelled the more I repeated my silent mantra. My hope would be my strength. Father had made sure my training included diplomatic negotiations. I would treat tonight's dinner with the same skill I used for diplomats I did not trust. My feelings hidden in order to protect the arbitration.

✳

THE BLACK BEADED GOWN DELIVERED to my room reminded me of the one my mother had worn to the celebration for my finished training. Father made his intentions known to name me his successor that night. Although it would be decades later before he would officially announce it. We imbibed between blood and wine and a mixture of both until our bellies were full.

Months later, I wore the same gown for a party, the last one we had before the world changed. Just before sunrise, we woke to a world bathed in bright alabaster shades. The ice and snow in Dallas in July the first since recorded history. At the gate, obscured by the blowing snow, was Vin.

His blue eyes, hazed and hopeless, looked at me. Pity formed in my stomach. I scooped him up and carried him inside before the first rays of sun could damage his skin. *How wrong I was then. I'd assumed he was created, but now we are in his mother's home. No, not home. Lair.*

I opened the door at the time the little card tucked in with the dress said in expectation of guards to escort me. Vincent's scent filled my nostrils. I soaked in the woodsy vampire aroma and met his eyes.

"I wanted to escort you to the dinner."

"Are they serving humans?" I looked down at his elbow, crooked for me to take. "We're supposed to maintain distance." I wanted to take his offered elbow, but there were rules. My shoulder brushed his as I passed him. The contact all that was needed to stir desire in my belly.

"An exception tonight won't hurt." His steps directly behind mine.

"Won't it?" My chin twisted over my shoulder; I raised an

eyebrow at him. Anger welled inside me. *Calidora manipulated us. Vincent was betrothed. Nothing about this made me want to comply, but yet I had to for appearances.*

"Don't forget this is for a reason."

"I haven't." My steps quickened.

"Your answers are too short. I know what that means."

"Really? What?" I didn't look at him, and I didn't know where I was going. I had to keep moving forward, afraid if I stopped, all my emotions would pour out of me like Vin's vomit in the tundra.

"You're pissed."

I shook my head side-to-side.

"You're really pissed."

"I'm worried, Vincent."

"And pissed."

"If you're trying to be funny, you failed." I slowed my pace.

"Hey." He took my elbow in his hand and stopped me. "We're going to be okay."

His confidence inspirational, but I couldn't share it.

"I'll believe that when we are out of here." I looked up to his eyes to find pink tears. My heart twisted so hard it seemed to turn inside out.

"Trust me to do the right thing."

I did trust him. I didn't trust the situation. "What's going to happen tonight?"

"A feast."

"Before your wedding?" I looked into his eyes.

His forehead bunched. "No, she hasn't chosen my bride, but we'll be long gone before then."

"Let's get this over with." I turned and stepped forward. Calidora's bridal selection party ranked at the very bottom of the list of things I wanted to see.

"Please trust me, Josie," he whispered.

The way he pleaded was enough for me to stop and let him take the lead.

Vin released my arm when we arrived at the entrance to a grand hall. The break in contact left me with emptiness. I noted the vastness of what I thought was an underground bunker. Calidora had built a kingdom underground. Not a bunker. I scanned the room for exits, but they were all blocked by guards.

The hall was decorated for a massive party in human fashion. Formal place settings adorned the tables with platters of human food. Some fruits thought instinct adorned the arrangements. Ushers seated Vin and me. Vin on the opposite side from me, so we faced each other. Every chair at the long table was filled with vampires.

Two guards darkened the doorway. The room stood to attention. The guards turned to the side. Calidora entered with a smile to match the grandeur of the room. She strode in like a queen. *An evil queen.*

The doors opened, and a line of humans filed in and lined the outer wall like staff in an old aristocratic home. *Where had so many healthy humans been found?* Hope sparked for success for the first time since the mission started.

The proximity of so much fresh blood flared the hunger in my stomach. I looked at Vin. Beads of sweat formed on his brow.

Another part of her plan I could see right through. She knew we existed on blood rations and was well aware of how hungry we were. All part of her game.

She approached the table.

"The is quite a group of volunteers. How did you find so many?" My eyes narrowed on Calidora.

"They wish to be part of something bigger." Her hands in a prayer position in front of her chest, she smiled at each one of them.

A door on the opposite side of the room opened. A woman about my height entered the room. Her wavy blonde hair cascaded around her shoulders. A true beauty among the vampire perfection we saw every day. That kind of beauty rare enough it often became a prize.

Vin gazed at her. His head turned and followed her graceful moves. Her movements drew me in as well.

She sauntered across the room, winding her way through the humans. Her fingers traced paths across arms, backs, and shoulders of the volunteers. The actions peculiar to me. It was like a ritual, but not one I'd studied. Each one leaned toward the woman like moons caught in the gravity of the sun. Her eyes locked on Vin.

My hands twisted into the beaded gown hidden under the tablecloth.

He shook his head and turned to me. Confusion lined his face.

A gasp drew my attention. The blonde had red hair wound around her hand. She used it to pull a woman's head back. The vampire bared her fangs. She bent closed and sank her fangs into the soft flesh. Pointed teeth sank slow and deep until blood pooled on each side. Her lips closed around them. Her green eyes watched Vin while she drank.

Disgusted, I looked away. Blood bags gave vampires control. Most vampires frenzied if they drank directly from a human.

Every vampire capable of discerning the difference between a human's heartbeat and a vampire's unneeded one. The human woman's heartbeat sped at a pace much too fast for a human until the vampire consumed most of her blood. Her heart slowed until almost non-existent. She died in the female vampire's grasp. The blonde vamp dropped the lifeless body to the ground.

My heart ached for the human. No one should die with such brutality. At least our donors lived a life and could have a family.

The others didn't move. Not even a flinch. *Drugged?* No, the blood smelled pure. *Either she or Calidora is a Controller.*

"Vincent, meet your fiancé." Calidora took his hand and pulled him forward.

He focused on me. The corners of his eyes turned down. His lips mimicked his eyes.

My own eyes closed to block out what I knew would come. *He'd play the part, because he thought it would save me.*

A shuffle on the floor.

"I'm Vincent."

My eyelids pried open to see him extend his hand to the blonde.

She bypassed his hand and pressed her crimson stained lips to his. "Natasha." Her name, a whisper against his ear.

I could kill her. Rip her head off and set her on fire. Along with Calidora. I glanced at Calidora. A smile plastered across her face. *Setting her on fire would be a pleasure.*

"I knew you would be perfect together," Calidora said. "And I'm always right." She pulled them both into a hug like a human mother would. "Let the party begin." She clapped her hands together twice, and the vampires started speaking like puppets.

I looked back at Vin, but he didn't dare look at me. *Could I leave him here? Would I be able to get back if I went for help?*

CHAPTER 11

VIN

Josie's facial expression crushed my insides like an ice pick on a block of ice. I'd warned her, but it hadn't been enough to prepare her. Hell, it hadn't prepared me. No other woman's lips created the warmth Josie's did. I faked it the best I could. *And I'll do it as many times as needed to keep Josie alive until I can get her out of here.*

"Natasha, you are as beautiful as your name." The words tasted bitter. I hated every one of them. Nothing about this woman's callous actions showed beauty.

"Vincent, your charm lives up to the hype." She smiled, much like Calidora, as she fixed her lipstick.

I nodded to her. "Charm is not one of my talents, but thank you."

"This feast is for you two. Enjoy." Calidora gestured toward the crowd of humans. None moved, even with the dead woman on the floor. No one screamed. No one inched away. No one closed their eyes. None reacted to the horror scene in front of them. Vomit would have been more pleasing than this sight. I tamped down the disgust to keep my face pleasant.

"I don't kill humans," I said. *Except in a memory, Cavanaugh.*

Natasha took my hand. "It's our right. Don't you miss the taste of fresh blood straight from the source?"

No. The only right we have is survival, and that can be done without bleeding humans dry of their life force.

"An old tradition vanquished when Josephine's father took power," Calidora said. Her lip curled up.

"Are these people drugged?" I waved a hand in front of a man's face. He didn't budge.

"Not drugged. They are in their personal paradise," Natasha said. Her sweet smile may have deceived the humans, but not me.

"You did this?"

"She's special like you," Calidora said.

Josie would offer guidance if it were just us. Don't ask in front of these two. Don't even look her way. They watched me too closely to chance it. Josie's safety depended on my compliance with this game. I focused on the love of her to hone my focus.

"I'm nothing special."

"Oh, but you are. Your tracking ability is just the tip of your capabilities." Calidora's smile spread across her face.

I considered her words. Her claims didn't make sense to me. I'd never noticed anything other than my tracking abilities.

Natasha held up her hand to shoulder height and wiggled her fingers. "Humans don't require my touch, but with a touch I can send a vampire into their special place as well." Her fingertips grazed my temples.

Sun bathed my skin. I rolled over in the bed to a pool of dark hair peeking out from under the covers. My fingers gently brushed the hair from her face. Josie smiled. Her eyes fluttered open. The palm of my hand slid across her milky white skin. She raised up. Her lips pressed against mine. Fingers grazed my temple.

My eyes opened. Natasha stood in front of me. The blood of her victim on my lips and in my mouth. A gag formed deep in my belly. I sucked in air to block it.

Calidora laughed. It echoed off the walls. "You two go get acquainted. Josephine, come with me."

I swallowed a growl to keep my outer composure. Inside, I thought of ways to rip Calidora's head from her shoulders.

Josie stared at me but walked to Calidora. Her face flushed. Red wine colored tears dotted the corners of her eyes.

My hand raised from my side, and I shoved it in my pocket to keep from reaching for her. *I'd make her understand later. I'd beg if I had to.*

"I take it I wasn't your fantasy," Natasha said. Her innocent beauty a mask of the evil inside.

"Did Calidora do this to you? Make you kill for her?"

She laughed. "No, silly. She found me and offered me an opportunity for my special skills."

"You enjoy the kill." I tamped down another gag.

"I do. Don't you?"

"I don't kill." I took a step away from her, no longer able to occupy the same space.

"But you're a vampire who has been through an Awakening. We all kill."

Anger built, and I peppered my words at her. "No, we don't." *Calm. I need to stay levelheaded.*

"You are a hypocrite. Your precious Ezra and his followers have collection and storage facilities. The death may be slower, but the humans still die." She frowned. Her movements as fake as Calidora's. The heel of her shoes clicked on the floor when she advanced towards me.

I stepped back my full stride. "You don't know what you're talking about." My arms crossed over my chest with my elbows pointed forward to keep her from closing the distance.

"Actually, I do. I've seen the facilities."

"Our humans are all volunteers. And what does that make you?"

She laughed, a wicked grating nails laugh. "So you think. It's his charade to make everyone, vampires and humans, believe his fake peace bullshit."

Not for the first time, I questioned Ezra's choices, but it was the first an outsider caused the examination. My own feelings reflected in her opinion and not unlike what I had said to Josie.

"Why would you tell me this?"

"Because you think your princess and her father are your saviors, but they are your damnation," Calidora said. Her shadow cast over us into the room. My tracker instincts failed to sense her arrival. *This place. Gods, let Josie be okay.*

"She's not a princess." Josie herself had said the same thing to me, and I used the line to defend her.

"Oh, but she is," Calidora said.

"Where is Josie?"

"Josephine is in the communication room learning about her history." She touched my elbow. "Yours is there too. When she finishes, you can have your turn."

My eyes cut to her hand. Pins and needles pricked my skin where her fingers laid. I pulled my arm back. "I don't like to be touched." Every time she touched me, dread grew. *How much longer can I stand this? Until Josie is safe. That's how long.*

"I know you don't trust me yet, but you will," she said. "In

IN BLOOD & ICE

time." Her arm extended around Natasha's waist. "And I think you will trust your future wife too."

I nodded. *I'd give my own life for Josie. Even if that meant marrying another to keep her safe.*

"Now, enjoy your party. The others are hungry. Choose your favorites before I let them go."

The innocents stood like statues. It disgusted me. If I tried to rescue them, Calidora's guards would just kill them, anyway. "There's no challenge in that. No honor. It doesn't appeal to my appetite. Let them go or release your minions. I'll be in my room." *This battle could not be won tonight. Murder would take place, and I couldn't stop it.*

Screams echoed down the hallway. The screams belonged to the celebration of vampires who feasted on the innocents. The metallic scent of blood filled my nostrils. "Fuck." I let out a sigh and closed the door to my room. The cries diminished one by one until silence reigned again.

I'd spent the last hundred years thinking I was once human. I thought I understood them. Whatever my kind, I didn't want the blameless to be harmed. *Murdered. Not even able to defend themselves.*

I hauled my arm back and punched the door to the private bathroom. It flew across the room and hung in the wall. The doorknob acted like a nail. My strength surprised me. Force not my usual method of resolution. Unlike Killian. *Where the hell is he? He should have found us by now. Unless...*

The bedroom door banged against the wall. I stepped into the hall and took a big whiff. Smells from all across the complex assaulted my nostrils. Fresh blood, the strongest of them. The scent should have sparked hunger in me, but it turned my stomach to think of the lives lost. I ran down the passage to the bend and inhaled again. The slightest hint of his scent detected offered hope.

It strengthened the closer I got to the end of the hall, but not strong enough for me to pinpoint his location. Just the direction. I spun around and tasted the air each way to confirm. The trail led me to wall. *Dead end.* I drew my hands back and shoved them against it.

Bits of the stone crumbled under my fingertips, but it moved. *Yes!* I pushed harder against it. My feet dug into the floor. The wall swung open to reveal the door it was. "This place has more hidden doors than a castle."

"It is a castle to her, dickhead." I smiled in the dark at the familiar voice.

I sucked air into my nostrils. "Killian?"

"Who else?" His voice echoed from the distance.

Only one vampire nearby, so no guards. "You're alone?"

"You're the tracker ass. You tell me."

I sprinted down the narrow hallway. At the end, a small cluster of reinforced cells resided. No lights anywhere nearby. Not that we needed them, but it told me what this was, a holding area strong enough to hold vampires but built to hold meals.

"It smells like humans." I looked for the keys along either side of the hallway. They'd been held here before being served as a feast. A terrible place to be the last memory before death.

"There's a doorway to the banquet hall over there. At least that's what the guards said when they took humans that way." Killian confirmed my suspicions.

I cringed. He deserved an explanation later. "I suppose you already tried to get out on your own?"

Killian crossed his arms and lowered his head. "No, I made this my vacation home."

"Do you know where they put the key?"

"I wasn't awake when they brought me here."

Black and blue marks colored his face. They must have worked him over pretty good to be visible now.

"She's my mother. Calidora is." I checked every crevasse for something to open the cell.

"I heard," he paused. "She's an evil bitch."

"I don't want her killed." The words hadn't even been a thought before they came out. *Why wouldn't I want her ended? One cannot take the life of a born.*

Killian grasped the bars. "We may not have a choice. Do you know what she does?"

"She's a born vampire."

"There are still rules. Even for us. Where is Josephine?"

The rules existed to keep the classes in check. *Killing a born vampire is forbidden. The one exception is for a born vampire who kills another unless in self-defense.*

"In the communications room." *Wherever the hell that was.*

"You left her alone?" Killian slammed his fists against the bars.

"I didn't have a choice," I growled. "Calidora said Josie was learning about our history. I figured it would take both of us to get her out of here, and she wouldn't leave you behind, anyway."

"And you trust her? She could be lying. We are sworn to protect Josephine."

Pain slammed into my stomach. I expected to see Killian's fist buried there, but there was nothing. *Josie.* "We need to find her." Nothing but a whisper on my lips.

"Damn right," He said. "I think you were drugged."

"I didn't think we could be."

"There are some blends of poison that will do various

things to vampires. Make them easier to control. The garden at the compound has some of those plants."

"Make them ambivalent to the someone they love or dull the senses."

"Likely," he said. "Either get me the fuck out of this cage now or go find Josephine."

"I don't see any keys." My fingers found a grove. The indention the size of a palm on the wall next to Killian's cell. I placed my hand in it, and the locks tumbled.

The door opened, and Killian strode out. "That wasn't so hard now, was it?" He patted my shoulder. "Let's go find our girl."

"She may not be very happy to see me." *Why did we even come down here? If we'd just left the cabin.*

"What did you do this time?" Killian shook his head.

"Got engaged to someone I just met." I peered down the way I'd come.

"You're fucked."

"My mother arranged it."

Killian stifled his laughter, but his shoulders shook. "If that's your excuse, she's going to give you the cold shoulder for the next century."

"God, I hope not. I don't think I can go a century without her. This has been close enough."

"I understand, brother." He paused at the end of the hallway. "She needs trust to feel safe. Just don't give her a reason to not trust you."

Killian never called me brother before. *Progress. Maybe we didn't have to hate each other.* Our common goal to save Josie united us.

He stilled.

His arm shot out through the doorway like a viper. It

recoiled in with his prey. A guard on patrol. Killian snapped the guard's neck so hard it severed from the man's body. He tossed the head to the floor in the pool of blood. We watched it turn to embers and ash at our feet.

I hated to see an ending of a vampire, but regret was hard to come by today. "That's why they call you Killer Killian, dude."

"No, it's because I have more kills than any other vampire." He looked each way. "Where is the damn communications room?"

CHAPTER 12

JOSIE

I sank back in the chair, focused on the monitors. *The entire ice age a power play by the ruling vampires for control. My father, the leader.* A heaviness weighted me down to the chair. It embarrassed me how I didn't see it. That it was preventable.

My father's image, among the other vampires who'd ruled for a thousand years, clear and stoic. They conspired against the others. *Population control.* That's what they called it. Too many vampires and too plentiful food. *Food meaning humans.*

"Jos--" He cleared his throat. "Josephine?"

I swiped my fingers under my eyes. "Yes, I'm here." Forced a smile, and faced Vin. "I thought you…" Killian stood behind him in the doorway. I closed my eyes and inhaled their scents. *They are both safe.*

"You've been--" Vin started.

"They were performing population control." The flatness in my voice jarred me, but I continued. I needed to say it out loud. To solidify it in my mind. "The ruling vampires were positioning for control." My eyes diverted to the screen. "This is my heritage."

"You are not your father." Vin's hands squeezed my upper arms.

His touched soothed me, but it didn't fix the brokenness the tapes revived.

"We can't bring those people back, but we can make it right." His fingers wrapped around my shoulders and guided me to face the screen with him. He searched through the images.

I'd seen all I needed to see. No part of me wanted to see more. I watched Vin instead.

The corners of his eyes dropped. His mouth fell open slightly.

"Vin." I rubbed his arm.

"You haven't called me Vin since we broke up."

Not out loud, anyway.

Those big blue eyes darted to mine. Tears pooled but didn't spill over. His humanity so much more alive than mine ever would be. Maybe the years of believing he had been human made him different from the rest of us.

"I need you to get through this." Even as I said it, the thought fleeted. Amends needed to be made to so many before I deserved it for myself. *And we still have to get away from Calidora, and the sham marriage she is planning for him.*

"No, you don't, but I'm here for you." His eyes shot to the screen. Fingers fumbled with the control to rewind to what caught his attention.

"Who is this? She looks familiar."

"That was my mother before she died. It's her painting that hangs in the study at the compound." I trailed my fingers over the figure as she moved across the screen, flanked by her guards. *No, not her guards. Those were father's guards. Most of them gone now.*

Vin spun me into his arms. "Don't look. You don't need to see this again."

My forehead landed against his shoulder with a thud and echoed through the hollow vacancy in my chest. "He killed her. My father had my mother killed." Fresh tears burned their way down my cheeks. I stared off over his shoulder. "Why did he have her killed?"

"She spoke out against their beliefs, and the people loved her. As long as she was around, he would never have had the support," Killian said. He moved closer.

Vin's arms tightened around me, securing my body to his.

I raised my head up. "Did you know?"

Killian shook his head. "I knew they had fought about his treatment of humans and lesser vampires. Suspected? Yes." He leaned forward in the screen's direction. "But I never had proof."

"Now you have the proof," Vin said. "We've witnessed it. The next step is yours, Josie." He kissed the top of my head.

"No, the next step is getting out of here," Killian said.

I sat upright. "Why would Calidora let us have this information?"

"She wants your father destroyed," Vin said. "Something has broken down in their alliance."

"The population control has gone too far. They killed too many humans with the ice age. The current human numbers can't sustain the blood needed to support so many vampires." The whole thing sickened me and deepened the crevasse in my chest.

"Our mission wasn't what we thought," Vin said.

"No, he wanted to flush your mother out of the shadows." I said. The entire expedition had been so Father could locate his enemy. He had to have known we would find out her identity. Had he hoped I would kill her? Do his work for him?

"And we led him right to her. She's her own brand of crazy. I'm not sure which is worse," Vin said.

"They have both committed the same crimes against our people and the humans," Killian said. He looked at the video feed. "Can we broadcast it out?"

My father's reign would end if I broadcasted it. If he was ended from it, I'm not sure I could live with the consequences.

"The signal isn't strong enough from here." Vin shook his head.

"But it is from our compound," I said.

"That's a long way." Killian checked the hallway.

"No, not our home today, but the compound I grew up in. The Dallas base of operations."

"Yes, everything was still functional," Vin said. "I think it would work."

"Let's make it happen. Our people have the right to see what their leaders have been up to." I turned and took a step towards the door. Rationalization took hold, and I stumbled slightly. "Chaos is going to erupt." All those we lost, and we could lose many more if we handle this wrong. I stepped back and rubbed my temples. My head pounded.

"A rebellion will be costly," Killian said.

"Sacrifices pave the way for change. We can't stand by and allow them to rule. Not just my mother and your father, but all those in the video." Vin stood with his feet firmly planted in place.

"Most of them are already dead and their successors have long been at the helm. Those groups will likely not care about penance for the sins of a past leader," Killian said.

Vin gripped the edge of the desk. "He's right. Too much time has passed and too many leaders have changed hands."

"You think, as a race, we would not feel the overarching need to correct this horrible act?" I couldn't believe what they said. My heart fractured they would give up so easily.

"No, I think change is needed, but expecting the predecessors to give a shit about what others have done is not realistic. Our race is a bunch of selfish bastards." Vin pointed to the video screen.

"They won't willingly give up an ounce of power," Killian paused. "Our forces are not large enough to protect our home and wage war."

"But if Ezra and Calidora joined forces, they would be..." Vin whispered.

"We have to stop them." I looked first to Killian, then to Vincent. Their faces somber. "No matter what the cost."

Vin nodded. His fingers navigating the keyboard with commands. "I'm transferring the files to our servers."

"We have a new mission," I said. "After we get out of here."

My father always thought his way was the only way, and my eyes were wide open to what an ass he could be. Even so, I didn't know evil of this magnitude was in his repertoire.

Could Vin kill his mother if it came to it? Could I kill my father?

"We'll do it for each other if we can't capture them," Vin said, as though he read my mind. "Our parents."

"I will give myself in sacrifice for our true leader." Killian bent at the waist in a traditional deep bow to me. While he had been my lifelong friend, Killian's loyalty never swayed. He was a citizen of the nation. A warrior of the private guard. His pledge fed my confidence in my decision.

I rested a hand on his shoulder. "Thank you, my friend. I cannot repay your loyalty." I said. "We need numbers."

Killian stood. "The real problem will be the ones loyal to them. What about your bride-to-be, Vin?"

My teeth ground together. Killian picked at Vin, but I couldn't stand the thought of another woman being Vin's bride.

"It's not real. My mother's doing." Vin didn't even look up from the keyboard. "Leave her here."

"You're not leaving me anywhere, darling." Her fake nice voice grated on me. I thought she was smarter than to insert herself in a situation like this, but she had Calidora's favor. We couldn't take her with us, but we couldn't leave her to tell our plans, either.

"You're not going with us." Vin jumped between me and Natasha, blocking the entrance to the room.

"I'm going to scout for some transportation. Be ready to move upon my return." Killian took off down the hall. "You're on your own, dumbass."

"Thanks, brother," Vin called after him. "Come back soon."

I bit back the urge to laugh, still angry at Natasha's presence.

"The novelty of a princess has worn off. The value is in the video, and you will never make it out of here without me. I'm the only one in the room who can come and go as I please and with who I please."

"Or I could just snap your neck." I lowered my voice.

"You do love my fiancé. Don't you?" Her eyes narrowed and her red lips turned up at the corner.

I drew my hand back to knock the smirk off her face, but it hit hard against a wrist bone not belonging to Natasha.

"Not now, Josie," Vin said.

I growled, but backed down. We couldn't afford for her to run back to Calidora now.

"Look at my future husband taking up for me," Natasha squealed.

I lunged forward, and Vin's hands wrapped around my waist. Warmth radiated through me. His touch in control of the thermostat. I leaned back into him. *He loves me. Not her. You know this, Josie. Release the anger.*

"But his arms are around me." I rested my hands over his.

"I forgot how jealous you can be," Vin whispered in my ear. "If we were somewhere else, I'd show you how I feel about it."

"I forgot how you like women to fight over you." Decades old memories resurfaced of the events leading up to our breakup. I pushed out of his muscular arms. He really hadn't encouraged Charlotte's stalker obsession back then or Natasha's advances now.

"You know that's not true," Vin said. His hands fell away.

"We have penance to do for the hell our parents have created," I said, changing the subject. I didn't want to discuss our past in front of Natasha. "Let's get the video and get out of here."

Vin dropped into the seat without a word and finished his task.

Killian emerged through the door. "I've located a vehicle we can use."

"Good. I've got the video." Vin pulled some pieces from the computer equipment.

"Let's go enlighten the world." I rotated to Natasha. "If you're coming with us, you will keep your mouth shut or I will yank your fangs out of your head." Perhaps it was pity that caused me to concede to bring Natasha.

Killian snickered and led the way down the hall.

Steps echoed behind me. My vampire hearing pinpointed the order. Vin took up the rear behind Natasha. She was close on my heels. Close enough, the urge to throw an elbow into her nose came to me.

"There weren't any guards this way?" I asked.

"No," Killian said.

"That doesn't seem strange to you?" I asked. *No guards. What game is Calidora playing? Is she just going to let us walk out of here?* I glanced at Natasha. *Maybe Calidora was letting us go because her spy is with us.*

"Yes."

"You're one-word responses always make nervous, Killian." I scanned the space.

"That makes two of us." He motioned for us to take cover behind a small vehicle..

Vincent peered over it. "Do you think she is letting us go?"

"Not without a purpose," I said.

"There's the vehicle." Killian jerked his head to the right.

I followed his motion to see a modern and well-equipped transport. "She wants us to go."

"I don't care what she wants. We need to get you out of here," Vin said.

Not just me. We all need to go… except Natasha. I already regretted letting her travel with us.

"Did you check for weapons?" I asked Killian as we approached a sleeker version of the tundras we were use to.

"No, but…" He opened a rolling cabinet next to the vehicle and grabbed three Vampire Killers. The powerful guns built to rapid fire small stakes. The size of the stake never mattered, as long as it pierced the heart in the right place. He handed one to Vin and me and took one for himself.

"What about me?" Natasha asked.

Let her try for one.

"No," Killian said.

She reached across in front of him. *Predictable.*

Killian's quick reflexes caught her wrist and pulled her hand up, away from the weapon. "No."

Natasha ran the back of her fingers against his cheek. A smile crept across her face. "You are interesting."

Killian's jaw tightened. He guided her toward the vehicle and let go of her when they reached the door.

Vin stood behind me. "Get in, Josie."

I climbed in and took a seat in the instrument room. Natasha sat buckled into a seat at the back. Killian's doing, no doubt. I concealed a smile.

"Let's go." Vin closed the door with a loud thud.

No one showed up to stop us. *Definitely a trap. We couldn't pass up a chance to get away, so into the trap we must go.*

We took off through the snow toward the Dallas compound. When we reached a safe distance, I spun my seat around to face Vin.

"Don't you think it is odd that after everything Calidora went through to keep us there, she just let us go?"

"She's insane."

"No, she's very sound minded. She's sadistic." I paused. "Apparently, it is something she and my father have in common."

"Josie, I know this will not be easy for you."

"Or you. Your mother is going to be a formidable adversary, but you don't really know her intricacies. At least I've had all my life to see how my father is."

Vin tensed. "She's not my mother. My mother is who raised me. I have no loyalty to Calidora."

"You say that now, but she has her ways. You will not be able to stand against her," Natasha said.

"Stay out of our conversation," I said.

"It's okay," Vin's voice softened for me. He looked over his shoulder at Natasha. "What do you mean, she has her ways?"

"She's like me, but different. Her strength is in her ability to control and bend people to her will. I had no desire to leave the comforts I enjoyed when she showed up at our home. Somehow, she convinced me to return with her, and I don't even remember how. The next thing I knew I was a prisoner and no hope of survival unless I did her bidding."

Vin studied Natasha. His posture relaxed. He seemed to soften towards her.

The urge to gouge out her eyes overwhelmed me, and I dug my nails into the armrest to keep from doing it. *This damn jealousy would be my undoing if I didn't get it under control.* I inhaled a deep breath. "Why should we believe you?"

"Don't. It doesn't matter to me. Either she kills me for failing to seduce her son. Or you kill me for being engaged to your lover. My life is forfeit regardless." Natasha shrugged, matter-of-fact about her potential ending.

"You haven't exactly made me feel sorry for you," I said.

"Josie," Vin said. He arched a brow my direction.

It was harsh on my part. There wasn't a bone in my body that trusted her. I crossed my arms and leaned back against the seat.

"What does she do to control them? Is it the same thing you do?" Vin asked.

"Not at all. I seduce to bend them to my will. They are like zombies under her control."

"Zombies?"

Natasha scoffed. "Well, they don't eat brains, but they

aren't exactly conscious either. I remember nothing about how I traveled to her home."

"That makes sense," Vin said. "I thought they acted like zombies when I was standing in front of them too."

I looked at Vin. "Why didn't it work on us?"

"I don't know." He sank back into the seat. "Natasha, are you a pure blood vampire? Born of two borns?"

"Yes." Natasha's voice timid and soft, like she didn't know of the vampire law that a born cannot kill a born without just cause. It was the first time I sensed fear from her. "Calidora wouldn't have sanctioned our marriage if I wasn't."

"Then I don't know why we are different."

"You are from her bloodline. That might be reason enough for you," Natasha said.

"But not for me," I said. Nausea formed at the top of my stomach. My eyes widened. "We're not. Right? We can't be?"

"We're not, Josie. Take a breath. There's another explanation. You are from the strongest and most powerful line of vampires."

Natasha let out a loud laugh and doubled over in the seat. "Does this mean the engagement is back on?" She wiped at her eyes.

Hate might not be strong enough for her.

"Someone shut her up. If I have to stop to do it, she will be left on the side of the road," Killian said. Not typical of him. The tundra went silent.

Natasha's mouth snapped shut. Her eyes narrowed in his direction, but her lips curled up at the ends.

I turned my seat around and focused on the road ahead. My head fogged some at the task ahead of us. I would need all my strength to complete it. Betrayal wasn't something I dealt. Ever. Yet, my next move would be a monumental betrayal against my father. My reflection in window showed a wrinkled forehead. The burden of what waited ahead written there for everyone in the vehicle to see. Including fucking Natasha. I glimpsed her reflection in the window too. Her fixation was on Killian, not Vin. My heart did a little leap at the thought she might have other interests in our escape. Regret replaced my momentary joy. Natasha's fangs better stay away from both of these men.

CHAPTER 13

JOSIE

Blizzard like conditions made the drive back long. I sat on edge the entire trip, worried Calidora's forces would attack. The compound looked like a mausoleum in the fresh snow. It should be a relief to arrive home, but the giant C on the roof prevented it. I clamored out of the battle vehicle.

"And you're sure no one followed us, Killian?"

"Josie, Killian is tired of your questions," Natasha said. She reached her long fingers out and rubbed along his shoulders.

Vomit rose up into my throat. I checked my instinct to foot sweep her ass.

Killian relaxed at her touch. *Of course he did. He had no real armor to the power over vampires and humans.*

Killian started his job to lockdown and conceal the truck.

"You two can go inside and relax. I'll help Killian." Natasha smiled.

My eyes landed on Killian's with an arched brow. He nodded. His strength wouldn't be a match against her gift.

I narrowed my eyes at Natasha. She fidgeted.

"Her power is to create a paradise in your head. Just

remember that," Vin whispered to Killian loud enough for all of us to. *Good.* Vin didn't trust her alone with Killian, either.

"You're no fun," Natasha pouted.

Vin and I walked toward the door. The normal sounds and scents drifted to us. Nothing out of place. Calidora could have sent forces while we were captive, but she didn't. I was grateful those here were safe. It left one question on my tongue. *Why?*

"Have you made peace with the civil war we are going to start?" Vin's hand rested on the small of my back as we walked into the foyer.

Tingles from his touch aroused familiar desire. Never forgotten. Always there. I swallowed hard. I opened the door to the office off the foyer.

"No, I'm not sure I'll ever make peace with it or with the fact the rest of our crew is gone. My father is likely to die the ultimate death from my decision. There's not much peace to have with that. My solace is in justice for my mother."

"We don't have to do it."

I fixed my eyes on him. When I thought he couldn't dig a deeper place in my heart, he did. Only love could lead the offer he gave me, but the humans and vampires deserved more than this. The crew who sacrificed for this mission deserved more. "Yes, we do. History can't be repaired, but we can set it right for the future. What the world does with it is up to them."

Vin's mouth formed into a sad smile. "The Josie I know couldn't dump news like that and walk away. They will need a leader."

"I'm not that person." They needed someone not born and groomed for it. Maybe even a created.

"You are. You're a leader who will make sure the truth guides the way."

"We're still vampires, Vin. Blood is always going to be the strongest commodity. Allegiance is bound in blood."

"And in ice."

I can do this. I've been groomed to lead all my life. Maybe not to betray my own father, but he betrayed the entire world. This is the right path. It's the way Mother would have chosen if she were here. There is no other way. I will lead us to a future where Mother would have been proud. "Let's get it all set up."

"You can always change your mind until the button is pushed." His hand cradled my cheek.

I leaned into it. "I'm not going to change my mind."

"No one expects you to turn against your father."

"No, they don't. He doesn't either. It will crush him." Tears warmed my eyes and spilled down my face.

Vin's other hand rested against my cheek, and his thumbs smoothed away tears.

"Why am I crying for my mother's killer?" A sob erupted.

Arms wrapped around me and pulled me to him. I bawled into his shoulder.

"His choices were his, and yours are yours alone. You do not have to deliver his death sentence."

"Whether the current power hungry vampires want to be on the right side or not, they will likely use it to seize power. I'm not rethinking what to do, but I am rethinking doing it here, so far from most of them."

"He'll never let it happen from the Southern Compound."

"No, he won't." I sucked in a breath. "Then it has to be here."

Vin leaned in and pressed his lips to mine. Our lips parted.

SUSAN PERSON

His tongue probed. The sweet and salty metallic taste filled my mouth. The rapid beat of my heart thumped in my ears.

He pulled back slightly without breaking contact. His breath hot against my cheek.

I threw my arms around his neck and kissed him hard on the mouth.

"Hmmm. Hmm." Natasha giggled.

Annoying little troll. "Fucking hell," I mumbled. "Natasha, are you and Killian done already?"

"Yes, but I think the ice is melting outside from the two of you."

"Where's Killian now?" Vin asked.

"He went to check the security cameras, and he told me to find you two."

"I better join him," Vin said.

"You might take a walk outside first." Natasha smirked and twirled her finger in a circle while pointing to his crotch. "Maybe drop some ice down your pants, because that is going to hurt in a few minutes."

Vin kissed my cheek and left without a word. My embarrassment likely enough for both of us.

"You love him," Natasha said. "Calidora didn't know there was a bond between you two."

"It's none of your business." I put my hands on my hips and stared her down. "I don't think Calidora cares. Nor do I think you do either."

Natasha shrugged. "What's the story with Killian?" She looked down and pushed the rug around with the toe of her shoe.

"Ask Killian."

"He's not much of a talker." Natasha fiddled with the hem of her shirt.

"You like him."

She stared at the wood floor.

"You do." I crossed my arms. "And you want my help with him."

"Yes!" She bounced and took a step towards me.

I stepped back. "I have bigger priorities than making a love match between you two. Besides, I care about Killian too much to push him into your arms."

"Are you in love with him, too? He certainly cares a lot about you." She hugged herself.

"Oh, you are fishing to see if there is anything between Killian and I." I nodded. "No, Killian and I are friends and only friends. Not that it helps you any."

"Are you always such a bitch?"

"Says the woman who tried to marry the man I..."

"Love? You can't even say the word. If you think I'm fucked up, you need to look in the mirror."

My insides went cold. Time taught vampires nothing. We lived forever as long as there was food. The cruelness in us festered and blocked any humanity in us. *If there were any.* I forced out a breath. *Putting trust in Natasha equaled stupidity to me. She's probably spying for Calidora. Gods. Fine. I'll try to be nice.*

"I'm not much of one for female bonding. I was groomed to lead, not make friends. What do you want, Natasha?"

"Tell me what Killian wants in a woman."

This will probably be messy, but Killian had taken notice of her too. "Killian is straight forward. He values honesty above most everything. If you want a chance with him, you need to let go of this fake persona you put on and be the real you."

Her eyes widened and narrowed in a heartbeat.

"You don't know who you are without all this facade. Do you?"

She bit her lip.

"You need to figure out who the real Natasha is before you can think about anything with Killian."

Her hands flailed up around her head. "Who knows if I will ever figure that out after all these years of being this Natasha."

"He's not going to entertain anything if you can't. Sounds like you need to figure out if he is worth it to you." Love life advice wasn't on my list of skills, but Killian tossed fake vampires aside like garbage.

"Is there somewhere I can freshen up?" Her face hardened again, like a beautiful stone.

"Yes. Let me show you."

THE DOOR CLICKED as I pulled it to behind me. I made my way to the control room to find Vin and Killian. The empty hallway created space for my thoughts, and I looped back to the conversation with Natasha. *Was Natasha different from me? I wasn't sure who I was either, and I had taken orders from a leader who committed shameful acts. Our differences might not be as vast as I first thought.*

I leaned against the doorjamb. Vin's head turned in my direction like he knew I watched him work. He held his hand out for me.

I slid in next to him. My hip tucked against his shoulder. "Almost done?"

"Yes, but I will give you the honors of pushing the button."

He made a few last commands. "All yours whenever you are ready."

"So much weight resting on that button." My world. Vin's world. The entire world would change once we sent this message. It could be chaos or anarchy, or vampires and humans could see the new vision and want to help see it through. *If they join us, we might actually have a future. That's what I need to make them see.*

"Yes, there is," Killian said from his seat on the other side of the room. "Natasha should be here for this. Whether or not she wants to be, she is part of this change now."

I trusted her not one ounce more, but she went from one shit situation to another. I could give some empathy for her.

"She is a product of her circumstance much like you, Josephine," Killian said.

Vin's fingers curled a little tighter around my waist.

"She might not be as heartless as I originally thought." I conceded to my thoughts on the way to this room. Natasha and I weren't so different. Her experience was not unlike the time I spent with my father after my mother died. Before that I had my mother as a buffer. I suspected Natasha never had a support system.

"I see you can't stop talking about me." She sashayed in on cue.

"Killian thought we should wait on you before throwing the switch," I said. "And I agreed."

"Isn't this basically an eFace post inviting everyone to kill us?" she asked.

Social media wasn't completely gone, but humans weren't the primary users any longer. It had become part of the spy network and a place to connect with mercenaries. Some vampires still connected there for the sake of connection with old friends.

"Not exactly. I have my own following, on and off of that platform, but we will need more numbers than that gives us," I said. "Hopefully, the message circulates quickly and the responses come fast."

"What's to stop your father and Calidora from sending their best mercenaries after us?" Natasha made an excellent point, and one I had considered. She understood the risk better than I imagined.

"Nothing specific, but knowing my father, I'm betting they will want them close to protect themselves against the factions who will want vengeance. If they don't, then we will be prepared for it." *If we can't prepare for that, we don't stand a chance at battle anyway.*

"I don't see how that differs from what they are doing."

"Their motives are power driven. Ours are setting things right."

"Hmm.. Maybe," Natasha said. "Post your video whenever you want. I'm going to the kitchen to look for wine."

"Doesn't seem like you to miss a show, Natasha," I said.

Killian's face hardened. "Stop it, Josephine." He walked out of the room in the same direction Natasha went.

"You don't have to be so hard on her. You have everything in her eyes, and she has given up the only security she had to help us."

"Has she really helped us?"

"I think she might have had something to do with us escaping so easily."

My gut twisted. "How did we get out of there so easily?"

"It wasn't an accident."

"No, I don't think it was." Natasha's gift could definitely have helped clear the path. If she did, was it for personal gain?

"Are you ready to do this?" Vin squeezed my hand.

I paused with my finger over the key. The future we wanted to build began as soon as I pressed the button Vin indicated. "For my mother."

"Second thoughts?"

"No," I said.

The power blinked on and off a few times. The screens went blank, and the room went dark. *Coincidence or sabotage.* "Really? Now? Think it's a sign?"

My vampire vision adjusted and cut through the darkness. The furnishings came into focus. A blue glow came from Vin's eyes. Most vampire eyes had an aura in the dark, but his were particularly brilliant.

"No more so than our escape." Vin stood up, and he continued to hold me close.

"If it was another situation, I would find this funny. Today, it's like dropping a brand new cellphone on a rough cement surface." *Bloody hell.* We knew from the C on top of the mansion Calidora had been here. I'd be surprised if she didn't have a kill switch on the power. Maybe the plan was to trap us here. But why? A bigger blow to my father to do it here.

Vin stepped into the hallway. "I need to go check the electrical room."

"Maybe Natasha did it," I said.

"I don't think her skills include cutting off electricity."

"The worst mistake you can make is underestimating a woman like Natasha." I'd witnessed my father's regimen for spy training, and if Calidora's was half as good, her spies were dangerous. Natasha seemed genuine in her desire to get away though.

A scream reverberated off the walls. I jerked around and peered into the darkness. "Was that her?"

"It sounded like her." Vin motioned in the direction of the sound.

We scrambled toward the direction where the sound came from. As much as I wanted to hate her, I didn't. At least not anymore, and I didn't want her to be ended without cause. Two steps inside the kitchen, and we found Natasha and Killian laughing.

I glanced between the two of them. There was nothing funny about the power being off. A good slap might stop the madness.

Natasha glimpsed us and kept laughing.

"Sorry. Killian snuck up on me." She slapped his shoulder playfully.

"This is not playtime," I said. "We have a situation."

"My apologies." Killian bent formally at the waist toward Natasha. He turned to us and did the same.

Natasha giggled and covered her mouth.

So immature. My head cocked over to the side. "Maybe we don't sneak up on each other given our lives are about to be endangered."

Natasha's hand dropped to her side. "Good idea."

"I'm going to the electrical room," Vin said.

"I'll go with you," I said.

"As will I," Killian said.

"And I have to stay here by myself?" Natasha's bottom lip jutted out.

"All four of us don't need to be in the electrical room. Killian, why don't you and Natasha go back to the computer room and start the reboot when we get the power back on."

"That is an excellent idea," Natasha said. She clapped her hands together twice.

Killian's face hardened into his warrior look. "It is my duty to protect you, Josephine. Even more so now."

Even in the darkness, the disappointment covered Natasha's face.

"So formal," I chided Killian. "Seriously, the quicker we get the computers rebooted, the better. Vin can protect me from the spiders in the electrical room."

Natasha's grin returned.

Her happiness too much for me, but I wanted to warm to her if she made Killian smile. And if she wasn't a spy.

"As you wish," Killian said. His hand extended toward the doorway. They lingered in each other's gaze before heading down the hall.

Vin stepped up beside me and slipped his arm around my waist. "Is there something going on with those two?"

"I think there is about to be." I smiled. "As much as I don't want to like her, I'm starting too. I haven't seen Killian look that happy in a long time."

"Poor Killian." Vin guided us in the opposite direction. The hallway was dark even for vampire vision.

"I know. She really wants to get to know him." *Like really.* "I don't think she knows who she really is. Something I understand very well." I paused. "Something I would think you would understand too."

"I've never seen a vampire with such desire to help others."

"I get that from my mother." A twinge in my chest reminded me of her absence.

"You mother must have been very special."

"She was. She was the epitome of kindness, which makes it all the more egregious what my father did." A pang in my stomach triggered nausea. "I cannot put into words the anger I feel for him."

"You know, Josie, sometimes actions done in anger lead to regret. Maybe you should wait for the anger to pass before you act upon it."

"It's never going to subside, but this isn't about revenge on him. It's setting the world right," I said. "Or resetting."

"This is the room." Vin blocked the doorway. His hand touched my face. Gentle brushes from his thumb drove the nausea and anger away. "Don't let it consume you. Don't let it make you into someone like him. Maybe take some time to think about what your mother would want you to do." His blue eyes glowed and went dark. He bent in to kiss my forehead.

Mother would always do the right thing despite status or popularity, which is why she was so loved. How I missed her guiding hand. Grief settled in my chest. I didn't need my lungs, but they couldn't get enough air despite that. Vin's words hung deep in my chest. Pain seized me. My knees buckled and thudded the marble floor. Shrill noises echoed off the walls. *Sobs. Mine.*

"Fuck. Josie. I didn't mean to upset you. I'm sorry." His voice close to my ears. He sat on the floor in front of me. Arms encircled me. He pulled me into his lap and held me tight against his chest.

My eyes opened to find the hot tears that burned down my cheeks and off my chin formed a pink circle on Vin's white shirt. I swiped my fingers across it and met his gaze.

"She wouldn't want me to punish father. She wouldn't want anyone to suffer. If releasing the tape would cause more pain than the good it would do, she wouldn't want it released."

"Have you changed your mind?"

"I want to be more like my mother than my father. Her path was defined by doing the right thing for the greater good. I need to be able to say I am doing what is best for people."

"Good choice." He kissed the top of my head.

"We still need to remove my father from power, but not at the cost of so many lives. I can't guarantee protection if we release it now, and the last thing I want is to bring death to the people who have put their faith in us to help them survive." I rubbed the dampness from my face.

"That's the Josie I know. I'd support you either way, but I like this path better."

"I'm so afraid I am more like him."

He crooked his finger under my chin and lifted. "You're not. As long as I've known you, the desire to help people has been there."

"It's going to be much harder ousting my father face-to-face versus with a revolution. The thought of having to look him in the eyes is like a human raking their teeth on a fork." I cringed. He would not go easy, and it would be a loud and painful exit.

"The right thing to do will come to you." He stood up and took me with him. His firm grasp setting me straight up on my feet. "We need to get the power back on. There's no telling what Natasha is putting Killian through."

"So quick to take his side." I tapped my fist against his shoulder. "He's not perfect."

"No, but she is a product of Calidora."

"She was a prisoner for a long time. She deserves an opportunity to redeem herself. If she fails to do so, we'll deal with her appropriately."

Change needed for all of us, but it started within each of us.

"Impressive to see your attitude change."

I whispered in his ear. "I am capable of change."

"Are you capable of rewiring?" Vin held up a handful of wires.

"Shit," I said. "Do you smell that?" The singed scent swept up my nostrils. This was intentional.

"The fried wire burnt smell? Yes."

"And the cologne? It's a strong, woodsy smell. Way too strong for a vampire."

"If we have humans cutting power, we have a problem." Vin dropped the wires and sniffed the air.

A human attack wouldn't be a threat to us personally, but it threatened the overall mission. Our numbers couldn't take on two battles, and we needed the trust of the humans.

"We need to find Killian and Natasha." I backed out of the room.

"Quickly," Vin added. We took off in a dead run of silent supernatural steps on the slick marble.

Vin rounded the corner into the room a few steps ahead of me.

I slammed into his back. "What the hell?"

He turned around and tried to usher me out of the room.

"Let go of me." I pushed around him. "Oh..." I covered my eyes. Killian and Natasha together burned into the back of my lids.

I buried my head in Vin's chest as he walked me backwards out of the room. Vin scrambled for the doorknob and shut the door.

CHAPTER 14

I led Josie to one of the unused rooms. The dark office dustier than some of the others from a lack of use. Electricity blinked back to life around us. I inhaled, looking for scents, but the dirt particles we stirred up masked it. No humans. No unknown vampires.

"I'm not sure I will ever get that view out of my brain," Josie said. "There's not a room dark enough to hide that."

"I tried to turn you around and make a quick exit."

"Vin, you need to work on how to communicate people having sex in a computer room." Josie laughed.

"I think I did a pretty good job, and I got the door shut behind us." I chuckled.

The door flew open. Natasha and Killian emerged clothed in an interesting fashion.

"Our apologies," Killian said, his voice extra low and quiet. He straightened his shirt.

"How about that kind of stuff happens in a bedroom next time?" Josie's eyebrow shot up .

"Anywhere other people can't come along." *Ugh.* "Poor word choice."

Natasha looked at her fingernails. "Boring," she said under her breath.

"Better than being walked in on," Josie said.

"We will make sure that if it happens again, it will be in a bedroom," Killian said.

"If?" Natasha's voice an octave higher than before. She spun on her heels.

"Natasha wait. Notice the power isn't back on? We have a problem. A human problem," Josie said.

Her foot froze in mid-stride. "Humans? Cut the power? Isn't that more of a disadvantage to them than us?"

"It would be," I said. "Unless they have night vision, but then why turn it back on."

"Military..." Killian said.

"Anti-vampire military trained mercenaries is my guess," I said. Human militias died along with the population, but pockets of mercenaries who practiced warfare tactics still existed. They were few and far between but deadly the same, especially in numbers.

"How many?" Killian asked.

"We didn't see them. Just their handiwork," I said. "This could be a distraction."

"Our first duty is to protect Josie. We should get her out of here," Killian said.

"I will not run and hide. This is going to be our headquarters, and we will not be run out by human or vampire." Josie straightened so tall she almost seemed to grow. "I will not leave my home."

"If you are ended, it will not matter what your cause is," I said. "You are the only one who can make this change."

"How many mercenaries do you know that wear heavy cologne to fight vampires?"

"One idiot does not mean they aren't dangerous," I said.

"Agreed. I don't think they are here any longer. Take a moment to sense our surroundings and tell us what you find," Josie said.

I stepped into the hallway and closed my eyes. My mind focused on humans. Heartbeats. Blood. None. "I don't sense any humans on the premises." I relaxed, but the thought it was a distraction hung over my head.

"Why would they do it?" Natasha asked. "It doesn't really make sense. If they wanted to take over, killing the power seems like a stupid thing to do."

"It is a warning," Killian said. "They want us to know they can get in and out without us knowing."

"Confronting us was never the plan," I said. "You're right. They wanted to scare us off."

"We need to find them and exterminate them," Natasha said.

Spoken like an entitled born.

Josie touched my arm. The tension retreated from my shoulders.

"It is that kind of thinking that created this society. We will not kill them," Josie said. Her voice firm and decided. She understood the importance. I wanted to shout how much I loved her, but this wasn't the right time.

"Why don't you two go check the place out. This seems to be more of a message than an attack. Natasha and I can go check the blood reserves," Josie said. "My hunger spiked with all the activity."

In all the time I'd known Josie, she'd never admitted

hunger. I studied her. This trip changed her. It opened her up, and I loved her more for it.

"You're not the only one." Natasha smirked.

"Gross. We'll meet you in the kitchen," Josie said.

I kissed her forehead. Her lips lush and ready for more, but I wasn't sure I could or would stop if I touched mine to hers.

"Are you and Josie back together, finally?" Killian asked when we were out of earshot.

"Are you and Natasha together, or was that just fucking?" I ducked into one of the rooms, and Killian took the one on the opposite side.

"The fucking was good, but there is something unique about her that appeals to me."

"Yeah, she's a succubus, dude." I laughed and patted his shoulder.

"Choose your words a little more carefully." Killian looked at my hand.

My hand dropped to my side. "You do like her."

"I do." Killian sighed. He actually sighed.

I shook my head. "I don't know what Josie and I are right now." We needed to resolve some issues. The conversation scared me. "I want to take her away from all this and screw her brains out until all of this is a memory. She deserves to feel better than this shitty situation."

"You love her, Vin. I think the correct term is to make love."

"If she heard you say that, she'd probably deck you." I laughed so hard it echoed down the hall.

Killian shrugged and laughed. "You are right."

"She's decided not to release the video."

We had cleared three rooms and still had a dozen in the area we occupied. The humans were nowhere to be found. No scent in this area. They must have entered from a different direction. The entranced needed to be sealed off... if we could find it.

"Why?"

"She wants to be more like Adelaide than Ezra. She'll still take her father on, but she wants to do it in person."

"Adelaide would be proud. The battle will be much harder."

"It's safe to say she is aware," I said. Harder but reduced risk to the humans here and more control in an offensive situation instead of on the defense.

We made the corner on the last turn toward the kitchen. All the rooms clear of any signs.

"Raising an army will present challenges."

"It's going to be harder in every aspect, but there should be less death."

"Josephine can live with the consequences this way?"

"She believes she can," I said.

"Then we shall make it happen. She is much stronger than Ezra realizes."

A light peaked out from under the door of a storage close. A perpetrator could hide in there. The door opened with a stiff metal hinge noise. The supplies, mainly for human needs, organized with great detail. "Someone had a lot of time on their hands."

"Ezra had many more people in his employee then. Some human and some vampire," Killian said. "He is particular about how things are done."

"I've noticed. Still, this is a huge stockpile even for those times."

Killian stepped to the left and opened a large cabinet. Tools banged together and fell at our feet. We jumped back.

A rat scurried out from the bottom. By how fat the ugly thing was, it didn't lack for food. He ran across the floor towards a back door.

Killian picked up a bag from the bottom of the cabinet. "The smell."

"Josie and I smelled cologne in the electrical room." I breathed it in. "It's the same."

"Cologne is a commodity of humans in power," Killian said. "There are tons of tools in the bag." He pulled them out in handfuls and set them on the shelf in front of us.

"We're not dealing with mercenaries." This was a squatter who wanted to claim our home for his own from these signs, but the cologne said power hand in it... vampire power.

"No, but this desperate type of person is more dangerous," Killian said.

I looked over the various tools, and the majority were electrical equipment. "We need to find this human before he permanently damages the power system. It's not like the parts to fix it are easily available. We would be cut off from those we need to support us."

"Agreed. Take a whiff and see if you can locate him."

"I don't know if I will be able to with the bag so close. The scent is overpowering everything in the room." *This squatter might have known the cologne would mask vampire abilities.*

"Fine." He dropped it to the floor. "We can follow the rat's lead and try outside."

Fresh snow blanketed the already frozen landscape. "If he's here, I will smell him." I knelt down and scooped up some snow. The soft powder filter through my fingers. My lids shut tight, and I inhaled in search of the cologne. Pine filled my nostrils. Nothing but woods. *Ah. There he is.* My eyes flew open.

"Found him, and he's not alone."

"How many?"

"A lot. Possibly too many for the two of us." A hundred humans could take down two vampires, even ones like Killian.

Rosewater. Josie tried to sneak up on us, but the aroma gave her away.

"What about the four of us?" Josie said from behind. She and Natasha had sports bottles full of blood. "Thirsty?" Her fingers brushed against mine as she handed me the bottle.

My dick fought against the cool air at such a minor touch. I swigged a gulp of blood from the bottle. The metallic taste like fire as it traveled through my body.

"Well?" Josie raised a brow.

"We could, but there are a lot. We would have to kill them to do it. There's no way we could subdue that many at one time."

"Are they some of the vagrant nomads?" Natasha asked. Her hand firmly planted on Killian's ass.

Josie rolled her eyes. "They are too wild to wear cologne."

"Josie, it is your call," Killian said. His bottle half empty.

Mine was gone. "You going to finish that?"

Killian elbowed me and took a swig.

"I don't want to kill them, but I want to know what they were doing here," Josie said.

"This is a job for me." Natasha turned her bottle up and finished the blood. "Alone."

Natasha had an opportunity to prove her loyalty, but a vampire alone in a large group of humans presented risks. She wouldn't be able to fight her way out if caught, and we wouldn't be able to get to her.

"You will not be going alone," Killian said.

Natasha squeezed his ass. "This is the kind of thing Calidora had me trained for. I'm the only one that can move around humans undetected."

"What if they have seen you, Natasha?" Josie asked.

"They won't remember it." She winked. Her head tilted back to look at Killian. "Give me a good luck kiss."

He wrapped his arm around her waist. "I will walk a distance with you."

"Only if you promise to turn around when I ask," she said.

"If I must."

She moved away from Killian and gave Josie a one-arm hug. Her lips whispered something inaudible, even for my vampire hearing. *What could she say only Josie needed to hear?*

Josie nodded and whispered back. She held out a hand for Natasha's empty container and waited for Killian to finish his.

Natasha embraced her like an old friend.

"Be safe, my friends. May the darkness be kind," Josie said. It was an old vampire saying. Odd since few used it after the ice age started.

"I'll wait at a distance for her if you approve," Killian said.

"I do," Josie said.

I exchanged formal handshakes with Killian before I grasped his shoulder. "See you soon, brother."

I turned to Natasha. "Do not take risks. Better to come back."

"I've got this, but thanks for caring." She smiled.

I watched them dredge with little effort through the deep snow until they disappeared from sight. My arm draped around Josie's soldiers.

My words light but my heart anything but. "They'll return."

"If they are discovered, two vampires will not be much of a match for that large a horde. Killian's never been one to leave someone behind, and he will not leave her if it goes sour." She wrapped her hand around my waist.

"It's Killer Killian and Natasha the Succubus. If they can't handle it, there is no hope for our revolution."

She leaned her head against my shoulder. "I love your optimism."

I pressed my nose to her head and breathed in her scent. *Rosewater. Always.* I twirled her in my arms so our faces were close together.

She bit down on her lip. Her eyes locked on mine.

My dick hardened, and I pulled her closer. "If I wasn't so worried about what's in the woods, I'd be all over you."

"Damn your sensibility," Josie said. Her body brushed against mine as she rose on her toes. Soft lips urged mine to open.

I obliged and captured her mouth. My hands found her hips and pressed her against the mass in my pants. I pulled back. "If you keep that up, my sensibility will waver."

"Mission accepted."

"A worthy mission, but we have work to do." I contemplated grabbing a hand full of snow and ice to shove down my pants to cool my overheated sensibility.

"We do. Yes, we do." Josie sighed. "Maybe a little bonding will help the time pass while we wait for them to return."

I linked my hand in hers. "It's quite a job so we might not finish before they get back."

"I thought you always finished." She winked at me and took a couple of steps away.

Cold, wet snow peppered my face. "Did you just kick snow at me?"

Josie laughed and ran towards the door.

I grabbed a handful and formed it into a snowball. She was fast, but my aim was good. I drew back as far as I could and sailed the frozen globe straight at her.

"Asshole!" She brushed the snow out of her hair with her fingers.

"You hit me first." I crossed my arms over my chest and leaned against the doorjamb.

"I know." She laughed.

Still hard from her touch earlier, that laugh tickled me deep down in my cock. Her laugh would do it to me anyway, but it vibrated my dick tonight. *Focus Vin. You can't walk around with Fang Shui poking through your pants all night.* I cleared my throat.

"The tools and supplies are over here." I grabbed the bag. "We can rewire those stations in the computer room by the time they get back."

"As your apprentice, do I have to carry your tool...s?" Her eyes dropped to my crotch.

I adjusted myself. "You are in rare form tonight."

"It's just the two of us alone, and that doesn't happen very often."

"So, are you saying you want to give us a chance again?" My heart pounded in my chest. All thoughts left.

"If you can tell me why you did it, I can move forward." Her eyes fixed on mine in a tight gaze.

I put the bag down and inhaled her scent. Rosewater aroma washed over me. *Her. It had always been her from the day she found me at the gate.* I held her face in my hands. "I didn't cheat on you, Josie. Not ever."

"Then why didn't you come talk to me? I was so confused by the signals I got from you. What few words you said did not match your actions. I fell hard for you. And I could again. Did you love me like that?"

The words tumbled fast from her mouth. I paused to let them sink in. My tongue thickened and wouldn't work. I had to swallow venom to make it work. Everything was warm. *She loves me.* The world fell away. Josie was all I could see.

"I did, and I still do. Do you believe me?"

"I believe you. I knew I didn't want to lose you when you almost ended in the tundra, and I knew I believed you when we were underground."

"Then you will have me by your side anytime you wish." I lifted her from the waist and spun her in circles. My face hurt from smiling. *She still loves me.*

"Put me down." Josie giggled.

I lowered her slowly down the full length of my body.

Her eyes fluttered closed.

My mouth devoured hers with a deep need. I walked her backwards through the door. Once we crossed into the hallway, I scooped her up and carried her to the office I claimed. The door stood slightly ajar, like I'd left it. My foot connected with the bottom, and it opened. I kicked it shut with my heel.

I shifted her so her legs were around my waist and carried her towards the desk. Her lips were on my neck. A moan came from deep in my throat. I swiped the maps off the desk with one hand and sat Josie on it.

She peeled my jacket off.

I buried my hands in her hair and dipped my face to hers. Rosewater enveloped me. I need to touch her to feel her against me. My fingers fumbled with the zipper on her coat. The teeth came apart.

"Oops," I whispered against her lips. My thumbs brushed her collar bone. I cupped her shoulders and pushed the arms of the jacket down.

"Enough," she said. She hopped off the desk. Her hands moved fast to get out of her clothes.

"Perfection." Pleasure shivered through my body. I wanted to touch her. A growl came from deep in my gut. I followed her lead and tossed m clothes in a pile next to hers.

She pressed her hands against my chest and tilted her chin up to look at me. She took my lower lip between her teeth and bit down in a gentle nibble.

A groan rumbled from my throat. My chest expanded as my heart pounded. I lifted her up and sat her down on the desk. My fingers found her breast. I lowered my head and pressed my lips against her neck. My tongue traced a line down until my head rested between her thighs. I tasted her.

She bucked and moaned. "I need you, Vin."

Her raspy voice made it hard to concentrate. I swirled my tongue around.

Her moans grew louder. "Now," she said, breathless.

I kissed my way up to her breast and stopped to savor it a moment. I licked and sampled each nipple.

"Now," she said again. Her moans made me rock hard.

"Are you sure?" I pressed my lips against her neck.

Her head tilted back. "Gods, yes."

I slid into her and caught her moan with my mouth. My body quivered. I paused inside her to let the connection build. Electricity pulsed through me.

She turned her head to the side and bit down on my arm. Her teeth grazed my shoulder. "Vin."

More. I wanted more of her. Every inch of her wrapped around me.

"Josie," I whispered in her ear, my voice hoarse.

She ground against me, and I started to move. I needed this. She needed this. We needed to be one to heal. Our climaxes met at the same peak. I surrendered to the intense closeness. This was my Josie and a moment I dreamed of often. It caused my heart to beat in an irregular pattern. I took at as a sign of how strong our love was for each other. A sign I neglected and ignored years ago.

I rolled to the side of the expansive desk and pulled her to me. Her cheeks glowed with the flush, and the scent of sex in the air mixed with her rosewater. I wanted to take her again. To show her my love in every way, and to break that barrier that had existed between us into rubble. But duty demanded things from us.

"We'll never hear the end of it if Killian and Natasha find us here," Josie said, her voice raspy.

"You're right," my voice came out hoarse and rough. I didn't want to move, but I stood up and handed her clothes to her.

"Reality," she said. Her face dropped.

I took her hand in mine. My lips pressed against her fingertips. "It's all going to work out. You're on the right side of history."

"It would be great if we could skip all the bad stuff and get to the good stuff."

"Wouldn't it be great if it worked like that? We have to go through the rough times to get to the peaceful ones."

"You've become quite the philosopher."

"It might have something to do with the smart and sexy woman I'm seeing."

"This woman is tired of being in the dark literally and figuratively."

"We have the tools to fix that."

I locked the door. The maps scattered across the floor and shrugged. *Screw it.* I dropped my clothes and wrapped my fingers around the back of Josie's neck. *We have time for one more.*

CHAPTER 15

JOSIE

My eyes drawn to Vin. I watched him work with the computer stations. He moved quickly from screen to screen, working on the perimeter video. *Was I weak for making love with him? We still had much to resolve, but I did believe him. I should have all along.*

"Tell me when you have camera views up, and we will sync," Vin said.

I startled from my daydreaming. "Got 'em."

"On the count of three," he said. "One, two, three."

The cameras were a key part of the security system to use in protecting the people we wanted to shelter here. "Did it work?"

"We make a pretty good team."

"Yeah," I said. "That's the last piece, right?"

"It is," he said.

I jumped from my chair and fell into his lap. The chair spun around. "We need to repeat earlier activities to celebrate." Wishful thinking blurted out of my mouth. There was work still required to get us prepared for the future.

"Ready so soon?" Vin pressed his lips against mine.

An alarm sounded on the control panel. Vin spun the chair toward it. I blinked at the screen.

"What is that? Is it a vampire?"

"Two of them," he said. "Must be Killian and Natasha."

I leaned in towards the monitor. "Are you sure that's them?"

"This technology is old, and the picture is grainy from the darkness," he said. "But it has to be."

"Should we go meet them?"

"Not until they are closer. You'd think they would be in more of a hurry to get back."

"Definitely them." I paused. "I can't look anymore. Twice is too many times for me to see that." *And I felt guilty for my making love with Vin.*

"I guess that answers why they were going so slow." Vin clicked a button on the keyboard. The camera angle changed. "It's like watching a porno when you know the people."

"I'm sure they would feel the same way if it was us."

"And they don't know the cameras are working again." Vin punched keys and cameras moved around, except the one he had angled away from Killian and Natasha.

"Something tells me Natasha wouldn't care," I said.

"Killian would. He wouldn't want his Empress seeing him naked, among other things," Vin choked out between laughs.

I changed subjects to something I dreaded, worse than seeing Killian and Natasha having sex. "We need to gather supporters right away. Have you figured out a good way to get the word out quietly?"

"We have the equipment to broadcast a video securely. You can't stop others from sharing it, so it could get sent to Ezra or someone under his command. That's kind of how it works. Have you thought about how much you want to say?"

"I've been playing it around in my head." Heat filled my cheeks. I should have been speech writing instead of having sex. *The sex was good, though. Gods, it was good.*

Vin smiled. "What do you think about doing a video message versus an audio message?" He tinkered with an old web camera on the desk.

"That could work. If I'm visible, that will definitely send a powerful message. I like it." I considered it. "What if my father intercepts the message?"

"It's only slightly riskier than the audio message, but it ensures everyone knows it comes from you. These are all people you know to be loyal to you already, right? You're not reaching out to those who support your father."

I blinked at the blank wall over his shoulder. *This could work. A video message is more powerful than an audio message.* "I like the video message for those loyal to me. For my father's supporters, we know to be disgruntle with him, I want to reach out personally."

The Emperor's loyalists would require more special handling even if they are disenchanted with him, but if I can sway them, they would be allies with access to soldiers.

"We'll do the video message first, then. You'll want to have your message down when you reach out to the ones on the fence," Vin said. "Do you want to do it in here or in another room?"

I looked around the room. Few pictures on the wall and modest furniture filled it. "The others are too pretentious. This room is the least decorated. I want to film it here."

"Give me a few minutes to set up the camera."

I nodded and paced the floor. *Hi! I'm Josie! No, that's igno-*

rant sounding. Most of you know me as... Stupid. Today I come to you from my old home. This will be the base for a new area. Vampires who believe in humanity and who want to coexist with the humans will be welcome here. Our predecessors are not on a path to leave a legacy we can be proud of. I want to change that, and I hope you will join me. We must band together if we wish this ice age to end. We need change so humans and vampires can prosper instead of being exploited. Join me here as fast as you can.

"DONE," Vin said. "Do you want to see it?"

"No," I shook my head. "I'm not going to like it, regardless. Just tell me I didn't sound like an idiot."

He took my hand and squeezed. "You sounded like a leader."

My heart filled with love and pride. Vin brought out the best in me.

Footsteps with the lightness only a vampire could pull off had both of us on alert. "It's them," Vin said.

I smelled them coming. *Who could miss the pheromones?* I faced Vin. *Gods. Did we smell that strong?*

Vin's forehead wrinkled.

I tapped the tip of my nose with my finger.

He mouthed, "oh."

"This should be the answer when humans ask why we burn candles all the time." I composed myself for when Killian and Natasha made the corner.

"We're back," Killian said. He stepped through the door with Natasha's hand in his.

"Your return was on the monitors." Vin averted his eyes and stared at the computer screen.

"Not cool," Natasha said.

"We didn't watch," I said. I made eye contact with Natasha like an idiot. *Never make eye contact when you tell someone you've seen them having sex for the second time. Awkward.*

She slipped her hand into Killian's and leaned against him.

"What do you have up on the screen now?"

"Josie recorded a message for her supporters to join us here."

"We should hold off on sending it," Kilian said. "The humans are already afraid with vampires in this compound again. We might have a full on war with them if we bring more vamps here."

"Do they think we are going to imprison them?" I asked.

"They escaped from your father a couple of decades ago. They must have been children at the time, because many of them have children now." Natasha said.

No one escaped. They stayed until they paid their debt. I pressed my hand against my stomach. *Lies.* The pain there stabbed deep. Lies, I believed from father. Lies, I repeated for him. Lies I portrayed for him that humans willingly stayed until they fulfilled their contract. He reached so far and wide the humans came to this frozen abyss to escape him. His reign had to end.

"What did they do for him?" I asked.

"Some were blood bags. Some were indentured in his home," Killian said.

"I might know some of them." There had been children who served father when their parents needed help or to work off the contract faster. The practice sounded terrible to me.

"A few looked familiar to me, but those stayed on the outer perimeter. I didn't get much interaction with them," Natasha said.

"We should invite them here," I said. "We have plenty of available rooms."

"They are going to be cautious, Josie. They escaped from one prison and aren't eager for another one," Natasha said.

I leaned against one of the computer stations. "We're offering them safety, not imprisonment."

"Sounds a lot like the contracts your father forced them to sign," Vin said.

If the humans stayed outside, they would have to face the elements and any vampires. Calidora's guard could round them up. Rogues could attack them. It really wasn't safe for them to be out there. They had their freedom out there, and that was something I could understand. They need to hear from me. It's what I would need if it was reversed.

"True. Maybe I should go speak to them myself," I said.

"That is way too risky," Vin said.

"Once the video goes out, everything I do is going to be risky. We're doing the right thing. We're righting history. That doesn't happen without danger. If I'm going to be the face of change and the leader, I need to be seen. They need to trust me."

"She's right boys," Natasha said. "If she hides behind an army or even a couple of big strong vampires." She smiled and rubbed Killian's back. "Then no one is going to believe she is legit. That wouldn't make her much different from the leaders we have now."

The 'boys' were quiet, and I stared at Natasha. "You almost sound like you believe in this change."

"I do, Josie. I was a prisoner, too. Calidora might have treated me well, but I was still her prisoner. My ability to decide was stripped from me, and it made me feel like I didn't matter."

"And now?"

"Freedom is a powerful thing. The world is big." She paused and raked her eyes over Killian. "And everyone should have the opportunity to see how big."

"You said it better than I did in the video," I said. "I'm impressed."

"Does that mean you finally trust me?"

"We are getting there." I paused. "Time to put the call out and see what happens."

CHAPTER 16

The humans joined us and more appeared each day. I'd reached them with an honest appeal and a shared contempt for my father's ways. The vampire responses weren't as auspicious after a couple of weeks. Time marched at a lightning pace while their responses returned at a snail's pace. The stress caused my cravings to spike. The hunger made me edgy.

"Three of your supporters have responded," Vin said.

I circled the desk. "That's not enough, no matter which three. We need faster responses before our hand is tipped to my father. If it already hasn't."

"Ezra has spies everywhere, Josie. He could already know."

I sat in the chair and spun toward the computer screen. My fingers jabbed in my sign in and password to my personal correspondence account. "There are a few new ones today. They were afraid to respond on the other network." I couldn't blame them for that. It was their ending at risk if they were to be caught.

"Understandable." Vin nodded. "We need to strengthen the secure network we have established here. Now that we know you have supporters, we don't want to take any additional risks."

"Do we have the means to do it?" I asked.

"We do. We'll do a handoff in the system. I'll embed it so deep no one on Ezra's team will be able to find it."

"Make it happen." I nodded. "I'm going for a walk." I stood from the chair and stretched.

"Are you sure you don't want me to come with you?"

I maneuvered to his side. "No, I'm staying inside. I'll be fine."

He lifted his chin toward me.

I bent to meet him and pressed our lips together.

"Don't forget about me on your trip." He smiled.

"Never," I said.

My boots squeaked on the marble floor. The echo on the floor louder than it had been the last few days. I listened, and the silence startled me. While I reached the humans to join us, most stayed on the perimeter of the wall. The gate left open, so they could enter and exit at will in hope it fostered trust. Natasha had successfully got some of them to move into the mansion with us, and there hadn't been much silence since then.

Laughter trickled up from a distance. *Children's laughter.* They were outside. Natasha's voice among the laughter as she shared stories. Warmth filled my chest. *Progress.*

I wound through the hallway to my mother's old library. The door creaked open. The furniture was all covered in sheets from when we left. Very little dust clung on the sheets or the books. I yanked one of the linens off a chair. Particles scattered and rained down in the thin light from the window.

The bookshelves still filled with all the books my mother had procured during her long life. They represented such an important part of who she was. A teacher. A scientist. A parent.

Her favorite book popped into my mind, and I scanned shelf where it used to reside. There stood the flower book she so loved. The number of times I found her in here with this book countless. It contained all the plants she worked with in her garden, and she would point them out to me as we worked through various experiments. The powerful memories made me lightheaded. I flipped through the pages, and it opened to a heavily worn page on jimsonweed. I carried the book to the chair I'd uncovered earlier.

Notes covered the margins. Mother connected to this plant. She hadn't made such detailed notes on any others. *Why the interest in this plant?* Night-blooming Cereus may have been the medicinal one she fussed over the most when we would spend time in the garden, but jimsonweed, part of the deadly nightshade family, had her attention in a big way.

The hallucinogenic property attracted vampires and humans, but it was deadly even to us in certain doses. Those addicted to it would often end up overdosing in a violent fit. Humans survival rate rare compared to ours. This one rated even higher than bloodroot for mortality in both species to me.

I perused her notes for clues about why she was so interested in it. The page flipped, and a folded piece of paper wedged into the spine waited to be found.

The brittle paper required careful handling as I unfolded it. *Mother's handwriting.* The details emerged. She had written a recipe for poison. A potent poison that would kill someone, vampire or not.

I sunk back in the chair. *What was she creating this for?* Before the ice age, vampires killed vampires, but to kill a born vampire took skill. Since the list of excusable reasons to end a born vampire was short, making it look like an accident earned a position as a high paid spy.

She'd mixed the ingredients so that the death would not be quick. A counter agent to make the recipient think they were recovering, but then the second wave kicked in without warning, resulting in a death full of seizures, pain, and vomiting. Not an attractive image. She wanted to hurt someone, and she wanted them to know. *Who? Was it father she was after?*

"Josie?"

I jumped out of the chair. The book fell to the floor and dust flew into a cloud. "I didn't hear you, Vin. What's up?"

He cocked his head. "I can see that. Are you okay?"

Vin retrieved my reading material from the floor and handed it back to me. "Yes, just reading one of my mother's old books."

He gave me a tight-lipped smile. "Flowering Danger?"

"It was her favorite book." A giggle snuck out of my mouth at how absurd it sounded.

"Not only did your mother have a garden full of poisonous plants, but her favorite book was about them? That's a bit creepy."

"Not for a vampire." I sat the book on the seat of the chair.

He bent for the yellowed piece of paper with the recipe on it. "Did she make potions too?"

"She wasn't a witch, Vin. She appreciated the strength of these plants."

"And this one? Jimson?"

"Jimsonweed. If a vampire runs their fingers over the petals, they might have hallucinations. If they consume the seedpod, stems, roots, or leaves, it will definitely create hallu-cinations. If they consume too much, they will die, and it will be violent. "

"And this recipe?"

"Meant to inflict pain. It was written for someone she wanted to see suffer."

"Your father."

"My thoughts too." I took the piece of paper from his hands. "Why were you looking for me?"

"Some vampires have just arrived."

Thank the Gods. We needed the numbers. "Ones we were expecting?"

"No."

I ground my teeth together. "Father's spies?"

"I recognize them from the military."

Father can be predictable. "Killing them seems the most logical answer, but he will probably send more. We need to keep the humans out of sight until I can get rid of them. How many?"

"Five."

"Only five? He must not think much of our efforts." He threw an insult without having uttered the words.

"That's good for us."

"Will you go warn Natasha to keep the humans hidden? I'll take Killian with me, so maybe he will think I am still mad at you. The more he thinks things are status quo, the more time it buys us." *Gods, be with them, especially the children.* I prayed to Vin's gods more these days.

My shoulders squared and my face composed, I descended the stairs. Four of the five soldiers were familiar to me. A power hungry jerk I knew too well led them.

"Captain Scott." I nodded in his direction. His strawberry

blonde hair cut short but leaving some falling forward on his forehead with eyelashes the same color.

He took a knee, and the other soldiers followed his lead. They rose from the kneeling position as one unit. "Our future empress," Captain Scott said. "May we have a moment?"

"Am I not in front of you now?" The last thing I wanted was to be alone with him or any member of Father's guards. I wouldn't be able to take them all down if they got me alone.

"Perhaps there is a place where you and I can speak alone."

"Of course." I gestured to the room right off the entryway. At least a scuffle could be heard from this room. "Will this do?"

I closed the door to the old drawing room behind us with my eyes fixed on him. My back would never be to the snake if I could help it. "What brings you this far north, captain?"

"Your father has concerns about your mission. Your communication has been sporadic."

"What do you know of my mission?"

"I know you are to gather replacements for our stores, and by the looks of the backside of the compound, you have gathered quite a few."

Damn. Damn. Damn. "Not nearly enough to sustain us for long, though. They are weak specimens." *Better bluffs, Josie.*

"Noted. We can take them back while you continue to find more."

Over the ashes of my ending. "That will not be necessary. When we have rehabbed them enough for travel, we will bring all of them at once."

His face twisted into a fake half smile.

Nausea rolled in my stomach. Cruel like my father, he had asked to pursue me. Ezra let me make my choice. My father, rather than piss off one of his trusted guards, told him he did not want me involved with anyone. *Her focus should be learning to run the vampire world.* Of course, we found Vin not too long after that, and we were inseparable until we weren't.

"You are still challenging your father's wishes."

"I serve at his will like we all do."

"But you are the only one who will inherit everything."

"You know what I find interesting, captain. The last mission decades ago didn't make it, but here we are. Two missions that made it here."

He circled me like a coyote on a carcass. "As do I." His fake smile plastered on his pale white face. "We could make a good team, Josephine."

My mouth filled with metallic tasting blood. *Vampire vomit.* I swallowed hard to clear it. "I have my guards."

"I'm not talking about as a guard, but I heard most of your crew has died." He grabbed my hand. "I could rule with you."

His touch dirtied my hand. I gently pulled my hand from his grasp. The spy network must have found its way here, as we suspected. "I am very flattered, but my father and I have already discussed the plan for my rule."

"It is your choice. When your time comes, your father will no longer be able to tell you how to rule." *He's still jockeying for position. That's why he agreed to come here.*

A knock at the door interrupted us. "Josephine, shall I enter?"

"No, Killian. Everything is fine." Thankful for the interruption, but I needed to create an appearance of strength in front of Captain Scott. I couldn't do it if Killian loomed over us.

Captain Scott's eyebrow raised. "My help would be valuable to you."

"Tensions are high during a transitional time. It is hard enough to adjust to a new emperor. It's not a good idea." I sat behind the desk in the room, putting a physical barrier between us.

"It's that Vincent. Isn't it? From the day you found him, he has been a problem." He slammed his fist on the desk.

I didn't flinch.

"I knew he'd be a problem on this mission."

The door flew open. Killian's immense presence occupied the space. "Our emperor swore me to protect Josephine from anyone or anything I perceive as a threat. Are you a threat, Captain Scott?" Killian spat his name out.

"Of course not, Killian." He moved toward him. "Remind me what rank you are?"

"I am of the private guard. There is no rank. We report directly to the emperor." Killian didn't move. "Only the emperor can command us."

"True," Captain Scott said. "And the emperor is not here. So who commands you?"

"I have my orders from the emperor, and I do not need to disclose those to you." Killian's arms crossed in front of him.

"No, but I have my own orders from the emperor. My orders include returning with the humans you have gathered, and I need to leave with them in the morning. You can continue with your mission."

The options narrowed like the window for me to make a decision. No way was I letting them out of here with the humans.

"I am not releasing those humans to you." I stood and straightened my spine. "I've had no direct order from the emperor, and it was his order that sent us here."

IN BLOOD & ICE

"Then you will be in violation of the emperor's orders and subject to arrest. Both of you plus the rest of your team." He snapped his fingers. "That's right. The rest of your team died except for you two and Vincent."

He bated me with the pain of losing a team, and I almost took it. I clenched my jaw tight.

Killian didn't move, but his eyes drooped and a grimace formed on his mouth. Those were his friends.

"Someone might think you killed them off so you could start a little revolution."

Killian and I exchanged looks. Captain Scott knew, and if he knew, then Ezra could have the same information. *Not good.*

"Is that what you two are up to? And Vincent?"

"Did someone call my name?"

Relief and anger mixed in my blood. Vin sidestepped Killian and came to my side.

"You certainly have your share of protectors." Captain Scott's eyes bore into mine. "Where do you fit into all of this, Vincent?"

"Into what? Our mission to find food?"

"This rebellion plan."

I squeezed Vin's hand. *If only a touch could communicate thank you and don't say a word.*

"Has there been a rebellion?" Vin wrapped his arm around my waist.

"You're not exactly a vampire with voting rights." A smirk formed on his lips.

"I am a vampire just like you." Vin's answer was honest, without giving away too much.

Good job, Vin.

"Not just like me, or Josephine, or even Killer Killian."

If he pressed Vin, the Vin I know wouldn't lie. One final option came to me on how to handle the visitors. "Enough of the testosterone filled conversation. Captain Scott, would you and your soldiers join us for dinner in the formal dining room this evening? You do still partake in some human food. Don't you?"

"Of course." He smiled the same plastered fake smile from earlier.

"If you and your men would like to refresh first, there is a bar just off the formal ballroom. It's out this door and straight down the hall. The last door on the right." I held my hand out in the direction.

"Thank you, Josephine." He accepted my dismissal and walked toward the hall door.

Killian grasped the door, but I waved him off. A closed door would only look more suspicious right now.

"What the hell are you doing?" Vincent whispered..

I motioned for Killian to come closer.

"Killian, we need Natasha to do her Natasha thing on them," I whispered.

"Then what? Are we going to kill them?" Vincent said. "Your Father would send more in his place.

"No, that's not my plan."

"I'm not comfortable asking Natasha to do this, and I am considerably less comfortable at the thought of her doing it," Killian said. He had a point, but her gift was control. We needed her to daze them and control them.

"It's my idea. I will ask her then," I said. "Are you going to be able to forgive me for it?"

"You are my empress, Josie. There is no need to ask for forgiveness." His body stiffened.

"Maybe not, but I'm your friend and I'm asking."

"Yes, I will forgive you."

"Thank you, my friend." I touched his arm. "I need you both to keep your cool during dinner tonight. We can't afford any violence with the delicate nature of our efforts." I needed to keep my cool during dinner tonight, too.

CHAPTER 17

No deed dirtied my soul more than what I needed today. I condemned her for her gifts. Vampires like Calidora used her over and over, and what I asked was not different. It made me like Calidora or my father. I pondered if this was how it started for them. One act compromised the moral construct of my world. *Would it stop at just one or would I become like them?*

Natasha entered the office and smiled at me.

Guilt tugged on my brain, my heart, and my soul. Killian promised to forgive me. Natasha's forgiveness I didn't deserve.

"Natasha, I'm sorry to --"

"I already know what you are going to ask." She dropped into the chair. "I'll do it. It's my gift after all." She threw her hands up and spun around in the chair. Her foot drug along the floor so that she completed the spin facing me.

My guilt intact, I nodded. "Thank you. I will tell you what I didn't tell Killian and Vin."

She crossed her legs and leaned forward in the chair. "Now you have my attention."

"I found an old reference to jimsonweed in one of my mother's books today."

"You're going to poison them?" Her eyes bugged out a little.

"Not exactly. If balanced correctly, it will cause hallucination for vampires."

"Why would you want to make them hallucinate?"

"So you can mind control them at one time and send them back to my father. Have them take the slow route too." I hoped to buy us some time to finish gathering our forces.

She clapped her hands together and rested her chin on the tips. "I've never used my gift on someone under the influence of poison."

"It's a risk, but based on what I read in my mother's notes, it should work."

"I've become very fond of the children, especially the little twins, Casey and Calvin. He's as feisty as she is sweet. She tried to give me her only toy, a little doll that looked like her. He kicked me in the shin when I held her, like he was her sworn guard." She paused and blotted at her eyes. "What I'm saying is, if it will protect the kids, then I will to try."

My eyebrow raised in surprise at her confession. I expected her to agree, but her compassion for the children, human children, surprised me.

Natasha's palms ran along the length of the armrest. She shifted in her chair. "And Killian is okay with this?"

I stared at a hole in the rug. When I looked up, I met her eyes. "No, he's not, but I only told him I needed your help. I didn't share the details of the plan."

She sat straight up in the chair. "I wondered who he would choose if had to."

Insecurity from her seemed out of place, but her world changed as much as the rest of us. "Between me and you? I'm with Vin. You are with him."

"But you are his leader, and he cares about you."

"He cares about you, Natasha. He is always going to put duty to the vampire nation at the top of the list. That is who he is. How he is built. I think that is something you will have to accept about him if you want to be with him."

"Like Vin has accepted how stubborn you are."

I coughed through a laugh. "And I have accepted how pig-headed he can be."

"You are his soft spot, though. He'd give it all up for you no matter what it cost him."

My truth bubbled up from my heart. "I would for him too."

"You would?" Her voice rose a full octave.

"Yes, but he would never ask me too," I paused. "Nor would I him."

"You give each other the freedom of choice no matter how much it pisses the other one off?"

"More or less." I smiled at her. Vin and I told each other our opinions in some of the most passionate ways. She needed to learn her own boundaries with Killian. If time was kind, they might be a good pair.

NATASHA and I prepared a makeshift meal from the human cuisine. I thanked my mother in a silent prayer for sending me to cook in the kitchen when I was a child. Father protested, but he never denied her wishes. I glanced at Natasha and wondered if Mother might have been blessed with the same gifts.

The soft cadence of the music from the twenty-first century mixed with the small talk Vin and Killian made with the soldiers drifted into the kitchen. The time ticked closer, and my nerves flared for what I asked of our new friend. Natasha placed a hand over mine and smiled.

"Make sure Captain Scott and his men sit at the seats where we put the glasses rimmed with the hallucinogen." I handed her the pitcher of blood and wine mixture.

"Got it." Natasha winked and went in ahead of me.

Her actions suggested she enjoyed this game. She said there was never a choice before. I may have given her a choice, but it still sucked.

I waited for her to signal me.

"Josie, we have some hungry gentlemen in here."

I picked up the tray and took a deep, unneeded breath.

"The pantry has not been restocked in a while so I hope you don't mind that we made do with what we had." I sat the various platters on the buffet. If this planned failed, we'd be exposed, but we would definitely have to end their existence.

"Is that pepperoni?" One soldier asked.

"It is." I forced a smiled and hoped it looked pleasant. He entered the army by training in the same group I had. I questioned my plan, afraid the formula might not work right. *No. We have to push forward to save their lives and, more importantly, those in our care.*

"I haven't had that in decades."

"Well, it's from a group nearby that makes various meat products."

"Humans?" Captain Scott sipped the wine & blood.

"Yes, and vampires. They live together." If the poison worked and Natasha did her job, he'd remember very little, if any, of this dinner.

"Are these Ezra's..." He slurred. "Subjects?"

"Yes, but they had not been in contact for some time." I watched his pupils expand.

"Why don't we sit down now that everyone has a little something on their plate?"

All seated except Natasha. She swayed like she got caught up in the music. Her hips moved back and forth. She spun around.

"Is that an elephant in the other room?" One soldier asked.

Here we go. The hallucinations started. The poison worked.

"The stars are beautiful tonight. I see the big dipper," another one said.

Natasha placed a hand on the shoulder of each soldier and whispered into each of their ears the script we had rehearsed. Each one stood when she finished. She reached Captain Scott. She bent with her lips close to his ears. Her hand lowered to his shoulder.

He turned his head and dug his fingers into her hair. His lips pressed against hers.

Not good. She told me not to interrupt, but this wasn't expected.

Natasha's eyes widened. The soldiers shuffled. They seemed to respond to her fear. Her eyes closed, and the men stilled.

Killian, Vin, and I all jumped from our chairs, but Killian made it to her first and pulled her back.

"Josie, we could be so good together," Captain Scott said. His eyes glazed over and unfocused in Natasha's direction. "A powerful couple capable of leading the nation in the future. Power. Who would be more worthy than us?"

Bile filled my throat both from what he did to Natasha and his hallucination about me.

"I'm fine," Natasha said. "Killian, let go of me. I need to finish. They are waiting for his instructions."

Killian stepped back away from her and crossed his arms.

He's not going to forgive me, but he better not hold it against Natasha. This was my plan, and his anger deserved by me.

I walked over to the side of Captain Scott faced and stayed in his line of vision but out of his reach.

His line of sight trained on me. Natasha leaned into the other ear and whispered. Her fingers stroked his temple.

He stood like the others.

Relieved he obeyed her, I would owe Natasha my thanks for this effort.

Natasha's fingers trailed down his arm. She spoke additional instructions in hushed tones.

"Men, we will be on our way," Captain Scott said.

Thank the Gods.

Vin headed into the foyer to have the door open and ready.

They filed out one by one into the dark coldness of the night. Killian and Vin stood watch on the steps. Natasha and I hung back in the doorway. They bypassed their transportation and trudged into the drifts.

"What else did you say to him?"

"I told him to kill himself when he returned to the compound," Natasha said. No emotion in her voice.

Some would not approve, but his ending would have been worse otherwise. I slid my arm through hers and gave her a side hug. "I'm sorry he did that."

"Men have done much worse, but I was never in a position to make them pay. Tonight I was." She leaned her head on my shoulder.

"I hope you never have to be in that position again, Natasha. I mean it. We will make a better world."

"Your ideas give me hope, and they will give others hope too." Her voice barely audible.

Killian turned around and held his hand out to Natasha. He pulled her out of my arms. Her form molded to his. He scooped her up in his arms.

"Natasha needs to rest," he said.

"Of course."

Killian carried her to the top of the stairs and disappeared out of sight.

Vin still stood at the open door. "How long will the toxins keep them in that state?" he asked over his shoulder.

"Around forty-eight hours."

"That should be long enough."

"For them to get back to the compound?"

"At least closer there than here. We have two days to get a good representation of your supporters here." My concern grew over whether enough would support us, especially when the word got out about Captain Scott, but we had two days. We'd have to work at vampire speed.

"They need to be able to protect their own homes, though, too. I will not let their families be slaughtered."

"We'll tell them to leave enough defense at home to have ample protection, and to rally all available forces here," I said. "Is the secure network ready?"

"Yes."

"Then send the messages now to all that have responded and even those that haven't." Captain Scott might be under Natasha's mind control, but he forced us to move faster.

"I'll go to the computer room now."

"I'm right behind you." My hearing focused on the distant

sounds of the Captain Scott and his soldier's footsteps. They crunched through the deep snow. If they avoided the Rogues, they'd be fine. They would a horrible ending if the mad monsters found them first.

Alone at the door, I let the cold air fill my useless lungs. This game tonight was dangerous, but nothing compared to what awaited us from here on out. I'd asked my friends to make a journey with me, and I had no idea if we would all survive. My heart ached. The pain severe enough I would think it a human heart attack if mine actually beat.

"Josie!" Killian screamed. "Josie, help!"

My feet landed on every third step up the stairs. I found him at the doorway to Natasha's bedroom. "Killian? What's wrong?"

"She's incoherent. Babbling nonsense."

"Did she drink or eat anything other than what we had at the dinner?"

"No, not that I know of."

"She probably ingested some of the poison when Captain Scott attacked her." I forced my voice steady. "I'll check her out." I pushed past Killian. It shouldn't have been enough to affect her with hallucinations, and I worried it was something else.

"Don't touch me!" Natasha screamed. "Don't fucking touch me!" She thrashed around on the bed.

I eased onto the bed beside her. "Natasha? It's me. Josie. Can you tell me what you see?"

"He won't leave me alone." Her voice softer and calmer.

"Who Natasha?"

"Him." She pointed to an empty corner of the room. Her eyes clouded from the poison.

She hallucinated, and I'd need to mix up a counter for her.

"There's no one there. It's just me and Killian in the room with you."

"Killian? I love him." A smile spread across her face.

I glanced at Killian. "I believe you. How about you sleep? Can you do that for us?"

"Yes." She closed her eyes, and her body stilled. She needed a restorative sleep.

Killian sat on the bed beside me. "Is she going to be okay?"

"Yes, It doesn't appear she ingested much of the toxin in her system. Her lips are still pink and her color normal. It will probably feel like a pretty good hangover when it wears off, so have some blood ready for her."

"She wanted you to be proud of her," he said.

I smiled. She had done well, even with the unexpected behavior of Captain Scott and his delusions of marrying for power.

"I am, Killian. I think she might be braver than any of us," I said. "Vin is in the computer room sending the word out to gather here as soon as possible. I'll be down there if you need me." I lifted myself off the bed.

He stood stoic in watch over her.

I gripped his forearm. "She's going to be fine."

He nodded.

VIN SAT AT THE COMPUTER. His fingers flew across the keyboard.

I slipped in behind him and wrapped my arms around his shoulders. My lips pressed against his neck. Salt mixed with a woodsy scent filled my nose.

"The messages have all gone out," Vin said.

"Now we wait and see if enough to show up." I rested my temple against his.

He reached one hand and covered my arm. "If the response is any indication. They will."

"I hope their faith in me outweighs their fear of Ezra." *Gods, if you are there, please let me trust in us. In me.*

"We knew it was a gamble when you started the journey."

Fear seized me. I straightened up and tried to rub the ache from my chest. "Vin, do you really believe I can do this? It's undoubtedly the right thing to do, but am I the right person to lead it?"

Vin rose in front of me and took my hand. His thumb brushed across my knuckles. "Yes, I believe in you, and yes, you are the right person to lead."

"Do you think I made the right decision with Natasha?"

"She wanted to do it, Josie. You can't beat yourself up."

"I am responsible, though. For her. For Killian. For everyone coming to stand with us. And for you." I caressed his cheek. Precious lives. All of them, but especially Vin.

"Your responsibility is to make the best decisions for our future. We are all here to make that happen." He dropped into the seat and pulled me into his lap. "All the vampires coming her are coming because they believe in you as much as Killian, Natasha, and I do."

Our heads rested against each other. "There is this part of me that believes I can do this. Then there is this other part that is so worried someone is going to get hurt or worse."

"You need to accept their sacrifice if that's what they choose, but what will happen if we don't take action is much worse."

"That's true." I slid into the chair and refreshed the screen.

"I need to figure out where we are going to house everyone. Are you going to be okay here?" He pressed his lips to my forehead.

My eyes closed. "Yes, it looks like I have quite a few replies to send. Thank you for being my voice of reason."

"Always." He caressed my cheek.

"We need to block off the garden. There are too many dangerous plants there for anyone to be wandering there. I can see where some plants have been tampered with." I pinched the bridge of my nose. "Especially the kids. That worries me."

"Natasha blocked off one side when the humans moved in, but I will make sure the other entrances are blocked too."

"Maybe post a couple of guards there. I want to still be able to get in there."

"Making more concoctions?"

I met his powerful, questioning gaze. "You never know what it is going to take to win a battle."

"No, you don't," Vin said.

Several ideas crossed my mind about how to win a battle with my father, but the only one I could see to fruition required tactics I wasn't one hundred percent comfortable using.

CHAPTER 18

The next couple of days showed how beloved Josie was to the people. She had many supporters, some of her own and some loyal to her mother, but they sent armies and warriors we needed. My circle of friends remained small, but they answered Josie's call.

A knock echoed off the office door.

"Come in," I said.

A guard escorted a familiar face into the room and left.

"Elijah, my old friend." I extended my hand to the vampire dressed in flannel. "I see you're still dressing like a lumberjack."

He grasped my hand in his and gave it a firm shake. "I see you're still a sarcastic bastard, Cavanaugh."

I clapped his shoulder. "It's good to see you. Thanks for making the journey."

"I would have done it for you, but I could never ignore a request from Josephine. Her heart is of a true leader."

"I couldn't agree more. She wants to right the wrongs of our past, and I believe we can do it with your help."

"Then let's get to it. I brought some very skilled fighters with me."

"We still have some more we are expecting. If you'll join me in the war room, I can fill you in on our plan."

"Can do. I'm eager to hear how we are going to take down the fascist fuck."

"Let me show you where the war room is," I said.

We walked through the hallways. "This place hasn't changed much," he said.

Vampires and human conversation buzzed around us, working in unison for a common goal.

"I believe in what you are doing here," Elijah said.

Elijah trained with me back at the compound, and we both learned the hacking trade. He questioned everything and took more than one beating because of it. Ezra chose him for his team because he was a natural strategist. When he questioned Ezra one too many times, Ezra shipped him off to the west.

"This is the war room." I gestured to a door.

WE MOVED the maps around on the table. Each map represented a unique piece of the puzzle. We identified the most defendable positions versus the most vulnerable. It reminded us of some missions we completed together. We marked the known WIN strongholds. I overlaid the plan to it all for synchronized attacks.

"That's a pretty tight timeline, Cavanaugh. Everything has to happen in coordination. One thing happens out of sync, and the entire plan is at risk."

"Which is why we reached out to those we felt we could trust, and you were at the top of the list."

"All right. We are in. My troops will want to hear the goal and plan from Josie."

Despite my argument otherwise about the risk, Josie wanted to be in person with everyone. "She has plans to address the group once everyone is here. She is in another room trying to contact groups we haven't heard from yet."

Elijah frowned. "Some are living under the radar to hide from Ezra. They might not be getting those communications."

"We suspected that might be the case."

"Have you sent anyone out on foot to reach them?"

"We haven't had the bandwidth to do that." I stared at the map where the ones we were aware of were marked.

"Get me a list, and I will send a scout out to each location."

"Elijah, thank you. There are no words."

"Just doing my part, brother."

I scribbled down which camps still had not responded. "This is the list as of today. Josie will have updates."

"I recognize some that are completely off the grid. I'll get some folks on those right now." Elijah folded the paper and left.

I sat alone behind the computer. The screen flashed a response from one group. Our first decline. They wished to stay neutral and not pick a side. Anger built inside me. *Chickenshits.*

The plan file saved only on this computer and off network for security. I clicked on the file and went over it again. There was no room for error, and we were on a tight timeframe, not knowing if Captain Scott had made it back to the compound yet. It had been two days, so our window closed with every second.

"Hey handsome. Are you up for a walk in the garden?" Josie leaned against the doorjamb.

"I'm up for anything with you." I met her at the door and kissed her lightly. "You just missed Elijah." My hand found hers.

She smiled. "Was he wearing the red plaid shirt?"

I laughed. "He had the flannel on, yes."

"He's an awesome friend for bringing so many, but that shirt is a weird choice for a vampire. It's not like we get cold." She bunched up her forehead. "Killian said he brought well over a hundred, maybe two.

"Before he became vampire, he lived on a farm where it was a little more appropriate attire, especially on winter days."

"Created vampires are talking more about their human lives now that you want to level the playing field for everyone. His people are fitting right in from what I hear."

She waved to the guards as we entered the garden.

"That's a good feeling. We have made some strides in a brief time." She gazed off down the hall.

"After you take down Ezra, we will make more even faster," I said. "What brings us to the garden today?" I'd enjoyed our regular trips to the garden as she explained the different plants.

She glanced away. "There doesn't seem to be anywhere we can get alone time today. In two days, we went from a few guests to a full house. I am very thankful for how the events are shaping up, and I hope this luck continues for us."

"You didn't have to bring me down here for that. What's really on your mind?"

She clasped her hands in front of her. "When this is done and we oust Ezra, I still want this to be our center base of operations. I don't want to move back to the old compound."

I'd be happy anywhere with Josie and being away from the

Southern Compound, and those memories sounded good. "What about the weather here?"

"The humans have adapted, and it's not a problem for us. We might even be able to reverse it, at least partially with the information from Calidora," Josie said.

"She's going to come for us after Ezra is no longer in power." I said, unable to keep the hardness out of my voice.

"I keep thinking she is going to show up or we will run into her along the way. Our group is enough to stand against hers now."

"She will want to show up when she thinks she can do the most damage," I said. "The Southern Compound. She would have to do it before you actually assume power there."

"That is going to be a hard point for her to time," Josie paused. "Unless she has someone on the inside giving her information. We have to keep everything tightly guarded until right before it happens."

"Consider it done, but you can't get there and keep everyone in the dark either," I said. "All these people have come to support you, but they will not follow blindly."

She studied the new plants on the workbench where she cultivated the seedlings.

"They need to hear our goals and objectives." She drummed her fingers on the table. "I will give them as much as I can where I feel it does not jeopardize safety."

"That's all I ask." I squeezed her hand. "What flower shall we look at today? Maybe show me the one you used against Captain Scott?"

"Any word on him?" Her tone grim.

"No, they should be close to the Southern Compound by now. It shouldn't be long."

"The flower I used on Captain Scott and his men was

jimsonweed. Everything about the plant is toxic." She walked to the planter and, careful not to touch it, pointed it out.

"Everything?" A plant like that shouldn't even exist.

"The petals, the nectar, the seeds, the stem. They all have toxins at the moment anything touches them." She sat on the edge of the flowerbed.

"But you didn't give them enough to kill them?" If a plant that poisonous could be refined to prevent ending, it could be useful in battle to prevent casualties.

"No, a human would have died, but that minimal quantity just causes some interesting hallucinations for vampires." Her eyes unfocused. "Obviously." She shrugged. Her gaze still distant. She compartmentalized when she didn't want to deal with a situation and suspected she was doing it now. "If we had mixed the Bloodroot with it or given a bigger dose, it would have been death even for a vampire."

"Do you think we could do something on a bigger scale against Ezra's army?"

"Like poisoning their blood supply? You couldn't control the dosage. People would certainly die."

"Anyway to control it?" This wouldn't be a peaceful transition of power. Loss of existence couldn't be avoided. Vampires, and maybe some humans, would be lost. If we could limit the loss, minimize it, I could exist with it better.

"Not in the supply, because you can't control who drinks when and how much. Theoretically, we could disperse it into the air like a fog or mist. We would need an agent to make it dissipate, because inhaling it is tricky."

"Do you have enough plants to make it for that many vampires?"

"Yes, but it's easy to get too much that way. We could end up with dead vampires and definitely dead humans."

"What if we got the word out for the humans to wear some type of gas mask?"

She looked up and met my gaze. Her eyes alight. "If they were wearing it while the poison was in the air, it would work. How would we get the word to them without getting it to the vampires, too?"

"I'll think on that while you figure out how to get the mixture airborne."

"I already have an idea." Josie stood on her tiptoes and gave me a quick kiss. "I'm going to check on Natasha before I hit the lab."

"Don't forget you have the address for all the followers. We'll be broadcasting live for the first time."

"Don't remind me." Josie's shoulders slumped, and she didn't turn around.

The path she chose took us down some risky twists. She carried the burden inside, and I needed to take some from her. I wracked my brain on ideas of how to alleviate it without diminishing her role. With all the powerful women vampires, the vampire society still leaned toward male leaders. My role had to be behind the scenes, so no interference came from me. My need to protect her could never overshadow her as our leader. *Gods give me the strength to be what she requires.*

CHAPTER 19

JOSIE - VIN

I nodded to the guard Killian had placed at Natasha's door and entered the room. The door clicked shut behind me.

Natasha's eyes fluttered opened, and she patted the spot beside her on the bed.

I settled next to her and whispered. "Hey, how are you feeling?"

"Horrible," she said, her voice like gravel.

"You sound it too. Have you been taking the herbs I sent with your blood supply?" I glanced at the nightstand and saw both the herbs and blood untouched.

"I'm being punished."

"Are they not helping you with it? I will take care of that."

"No." She laid her hand on my knee. "I'm being punished for telling Captain Scott to kill himself, and all the other horrible things I've done with my existence." Pink tears pooled at the edge of her eyes. One slid down into her hair.

The remorse she expressed appeared genuine. "Natasha, you're not. You had an unusually strong reaction, and that

SUSAN PERSON

happens with some vampires. You need to drink the blood and herbs."

"I think it's time for me to die. To really die."

My heart broke for her. She sacrificed for us and proved her loyalty. "You don't mean that."

"I do. I've done no good with my time."

Vampire depression. She suffered from it. Jimsonweed triggered it in some vampires, particularly those predisposed to it, and the only thing that really helped was to get the poison out of the system.

I stretched for one of the blood bags and tore the top off of it. The straws unwrapped in a cup beside them. I dropped one in the bag and turned off my sense of smell.

My hunger spiked from the stress, and I tried to make do with the rations.

"Then now is the time to make up for that, because I need you and Killian needs you."

Her eyes widened. "You need me?"

"Yes, I need my advisor, and most of all, I need my friend." I touched the straw to her lips.

A small smile formed on her lips. "I'm your friend?" Pink tears flowed down her temples.

"Yes." Tears blurred my vision. After all she had done, I liked her, and I worried about her. "Now, will you drink the damn blood?"

Her lips wrapped around the straw, and the crimson liquid moved up the white cylinder until her mouth filled. Her small, slow sips turned into gulps.

I was glad to see her drink. "Easy. There is plenty more over there."

She swallowed hard. "I'm hungry."

Poison recovery made the hunger tenfold. I'm not sure how she resisted it before except to punish herself.

The door creaked open, and I adjusted to see who it was.

"Killian." Natasha's voice sounded more like herself, with a pint of blood in her.

His eyes widened as he closed the door. "You're eating."

"Yes, my friend convinced me I need to stick around a little longer." She pushed herself into an upright position.

I relaxed to see her strength returned at vampire speed

Killian rearranged the pillows behind her. "You are both a mess. Had I known crying was the trick, this would have been a lot easier."

"Could you have made me cry?"

"Not on purpose. I never want to see you cry." He ran a finger along her jawline.

The tenderness of his touch brought color to her cheeks, and I felt like a third wheel.

Fresh tears spilled down her cheeks. "Okay. Let me eat without making me cry, you two."

I tore open another blood bag and added the herbs to it. The herbs contained the equivalent of the energy drinks humans were so fond of a century ago.

She tossed the empty one on the nightstand and reached for the one in my hand. "I'm feeling better already."

"We're vampires. We need blood to heal." I watched her drink at a slower pace. A good sign her hunger returned to a manageable level. "And you've been fighting one of if not the most toxic poisons on the planet."

"It's no joke. I hope we never have to use that again."

"Actually, Vin had an idea to use it on Ezra's army like we did the soldiers here." I surprised myself at the candor I shared with Natasha. Her gift might not work on me, but she had chipped into my small circle.

Natasha's face froze in a frown. The crimson liquid slid back down the white straw.

"How can we even consider using it? Innocent casualties are not acceptable," Killian said.

"I wasn't exactly innocent, Killian." Natasha touched his arm, not to use her powers but to reassure.

"His idea was to make it into a gas or mist," I said. "And I should be able to do it." It's a solid idea if we can get the message for masks to the right people.

"So we are just going to commit mass murder? Not even give them a chance to convert or surrender?" Natasha asked.

"They would hallucinate. It wouldn't kill them." It concerned me too, but I was confident I could make the right mixture.

"You can't control those levels," Killian said, his voice grim.

"If I make a gaseous form with the right weight, I can time the dissipation so that no one dies, or we can condense it, so they do." I swallowed hard. The condensed version not the way I wanted to go. "Mass murder like Natasha said."

"The mist. It would have them in a cooperative state?" Killian asked.

"Yes, it should work."

"And the humans?" Natasha's fingers wound around my wrist. Her eyes wide, she waited for my answer.

"We will get word out to them ahead of time so they can be ready with masks to protect themselves," I said.

"The odds do not balance in favor of anyone residing in the compound. I'd rather have fair combat. No honor if the scale is tipped in the warrior's favor."

"It's not the normal warfare, Killian, but I don't see another way for us to have any kind of advantage with Calidora waiting in the wings."

Natasha stiffened at the mention of her last prison master.

"Was this Vin's idea, Josie?" Natasha asked. "It sounds a lot like something Calidora would do."

I leaned back. *What exactly is she insinuating?* I didn't want anyone to die, but people already had. Vampires. Our friends. Humans. The end of existence as we knew it. We lived a hundred years this way and watched many people we know die because of it.

I looked them in the eyes, one at a time. "I'm committed to minimizing the death of both human and vampire, but it will happen before the war is over. We will see people we know die. Are you still able to stand by me and our cause knowing this?"

"I've seen my share of death, but it has rarely been to right something I knew was so wrong. My allegiance has been and still is to you," Killian said, and fisted a hand over his heart.

Killian's allegiance had always been to the empire, but when Ezra made him head of my guard, he took it to the next level. His gesture to me meant he accepted me as the new leader of the nation, and that came at substantial risk.

"I support my friend and trust her judgment," Natasha said. "Just promise me we protect the humans when we can."

I nodded. "Then I hope you will both be by my side when I address the forces tonight."

I LOOKED over the map on the desk. And the gas should help us accomplish the goal of removing Ezra with minimal loss of vampire or human life. Josie's idea to use it to make the vampire army compliant made sense. My back to the door, the hair on the back of my neck stood up.

"Vin?"

I spun the chair around to see Natasha standing in the doorway.

"You look a hell of a lot better." I gave her a smile. Josie mentioned Natasha was better, but I didn't expect her to bounce back this fast.

"Thanks," she said. "Evidently, my friends see value in my presence." Josie's trust had grown in Natasha.

"Josie is in the lab if you're looking for her."

"No, I came to find you, and I only have a few minutes before Killian comes after me. He treats me like a fragile human." She sounded like the normal Natasha.

I tossed my papers down on the desk. "You looked rough there for a while."

"Yes, and I love that he worries about me. That's not why I'm here though."

"What's up?"

Her forehead wrinkled up, and she rang her hands. "This whole poison mist stuff. Was that your idea?"

"We came up with it together. Why?" She's killed before. Why would she be nervous about the use of a gas?

"When Josie was describing it to us, my first thought was Calidora. Her need to control."

"What are you saying, Natasha?" I leaned back in the chair to distance myself. If she implied I acted like Calidora, I'd probably lose it.

"I'm concerned we are trading one corrupt leader's tactics for another. Ezra's for Calidora's."

My hand fisted, and I dug my nails into my palm. "Are you comparing Josie to Ezra and Calidora?"

IN BLOOD & ICE

"No, I don't think this was her idea. I think it was yours, and Calidora is your mother. Surely, you want to avoid following her path." Her words came out in a flurry, but she stayed firm.

It burned almost as much as my throat when I blood vomited from the Call. I blew out a breath and held it there. Her adrenaline overpowered everything in the room, and I couldn't focus while smelling it. This conversation scared her, and fear wasn't something she wore on the outside. "I'm nothing like her."

"Of course you're not. You are a much better person than she will ever be. That's why I thought you would want to be aware."

I'd never take a life on a whim the way Calidora killed, or the way Natasha had killed for her.

"You're pissing me off, Natasha. I don't know what game this is, but I'm not playing. Go find Killian." The fear she exhibited was real, but she mastered manipulation a long time ago. I believed it to be another facade of hers. She was here by default and needed to earn her place. I'd been there, but I earned mine through honesty, not deceit.

"I'm not playing a game. Calidora favored me, but I was still a prisoner. A prisoner who studied her for weaknesses, and there weren't many. She acted without conscious." She braved a step forward.

"My conscious is intact. My desire to solve this as peacefully as possible is intact too." The comparison she drew from me to my mother made me sick. My nails pierced the palm in frustration. A rotted metallic scent hit the air.

"I have no doubt it is, but there has to be another option."

"If we had more time, there would be tons of options. We have to make it happen in a very small window which limits our choices." I'd went over the options in a dozen directions. The gas was the only option where we could keep the timeline short and the loss of life low.

"Maybe you're right. The twisting pain in my gut says we need to think it through some more."

"Noted. Now, are we done?" The blood pooled in my hand.

"I guess so." Natasha walked to the door. She tossed her hair over her shoulder. "I'm not the enemy, but I am the only person who understands how your mother works."

"She's not my mother. She's just the vampire that gave birth to me."

"Whatever you want to call her." Natasha didn't even try to hide her steps. The echo deafening in the wake of the silence her comments left.

"Fuck." I slammed my hand on the desk. A bloody hand-print marked the spot. I scrolled through the files until I found one of Calidora meeting with Ezra. *Do I act like her? Do I think like her?*

"Have you ruined me? Are my decisions shit because of your genes?" I asked about the image on the screen. "I refuse to believe I could be anything like you."

The decision to use poison on Ezra's Southern Compound resulted from brainstorming ways to end the war quickly with the least casualties. Death wasn't my desire, like Ezra and Calidora. *Was it? Fuck. I refuse to be like that woman.*

"Damn it to fucking hell." I cleared the desk in one sweep of my arm. Equipment banged. Pens bounced across the floor. Papers flew through the air. My head dropped into a prayer position, but I didn't pray to the Gods. Josie and most vampires didn't believe in them. *Why did I? Was it a left over memory from the fake ones Calidora planted?*

"Vincent? Is everything okay in here?" Killian asked.

My restraint near the point it I neared losing it. *Maybe I was like Calidora.* I didn't raise my head. Josie wasn't the only one that compartmentalized. I'd done a job of it myself. "If you're looking for Natasha, she went to find you."

"She's out of bed again?"

"You can't make her a prisoner in her own home. She's had that already." I pushed back and up out of the chair. Rage clung below the surface of my neatly contained composure. Killian was at every turn. Always in our business. He told Josie the lie that separated us in the first place.

"That's not what I'm doing." Killian squared his shoulders.

"Isn't it though?" I stepped up in his face. He tried to control Josie by breaking us up, but that didn't work for him either. Now he tried to control Natasha. "You're controlling her to the point she has to sneak around."

"You don't know what you're talking about, but I can correct that attitude for you." Killian put a hand on my shoulder.

I shoved my hands hard into his chest. He slid out the door and leapt back into the room.

"I will tear you apart, little vampire," Killian growled.

"Let's see who tears who apart." I jumped the distance between us. The floor rumbled.

"What the hell is going on here?"

Shame washed over me. I cocked my head around to find Josie in the doorway. The glare on her face cut into me.

"We were having a discussion," I said. My temper eased back.

"It looked like you two were about to have some epic battle." She crossed her arms and stared us both down. Her brows pinched together. "Who's going to tell me what caused this?"

"He was trying to tell me I was keeping Natasha prisoner." Killian pouted. An adult warrior vampire pouted.

"You are being way overprotective. Back off and let her breath. Now, take a walk. Preferably in the snow to cool off." She pointed a finger at the two of us. "You two cannot be seen as in opposition. We need to be on the same page or no one is going to trust us."

It bit at me how right she was and how stupid I acted with Killian. I extended my hand to him. He accepted it in kind.

My bloody handprint looked like a badge on his shirt. Killian's shoulders slumped like a scolded child. He turned without a word.

"Now, your turn. Why are you starting fights over Natasha?" Her voice low with a twinge of hurt. *My turn for a well-deserved scolding.*

"He's treating her the same way Calidora did." I shrugged my shoulders more because the words felt wrong.

"Not even close. What's the real issue here?" If Natasha mastered manipulation, Josie mastered reading me. I couldn't let her see the part of Calidora in me. All the times I accused her of being like Ezra or a product of his indoctrination, and I'm like Calidora even when she didn't raise me. Born or created didn't matter. She decided to break a cycle, but I found myself unable to break away from a past I didn't know I had.

"There's not one. That's it," I said.

"Even in this state, you know that is a lie. Are you going to give me the truth or do I need to get Natasha down here to help you talk?"

"Gods damn it, Josie." I backed up until my legs hit the desk. I try to shove it all down inside, but her presence kept me from building a wall around it. "Leave me alone."

"What is up with you?" Her voice softened. She stood between my legs and rubbed my arms with her soft hands.

Her touch a reminder of what I had to lose. *But I am Calidora's son.* I focused over her shoulder on some shit picture on the wall. "I want to be alone."

"In all the time I've known you, and that's a long time, you have never refused my company. I see pain in your eyes, and I'm not leaving until we talk through it."

My fingers wrapped around her upper arms, and I gently pushed her away. I moved over to the far corner and leaned back. The anger and disgust in me was like a sharpshooter with an itchy trigger finger, and my trust in myself faltered. Josie wasn't the only one with a wall up. I'd built one around myself when I found out I was born from evil. If I hurt Josie, I'd punish myself straight to my ending.

"I see Calidora in myself, and it outrages me."

"Everything about her should outrage you except yourself. You're not like her. Did Natasha say something that made you think you were even a smidgen like her?" Her voice even and soft. It soothed the agitation.

"It's not Natasha's fault. The truth is, I am her son, and it was my idea to use the poison mist on the Southern Compound." It was still the right decision, even if it made me a monster like Calidora for thinking it.

"Natasha's scared and reacting to her fear. You and I came up with that idea together."

"But it was mine." I buried my fist in the plaster, trying to punch the connection away.

"Stop." She showed zero fear of me and pulled my hand out of the wall. *How is she not afraid? Because she's Josie, and she has no fear. She's special.* She dusted off the plaster and pressed her lips to my knuckles, covered in abrasions. "You are not like her. You do not revel in the death and misery of others. You have shown kindness to me, other vampires, and humans. Even when you thought you were created, you showed compassion for all. That is who you are."

The anger within me eased. Josie took the edge off of it. I sucked in air. Her rosewater scent filled my space. "You are too good for me."

"No way. You opened my eyes to how the world should be."

Me? She would have figured it out. "Calidora gave you the video."

"But you and you alone guided me to the right side of history," she said.

"You would have found your way there, eventually." My neck softened, and the tension left my shoulders. She had this effect on me. Her love never wavered, even when she hid it.

"No, I don't think I would have, Vin. Your perspective is what made me see the change we needed." She took slow steps towards me.

I didn't back away and stretched my hand out to her. *She gave me more credit than I deserved, especially after my immature behavior with Killian.* "You are my voice, Josie. You are the voice of us all. The voice we need to hear. I most of all needed to hear it tonight." I held her tight against my chest. The connection with her intimate and strong. She'd brought me out of a spiral. *Only love could do that.*

"My voice is yours anytime you need it," she whispered.

"I never want to be what she is or do what she does."

"Then you never will." She looked up at me and rested a hand on my cheek.

"Then why am I so scared?"

"Because you care."

I cared about what happens to this world. To the vampires. To the humans. Most of all to Josie.

"I care about you. Josie, I love you."

"I love you too. Can you just tell me that next time and not pick fights with Killian?" Her lips pressed against my neck.

My body ached for her. "If you promise to keep doing that, I will."

"I would love nothing more than to keep kissing your body. Every inch of it." She planted a long kiss against a lower spot on my neck. I longed to feel her to be naked and in my bed or right here on this desk. "But I have an address to give. You're going to stand by my side for this. Aren't you?"

"I'd stand in a pyre of stakes for you."

She gave a weak laugh, like she wasn't sure if I joked or not. "No need for such a showy proclamation of love. By my side at this gathering will do."

I pressed my lips to hers and let the warmth of her touch heal the seared hole in my soul.

CHAPTER 20

VIN - JOSIE

I stood with Josie out of sight from the crowd and glimpsed a view of the courtyard. More supporters arrived. Vampires gathered on one side and humans on the other, like junior high kids at their first dance. The divide might as well have been a chasm. Night had fallen some time ago. The gathering time chosen to accommodate as many as possible. Josie shifted from foot to foot and picked at non-existent lint on her outfit.

"Are you nervous?"

"I'm about to address the vampires who left the safety of my father's reign to stand with me. Yes, nerves are a factor." Her hand ran through the loose waves of hair.

"There is a reason they chose to stand behind you. Remember that. Remember, you are here to fix what our parents broke."

"Haven't you heard? You can't put Humpty Dumpty back together again."

"No, but you can get a new egg." My humor wasn't the best, but I wanted to lighten the mood.

A giggle erupted from Josie. "Yes, you can always get a new egg as long as there are chickens to lay them." She shook her head.

"And that's what you are doing. Securing a future of egg laying chickens."

She slapped my arm. "Okay, Old McVincent, don't put me in the chicken coop yet. I still have a speech to give. Message received."

I chuckled. "Tell me when you're ready, and Old McVincent will start the live feed. Killian's already on stage doing his thing." Killian scouted the audience for any perceived threats under the guise of welcoming everyone and giving updates on the start time.

Josie's throat moved as she swallowed hard. She took a deep breath. "I'm ready."

I gave her a thumbs up.

She took deliberate steps onto the platform we had made in the rear ice-covered courtyard, the only place large enough to hold this many people.

"I welcome you to the Northern Compound and thank you for your loyalty. Tonight I share with you the truth that led to the decision to separate. My father and other vampires in leadership a hundred years ago were power hungry and sought to increase their own strength."

I projected the videos on the wall behind her. Gasps sounded from the crowd as they saw the experiment results on the whiteboard behind Ezra. The humans and vampires talked over each other.

Josie cleared her throat, and they fell silent again. "I stand before you tonight to tell you my father, Ezra, along with other top vampires, conspired against their competition and the human race. Their plan was to strategically kill off the human populations with an ice age. It did not go as planned, and ended up plunging the entire planet into an ice age and killing off most of the humans. This left many vampires starving and eventually turning Rogue or dying."

Josie's eyes cast down. We'd prepared for this moment. Her decision did not come lightly for the next video.

"My own mother found out the plan. She initiated a tactic to stop them. Ezra found out." Josie cleared her throat again. "My father had my mother killed to protect his secrets."

A dull roar erupted from the crowd.

Her fingers ran under her eyes to wipe the pink liquid away.

"If you will stand with me, we will end the reign of the perpetrator. His evilness has written terrible chapters of history. We are the ones who can bring back balance and rectify the mistakes. I want to use the technology they have to attempt to reverse the ice age. It will be my goal for the rest of my existence to right what my father did."

The vampires moved toward the stage. Killian snapped to attention and glued himself to Josie's side.

"Will you join me in our new crusade?"

Cheers erupted from both vampire and human. I couldn't yell it out like some of the other cheers, but I was proud of her. Josie did not know what a gift she had with people.

Random hands from the crowd extended up to her like concert goers reached for the star. That's how bright she shined. Killian's expressions rigid in contrast to Josie's genuine love of the people. She touched a hand, and that person would move out of the way to make room for the next. It went on until she had reached them all. She'd single hand-edly touched every one of her followers personally. Our leaders had never done before.

The change had begun, and there was no turning back now.

When everyone had gone, she sought me out. Her arms wrapped around my waist. We walked down the hall towards our rooms.

I hugged her to me. "You have no idea what you did. Do you?"

"I told the truth."

"You started a revolution."

"It sounds unbearable when you use that word."

She'd grown up with the indoctrination that revolution meant treason. That perception was an old tape that needed to be changed. "It's not a bad word. Sometimes it takes a revolution to save the world."

"I hope I can live up to the expectations."

"You are already there. I'm very proud of you." I pressed my lips to the tip of her nose. "How about some more of those kisses you were giving out earlier?"

"That might be the best thing you've said to me." She kissed me hard on the mouth.

My dick twitched. I scooped her up in my arms and carried her inside.

Her head rested against my shoulder.

My hurried steps not as silent as they should be on the marble floor.

Killian met us at the edge of the hallway of our apartments.

I sat Josie on her feet.

"Hey, we need to talk about some of the security issues in the morning," Killian said. "Nothing immediate. Just observations."

"Noted," Josie said. "I'll see you in the office later."

I quickened my steps and stirred up a breeze. "Later. We're having a private debriefing right now,"

I STRETCHED my arms up over my head. Vampire sleep engaged restorative healing. We could go days without it unless bored, but the wake from it was like drinking ten blood bags. My hand dropped to the space next to me. *Empty.* The hollowness in my chest mirrored the vacant spot in the bed. I sat up. "Vin?" No answer.

A twinge in my gut twisted around my inactive organs. My usual pace of taking human time to get ready abandoned. Vampire speed kicked in for me. I ran through the shower and dressed in full vampire mode.

The same urgency carried me to the voices echoing from the computer room. Unlike my personal time in the poison plant garden, this room had become our little group's sanctuary away from the now crowded house.

Vin and Killian sat at one of the desks, so focused on the monitor they didn't look up when I walked into the room.

"This is someone very loyal to Ezra," Killian pointed to the screen.

What are they looking at? Who is loyal to my father?

Vin looked over his shoulder. "Hey, babe." His voice light. He held his arm out for me.

"Babe?" I leaned in against him. *Babe is an interested replacement for Josie.* It warmed me all over, but it had an even stronger affect below the waist.

His arm rested lightly around my hips. "Do you recognize this man?"

I studied the picture and recognized the vampire. "My

father promoted him before we left. He used to report to Captain Scott before that. Steven something."

"Steven Smith," Killian said. "He's a known drug dealer turned abuser after his wife committed suicide. I questioned why Ezra promoted him, and Ezra chastised me for questioning his decisions instead of answering."

"Sounds familiar." I grimaced. "He'd do anything for his next hit. Ezra could use that to control him. That, also, explains who has been in my garden."

Vin and Killian both turned their attention on me. I told myself curiosity led someone there, but deep inside, my instincts had contradicted it.

"Has he approached you?" Vin asked.

"No, I noticed someone had been taking some plants or parts of them rather," I said. "I thought it was someone who missed the variety of plants."

"How did he get past the guard?"

"He's an addict," Killian said.

Vin's grip tightened on my hip. "That's Josie's safe place. We need to figure out how he's getting in there and close it off."

"We need to eliminate him, period. He threatens her safety just by being here," Killian said.

Good gods. Can they talk to me about it? "I'm right here guys."

They looked at me again.

"Remember me? The leader of this revolution. I don't want him killed. If you want to detain him and question him. Fine. No killing on this compound unless we are attacked. We will not be like Ezra."

"As you wish. I'm going to look for him now," Killian said. "Alone. He'd smell you two."

Vin kicked Killian in the shin. "Let us know what you find,

asshole."

Killian laughed. "Dickhead." Then turned to me. "My apologies for the language, Josephine."

I waved him off. Vin and I sat alone. I slid into the chair next to him.

"You two have to quit trying to protect me without consulting me."

"We weren't. You just looked so beautiful sleeping." He leaned over and his lips brushed against mine. "We do have to think about your safety, Josie."

"Not just mine, but yours and Killian's and Natasha's and everyone now in my charge," I said.

"You are the leader. The face of this revolution. If something happens to you, it would be over. These people didn't show up here for anyone else. Vampires and humans came to support you. It's so unprecedented." Vin took my hands in his. "I don't think you fully realize how much you're impacting the world."

I sighed. There would need to be a leader. While I wanted to right the wrongs of the vampire regime, I didn't think my name should be the one in the leadership spot. "I'm trying not to think too hard on my role and more on what we can do in the future."

"Because you don't want to consider what might happen to your father when we succeed?"

Tears burned my eyes. I managed a nod. There had been vampire revolts in other empires. Vampire leaders had been ripped into pieces and burned. *Nothing but ash.* I felt sick. I hated what he had done, but he was still my father.

Vin pulled me tight to him.

My head thudded against his chest and stayed there until I gained my composure. Emotions in check, I looked up into his eyes. "He's a bastard. I'd never make an excuse for him, but I'm scared for him. What if they tear my father apart before I get to him?"

"He's smart and has ruled long enough to have seen rebellions in the past. There is always a chance he may surrender to you when he realizes how strong your forces are."

I wished that were true. "No chance of that. He would rather die than willingly give up his power."

"The truth is, we have no idea what he will do, but you cannot base your decisions on a future you can't see. Do you clearly see a new age for vampires and humans?"

"That is one thing I know has to happen." My father acted on strategy. Every moved he made calculated for every variable. He enjoyed the challenge. I had to match him move for move to bring about this change. If he were to get one step ahead of us, our chance for change might disappear and us along with it.

"Then keep focusing on that when you get worried," Vin said.

If only it were that simple. "I'll give it a try," I said.

Light footsteps padded down the hall. Vin and I both darted to the door to meet her.

"Natasha, why are you running?" I asked.

"Killian needs you in the garden." She glanced at Vin with a grave look. Then to me. "Both of you."

There must have been another case of an intruder. *How did they keep getting in there?* We ran to the garden. Natasha waited at a distance. The corpse flower stunk up the air.

Killian crouched over something. *Clothes?* Crimson red pools met the toe of his shoe.

I covered my mouth and nose. It wasn't the Corpse Lily.

"Is that--" Vin said.

Killian interjected. "Steven Smith."

"You killed him? Why? I told you not to do it." I stared at the body. He'd expelled the blood from his body. *Poison.*

"I didn't kill him," Killian stood up.

I looked at him. *Of course he didn't. Why did I even say that?*

"Overdose on the jimsonweed?" Vin asked.

"No, I don't think so."

"If he didn't overdose, then why is he in here?" I asked.

"Someone was trying to frame him, but I'm not sure why." Killian stared at Steven's lifeless body.

"Frame him for what?" Vin asked.

"For being the one taking the plants from the garden."

"I'm sorry. I'm not following. Why do you think he was framed?" Vin knelt down.

"The jimsonweed is in his right hand," Killian squatted down and gestured to the other side. "But he has scars and marks on his left hand from before he was created. Clearly his dominant hand. Also, there are large chunks of the plant shoved in his mouth, but he was vomiting blood from his exposure. He wouldn't have been able to hold that in his mouth as violent as the scene was."

"Someone was here with him," I said. This was an elimination of a threat. *But for what?*

"His existence was deliberately ended," Killian said.

A sweet scent tickled my nostrils. *Bloodroot.* I pivoted to face its location. It was on the other side of the garden. *Where was the smell coming from?* My eyes looked at Steven's blood-covered face. The roll in my stomach said I was on the right track.

"Scoot back and let me close." I maneuvered in a position where I wasn't standing in his blood, but could bend down close to his face. My nose to his mouth, I inhaled deeply. A cough gagged out of me from the strong, sweet smell. And again, until some of my own blood melded with Steven's on the floor.

"God, Josie. Are you okay?" Vin pulled me some distance away and blocked my view of the body. He ripped some fabric from the hem of his shirt. He balled up material as a makeshift rag to wipe the blood from my face. His hand cupped my chin. "Talk to me."

"Someone really wanted him dead. They mixed bloodroot and jimsonweed together. They tried to cover it up by putting him near the Stinking Corpse Lily." This is sloppy. Too sloppy for a good spy.

"A vampire should know our sense of smell would detect that," Killian said.

"Exactly," I said.

"Either we are looking for a very dumb vampire or a human did this." Natasha ventured closer to us by wide berth of the body.

"So which is it?" I peeked around Vin's frame at the body. "And why are they stealing my plants?"

"Why don't you two go back to the computer room and see if you can find something on the videos?" Killian asked of me and Natasha.

"What are you two going to do?" I asked.

"Investigate," Vin said.

"I want to know as soon as you find something," I said.

Vin kissed my temple. "Of course."

Natasha and I walked halfway to the computer room in silence. Spies sent by my father. It had to be. The haphazard scene was a message *Maybe humans braved poisonous plants to kill my father's spies.* Chaos developed in my house.

"The humans didn't do this, Josie," Natasha said. She

stirred me from my thoughts.

"I know you've been spending a lot of time with them, but we can't rule them out just yet." I'm not even sure the humans could have discovered him, much less acted on it.

"They are excited about this new world you want to create. There is much more for them to lose than us."

I froze. She was right. The humans did have more to lose. More than they had in almost a hundred years. "Humans would have an equal say."

She looked me in the eye. Fear lined her face.

"Vampires who don't want them to be equal would benefit from staging a vampire's death to look like the humans did it." A vampire would know to make it look messy to frame the humans.

"Mmm hmmm. That's what I was saying," Natasha said.

"We have a problem," I said.

"We sure do."

"Those videos better show us something, because we need answers fast," I said. "If we have vampires willing to frame humans, they will not stop with just one incident."

We got to the room and combed through the tapes from today.

"Any luck?" Natasha called from her computer.

"No. You?"

"I wouldn't be asking if I'd found something." She frowned and looked back at the screen.

Vin and Killian skidded around the door and slammed into each other. *Geez. Like toddlers.*

"Were you two racing?"

They exchanged a look, but neither answered.

"Killian, go ahead," Vin said.

"The killer is probably sick. No, you figured it out. You tell her," Killian said.

What the hell is up with the two of them?

"No, you saw it."

I threw my hand up in the air. "One of you tell me."

"They touched the jimsonweed. You said every part of it is poison," Vin said.

They could have worn gloves. "How do you know they touched it?" I asked.

"There was a snag of fabric and some tissue on the small fence around the planter. Vampire tissue," Killian said.

"That doesn't mean they physically touched it," I said.

"No, but we were hoping you found something on the cameras," Vin said.

"We came to the conclusion it was vampires. The humans stand to lose a lot more, so it doesn't make sense," Natasha said. "But we haven't found any evidence on the cameras."

"We came to the same conclusion when we were in the garden," Vin said.

"Are we missing something?" I asked.

"No, the perpetrator is very good at covering his tracks," Killian said.

"To answer your original question. If they barely touched the jimsonweed, they would only have hallucinations. The more contact they had, the more likely they are to become ill or die. You saw what happened when Captain Scott kissed Natasha."

Killian stared off at the wall.

"Let's go find a sick vampire then," Vin said to Killian.

"I guess you're going to ask Natasha and I to stay here?" His need to protect me was sweet, but unnecessary. I'd bested most of the elite fighters in sparring matches and could do it again if needed.

"Yes, if you would."

"You know that's not going to happen," I said. Vin glared at me. "Just go. We'll meet you later."

I turned back at the computer screen and scrolled. I had my own ideas on how to catch the perpetrator.

"Are we really staying here?" Natasha asked.

"Hell no." I cut my eyes at her. "A poisoned vampire is going to want blood."

"So we're going to the blood storage room," Natasha said. "You're too good, Josie."

"I never thought learning about the plants I once thought were frightening would ever come in handy."

No one met us in the hall as we walked towards the kitchen. We had a compound full of vampires and humans and not one walked this hall. The sunny day drew them to the courtyard. *Who wouldn't want to feel the sun on them as many days as we spent without it?*

The door to the giant refrigerator stood ajar by an inch or so. We entered the room slowly. I scanned for signs of an injured vampire. Blood splatters and empty bags laid strewn across the floor. *We have a sick vampire on our hands.*

"Looks like we didn't figure it out in time," Natasha said. "With this much blood, will they already be back to normal?"

With this much blood, either the vampire's symptoms were extreme, or they were on their way to being healed. "It's hard to say. Not everyone has the strong reaction you did. It really depends on how much they consumed and how it was ingested."

"Could we be missing anything in here?" She kicked some of the bags around on the floor. "Why would someone who was so meticulous with the murder be so sloppy here?"

"The bloodroot poison is excruciating, even with our

threshold for pain. I'm sure the vampire was desperate," I said.

"What else makes a vampire desperate?"

"The unbearable thirst of a newly created vampire. I've seen them do some horrific things for that thirst." A new vampire with poison in them fit the observed behavior. *Sloppiness. Not understanding the poisons. Thirst.*

"Me too. Like rip a human to pieces while they drank from them." Natasha shuddered.

"A created vampire that thirsty around spilled and tainted vampire blood would likely be driven into a frenzy of hunger."

Natasha nodded. "The tainted blood would repel them, but make them fiercely hungry."

"What would make a newly created vampire wouldn't kill another vampire, though?" They wouldn't, couldn't really, kill their creator. The bond would be too strong.

"Revenge," Natasha said.

"Steven was an addict. Maybe he turned them," I said.

"Or someone turned them specifically for this purpose," she said. "Maybe they were trying to create chaos."

"Violence," I said. *Strategy. Ezra was the king of it as much as he was Emperor of the nation.* My jaw ached from clenching it. I rubbed it. "A small army inside our revolution to tear it apart."

"You think there is more than one?"

I surveyed the number of blood bags on the floor. Twenty pints of blood consumed equated to about two humans. Rogues excluded, a vampire alone even in starvation would only consume four to six. The vampires drank fast, so hunger factored in for sure. The sloppy scene suggested youth or pain or both. I knelt down and inhaled. A mixture of vampire scents hit me. I couldn't determine one from the other. Vincent needed to give it the sniff test. His tracker skills more developed for this mess of smells. "Yes, I do."

CHAPTER 21

JOSIE

Vin dropped into a crouched position. His eyes closed, and he sucked in the air through his nose. Time ticked by, but Vin sat motionless. He inhaled again.

"I can't separate them. Steven Smith is the only one I recognize. They probably had some of his blood on them."

A random vampire spy created a risk, but a usable one. The potential of multiple vampire spies who framed humans for their actions raised the level of peril for our followers. *An extermination squad.* A killer or killers among us threatened the delicate balance and could throw the entire plan into chaos. No one would feel safe.

"We need to get them rounded up, but there is a bigger question," Vin said. "Who is controlling them?"

"Is that really a question? It has to be my father."

Killian picked up an empty blood bag and tossed it into the trash can. "From a distance, but there is a traitor imbedded here, creating them and controlling them."

"There are too many people to interrogate one by one." Vin flung the bags he held towards the trash can.

"I wouldn't want to do that anyway," I said. "Panic would erupt the second we started." I picked up a handful of the bags and tossed them in the trash.

"How are we going to tell which ones are new vampires? It's not like they are wearing a new vampire sticker," Natasha said.

"They will congregate together," Killian said. "Especially if they are freaking out."

"So, if we were newly created, where would we go?" Vin asked.

"The woods," I said. "The craving would be stronger around the humans. If they are smart and being guided, they will be in the woods and out of sight."

"We need to find their leader," Vin said.

"If he wanted chaos, wouldn't he just turn them loose?" Natasha chewed her fingernails. Nervous was a new look for her.

"Ezra prefers controlled chaos. He'd want his finger on it," I said. "Even if it is through a minion."

"Yes, he does not like anything left to random acts. Everything he does is deliberate and planned," Killian said.

"Drawing a skilled soldier of Ezra's out in the open will not be easy," Vin said. "If it was one of the elite guard, you would recognize him, Killian. It must be someone else."

"He always has a couple of spies only he knows. They sneak in and out of the compound."

Those spies often blended in with the crowd. They followed me throughout my childhood. Ezra not the one who told me. As a teenager, Mother warned me when curiosity led me into some precarious paths. Her arms had went around me in a hug and she whispered the warning. Mother's warning stood out in my mind as the only time I ever saw genuine fear from her.

"Then we have no clue who the fuck we are looking for." Natasha threw her hands up in the air. "This is hopeless."

Killian wrapped a hand around the small of her waist and pulled her to his side. "Hey. What's going on with you?"

"If we don't figure it out quickly, the word is going to leak out about the death, and the vampires will turn on the humans. There are children." Her head dropped, and she pinched the bridge of her nose. "We can't let them hurt the children." Pink tears spilled down her checks.

The real Natasha had a heart and some humanity. She'd spent time with the human children and cared for them. Her instincts motherly even if we would never have children of our own.

Killian enveloped her in his arms. She leaned into him like she sheltered in her own personal Killian cocoon.

I rubbed her back and looked up at Killian. "We will not let anything happen to those children, Natasha. I promise you that. If we can't do anything else, we will protect them."

"Maybe we should look at moving the humans to another location," Killian said.

"No, they are better off here, where we are close enough to respond if something happens," I said. "Besides, I'm not sure where else we could move them.

"We need a way to get details on all the vampires without being obvious," Vin said.

"We tell them we're organizing the troops. We'll create questionnaires. Find out name, home location, specialties, and where they trained," Killian said.

"Perfect. We have an approach. I'll go to the computer room and make sheets. Anything else we should ask?"

"I saw some clip boards in one of the offices. I can go get them," Natasha said.

"I'll go with you," Killian said without breaking contact with her.

"And I'll go with Josie," Vin said.

I smiled at him. He took my hand in his and pressed his lips to my knuckles in the same I had when he punched the wall. His instincts in tune with what I needed. Reassurance. Kindness. Love. Our mantra for the future.

The word processing application almost created the sign-up sheets for us. We were done in a few minutes.

"I'm making two hundred copies," Vin said while I sat next to him in the computer room. "I counted thirty-five hundred yesterday and more have arrived."

"It has to be most of the northern territory and then some." I turned my chair to face him. "Do you think this will work?"

Vin shrugged. "It seems like a reasonable request. We need to make sure we do something with the information to help quell suspicions."

"We'll know what groups to put where, and that will help make us more effective," I said. "It will give us a chance to look in the eyes of our followers too."

Vin walked over to stand in front of me. "Your followers, Josie. You are the one they all want to see and hear." For the good of humanity and the vampire, I had no choice but to step up. My name had power behind it, and we needed some power right now.

"Does it bother you?"

"That they want a piece of you?" He rested his hands on either side of me and leaned in close. "Yes, because I'd rather have you all to myself all of the time." He pressed his lips to mine. A soft touch only a vampire could do with the immense control we have. He pulled back. "When this is over, we will take a trip to a cabin."

"You realize it might be awhile before it is over. Right?"

"Luckily, I'm not getting any older, and I have plenty of patience. Look how long I waited for you."

Vin made me feel safe even when the world was far from it. I slid my hands into his hair at the temples and pulled his face to mine. My lips demanded a response from his. I rose from the chair without breaking the contact. I craved his touch more than I ever craved blood.

Vin's hands gripped my waist and pushed enough to urge me to step back. The edge of the desk dug into the backs of my legs. Vin lifted me onto the desktop. His tongue plunged into my mouth. Our venom mixed.

"Hmmm hmmmmm."

Great. My cheeks burned. *Probably bright red.*

Our foreheads leaned against each other. "Later," Vin whispered and placed a soft kiss in between my eyes. "What's up, Killian?" Vin let go of me and faced the giant figure hovering at the door.

I slid off the desk and turned around.

"You two need to be more alert," he said.

"Like you two were?" Vin asked.

Killian looked over his shoulder at Natasha.

She shrugged. "I didn't say anything."

"We retrieved some clipboards," Killian said.

"But we found something interesting in the process," Natasha added. She reached into her pocket and handed me a picture.

I ran my fingers across my mother's face in a photograph I had never seen. Just the two of us in it. I was maybe six, and she knelt down beside me. No memories came of the day, but her face looked happy. "This was in the office? I've never seen it before."

"That's not all. This one was with it in the drawer." She handed me another one. The urge to rip it to shreds came on strong, but I settled for getting it out of my hands.

"Why am I not surprised?" I passed it over to Vin.

"Calidora with Ezra," he said. "In the lab nonetheless."

"These were together?" I didn't have many photos of my mother, but I could do without the one of Ezra and Calidora together. *Why were they together?*

"Yes, along with these notes from the scientists your mother was working with before she died. They were very close to finishing a plan on how to reverse the ice age." She passed the rolled up pages to me. "We think you could finish it."

My mother's research. Had she left this for me to find? I unfolded them to see my mother's handwriting. The detail was impeccable. "A final gift from my mother." I blinked back tears. "We're really going to save the world for vampires and humans." My hand squeezed Natasha's. "Thank you."

It wasn't complete and would need work, but most of the work had been done.

Vin took a page from my hand and chuckled as he perused it. "Those damn plants are the key ingredient. The toxins are neutralized enough to prevent death or serious side effects with certain combinations."

"Was this just out in the open and I missed it?" I went through the desk when we arrived and opened every drawer.

"No, we noticed the bottom of the drawer was a false one when we pulled the clipboards out," Killian said. "And by we, I mean Natasha." Killian gazed at her with love. His poker face gone.

"The pictures were taped to it. When I pulled it out, the false bottom shifted. The papers were there. She led us to it."

Her reasons for doing it in the first place. To stop Father and Calidora and save me.

Hope flitted around me from the time we started talking about a new future. With this present from my mother, hope settled for this time in my heart. Hope left by my mother as if she had known our paths would lead her.

"A simple clue that wouldn't be obvious. This is my legacy. She knew she was going to die, and I would have to finish it. My mother is saving the world from her grave." Tears rolled down my face. "This is something we can share with the people today. We are going to make it happen.."

"What about this picture?" Vin asked.

"It was loose in the drawer," Killian said.

"We're not going to use it, Vin. We've presented enough evidence of guilt. It's time to move our people forward. You've reminded me and shown me many times that is the direction we need to take," I said.

"What about the battle? Does this mean we can skip it?" Natasha asked.

"I wish that was the case, but we have to disempower Ezra or this doesn't end," I said.

Vin stared at the picture of Ezra and Calidora. "We have to remove Calidora's power, too. She wants us to take Ezra out to clear the path for her. We can't let that happen, either."

"We'll be vulnerable here when the troops go to the Southern Compound. The humans will not have protection." Natasha's eyes widened.

I focused on her. Her worry sincere. I could see the concern and shared it. "Take a breath. They'll come with us."

"Then the compound is wide open," Killian said.

"Do we have enough to split the forces?" I asked.

"We'll know after we finish our meet & greet," Vin said.

I grabbed the stack of papers from the printer and divided them among the four of us. "We just became census takers for the day."

"Don't forget the biggest reason we are doing this is to find Ezra's spy," Vin said. "But we are looking for skills that can be useful too."

Natasha stepped forward and froze in mid-stride. "What if it's Calidora's spy and not Ezra's?"

" I know you hate her for what she did to you. I'm not saying it isn't possible, but she let us go." Vin kept his voice low.

"I was throwing an idea out. Nothing more." Natasha held her empty clipboard to her chest like armor.

"You two go ahead. We'll be right behind you." I waited for Natasha and Killian to leave. "I thought you were doing okay after we talked."

"It's stupid, but I had some hope she would somehow be on our side. I know she's not, but something deep down in me really wanted her to be."

"Calidora?" I dropped my clipboard on the desk and clasped my hands around the back of his neck. "She's your mother. Of course, you want her to be good. No child wants their parent to be a psycho. Yet here we are. Two grown vampires, each with a psychotic parent."

"You have good in you. Your mother made sure we had what we needed to fix everything."

"Not everything, but I know where you're going," I said. "You don't know your father. He might be as good as my mother."

His chin rested heavy on my shoulder. "We don't know, and if Calidora chose him, he's probably as wicked as she is."

"Hey. You can't think like that. You are a good person." I leaned back and waited for his eyes to meet mine. "If I have to tell you every day for the rest of our existence, I will. I'll make sure you never forget that you are good to the core."

"You have a good parent to look up to."

"And you might too. You don't know, and that's scary," I said. "Our parents are guideposts. They don't define who we are. We make our own decisions. Just like I made the decision to pursue this revolution with your help. You have made moral decisions your whole life. I can't say my track record is as good as yours."

He smiled, small but genuine. "How did I get so lucky to find you?"

I smiled back. "Fate," I said. One word. A word that defined so much of our existence. *Love. I loved him and would support him however he needed.*

"Where's my census taker's hat?"

"You look better without one." I ruffled his hair.

He smoothed it down. Gave me a quick peck and passed me my clipboard.

THE QUESTIONING DIDN'T TAKE AS LONG as expected. Vampires eager to stand out flooded us to get on the list. Not exactly what we needed to flush out the spy. We had stacks of sheets on the desk in the office, where Natasha found the pictures. I chose this one, because it was the place my mother left her clues.

SUSAN PERSON

Natasha counted the pages at vampire speed. "One hundred and eighty-eight."

"Around thirty-seven hundred. That's a good number," Vin said.

It was more than we hoped for, and I was thankful. "We'll be able to leave some here to defend our home then."

"Not a clean fifty-fifty split. We should take at least two thousand with us to the south," Killian said.

"Did anyone see someone they thought was suspicious?"

Killian thumbed through the papers. "No, nor did I see any new vampires."

Our newcomers were good and hide-n-seek. A problematic skill for us. I tapped my fingers on the desk in a rhythm to help me think.

Vin covered my hand with his. "So, they are hiding as we suspected."

"It's too easy to come and go here," Natasha said.

"We have been lax on the control in and out of the compound. Killian, I assume you'll want to lead that effort," I said.

Ezra wouldn't have made that mistake, and I shouldn't have. I just didn't want anyone to perceive this place as a prison or anything like the Southern Compound. *Lesson learned.*

"Yes, I've already identified some vampires who have the skills for it. They'll lock the open gates and manage the entry and exit."

"Do we need to start moving them over to a list?"

"I marked them on my pages and already recruited the ones I trusted immediately. Those names have an 'R' beside them." He handed me some pages. "They just need orders."

"Always one step ahead, Killian. That's why you're the best." Vin patted him on the arm.

"Go on. Once you have your mind made up, you like to act."

"Natasha, would you like to come with me?"

"Unless you need me here, Josie?" Natasha asked.

I raised an eyebrow. She rarely strayed far from Killian. "Nooo, I think Vin and I can handle this for a while. Meet us back here when you're done."

"Let's divide the forces in two. The one that will stay and the ones that will go. Then we can split the ones going with us based on the strategy we discussed." Vin grabbed a stack of forms and sat them on the large map table by the windows.

I grabbed a stack and followed. "We're going to need to figure out what to do with the vampires hiding in the woods." The papers landed askew on the table.

"Yes, but we need to wait for Killian and Natasha to secure the perimeter. Then we can see the comings and goings of the compound."

"What if we don't find them before we have to leave for the Southern Compound?"

"We will, Josie. They'll be easier to track with a perimeter intact," he said. "I'm kind of curious when you will deploy the reversal for the ice age."

Reversing the ice age wasn't as simple as following Mother's notes. The formula and process were unfinished and untested. It could take months or years for me to work through it. I'd need help if there was anyone left to help.

"I still have to finish it, and I'll need the technology at the Southern Compound, along with some scientists, to do that. Did anyone list scientist as their profession by chance?"

"I haven't seen one, but we still have plenty to go through."

I'd never realized how groups clustered together. The list across three pages even told a tale. Ten vampires in a row who listed archery as a skill. Twenty-three names with the sharpshooter moniker. Five included wrestling versus nine called themselves boxers. Thirteen indicated hand-to-hand combat was their specialty. They identified themselves with what they had known the longest. The pages drew a drastic picture of vampire behavior.

"Do we need any pilots?" Vin asked. "I've seen several here."

"Are they not already flying?"

"It doesn't appear so. The temperatures here aren't as conducive as in the south. I'm not even sure the northern camps have aircraft of their own."

"We should get them trained and in the air for some practice."

"Making that list now," he said. "We need to see if those old helicopters and first edition tundras still run, so we can put them to use there."

My hand brushed a stack and sent the top half tumbling to the ground. I slid from the chair and crouched down to pick them up.

Vin joined me on the floor to gather the papers.

My hand reached for a piece of paper under the table. I stared at the name. It glared at me like I should know it. I raised up and my head thudded against the table.

"Fuck." My eyes squinted shut. I touched the back of my head.

"Are you okay?" Vin sat on the floor beside me. He tilted my head without touching the actual bump.

"I'm fi--" The name. I knew exactly who it was. "Fuck!"

CHAPTER 22

JOSIE

Killian stared at the names on the list. His recognition less than mine.

It was her and all her nastiness. I couldn't forget her.

"And you're certain?" Killian asked.

"Yes, I remember her," I said.

"There's only one Livia I know," Vin said.

"My father's infatuation and spy." My lips twisted on their own.

"And she made sure she got in my line, because the three of you would recognize her," Natasha said. "Why wouldn't she just hide? And why use her real name?"

"She was already in the compound. It would draw more suspicion," Killian said.

"We are looking for a woman about Natasha's height with long red hair. She has a thing for sweets. She prefers to have human blood after they have eaten sweets as well," I said. "Her combat skills are primarily martial arts, and they are better than anyone she sparred with that I saw."

"So, she's beautiful, hungry, and an excellent fighter. A real triple threat," Natasha said. "I don't remember anyone coming through my line who fit that description. What did she list for skills?"

"Only one," I said. "Emissary."

"Emissary?" Vin said. "She's trying to hide in plain sight."

"Or she wants to get caught." Natasha said. "I would have noticed if someone put emissary down. She's got other skills than what you think."

"The top of our to do list is to find her and lock her up," Vin said. "Then we should be able to find the new vampires with her assisting them."

"Lock her up like Calidora did to Josie by confining her to a bedroom, or like she did to Killian by putting him in a cell? We don't even know she did it." Natasha crossed her arms and raised an eyebrow. She seemed intent on challenging everything Vin said.

I stood between them and put a hand out towards each of them. "What is it between you two? The animosity has to stop. It's going to tear us apart before we even get to the battle."

"I'm sorry." Natasha said.

Killian slipped protectively to her side. He didn't touch her. Instead, he let her have the space she needed, but he remained close and silent. His actions subtle.

"Why don't we just mingle with the crowd and see if we get a glimpse of her?" Livia would see us coming if we didn't act casual.

"It's worth a try," Vin said.

We made our way to the open space the vampires preferred. Some humans mixed with them. The conversations relaxed. Crowds worked their way back to their clusters.

Dark red hair caught my eye. She sat near a group but off

to herself, similar to what she did on the Southern Compound.

I signaled the group and approached her.

"Livia, would you join us for a moment," I said.

She pursed her lips but came willingly. She fell into step with me and Natasha. Killian and Vin took up behind her.

I gestured to a chair in the office. "Have a seat."

"What have you told Ezra of our plans?" Killian asked.

Livia looked at me. "Josie, it's not what you think."

She was the person father sent on his most secretive missions. Not a chance I'd believe her. "Isn't it? My father sent you here to spy on us."

Vin leaned toward her. "We'll let you live if you answer our questions. If you don't, well I hear poison is a terrible way to die." He paused. "Your friend, Steven, would agree."

"Steven is here?" Her mouth gaped open. *Does she really not know he is dead?*

"Was. Someone killed him, and my guess is, it was you," I said.

"No, it wasn't me," she said. "I loved him. I wouldn't kill him." Tears welled in her eyes. Ezra's spies trained in emotion control. She could fake tears.

I studied her every movement, down to the tiniest twitch in her eye. "You loved a poison addict?"

"He wasn't doing that anymore. No poison. No drinking for either of us."

"Someone wanted us to think he had overdosed, but we found proof he hadn't," I said. Livia was used to lies weaved with half-truths. I hoped honesty would flush out if she was lying or not.

Pink tears covered her cheeks like had once covered mine and Natasha's. I questioned her sincerity, but I couldn't deny how women in our society were treated and how her life was shaped by that. Leadership wasn't kind to us, and Calidora was not a role model any more than Ezra. The drive for freedom that was common to all three of us. Livia had sought hers in the form of solo missions. I'd never been allowed solo missions because of status, but I appreciated the freedom the expeditions gave.

"Why would you both come here if not to spy for Ezra?" Vin asked.

"We wanted to get away from our pasts."

"Ezra would never let that happen. We all know how he deals with what he considers traitors." I said.

She clutched her stomach and grabbed the back of the chair. "Your father didn't want me to go, but he would not allow our relationship." A sob wrenched from her gut. "The only way for us to be together was to leave."

I started to believe her, but her profession nagged at me. "That's the first thing you said that sounded like it might be the truth."

"It is." She wiped at her face. "That's why I didn't lie about my name or who I was."

My gut twisted like a lie detector going off. "Something doesn't sound right though," I said. "You went through Natasha's line. She can't remember you, but you wanted to start fresh."

She wiped new tears from her face. "I'm not stupid. My time with Ezra puts a price on my head. Switching sides does not always help someone like me. The longer I remained hidden, the better my chances."

"What about the new vampires?" Vin asked.

"New vampires?" She asked, wild-eyed.

"Yes, the newly created ones? What was your plan with them?" I asked.

Her eyes widened. The scent of adrenaline filled the air. The news frightened her. "I know nothing about them, but if there are newly created vampires here, we need to all be careful. Who is teaching them?"

"My guess is you are the one creating and leading them," Killian said. "How many are there?"

"I honestly have nothing to do with them. That's not my style. I have superb control of my venom and who I share it with."

"And what about Steven?" Vin asked.

Fresh tears rolled down her cheeks. "He had a lot of enemies and owed a lot of favors. Could he have been involved in something I didn't know about? Sure, but I doubt it."

"Why?" I asked.

"He broke ties with all his old 'friends' when he quit using. He had new friends." Her eyes cast down. "And new activities."

"What kind of activities?" Killian asked.

Natasha tapped his arm with the back of her hand. She leaned in to whisper in his ear, but I heard her. "She's his lover."

I shook my head. "Don't answer that, Livia." I didn't need details of their sex life.

"Can I see him or did you stake him to destroy the body?" A wave of pink tears rushed down her face.

"We did not turn him to ashes yet," Killian said. "I'll take you to him when we are done."

She pressed her lips together and nodded.

"Why here, Livia?" I asked.

"We thought we could hide without hiding," she said. Something in the way she answered made me believe her.

"Did you think Ezra would let you go without consequences?"

"No, but I thought he would wait until after the impending battle."

So she knew a battle was coming. *That means Ezra does too.*

"He has great patience, but he will never turn down an opportunity to strike. Someone so close to him would know that," Killian said.

"Believe me. I did. My hope was the opportunity would be later," she said. "That I'd have some time to figure out a long-term plan."

"Or he would be ousted from power and the pressure removed," Killian said.

"Yes, that might have been my long-term plan." She looked sheepish, like she didn't think we would figure that out.

Killian put a hand on each of the armrests and leaned down, putting him at eye level with her. "What can you tell us about Ezra's plan now?"

She considered the question longer than made me comfortable. More than enough time passed to fabricate a story. It convinced me anything after that long a pause would be a lie.

She blew out a long, slow breath. A practiced human action used by spies to infiltrate. "We were gone for weeks before we got here. He hadn't made any permanent plans before I left, but he knew something was going to happen. The number of troops at the compound had increased. It made it hard, even for someone like me, to get in and out unnoticed. That's why we left."

"I noted that before we embarked on our mission, too," Killian said.

"There is some truth in what you are saying, but I'm not sure I believe you've told me anything useful nor everything you know." I turned to my friend. "Killian, take her to see Steven, and let her say her goodbyes to him. Return here afterward." I wouldn't deny her a last goodbye to her lover nor imprison her without proof. There would be eyes on her. She wouldn't make a move that we didn't know.

"Thank you," she said. "What will happen to me after that?"

"I haven't decided, but you're not to leave the compound without my permission."

"You're not going to confine her?" Killian stepped back from the chair.

"No, not right now. I don't have anything that would justify it. If what she said is true, she's no different from the rest of us." *Except she is. Letting her loose on the compound gave her the opportunity to choose our path or fuck up.*

"Your father is a real bastard, Josie. I don't know how you turned out so differently," Livia said.

"He gave you a comfortable life in an uncomfortable world," I said. "You certainly didn't turn down his offers down nor his affection." In my mind, she had no room to talk about anyone else.

"There wasn't a choice for me. He held my human family over me. The last relation died earlier this year." *Interesting in that Father had said she had no family. One of them lied.*

"His leverage was gone," I said. Ezra generated influence when none was to be found. He'd have manifested something to control.

"Until he found out about Steven."

"I never knew you were created. Who is your creator?"

"Not Ezra," she said.

Vin studied her. "You don't know."

"No, I was created and left to find my way just like you, Vincent." *No, Livia. You are not like Vin at all.*

I waited for Vin to meet my eyes and gave a small shake of the head. Livia could still be spying. The less information she had on him, the better.

"Or did you finally figure out the truth?" She sat back down on the chair. "The truth Ezra kept from you for a century. You're not one of us low class created vampires. Nope. You were born to two of the most gifted vampires ever to grace this earth."

She knew. Father not only knew, but he confided in her. And not me. No wonder he always wanted me to forgive Vin. My palm lifted. I wanted to slap her, but I shoved my hand into my pocket instead.

"Why are you telling us this?" I asked.

"I'm not telling you." Livia looked from me to Vin. "I'm telling him. Haven't you wondered why Ezra kept you so close?"

"Never trust a woman who is trapped," Natasha leaned against the desk. "If anyone should know, I'd be the expert."

"Calidora's puppet." Livia spat at Natasha's feet.

She's crazy if she thinks Natasha will let her get away with that.

"Then that would make you Ezra's stooge," Natasha snapped back. She took a giant step towards Livia.

I put myself between them. "Both of you stop."

Livia looked me up and down. "You, sadly, are Ezra's real child."

It was like she was trying to provoke us into hitting her, but that statement didn't get a rise out of me. She'd been roughed up on plenty of missions for my father. I'd seen the bruises when she returned.

Vin jerked Livia's chair to face him. "I know who my mother is. Who is my father?"

"Why don't you ask Calidora? Didn't you pay a visit to her?"

"Take her out of here. I'm tired of her games," Vin said.

"No games. I do know who your father is." She smirked.

"Then tell me, damn it." Vin's voice bounced off the walls.

"Where's the fun in that?" Livia laughed. Her posture changed from the slumped, scared person to the relaxed and cocky Livia I remembered. *I wanted to believe she wanted out, but she stayed deep in the usual games.*

"You're fucking playing us." Vin spun around and punched the wall.

That bitch. I wanted to console Vin, but my anger was not in check.

"You weren't seeing Steven," I said.

"No, he was my mission, but he was good in bed. I hated to kill him."

I took a step forward. Killian linked his arm through mine. I appreciated he gave me pause, but touching me was a bad idea at the moment.

I looked down at the contact and up at him. He'd sparred with me enough he must have recognized my stance.

He backed his arm out. "Don't do it, Josie." His voice barely a whisper.

I rounded on her and planted my foot against the chair. It flew out from under her, and she landed on her ass.

My hands fisted in her shirt. I lifted her off the ground and shoved her hard against the wall.

"Humph."

"I want nothing more than to kill you right now, and if you think I don't have any of my father in me, you are wrong."

"I like it rough. Didn't Ezra mention it?" She smiled.

I shifted her weight to one hand. My elbow connected with her temple. I let go.

She slid down the wall and slumped onto the floor.

"That should shut her up for a while." I turned my back to her. The sight of her made me ill.

"What the hell just happened in here?" Natasha held her hands at her temple and opened them outward. "Mind blown."

"She had us fooled. Why did she reverse course?" Vin said. "Nice hit, by the way." He smirked.

I wished I could say I regretted it, but I didn't. It felt good to take her cocky attitude down.

"Thanks. It's been a while. Why would she go through all that drama other than to make us look foolish?"

"She was successful," Killian said. "We fell for it."

"Um. I didn't,," Natasha said. "The bitch is a spy caught in the act. If she killed Steven, then she definitely is the one who is controlling the new vampires."

"We can't prove any of it, and I doubt she'd admit it in a larger setting. She has her other act down perfect. I can't pass judgement without proof. That would make me as ruthless as Ezra in the eyes of our supporters," I said.

"And she knows it," Vin said. "Do you think she was telling the truth about knowing who my father is."

"I don't know." I rubbed his arm. "Killian, we need to put her somewhere she can't have contact with anyone, and I do mean anyone other than the four of us," I said. "Do we have a place that can work for that?"

"The basement."

"I wasn't allowed down there when we lived here."

"It has several cells, including one built for solitary confinement," he said. "It's soundproof."

"That's the one then."

He nodded, and bent to scoop Livia's limp body up. "You'll know where to find her when you're ready to chat again." He glanced over his shoulder at Natasha. "Do you want to make sure no one sees us?"

"Sure," she said. "If she wakes up, can I knock her out again?"

Killian chuckled. "I suppose that would be justified."

"Then I'm the woman for the job." She pulled the door open. "After you." Her hand grabbed his ass as he passed by.

"Not doing that in front of us would be preferable," I said.

"Sorry. Not sorry." Natasha closed the door behind them.

My anger left the room with Livia. "Alone for a moment," I smiled at Vin.

"Think you could grab my ass like that sometime?" Vin sat on the edge of the desk.

I laid my arms over his shoulders. My wrists rested on his collarbone. "Didn't I grab it better than that last night?"

"Yes, much better." His head lowered.

Warm lips covered mine. Strong hands cupped my ass and lifted me up. My legs wound around his waist, and he back me up against the wall.

"I can grab asses too," he whispered in my ear.

"Better only be one ass," I said.

"One forever." His lips trailed a blaze down my throat.

His love settled me inside, and I was centered again.

CHAPTER 23

VIN - JOSIE

After checking that Livia was secure in the cell around first light, I found Josie in the office. She sat at her mother's old desk. Her long dark hair hung loose around her shoulders. I inhaled as I leaned down. *Rosewater.* My lips mashed against her temple.

The sun flooded the room with morning light. I sat on the edge of the desk and basked in it. My eyes closed. *Thousands of days I missed believing I was created, not born.* The warmth reminded me of how Josie's touch warmed me.

"Feels good, doesn't it?" Her chair squeaked.

I opened my eyes to find her face tilted to the sun. Her forehead wrinkled, but she gazed off in the distance. The light bathed her pale skin in a warm glow. Her dark hair picked up hints of gold. The sun faded compared to the beauty inside her. It radiated brighter than the beams streaming in the window.

The wrinkles on her forehead deepened. "You look more stressed than usual."

"That's my normal state." She turned back to the desk. "Any leads on our new vampires?"

"Yes, that's what I came to tell you. Killian thinks he located the general area of their camp. They are attempting to confirm now."

"Good. You could have led with that, you know."

"What are we going to do with them?" I asked.

Her fingers tightened around the pen she held. "I don't know. Not kill them, but we can't let them jeopardize our position or strategy either."

"Killian and I are going to lead a team to round them up this morning. They'll feel weak because of the sun, and I'm sure they've figured out they can't be in it more than a few moments."

"How are you going to get them back without turning them to ash?"

"We're using the tundra vehicle we brought from Calidora's stronghold."

A soft knock on the door made her jump. Her elbow landed on the desk, and she dropped her head into her palm.

"Easy." I squeezed her shoulder. "You are jumpy." I crossed the room and opened the door. "Right on time."

"Hi, Natasha." Josie smiled, albeit weakly, from behind the desk.

She gave a tentative wave. "Keep my man safe, Vin."

"He's the best there is." I smiled to reassure her.

"Yes, he is, so make sure he comes back."

I nodded to her and faced Josie. My hand covered my heart.

She smiled at me and placed her hand over her heart.

❆

"How does it feel to be my babysitter?"

Silence followed my question. I looked up from the ice age documentation. The failed attempts outnumbered the successes, and it drained me. I stitched together the equivalent of a thousand miniature puzzle pieces.

She was facing the door. "Natasha?"

Nothing. *Was she in a trance like Vin had been in the cabin?*

I slid my chair back. "Natasha?"

She turned. Her forehead creased tight.

"Are you okay?"

"Sorry. I've never worried about someone so much."

"He's been on many missions and most more challenging than this. Pull up a chair," I said. "Join the club."

The wingback chair scraped against the wood floor. She positioned it close to me. Her gaze focused on the papers. She scooted the chair a little closer. A shadow cast across the papers in her likeness.

"You are in love. That's the endless worry you feel for him."

"Wow. I've never been in love before. This is a whole new experience." Her words tumbled out fast and strung together. "Lots of lust, but never love. Could it really be love?"

"Yes, you are definitely in love."

"Is this how you knew Vin was the one?"

I twirled the pen in my fingers. The internal spastic thoughts sounded familiar. I smiled. "It's not easy. Relationships." I paused. "I knew the moment Vin spoke his first words to me I wanted him in my life. Worrying about his safety has been a constant ever since then. Even when I was so angry with him."

"Do you think they will have to kill today?"

I blinked rapidly. "I hope not, but it is a potentially dangerous situation."

She bit on her lip. "It changes you when you kill. That first kill changes everything."

I suspected she was talking more about herself than Killian now. "I have killed, Natasha. So has Vin, and Killian's nickname is Killer Killian for a reason." I hated the reminder, but it was true. To deny it would be denying a piece that shaped me.

"It gets easier after the first one. It's like your moral compass changes. That one act that pushes you over the line, and then each kill after that gets easier and easier." She pushed back in the chair and went to the window.

Ahh. Her kills. "My experience is a little different. I've never found taking a life or an existence to be easy. A piece of them, good or bad, goes with me every day."

"That's definitely not Ezra in you. It must be your mother." She smiled at me. "Since I've been here, it has bothered me more. It's like the guilt is coming back to remind me of each life I took. I've killed way more humans than vampires. Vampires were out of desperation or preservation, but humans." She swallowed. "Humans I killed for sport. Pure unadulterated pleasure of sport. I was such an awful fucking being."

If I'd only known the Natasha from Calidora's underground lair, I would have agreed, but that wasn't who Natasha really was.

"No, you survived," I said. "You are a survivor, and now you have a chance to evolve into something more. Look at the bond you have built with the children. They love their Natasha."

"And I love them. They make me happy." She'd been there every day to visit them. One little girl, Trina, even followed her around when she visited. Natasha gave her a doll she found, and it hadn't left her sight. Her mood lightened, and her posture eased.

"It shows. Have you and Killian talked about a future?"

"No, it's too early. It's not like we are going to grow old. We have centuries to decide. What about you and Vin?"

"No, we barely get any alone time, and we probably won't until after we oust Ezra." I understood the human need to sigh more. It offered a temporary relief to frustration.

"You would have some beautiful babies," she said.

"So would you and Killian, but we have to get our planet back first. Then we can see if there is a way to correct the infertility."

"Yes, we do. So, how is that going?"

"There are some big assumptions in their plan, and we don't have a way to test it. I'm hoping the lab at the Southern Compound will have enough resources to run a small test."

"What about the missing piece of the formula you mentioned the other day?"

"I'm pretty close to it. I need a bigger brain than mine on it to confirm," I said.

"I can't imagine a scientist who understands it better than you." Her voice softer than normal.

Was that how she used her gift? "That's flattery, Natasha. What do you want?"

She cleared her throat. "Sorry. I'm used to... well, you know. I want to talk to Livia."

I slid my chair back from the desk. The request left me skeptical. "Why do you want to speak with her?"

"No one else has my skills, and I can't do it with Killian here," she said.

Her gift would get answers. "There is no way I would ask you to do that. I'm not Calidora, and you don't have to do that ever again."

"It's my choice. My opportunity to help."

Livia knew planned to battle. She had valuable information locked away in her head. It could give us an advantage. "If you're determined to do it, I'll go with you. She too dangerous for any of us to be alone with her," I said. "Before we go though, are you sure you want to do this, Natasha?"

"Yes, I've known since we locked her up. You and I both know that the information she has in her head could tip the scales for us."

"I agree with the latter. Sending my friend in to extract the information from one of Ezra's most lethal assassins is not a risk I want to take," I said.

"But I'm going to do it, because we are out of time. We all know need answers now."

"If we're going in, we need to do it now. When Killian and Vin bring back the new vampires, they are going to put them in the cells in the basement. We need to be out before they get back."

"She mentioned she is created. Is that true?"

"As far as I know, it is. Does that change anything?"

"They are easier for me to control," Natasha said, her voice fixed. "I'm ready."

I placed a bag of Jimsonweed in my pocket and attached the sunshine stick from my desk to my belt.

Natasha navigated the basement with ease from her trip with Killian and Livia. It was darker than any place on the premises, but the resemblance to the one at the Southern Compound glared at me. *Ezra's design.* The one in the Southern Compound more modern, but death clung to every

IN BLOOD & ICE

crevasse of the stone walls. It reminded me of the tales of dungeons. The thought of what Ezra had done here turned my stomach.

"What is that?" Natasha pointed to the weapon on my hip.

"Sunlight taser the scientists created before we left this place," I said. "Or as I like to call it, sunlight in a stick. Otherwise known as the predecessor to the sunshine sticks we have now."

"And it still works?"

"I fixed it. Works like a sunshine stick now."

"Does it kill the vampire?"

"It was designed to go from inflicting pain to death," I said. "When the Rogues grew in number, the scientist adjusted the version we have now to straight kill."

"You're not going to kill her, though."

"That's not the plan, but if it comes down to her or us, I will have no hesitation." I paused. "She's a mercenary, not an emissary, Natasha, but I will start with pain first if it even comes to that."

The basement didn't have the usual dampness associated with the underground rooms. The air circulated, kept it dry. There were fluorescent lights hung at wide intervals. *Not for vampires.* We didn't need them. The environment almost sterile with the painted white walls. It had a mad scientist vibe that screamed of Ezra.

Interrogation rooms were at the front, but the cells for the prisoners Ezra didn't want anyone to hear were further back. We walked past empty cells to the soundproof one on the end. I fumbled for the key in my pocket. I had little fear facing Livia, but worry for Natasha grew. *She volunteered. You wouldn't want to be denied the opportunity if you had volunteered.*

"No guards?" Natasha asked.

"We are keeping her presence a complete secret."

"Was she fed?"

"No, I wanted to keep her weak, but that means she is going to be desperate with hunger after the emotional display upstairs," I said. "I brought a tiny amount of jimsonweed if we need it."

"Not before I do my thing. We can't trust what anyone says on that stuff." Her experience far worse than most, but she had a point. Livia likely had a practiced tolerance for it as a spy. Some of Father's spies were poison experts even.

The key slid into the lock. Tumblers clicked into place. The door opened wide.

A hiss greeted us from inside. "What do you want?" Livia crouched in the corner. Her hair disheveled and skin pale even for a vampire. She'd been scratching her arms from the hunger. Created vampires needed more blood than born vampires and at more frequent intervals.

"I just have a few questions." Natasha stepped through the door.

I stayed close behind her.

"Give me blood, and I'll give you answers."

My body tensed. I was ready to knock her out again if needed. Natasha came close to Livia. *Too close.*

"That will not be necessary." Natasha knelt. Her hand laid against Livia's cheek. "You want to give us answers."

Livia blinked a half dozen times. "I do." Her eyes glazed over and became unfocused. She was under Natasha's control.

"Good," Natasha said. "Let's start with where you came from."

"The Western International Nation," Livia answered in a robotic like voice.

"When did you come to this area?"

"A few weeks ago."

"What was your mission?" Natasha continued to stroke Livia's cheek. Livia's look similar to Captain Scott's when Natasha made him march to his death.

"Classified," Livia said.

"Why did you come here?" Natasha rephrased.

"Classified."

Natasha's other hand went to Livia's face. Her thumbs brushed the temples as she turned our enemy's face towards hers. She pressed her lips to Livia's and leaned in so she could whisper in her ear. The words intimate to them and inaudible at this short a distance. Natasha had been here before and knew what it took to coax answers from an assassin.

"We were sent to retrieve humans and prevent the previous mission from returning."

"Previous mission? Us?" I swallowed hard. Venom hung. My hand went to my throat. Father sent her to make sure we didn't return. *Was she the one who took out our tundras? Killed my crew?*

Natasha looked at me. Her hand came to her mouth and one finger over her lips. She turned her attention back to Livia.

"No survivors from the previous mission?"

"None," Livia said. "Except the future Empress. We were to keep her alive."

Father thought everyone else was expendable except me. I grabbed my stomach. *Why even send us?*

"Why were they to be killed?" Natasha asked.

"The children."

Natasha and I gasped at the same time.

"What children?"

"I have to protect my baby." Livia's eyes began to clear.

Her baby? She's created. Even if born could still procreate, she wouldn't have children. What baby is she talking about? Vampires raised stolen human children from time to time. Father didn't approve of the practice, mainly because he believed them inferior, but he hadn't stopped it either.

Natasha stepped back and shook her head. Her pheromone spell was done for now. It wasn't enough. I'd wanted more information.

"We can try again later," she said. "But it doesn't work immediately after they come out of it."

"Did you come to bring me something to eat or just stare at me?" Livia said.

Natasha reached into her jacket and tossed a blood bag to her. "Are you pregnant?"

Livia ripped open the blood bag. She didn't say a word. Livia's training would tell her to manipulate the situation, and I'd seen enough of that for one day.

"Let's go," I said.

"Don't you want to talk? I have so much to say."

"If that were true, you could have spoken the other day," Natasha said.

"Not in front of the men."

"Whatever." Natasha walked out the door.

I crouched down to Livia's level. "Why not in front of the men?" I knew it was a manipulation, but my curiosity led me to ask.

She sucked the bag dry and tossed it aside. "It's not their purpose that's important."

"You're babbling." I backed out of the room. My eyes glued to her every move.

"Don't you want to know how I'm pregnant?"

The door slammed shut. I slid the bolt into place and locked it. A created cannot reproduce, other than creating another vampire. Pregnancy. Birth. They weren't possible for them. The transformation from human to vampire caused sterilization.

"Do you believe what she said?"

"Wait until we get back to the office," Natasha said.

I hurried up the stairs with Natasha and down the hall to the next set of stairs. The closer to the office we got, the faster we walked.

Natasha slammed the door. She leaned back against it and giggled. "We must have looked like idiots to anyone that saw us."

"No doubt." I wiped the smile from my face. "Now, do you believe her?"

"I do, but her answers seemed a bit jumbled. Like someone had messed with her mind."

"What did you whisper to her?"

"I told her blood and pleasure awaited her if she would only give me the answers I wanted."

I gagged. "Yuck."

"It's surprising how that always works, though," she said. "What about the children comment? Are they coming after the human children? I will rip them apart." She clutched her stomach.

"Unlikely, Ezra would care about human children other than as pawns. There haven't been any born vampires in decades, but it's not like it has hurt our population."

"Vampires have continued to create vampires though."

"But created vampires can't have children," I said. "Only born could."

"Then it has to be the human children," she said. Her

fingers wrapped around the top of the chair. Knuckles whiter than usual. "I'm going to be sick."

"I know it's disgusting to think," I said.

"No, I'm really going to be sick."

I helped her to the bathroom and held her hair back.

Her hands on either side of the toilet seat, she wretched repeatedly until the bowl was full of blood.

"I think I'm done," she said.

I wet a washcloth and wiped the blood from her face. She shouldn't have any traces of poison left in her body, but her reaction was strong. "This must be some residual effects of the poison in combination with the strain you put on your body today. I think we need to get you to your bedroom for rest."

"Yes, I feel weak," Natasha said.

"Can you lean on me to walk?"

"I think so."

I guided her with slow and steady steps down the hallway to her room. Inside, I helped her out of her jacket and shoes. She slid into the bed.

"Do you think she's really pregnant? We can't leave her in the cell if she is." Natasha asked, her voice a tiny whisper.

"She's a master at games. You never know when she's telling the truth or not. We'll find out and move her somewhere more comfortable, but still secure if she is." I covered her up and tucked the covers around her like my mother used to do for me. "I'm going to get some blood for you."

I kept my face neutral, but my worry for her turned my stomach.

"When Killian gets back, can you send him to me?"

"You'll likely be his first stop." I forced a smile to hide my worry. "Close your eyes and rest. Thank you for what you did today."

"Use it for good. Let's make a better world."

"We will." I squeezed her hand and left her to rest.

By the time I returned with the blood bags and herbs, Natasha rested in a healing sleep. I touched her arm. Good lived in her. The more I learned of her true nature, the more I realized I liked her.

My steps back to the office as slow as the ones to Natasha's room even though I no longer had her physical weight on me. I slumped into my chair. The sun started to set and the windows on the other side of the room cast shades of pink the color of vampire tears. My head back and eyes closed, the conversation replayed in my head. *What had Livia really told us?*

The door creaked open. I raised up at the noise.

Vin and Killian strolled in, dirty and disheveled. My heart pounded. Vin's arms opened up.

I ran to him and threw myself against him, ready for his touch to wash the stress away. "You two look like hell." My arm stretched out to Killian's. "Go see Natasha. She's in her room."

His face dropped. "What happened?"

"She's weak. Maybe from the poison still. I told her you would be her first stop. Don't make a liar out of me," I said.

He tore out of the room in a blur.

I reached around Vin to push the door shut.

"You really look awful. What happened?" I brushed dirt from his cheek to reveal dried blood. "Is this blood yours?"

He kissed my temple and pulled me tight against him. "No, they gave chase. One was in the sun too long," he said.

I shivered at the image of a young, frightened vampire on fire. "That's terrible."

He angled back. "It freaked the others out so bad. They

273

gave up then. I think they thought we made him spontaneously combust." He shook his head.

"So, the rest are here? Where did you put them?"

"Yes, in the cells below."

"I want to see them." If they divulged Livia was their creator, that would be some evidence. Information was easier to extract from newly created ones.

"There's something you should know first," he said. "They are marked with the same military symbol we saw on the Rogues when we first arrived in Dallas."

"The ones on the outskirts of the territory that Killian ended?"

"Yes, exactly like it."

"But they were Rogues," I said. "But these new ones aren't?"

"These were headed that way. They were starving. Livia must have been keeping them supplied in blood."

"Did they say anything?"

Vin shook his head. "No, they were all pretty freaked out. They haven't been vampire very long."

I grabbed onto the chair and slid sideways into it. "But she recruited them at the leisure of my father's hand. What the hell is he up to?"

"He's building an army, but what kind of army is the question."

Ezra's value on the created ranked almost less than the humans. "An expendable one. Although I would bet they don't know that."

"Safe bet."

"I need to talk to them. Are they all together?"

"Yes, do you want them separated in interrogation rooms?"

"No, I think they will give more information together."

Ezra created an army right under our noses. His maneuvers continued to be a step ahead of us. Livia told us the truth. *Why kill the entire mission except for me? Why have Killian and Vin killed?* I knew how to get the information we needed, but if I stooped to Ezra's methods to get it, our vision of a better world died.

CHAPTER 24

I n the basement with the new vampires, Josie thought the way to a created vampire included the blood bags on the tray in the guard's hands. I glared at her. I didn't want her close to them, and they didn't need a strength boost.

"I'm not opening the cell," I said. I refused to risk them getting their hands on her. Ezra's evil lab started here. The stench of it drowned everything else out. Memories of his assigned tasks filled my mind. I didn't take a life here, but I came close. His decision to send me to the computer group perceived as a punishment rather than the promotion, he told everyone.

"Vin, they will not talk through bars."

"The sun is setting, and they will feel stronger whether or not they've had blood." For a hundred years, I thought the surge of the sunset strengthened me. *More of Ezra's lies.*

The guard Josie sent for blood stood beside us. His eyes averted.

Josie took the tray from him. "Fine, but I'm giving them the blood before I ask them questions. They are starving."

"As you wish," I said. "As long as it's through the bars."

Her stubbornness attractive. Her decisiveness even more so. If only she would let me protect her like I wanted to. She could protect herself, though. She'd proved it time and time again. Another quality I loved about her.

"Vin?"

"Sorry. What did you say?" *Shit.* I focused on her with refreshed determination.

"The guards stay out here."

"They are trusted." Killian and I had posted four guards at the door.

"Not by the new vampires. It will be hard enough with the two of us in there, much less a bunch of guards."

She placed a hand on my arm. My body warmed to the touch. Against my better judgement, I compromised. "Then I will place a chair a certain distance from the bars, and you will not get any closer than that."

"I can live with that."

I put my palm up to the guards and opened the door for her. "Hold for my signal."

The odor putrid as we entered. I held my breath.

Josie coughed and gagged. "Have they not been bathing?"

"They were living among dead animal carcasses." The odor stunk worse since we picked them up.

"They drank animal blood? They were already getting desperate. Nothing tastes worst on the pallet than gamey animal blood."

"It's not that bad, Josie." Many of the vampires resulted to animal blood after the ice age hit. As animal populations dwindled, more pockets of Rogues popped up. I'd drank it in an effort to consume less human blood and even diluted human blood with it to make it last longer. The latter a common practice with the rations Ezra supplied to the created on his compound.

"Sleeping with a pile of remains is."

"Is that blood?" One of the new vampires came to front of the cell and pressed himself against the bars. He wore blood-stained clothes, and his eyes were dark with hunger. All of them looked to be young adult humans when they were created.

"Yes, I have some for each of you," Josie said. She took a step forward.

"Wait." I held out my hand. "Chair." I took the chair from the corner and placed it a couple of inches further than my arm's length.

She sat in the chair and leaned forward with the first bag of blood.

The vampires pushed forward in mass.

"I have one for each of you, so no need to push. You will all get your own."

They responded and formed two lines. The line on the right was one person shorter than the left. The vampire that exploded this afternoon was missing. This wasn't the first time they lined up like this. Livia had trained them to follow orders and used food as the reward.

"Does everyone have some?" Josie asked.

"When you are finished, place the empty bags here on the outside of the cell." I pointed to the corner away from Josie.

She nodded at me.

One by one, they piled them up in a neat stack as directed. My theory proven.

"I'd like to ask you some questions," Josie said.

They all directed their attention to her like a herd of hungry cows.

"Do you remember being human?"

The horde exchanged looks, and one dark-haired guy stepped towards the front. "We woke up as vampires and were told our life before didn't matter. We don't have knowledge of what happened before that day."

Josie cut her eyes toward me. It sounded familiar. A tale personal to me. One we heard in repetition.

She pushed forward with another simple question. "Did you all wake up at one time or on different days?"

"We all had our awakening on the same day," he said.

So they killed humans, but the choice of word used the wrong way. Created vampires often killed right away where born vampires did once they reached adulthood. Livia taught them something wrong. *Why?*

Josie cleared her throat.

"And who created you?"

He cocked his head to the side.

"Who awakened you?" The terminology was wrong, but he understood.

His eyes darted around the room. "Mistress Livia was our awakener."

"Did Mistress Livia give you a name?"

"I'm Alex," he said.

"Alex, why were you living in the woods?"

"We were told to remain in the woods until other directions arrived." No interaction with other vampires except her. The isolation would drive them mad without someone to guide them.

"What have you done since your awakening?"

"Whatever Mistress Livia instructs us to do."

"Can you give me an example of something she instructed you to do?" Josie asked.

"We extracted some plants from the garden for her."

Josie nodded. "Did you interact with any other vampires? Other than Livia or your group?"

"Yes, we have interacted with many others."

"Did you have to end any vampires?" I asked.

"As part of our training, we were asked to end vampires who had broken laws." They were mindless assassins and had no idea. *How many had they ended?*

"Who's laws?" I asked.

"Our Emperor's laws, of course."

"And have you met the emperor?" Josie asked.

"No, he is much too busy. He sends his missions to us through Mistress Livia."

"Thank you," Josie said. "I'll make sure you are fed regularly." She pushed out of her chair and rushed out the door.

I caught up with her on the other side of the door. "Close it." I gestured to the guard.

We headed up the stairs. The door closed behind us. "Slow down, Josie."

"It's not like we need to. We don't get tired." Her body as stiff as her answers.

When we reached the top of the stairs, I guided her into the tiny butler's office. "What set you off in those questions?"

"They pretty much confirmed what Livia told Natasha and I earlier."

I crossed my arms in front of my chest and narrowed my eyes at her. "You went to see Livia while me and Killian were gone?"

"Oh." Her eyes got wide. "Yes, Natasha put her voodoo goddess stuff on Livia."

"And here I was worried about you with a handful of new vampires this evening when you spent the day with an assassin." I threw my hands up. "What in the hell were you thinking?"

"Natasha was determined to do it, and I wasn't going to let her go alone."

"She should have known better, too. It has her laid up in the bed."

"Can't you understand she needs to feel useful? It was her choice."

"A foolish choice that put you both at risk."

"A choice that got us information the vampires in the basement corroborated," she said.

"So what did they confirm that sent you flying out of the room?"

"Before Natasha's gift wore off, Livia started to tell us about some plan with children. Something Ezra is working on with the scientists. Since born vampires haven't been able to have children in a while and created can't, we figured that meant he was after the human children."

"The vampires in there are young, but they are adults," I said.

"There was something else she said. Her mission was to make sure ours failed. No one was supposed to survive but me. Somehow that ties into the children."

"Ezra almost got his wish there," I said. The explosions from the tundra played through my mind. Terror rattled through my body. I thought I might lose Josie that day.

"Why would he want to kill you and Killian and leave me alive?"

"To break you, Josie. He needs you, but you have a strong will and friends who will die for you." *Could that be why Calidora intervened? She learned of Ezra's plan?*

"Like my mother. He was never successful at breaking her spirit, so he killed her." She wrapped her arms around herself.

I lifted her chin. "We will not let him. We will succeed."

"I don't understand him."

"Come here." I pulled her to me. "I know you want to find answers, but it might just be the way he is."

"You mean just accept that he's a bastard?"

I snickered. "Something like that."

"We need to move forward, and we need to do it quickly. Ezra's plan has to be bad, and the longer we wait, the more of an advantage I feel like we are giving him."

"When Killian meets up with us, we'll decide on a date," I said.

"I want to show you something I've been working on in the big office."

"Your office. It's okay to call it that, Josie." She considered it her mother's office. I guess a part of her needed to think of it that way to keep the memory alive.

"It doesn't feel natural."

"But it will. Get used to it." I took her hand and led her down to the other office.

She opened the drawer and pulled out some papers. She unrolled them across the desk and placed paperweights in the corners. "I think I'm on the verge of breaking this, but I'm going to need some very specific equipment at the Southern Compound to do it. I could use some of the scientists, but I'm not sure there are any we can trust."

I studied her work. It looked sound, and she understood this science better than I did. "That's why you're so eager to get there."

"And I want to stop whatever plan Ezra has in motion."

I nodded. *Redemption.* It was important to her. Dark circles stood out under her eyes. She'd spread herself thin across Livia, the rebellion, Natasha... me.

"Why don't we go check in on Natasha and then go to the garden for a while? I think you need to recharge after all the stress from today."

"I don't know if we have time to take a break." She rolled up the papers.

"If you don't recharge, you are no good to any of us," I said.

She wrapped her arms around my waist. "I would like to see how Natasha is doing," she paused. "If Killian doesn't kill me for agreeing to her plan."

"I'm sure he understands her determination." I put my arm around her shoulders for the short walk to Natasha's room.

We stopped at the door, and I rapped on it with my knuckles.

"Come in," Natasha said. She sounded normal to me.

We entered her room hand in hand.

She sat in the sitting area looking refreshed. There was even a rosy cast to her cheeks.

"You look so much better," Josie said, her voice full of relief.

Natasha patted the spot beside her on the loveseat. Josie plopped down next to her.

Killian laid, stretched out on the couch. He sat up. "I can smell the new vampires on you two."

"We paid a visit to them." I sat down on the other end of the couch.

"Anything come out of it?"

"Yes, and no. They don't know much, but they were able to validate what Livia told Josie and Natasha earlier."

Killian glanced at the loveseat. "Natasha filled me in on that. Ezra's up to something."

I nodded. "Josie wants to move forward as soon as possible."

"Strategically speaking, that makes the most sense."

"When would you suggest we go, Killian?" Josie asked.

"I'd like a week to organize, but I suspect you want to go sooner."

"Can we be ready in three days?" Her voice frank.

I expected her to say tomorrow, so three days showed patience and restraint. *A leader.* Ezra underestimated her, and for our sakes, I hoped he continued to do so.

"Depending on your definition of ready."

"Ready enough to take on his forces."

"We have the numbers."

"But not the skill?" Natasha asked.

"No, we have the skill. Typically, we would have trained together on our plan. It builds loyalty and comradery among them. Not to mention the ability to fight as one unit versus two thousand individuals."

"These groups have all trained together themselves. Right?" Josie said.

"Yes, and that definitely is an advantage," I said.

"I'll pull their leaders together tonight and discuss the plan. Maybe we work as small pockets for the larger whole. They'll need to see the map in your office, Josie." Killian looked at her.

"No problem. I will put the research up in my desk when we leave here."

"Do you need us there for the meeting? I was going to walk Josie through the garden so she could decompress a little."

"Can you make an appearance at the end? The more they see Josie, the more motivated they are."

"We can do the garden afterwards. My voice should be part of this," Josie said. The dark circles more prominent.

I nodded. She needed food or rest. Maybe both. She pushed herself, but that wasn't new to her.

"Anyone hungry before they go to the big meeting? Killian brought enough blood up here for half the army." Natasha waved her hand towards the tray on the side table. "There's wine too. I couldn't stomach that, but it is sounding better now."

"I'll take a glass full without the wine." Josie stood to pour. "Anyone else need to power up?" She looked at us all. "Natasha appears to be the only one who has eaten today." She filled up the glasses and passed them out to each of us. "Sure you don't want some more, Natasha?"

"No, I ate enough for several people earlier." She smiled. "I did not know poison would linger like this."

"I hope that is the end of it for you," Josie said. She tilted her glass up and drank deep.

I licked my lips at the sight. Hunger twisted in my gut, but the sight of her went lower. Strong, confident, beautiful. I tipped my glass and chugged it down. The metallic slickness coated my tongue and down my throat. A charge ignited through my body and rejuvenated the cells.

"Want to help me clean up my office for the meeting?" Josie held out her hand to me and winked.

I took her extended hand and let her pull me to my feet.

CHAPTER 25

JOSIE

I spoke from the heart to the leaders, both vampires and humans. Both skeptical of the other, but we achieved a common ground. We all sought defeat of my father. To my surprise, the humans offered to fight with us when we only planned for vampires. Once again, my faith grew and hope expanded for a new path.

"That went better than I expected," Vin said.

"They've been preparing for civil war for a while," I said. "Humans and vampires."

"It's been our practice to be ready for war at all times," Killian said. "I'm not surprised they are prepared. I would prefer we tell them about Livia and the new vampires." He turned his stern expression to me.

I deserved it. Secrets threatened us, but also kept us alive. Too much information led to misinformation as it passed along. No story ever stays the same after it is passed around from hundreds of mouths. "What would change with them knowing?"

"It makes them more informed of what they are walking into with Ezra."

The more knowledge provided put the leaders in a better position. I mulled it over for a moment. "I hear what you're saying. We will tell the leaders together in the morning but under confidentiality. If we lose any of them, will we still have the numbers?"

"We really need them all," Vin said.

"If we lose more than a thousand, we will not have enough to split forces adequately."

"That's an enormous risk, Killian. You think it's worth it?" Vin asked.

"I think they deserve to know the truth."

I considered it. *Maybe my fear of sharing the secrets came from the ways learned by my father. Habits can be hard to break. Ezra's lies got us here, but that didn't mean we had to keep reliving them.*

"We'll take the risk," I said. "I would rather build our new world on a foundation of honesty than secrets, even when I think we are better for keeping them. We've seen what that world looks like. Time for something new."

"If you'll excuse us, we have a date in the garden." Vin held his hand out. *This was love.* He knew what made me safe and gave me strength.

My fingers entwined with his, and warmth wrapped around me. The way it enveloped me surprised my senses each time.

The guard smiled and opened the door for us. I smiled in return. Our training included a side of humanity with it. We were not building the discardable army Ezra enforced.

"As long as we're not finding dead bodies in here, your forehead isn't wrinkled," Vin said.

I laughed. "Is it wrinkled everywhere else?"

"Most of the time," he said. "Except when I have you."

"You mean when I have you." I poked him in the ribs.

"Both," he said. His hand on my waist, he pulled me to him and crushed my lips under his.

"I like both," I said. "Why was it so important to come to the garden tonight?"

"I figured it would be our last chance to be alone before we left."

"You're right. Things are going to change in a few days." I lowered myself on the stone perimeter of the rose flowerbed. The soft scent drifted up. *Heaven.*

Vin sat beside me. "I was thinking about the children Livia brought up. Could Ezra have been researching a way for born vampires to conceive again?"

"That doesn't really seem like something he'd pursue. He doesn't really like children, or young vampires, for that matter. He wanted there to be fewer born vampires, after all. Why do you ask?"

"I swear I keep hearing a faint quick heartbeat like a baby's."

I giggled. "It's probably a human baby on the compound."

"No, it doesn't sound human. I don't hear it in the garden, which is interesting, but other parts of the compound, it's louder than others."

"If a vampire actually conceived, you wouldn't hear a heartbeat through the placenta. It's like a barrier. It would have to be one of the humans." *Could Livia actually be pregnant? No, a created can't conceive.*

"Have you heard of any?"

"No, not recently. Before the pregnancies stopped all together there were a lot of miscarriages though, but I never heard a heartbeat, at least not early in the pregnancy, unless it came from a human." I said. "Did you bring me down here to talk about pregnancy?" A nervous laugh escaped. If he wanted babies, that was literally the one thing I couldn't give him. No female vampire could.

"Not exactly," he said. "It was just on my mind, because I heard the sound before we came down here." He fidgeted on the stone seat. "What I wanted to ask you..." He cleared his throat. "What I wanted to ask you is if you wanted to officially move in together. We already spend our time together, but we still have our own suites. Would you want to share the same suite? Assuming we survive the battle of course."

I smiled. He didn't get nervous, and it was sweet. "Aren't we already pretty much living together?"

He deflated. His shoulders dropped. He wanted our stuff, not that we had brought much with us, co-mingled.

I loved you, Vincent Cavanaugh. For all of you, and one day I would tell you how much. I squeezed his knee and locked eyes with him. "I love the idea of officially moving in together." I paused. "My room is bigger though, so I hope you will want to move into it." I giggled like a schoolgirl.

"I'd move into a closet if it meant sharing space with you." He tugged me into his lap. "I love you, Josephine." He pressed his forehead to mine.

"I love you," I said. "But call me Josie." I could melt the ice and snow outside when my name rolled off his tongue. The only name I ever wanted to hear him call me was Josie. I pressed my lips to his.

He devoured my mouth. "Josie," he whispered against my cheek.

My eyes opened and landed on the lavender trumpet-shaped flower. "I need to pick some more of the jimsonweed to prepare the spray. The team preparing it is caught up with what I brought them already, so we are on schedule."

He kissed my forehead. "All right. Then I'm taking you back to our room and having you."

The words tickled me inside from my heart to my toes. "Not if I have you first." I laughed and moved over to the planter with the jimsonweed. A lot was used. I put on a pair of gloves. "Can you bring those containers over? I need to extract the seeds to replant."

He sat them down on the workbench, and I noticed a mark on a piece of paper stuck to one. "Look. It's that military mark tattooed on the new vampires." I looked around, but there wasn't anything else. *How did we miss this?*

Vin shrugged. "It looks like a pattern. They probably dropped it when they killed Steven Smith."

"Probably so." I stared at it. Maybe the new vampires lost it. Maybe Steven had it. Maybe.

CHAPTER 26

JOSIE

The leaders reviewed the plan one last time, and we exited the war room to find everything readied. Equipment had been doled out. We found only a hundred or so metal chest plates to cover the heart. They were in storage and were handed out to those on the front line. I tried to refuse mine, but Vin insisted I take one. I only agreed if he would take one as well.

With the teams assigned, we traveled to the south on foot at vampire speed. The few humans who journeyed with us came in the old repaired equipment. The betterment of the once decrepit equipment impressed me. Humans and vampires worked together. Our caravan included some new tundras we found stored at a nearby hangar. The structure was built well after we vacated during the onset of the ice age, and I suspected Calidora planted the vehicles on the Northern Compound to aid in our ousting of my father. We needed the vehicles, so I wasn't in a position to not use them. Created vampires traveled in those newer vehicles because they blocked the sun out better than the older equipment.

We arrived just before sunset in the Southern Territory. It felt like foreign land to me. Once a resort area on the coast, the beach now spent half the year with a dusting of snow. The sand faded behind us as we took our positions near the Southern Compound.

The machines, prepared by our allies here, stood in position, ready to administer the deadly mist. Vampires would die. I'd made the decision to use the condensed mist and pushed it to the back of my mind, but it faced me now. It would go with me from this day forth. *Mass Murderer. My new title. I'd only give the order if they didn't concede. They would have a choice.*

The vampires came into view. *Rogues.* He put Rogue vampires on the front line. As disgusted as I was to see them, it made the decision to use the gas easier. I hadn't tested the solution on them, and they had never reacted to anything like a normal vampire. For the first time, I considered we might actually lose this battle. Fear spiked, and adrenaline scented the air, not just from me. *It has to work. It has too.* A humanlike breath escaped from me. I found little relief but it would almost be a mercy for the Rogues.

My body started shaking. Vin slipped his hand in mine. The touch steadied and calmed me. My eyes closed, and I prayed. *Gods be with us today. Let us be successful.* If my soul was gone, then it didn't hurt, but if it was there, it sure might help.

"We haven't tested it on their kind."

"They're still vampires. It will work," he said.

The Rogues moved in strange back-and-forth motions. Grunts and growls similar to a dog came from the horde. So many of them stood there before us.

I stood on top of the vehicle with Vin beside me. "Your people are ready. Give the order when you feel the timing is right." The others confirmed by radio, they followed suit into the planned positions.

The timing would never be right. Not now. Not in ten years. Not in a hundred years. Natasha was right about the guilt of the kills. Even staring at the Rogues, I didn't want to be the one responsible for giving the order to kill them. It seemed too easy to command my people to kill them even though it was more of a mercy than a sin.

Alone, I looked out in front of me at what many of our kind thought was the worst version of us. They were wrong. The worst of us were behind them. He hid behind an army of beasts he created. *He is my father, and his reign ends today.*

Vin dropped into the vehicle. "We're here, Josie. It's your decision on how we proceed, but waiting will not make the decision lighter." He looked up at me.

"No, it won't. It's going to be heavy on me for the rest of my existence. Every death will go forward with me."

"That's not what I meant."

"It's time." I raised my hand in the air. My heart beat fast in my chest. Useless as it was, it made me feel alive. *In a moment, there would be no option to turn back.* Not that there had been once I made the decision and the journey started.

I dropped my hand to my side and remained still for a moment. I slid inside the tundra vehicle. Everyone that could fit in a vehicle for our first wave was sealed in. The rest of our group remained at a safe distance away.

Vin closed the hatch and secured the seal. "Natasha, turn the support system on."

"We don't need the oxygen," she said.

"No, but we want to make sure that if any poison leaks in, it is filtered out."

Natasha flipped the series of switches, and the filtration system kicked into full blast.

I reached for the radio handset. The heaviness of the verdict I handed down today weighed thousands of pounds on my shoulders.

"Thank you all for your belief in this cause. If you have not already done so, secure your preventative measures."

"We don't have to release the gas," Vin said. He wanted to relieve the burden, and I loved him more for it. My decision firm.

"Killian, what is our best option tactically?" I kept my gaze on Vin. Sympathy filled his face, but I wasn't sure if it was for me or the lives we would end.

"Discharge the mist," he said.

I placed a hand on his shoulder. "We're releasing it. Our entire plan revolves around this initial surprise. It's our only chance to throw Ezra off kilter."

"It's still your decision," he said.

I looked away and depressed the lever on the handset. "Deploy the mist on my mark," I paused. "Three... Two... One... Deploy."

The trajectory was correct. The dark cloud formed over the Rogue vampires and moved toward the compound.

Everything in me urged to look away, but I owed it to them to watch them die. Ezra may have commanded them to fight, but I sentenced them to death. I watched the poison creep into their orifices. The Rogues' heightened sense of smell their downfall. They inhaled the poison, and I could see it drift up their nostrils.

They writhed. Bodies convulsed. Blood flooded the ground around them. Screams and grunts filled the air. They'd only turn to ash if someone staked them. No one braved the mist to do so afraid they would suffer the same fate. The scent of rot in the air couldn't be filtered out.

Tears fell from my eyes. I did nothing to stop them, just like I did nothing to help the Rogues. The night would be long. My heart would be heavier in the end.

"How long before the cloud dissipates?" Natasha said.

"About thirty minutes." I forced myself to watch the movement in front of us cease.

"So we just sit here and let it kill everyone," she said, a statement not a question.

"Not everyone," Vin said. "But that is the plan."

"It's not going to be easy just because we are doing this. These thirty minutes are precious minutes Ezra is no doubt using to fortify and block us," I said. "It does, however, preserve our numbers with no losses against his frontline."

"He will not let us just walk in there, even after the poison cloud," Killian said.

"No, he's not. It's going to get dangerous, and it will happen fast," I said. "I need you all to be ready. You three are the most important to me in this. The only family I've known for the last hundred years is a monster. You are my family now, and I could never do this without you. Stay ready. Stay close. Don't take unnecessary risks."

"Josie, realize we are here to die for you, if that is what is required," Killian said.

"It's not only the allegiance we swore to you, but it is our choice. A choice we willingly make for our Empress," Vin said.

"I'm your friend, not your Empress. I will never presume to rule the three of you. We wouldn't be here ready to make a difference in the world without the honesty and support you give."

"Death will not be my choice today," Natasha said.

"It will not be the choice for any of you," I said.

"The mist is clearing," Killian said. "Ezra's guards will not come out to meet us. This will be hand-to-hand combat in close quarters. A way for his guards to control the movement."

"We're cutting a path straight to the control room," I said.

"Do you think he'll be there? I mean, doesn't he have some kind of panic room?" Natasha asked.

"I never saw a panic room, but I don't think he expected anyone to rise up against him, even with his spies and treachery," I said.

"Do you think he knows Livia is pregnant?"

"No, I think he would have sent someone after her if he had known. She's the first created vampire to conceive a child. Obviously, he has been working to make that happen, and she is an experiment to him."

"I hope we made the right decision leaving her there," Natasha said.

"We couldn't bring a pregnant person to a battle. I might hate her, but it's not the baby's fault she's its mother," I said.

Natasha looked away. "She might have been a good bargaining chip if we needed it though."

"Not a risk I would take with her unborn child," I said.

Natasha never looked back. She nodded with her gaze fixed outside the window. "I'm glad to hear you say that."

Vin took my hand and squeezed. "You have my heart. Today, tomorrow, and to the end of our existence together."

"Keep those sentiments for when we win today." I returned his squeeze. "There is something inside me that just wants to scream."

"It's tension," Killian said.

"Group scream," Natasha said, still not making eye contact.

"Okay. Let's do it," I said. "On three. One... Two... Three..."

The tundra vehicle rocked back and forth from our screams.

Small giggles bounced off the vehicle.

"I feel better," Natasha said.

"Everything okay over there?" Came over the radio.

Vin grabbed the handset from the cradle. "We're fine. Just practicing our battle cry."

I laughed hard. A dull roar made me stop. The vehicle fell silent.

"What is that?" I asked.

Vin spun the three sixty cameras around to focus on our army. The tundra vehicles shook like ours had. The troop transports flashed their lights, and the screams vibrated the ground and us in our seats.

"Your army is ready, Empress," Killian said.

"The first thing I may do is get rid of that title," I said.

"Maybe in time. There are other things you want to do first."

"True. End the ice age is the first," I said. "The mist should be close to if not completely gone."

"It looks clear to the entrance."

"And this is the one closest to his throne room?" Natasha asked.

"It's not a throne room, but his central command is close to it."

Killian fisted an arm over his heart. "With your permission, Empress, we will begin our movement forward."

"Don't be so formal, and you have my permission."

"Now is the time to be formal. Your followers need to see a clear line of command."

I nodded. *Clear line of command. This path chose me, and I'm giving it everything.* "Then this is my official order to move forward."

Killian moved our vehicle forward with the others visible on the camera.

"We're going in fast," Vin said. "Since we don't have humans with us, there is no need to stay low. A spike to the heart makes us dust. Most anything else we can survive. Eyes open, and our primary goal is to get the Empress face-to-face with her father in order to make a power exchange."

The thump thump of a rapid heartbeat leaked in around me. *Whose is that?*

"We've been over it a dozen times, Vin. We've got it," Natasha said.

I twisted my chair around to face her. "Are you okay? You can stay behind."

Natasha shrugged it off. "I feel so irritable. Everyone is pissing me off. Nerves I guess."

"You've been surly a lot lately. We took every precaution to make sure the remaining humans and their children are safe while we're gone." I reassured her.

"Yes, I don't think that's the issue. I can't put my finger on where it is coming from. Somewhere inside me."

"After we get through the initial change of power, then you and Killian can take a vacation and spend some time together."

Natasha leaned forward and placed her hand over mine. "We aren't going anywhere until you are established and secure in the leadership role. Besides, this might be a magnificent spot to be when the ice age reverses."

"I plan on going back to the Northern Compound once we make the breakthrough."

"You definitely seem at home there. I could see you running your kingdom from there." Natasha winked at me.

"It was my first home. The first place I remember. It is the place that reminds me of my mother most."

Killian stood. "We're here. Once the army is in place, we will exit the building."

Vin looked at each of us. "The army will enter from the three entrances on this end. The front five will go in first through the door closest to us, and we will go in behind them. Straight to the control room is our goal. We have good intelligence that Ezra hasn't left the room since he heard we were on the move."

"He never thought I would do it." *My betrayal must be especially bitter for him. Who am I kidding? He killed my mother. He doesn't truly care about anyone other than himself.*

"He's not one to underestimate his opponents," Killian said.

"No, but he never expected me to betray him either." I got up and prepared to open the hatch.

Vin pulled my shaky hand away. "You're not betraying him. He's the betrayer of all vampires and humankind."

"We'll exit the vehicle on my mark," Killian said. "Double check your gear and weapons."

I pressed my hand against the hard metal plate over my heart. My stakes were all in the holsters, and the sunshine stick was on my hip. This was as ready as I would be for this task.

We made our way forward and positioned ourselves at the door. Vin in the front. Killian in the back.

"Go go go," Killian shouted.

Here I come, Father. Sadness hit me with a swift touch, and I pushed it down.

Vin popped the door open and led the way down the ramp.

The army had cleared a path for us, and I followed the team and rushed to the door. The echoes of footsteps and the hard thud of fists connecting with vampire flesh bounced around me. I made it inside the door.

Once my home, the former safety it offered replaced with the sickened thoughts of Ezra's experiments. The beauty of the compound a facade that hid the evil he evolved here. If we burned it down in the end, I'd be okay with it.

Our front five engaged the guards at the barred door. Ezra had to be behind there. He'd want to look me in the eye as much as I would him. I recognized his personal guards. They were some closest to him. No surprise they would be willing to die for him. Other than the Rogues, his army was lighter than I expected. It left uneasiness pitted in my stomach. We missed something. *Something big.*

"If you were defending your reign, wouldn't you have more of an army ready to fight?" I peered around.

"They deserted," Natasha said. "That shouldn't be much of a surprise." A guard ran at her with a take in hand. She planted a foot in his chest.

"She's right," Vin said. His stake sunk into the chest of one of Ezra's vampires. "These are all that remain of those loyal to him. Even the money he offered could not tempt them to stay."

I'd heard rumors too, but the reality made it much sadder and heavier on my heart. My father, a bastard of a vampire, didn't deserve any sympathy, and he wouldn't get it from me either.

"Let's get the bar off the door before more come," Vin said.

"There will be one on the other side, too. This one was always for show," I said.

"We're going to break it down anyway," Vin said. "Killian? Natasha?"

"Ready," Killian said.

"Or we just use this." Natasha produced a small device from her pocket. She stepped to the front and attached it to the door.

"We need to take cover," she said. "10 seconds folks." She ducked behind the corner.

The rest of us followed.

CHAPTER 27

VIN

Killian wrapped Natasha up in his arms and turned his back to the direction of the door.

Josie faced the wall, and I positioned my body around her.

She resisted. She wanted to be strong, but this wasn't about strength.

"Don't," I said. Vampirism didn't make us immune from pain. I'd be damned if it happened to her while I stood near.

Everything nearby, including us, vibrated. The door shattered into a million tiny pieces and rained down on us. Slivers of metal sliced into the skin not covered by the thick plates I wore. Each tear in the skin like a torch pressed against flesh. I tucked Josie tighter to me. The blood seeped from my arms and onto her. My grasp became slick. The destructive drizzle halted, and I let her go.

"Vin." She spun in my arms. "Shit. You need some blood to heal."

"I'm good. Let's go claim your kingdom." I looked at Killian.

His own arms bloody from the debris. "We came here for a purpose. Let us finish it."

"All in here," Natasha said.

I stepped through the smoke and remains of the door. We crept deeper. Josie and Natasha's soft steps followed behind Killian and me. The hair on the back of my neck stood up like a pissed off cat.

"There is my lovely daughter." Ezra stood on the far side of the room. His hands resting on the top of the computers in front of him. A dozen elite guards flanked him. "Have you come home to take your place by my side?"

Josie positioned herself between Killian and me. Her feet planted shoulder width apart, and her hands fisted at her side. "I've come to lead our people to a future with the humans and out of the ice age." Her body still and solid. No tremors in her voice. She held her chin up. Her stance strong and bold as a leader should be.

Ezra brushed her words aside with the wave of a hand. "With me and following the direction I set forth is where you belong. The future we have in motion is the only direction acceptable, and you must concede to it."

Josie stood strong. "I'll not concede to something I was deceived about. I will not follow you blindly into a path of death. My army of supporters wants the same future I do. A future where we are all equals."

"If that is what you desire, you wouldn't have brought her here." He waved his hand toward Natasha. "Why else would you bring the pregnant one with you other than to prove your loyalty to me?"

We all turned to Natasha. *What the fuck is he talking about? Natasha wasn't here for him to experiment on like Livia.*

"I'm not pregnant." Natasha's eyes widened. "Like the rest of the vampires, I cannot conceive."

I looked at Josie. She met my gaze and gave a quick shake of her head. Natasha would have told her.

"No, a fetus grows inside you every day. Have you not heard its heartbeat? Even now, with all the noise around us, I can hear it beating fast."

Killian extended his hand out to his side and guided Natasha behind him.

"It's yours Killian? Then it will surely be a powerful addition to our team."

Natasha looked at Josie in disbelief. The long recovery time from the poison hid the early signs. Livia deceived us into thinking it was her.

Killian didn't speak, which spoke a different language. His body rigid and prepared. His stance a position he could launch into an attack.

Josie took a step forward. "Surrender now and acknowledge our change in command."

Ezra's head tilted back, and a deep boom of laughter erupted from him. "Josie, you can join me or become my prisoner and watch your friends die. The choice is yours."

"We will fight to the death if necessary, but we have taken measures to make sure you will go with us if it comes to that," I said.

She bluffed. We could burn the place to the ground, but I knew she'd never give that order. She needed the equipment in the labs here.

Ezra shook his head. "And you would willingly kill the first pregnant vampire in almost a century with that?"

"You don't know she's pregnant." Josie moved towards Natasha.

She and Killian eased into a protective stance around Natasha. I focused my hearing on the occupants of the room. One heartbeat in the group. Fast and strong. *The heartbeat I heard at the Northern Compound. Natasha is pregnant.*

"Vincent, life has always been important to you. Would you willingly kill an unborn vampire?" He paused. "I'm impressed that Calidora was successful before me. We were so close with Livia. Alas, she disappeared." He held his hands out, palms up.

He knows exactly where she is. Fake ass bastard.

Josie cocked her head my direction. The look answered my question. Livia was pregnant too. Ezra and Calidora had cracked the vampire fertility problem, and both the pregnant vampires had ended up in Josie's care. *Was it part of his grand scheme, or was it an accident?*

"What have you been doing to the vampire women?" Josie asked.

"We need survival of the strong and gifted," he said.

"We are immortals," Killian said.

"But we can be killed." Ezra took a stake from one of his guards and twirled it through his fingers. He flipped it up and caught it. In a swift motion, he thrust it into the chest of the guard. The guard disintegrated to ash in front of us. "We must be ready for it at all times."

"Killing your guards proves what?" Josie shifted her weight. She was reading herself for his attack. He wouldn't kill her. He needed her support.

"Only our strongest, wisest, and gifted should survive." His answer came without hesitation.

"Our cause is still the same, Josie. Does anything he says change it?" Natasha came out of her daze.

She stared at him. Her eyes narrowed.

"Did you hear me?" He sneered.

"Yes," she said, straight-faced.

"He needs to answer for his crimes," Killian said.

"We will not negotiate with you, Father," Josie said. "You can surrender or you can die, but we have the numbers to take the compound today."

"Neither of those options work for me. Stand with me."

"I'll never stand with my mother's killer," Josie said. She shifted between her feet. It cost her to say it out loud to him.

"Anything I've done has been for the betterment of the vampire kind," he said.

"Including having vampires killed?"

"I haven't ordered a born vampire to be killed."

"Except my mother," Josie said. "Oh, and the guard on my detail whose head rolled to my feet."

"And created vampires," I said. "Don't forget the hundreds of created vampires he killed or turned into Rogues."

"Killian, take Natasha out of here. Vin and I have this," Josie said.

"I'm not going anywhere," Natasha said. "I want to know what they did to me, and what is inside me."

"You'll need to ask Calidora." Ezra smirked.

"Stop playing games, Ezra," Josie said.

"Father. I am your father. Have you forgotten that?"

"I'm reminded every day when I see the destruction you wielded on vampires, humans, and the world." Life staged constant reminders of his treachery in front of me. There would be no forgetting. Not in my lifetime.

"Yet you're not angry at Vincent's mother? Calidora's hand in this bears an equal load to mine."

Venom poured into my mouth, and a growl came from low in my throat. "She's not my mother."

Josie touched my arm and squeezed. Her touch the source of calm for me. I swallowed the venom.

"And you drove us straight to her," Josie said. "She let us go without harming us."

"Did she?" Ezra tapped his finger on his temple. "Or was she positioning you to aid in her plan?"

"What plan would that be?" We guessed Calidora's endgame, but he didn't know that. I played along in hopes he had more information.

Ezra looked me up and down. "You are of her flesh. Do you not know how she thinks?"

"Vin is nothing like her. You should know that," Josie said.

Ezra inclined his head toward me. "One of Calidora's gifts is to make others think she cares in order to manipulate them. Is this something you possess as well, Vincent?"

"I've never been one to be fake." I wanted to stake him where he stood for implying I would ever pretend to care about Josie.

"Calidora wants me out of power, and she has sent you here to accomplish that task for her. What do you call it then?"

Josie and I exchanged looks. *Had we been unwittingly aiding Calidora? We knew what she wanted, and we thought being aware prepared us.*

Josie played along with his game. "What would she gain?"

"My area. My technology. My power."

"Those are no longer yours," Josie said. "She'll have to come after me if she wants them now."

Ezra's guards readied themselves to fight. He held a hand up. His sign to hold position. "Put down your weapons. I will not fight my own daughter."

Too easy. Even for a master of strategy like Ezra.

The guards laid down their weapons on the floor.

Josie looked to me. Her forehead wrinkled. She prepared for every outcome except a peaceful surrender.

"It's not like you to issue false threats," I said.

"No, but I will not harm my daughter. She is too special to me."

"Tell your guards to face the wall," Josie said.

"Do as she says."

"Killian, secure him," Josie said. She reached for Natasha's hand and pulled her between us.

Killian cuffed Ezra's hands with the sunlight cuffs. Any resistance would admit a burn strong enough to cause intense pain for a vampire. We created them under Ezra's leadership. He deserved to be bound by something he used against his own people.

The guards all dropped to their knees and placed their hands behind their heads.

I radioed for the team outside the door to take them into custody. "Do you want to lock them up here or at the Northern Compound?"

"Here for now, but I want to take them back to the north to stand trial."

"If you are going to..." I stopped myself from revealing her plans in front of him.

"What are you going to do, Josephine? How are you going to handle the famine we are facing? How are you going to handle the growing number of our kind feeding on each other? We are the minority to the Rogue. The scales tipped in their direction while you were out exploring with your friends."

Did the Rogues outnumber the born and created vampires now? That presented a danger to humans and vampires, and the answer would be to cull the numbers. The thought made me sick, but Rogues had no humanity. They'd kill to satiate their unsatisfiable hunger.

The team arrived from our army and shackled the rest of Ezra's private guard.

"Take him to the prison building and lock him in a cell far away from the others," Josie said. "Killian, you can show them where that is."

"I'll stay here," Natasha said.

Killian nodded. The team left with Ezra in shackles.

"Josie, I was just starting to think I might be pregnant, but I didn't know anyone else could tell. Now, I'm wondering what I am pregnant with that has a heartbeat."

"We'll figure it out." Josie squeezed Natasha's hand. "Livia is pregnant as well, and her baby has a heartbeat."

"You can't hear a normal vampire baby heartbeat. What is this inside me?" Pink tears dotted the corners of Natasha's eyes. "What kind of voodoo magic have Calidora and Ezra committed?"

"You're going to be fine, and you have no reason to believe this is anything other than a healthy baby growing inside you."

"How can two vampires produce a baby with an audible heartbeat?"

"I don't know, but we will figure it out." Josie hugged Natasha. "Maybe your placenta is thinner."

"We will protect you," I said. "Even if it is against what is inside you."

Natasha pulled away and placed her hands over her stomach. "The craziest thing is I feel protective of it already."

"It could just be a baby. There is the possibility they solved the vampire fertility issue," Josie said.

"This is your father and Calidora we are talking about. They have ulterior motives in everything they do."

"Natasha, sit down and relax." I held one of the chairs out for her.

She dropped down in it and folded her arms across her chest.

Josie moved to the keyboard and tapped away. "I need your skills over here, Vin."

I peered over her shoulder. "What are you accessing?"

"His communications. See here." Josie pointed to the screen.

"He's been communicating with Calidora." I scrolled down through the messages. "Every day it looks like."

"We played right into their hand. That's why they let us walk out of Calidora's and walk into Ezra's." *Damn it. I led us straight into whatever web he had spun. Which means he knew what would happen.*

I depressed the button on our radios. "Killian? Come back, Killian?"

"This is Killian."

"Leave Ezra's guards in the cells, but bring him back to the control room."

"Why?"

"We'll explain when you get here."

"Copy. Killian out."

"We need to check on the Northern Compound," Josie said.

"I told them I would open a chat when we secured the room so they are expecting us." I opened the window and executed my program to open the line.

The screen filled with their return message. "They are safe for now, but they have detected activity at the perimeter. It's a large force, but they are on foot."

"Rogues..." Josie said.

"You might be right, or maybe Calidora thought she could sneak past the old radars at that facility."

"She's smarter than that," Natasha said. I glanced over my shoulder. Her eyes focused on the floor. "She'd never send her forces in without all she could spare." Her head raised to meet us. "It's an army of Rogues."

Fuck. And less than half of our forces. They aren't trained to fight an army made up of Rogues.

Josie's eyes widened. "We need to get back there."

Our split forces opened a vulnerability for the humans and vampires at the Northern Compound. I ran through the number of those with battle skills who remained behind. *No more than five hundred with real battle action.* All the vehicles traveled with us. The Northern Compound sat wide open with little to defend them.

"How much poison do we have left?"

Josie shook her head. "It doesn't matter. We didn't leave enough masks for everyone there, and it wouldn't work."

"We're going to have to fight," I said.

"Not just us, but at the compound too," Natasha said.

"You're not fighting," Josie said. "It's too risky."

"It's going to take all of us," Natasha said. "I'm not injured. I'm pregnant. And I'm fighting."

"What's going on? Is everyone okay?" Killian stepped through the busted door without Ezra.

"Where's Ezra?" Josie asked.

Killian inclined his head towards the door. "I left him in the hall with some of our team."

"There is an army of Rogues descending on the Northern Compound. We might not get there in time, but we have to try." Josie paced the floor.

"How far away are they?"

"Take a look." I spun the monitor around for him.

"Can you use the--"

"Poison? No, Josie pointed out that we didn't leave the right equipment with our loyal supporters." I stared at the screen. *We need to go now.*

"Oh," he said. "We can travel faster on foot than in the tundra vehicles. Natasha can stay here."

"Would you people stop trying to leave me behind? I'm going and that's final." Natasha narrowed her eyes.

"Then you stay behind me the whole time," Killian said.

"No, I fight like the rest of you and our people," she said. "This dang armor covers my belly too." She gestured to the metal plates we were all wearing.

"He knew this was going to happen. I want to make an example out of him. If we're traveling on foot, we won't be able to take him," Josie said.

"I'll have the guards bring him in one of the tundras."

"Make sure they secure him where he can't get anywhere near the communications equipment."

"They're not imbeciles, Josephine," Killian said.

"I know. We need to be extra cautious with him though."

"Yes, I'm aware." They locked on each other like a brother and sister having a staring contest.

"Enough debating on who knows the asshole better. We need to go." Natasha stood at the once massive door.

Josie's face hardened with concern. She walked past Ezra without a word. *Lead by example.* Her example of how to be a better leader.

My stomach knotted tight. Blood sloshed in it in time with our steps. The odds stacked high against our return to the Northern Compound before the Rogues descended on it and our people.

CHAPTER 28

Killian locked Ezra down tight in the tundra before we took off with as many as could follow. The temperature dropped as we moved North at a swift pace. My mind trained on getting back to the Northern Compound. The thick snow drifts hampered our speed. Killian slowed. I fell in pace with him, as did the rest.

Killian pulled his radio out and paused his steps. "We will be out of range of the tundras in a short time. I will check in one last time before we lose contact."

I stopped beside him. Vin and Natasha took up either side of me. The shuffles behind us silenced. The army stopped to wait for their next order.

"It's going to take the tundras two days at that speed," I said.

"That's if they don't have any trouble along the way," Vin said.

I nodded. "How many men did you leave with him?"

"About fifty," Killian said. "Enough to man the vehicles and guard him. What are you thinking, Natasha?"

"Calidora wouldn't want him captured. Too many secrets to share."

"You think she will send troops after him?"

"I think she'll either capture him or end him," she said.

"Tell the warriors to save themselves if it comes to it," I said. "They're lives are more important than his."

"Are you sure?" Killian asked.

"Yes, I'm sure," I said.

We traveled on through the frosty night and made it several hours before sunrise. I swallowed down the panic that continued to rise up in my throat. Killian and a few guards checked the position of the Rogues. They would have to attack and be gone by sunrise or they would burn alive in the sun. Vin and Natasha stayed back with me. I gave my last blood bag to a weary created vampire. Her dark circles visible even in the little light from the moon. Vin shared his with another. Natasha tried to give hers away, but I put an end to the idea. She needed to nourish the baby.

Killian kicked up small white clumps of snow with his jog back to us. He came to a stop in front of us. His forehead wrinkled and lips pursed.

"There's more of them than we expected?"

"Too many, Josephine. I've never seen so many Rogues in one place."

No. We will not lose like this. I rubbed my eyes like that would erase it. "We need options," I said.

Killian's face was grim. "Maybe if we could use the poison mist—"

That was something Ezra would do. Not me. "And kill our own people? Then what would be the point?"

"Josie, he's just trying to come up with options," Vin said. "The tundras are still at least a day out."

"You're right," I said. "I'm sorry, Killian."

He held his hand up to cover his earpiece. "Copy. Don't pursue. Continue north." His face tight, he looked at me. "We have another issue. The caravan broke radio silence to tell us Ezra escaped."

"I can't say I didn't expect that to happen. No doubt he is headed here, then." I paused. I wanted to crumple to the ground and let the tears flow. Not a good look on a leader. *Next steps.* "What options do we really have? We're the best of the best, but we can't take on an entire army of Rogues ourselves." *Think, Josie. Think. There has to be a way.*

"They're not going to stop with you anyway," Natasha said. "Haven't you seen how they get into a frenzy and tear bodies apart like wild animals?"

I cringed. I'd seen the frenzy up close on a mission a few years ago and tried to block it from my memories. "Will Calidora negotiate, Natasha?"

She shook her head. "Not unless she's backed into a corner."

"And we're the ones backed into a corner so not happening," I said.

"Whatever we are going to do, we need to decide fast." Vin pointed to the position of the moon. It was like a ticking clock.

"The kids..." Fresh pink tears spilled down Natasha's face.

I wrapped an arm around her. "We're going to save them. They will be safe and warm with a glass of milk and cookies." Milk is to kids as blood is to vampires. *The blood.* "I have an idea."

"We can blend the mist into the blood supply. It should keep the poison from going airborne. Then we can spray the outermost row of Rogues," I said.

He nodded. "They will turn on each other."

"The poison will take care of the rest for us," Natasha said.

Killian inhaled and exhaled in human fashion. "The poison is on the tundras." He paused. "We don't have a day to wait for them."

"We didn't bring any with us?" Natasha asked.

"No, I am to blame. I didn't see how we would need it," I said. *Stupid. I should have brought it.*

"Is covering them in blood not enough to set them into a frenzy?" Vin asked.

"If it was fresh blood, it might be, but we would still end up with a significant number of them surviving. The poison would be a more efficient way," I said.

"The blood could facilitate wiping out enough of them that we would stand a chance," Killian said.

"It's a colossal risk." Vin glanced at the army. "Do we even have enough blood? We gave our last ones away."

"Anyone have any other options?" I paused. No one chimed in with alternatives. "Then let's figure out if we have enough and how we are going to spray this blood on them. If nothing else, we can buy some time for the residents in the compound."

"Time to what? Escaping a pack of Rogues this size isn't feasible," Vin said. "It will be like a mosh pit full of chainsaws."

"We have to try something." My hands jutted out, palms up.

"Okay," Killian said. "It's our only option regardless of the risk." He turned to Natasha. "I don't want you anywhere near here when this starts."

"There's nowhere else for me to go," she said. "Besides, I'm a much better fighter than you all give me credit for."

"We'll wait as long as we can to see if some miracle brings

the tundras here early," I said. "Prepare as if we will proceed without them, but hope like hell they show up."

"The Rogues are just ahead of us. We need to get the prep done and move into place," Vin said. "They will have to attack before sunrise to get indoors."

"That only leaves a few hours," Natasha said.

"Then we better get busy." I started looking through my bag for something to use to spray.

"We're going to need something to disperse it like a spray nozzle," Vin said. "There's an old abandoned house not too far from here."

"If there isn't anything, then we are going to be shit out of luck," Natasha said.

"There will be something we can use," Killian said.

"Well, hello Mr. Positivity," Natasha said.

I smirked. Natasha was definitely his match.

Vin belly laughed.

Killian smiled and shook his head. "Yes, that's me. I'll gather some help, and we can commence with the scavenger hunt."

I stayed behind and searched for blood. The army freely gave donations to survive. I used old blood bags and other plastic containers from our packs to store it. Rogue preference didn't include the origins of it.

The moon's position ticked towards daybreak. I thought of the pinkish orange hues it would bring, like an omen of our night ahead. My time as empress might be short, but at least I would go in a blaze of glory... or a frenzy of Rogues. *My friends, the only people left I loved, could die from my choices. That would be my only regret.*

Hands slipped around my waist and pulled me against a

hard body. Lips pressed against my cheek. "Don't be so pensive. It's a solid plan. We will succeed."

"You're so confident," I said. "We're using vampire blood and upcycled garbage to dispense it."

"Because I believe in you," Vin whispered in my ear. "And I love you."

"I love you too. It's hard for me to put into words," I said. "Here, in the evening's light, it is peaceful and never ending like my heart for you." I turned in his arm. "It turns to pain when I foresee what I've asked of you and everyone, but especially you. I've put you all in a position where you have committed to die for me. Is that any better than what Ezra has done?"

"Stop torturing yourself. The empathy you feel is what makes you different from Ezra."

A faint heartbeat thumped in my ears. I cut my head to the left and right, but I didn't see a human. "Is Natasha anywhere nearby?"

"She and Killian were doing one last check before we go. They are on the far end of the line."

"Strange," I said. "I could have sworn I heard a heartbeat."

"While we're alone, I want to say something," Vin said.

His hands trembled as they grasped mine. He dropped down on one knee.

Tears pooled in my eyes. *I didn't see this coming either.* Happiness blocked out the sorrow. My heart beat hard in my chest.

"Josephine, you saved me when I was lost, and you pushed me to find myself. You accepted me and loved me even when I wasn't sure I was worthy. I'm not sure I'm worthy now. I am sure that I love the way you have grown and how you have inspired me to grow. You are the moment in between a heartbeat. The important space I didn't know needed to be filled until I met you. Will you do me the incredible honor of being my wife?"

Tears rolled down my cheeks, and I didn't care. This was the wrong place and exactly the right place, all in one. "Yes." I threw my arms around him and pressed my lips to his.

He pulled back. "I don't have a ring. Sorry. I didn't plan this."

"No ring needed."

He coaxed me to his knee, so we were at eye level and covered my mouth with his.

My heart sank when he pulled back. The task ahead a cloud over us.

"When we win tonight, I want to take you to the chapel and make you my wife."

My heart fluttered and danced. Happiness filled the air around us. The tiny heartbeat pounded a rhythm. I looked for Natasha. I found her on the other side of the line with Killian.

"Do we have a minister to perform the service?" I asked, knowing the humanity in him would want a more human ceremony versus the vampire one. The human joining was warmer than ours.

"There's bound to be one among all these vampires and humans."

I laughed. "You're probably right. With that many people, the odds are pretty good."

Footsteps crunched in the snow behind us. "We're ready," Killian said.

I inhaled a deep breath and let go to the moment. "We will win tonight."

"The army is in position with the gear. You will be behind the line."

"I'll be on the frontline," I said. "This is our last chance. All of us."

"Don't argue this time. Our Empress does not need to be in the middle of frenzied Rogues," Killian said.

"I'll be with you." Natasha rolled her eyes. "We don't know if they will recognize the fetus and come after me either."

I shared her annoyance. Not only had I trained for this kind of combat, I'd fought Rogues before. My skills, just like all our best fighters, needed to be there.

"Vin, don't do anything risky."

"You know I can't promise that." He tucked my hair behind my ear.

"Time to go," Killian said. He placed a soft kiss on Natasha's lips. In one movement, he turned and leapt over the army to the front.

"I should join him," Vin said. "It shouldn't take too long."

"Come back safe."

He squeezed my hands and match Killian's leap.

"We need the strongest fighters up front, and you and I are some of the best. It makes more sense for us to fight than hide." Natasha waved her hands up and down her torso. "My body is a suit of armor around this baby, and I swear it gets stronger all the time."

I'd never allow myself an ounce of grace if my family got hurt or we lost because I wasn't there to help fight. "Are we going up front or what?"

Natasha's eyes widened. "I thought you'd say no."

I smiled. She should have known better. "I want to lead my people, not follow. I can't lead from the back of the room."

She took my hand. "We're going to have some pissed off boyfriends after this."

"Fiancé," I whispered.

She squeezed my hand. Her voice softer than the footsteps ahead of us. "It's about time. Congratulations." She nodded.

We jumped together like our men had before us. My feet landed in a small white cloud between Killian and Vin. Neither looked our directions. The dark hoard had made it midway to the compound wall, and all attention focused there.

"The agreement was that you would both stay behind the line." Vin's head locked on the target.

"Grrr." Killian faced forward with no contact.

"I'm the leader and more skilled than most of the others," I said. "My place is here where I can help my people live to see another day."

"And she wasn't going to have fun without me," Natasha said.

"Killian, you will still give the signal," I said.

"No, my Empress. You are here and should give the command for your army."

The transition happened in an unexpected way. Eyes on me to give the word and not only as a leader. My supporters, my friends, my husband-to-be, all looked to me as their Empress. Either to lead them to victory or to lead them to death on this night. My eyelids fell closed, and I focused on the task.

I opened my eyes and pushed my hand in the air with three fingers raised. No words to utter, only a hand signal for which the sharp vampire eyes waited.

My ring finger dropped under my thumb.

The surrounding air stilled in the already silent night.

My middle finger tucked under my thumb.

Vampires prepared the makeshift delivery pumps we'd created. Tension and anticipation electrified the air.

My forefinger left alone to indicate the exact time we would all leap to within a few feet of the Rogues. The final gesture done. My fist remained high above my head as I jumped with my people.

Growls and yells permeated the space and drew the attention of the Rogues. The packs spewed blood out in a wide spray. The inhuman version of our species stood rooted in place as the crimson liquid rained down on them. Grunts rumbled low from the devils. They sniffed and eyed each other.

"Come on," I whispered. It was taking too long. *We just need one to start the domino effect...*

A large Rogue tackled the one next to him. His teeth sunk into the exposed neck. The smaller one's arms and legs flung snow over them. The sight was grotesque. Worse than the sight of the poisoned Rogues in the south. Teeth clanged like bear traps down the line. Tissue soared through the air and landed on the snow. Red pools formed against the white snow. The frozen blood a maroon slush.

"It's working," Vin whispered. His face contorted in disgust.

"Some will break the line. Be prepared," Killian said.

One sunshine stick was already in my hand. I drew the other one.

The blood in the packs sputtered out the last few drops. Soldiers shouldered the packs off and stepped back to retrieve their weapons.

The exterior perimeter we formed stood strong against the first impact of the Rogues. The second wave found a weakness, and a few came through.

"Now," Killian said. He and Vin leapt into the middle of the Rogues. Some fighters followed them.

I lost sight of them. A queasy pit formed in my belly. My head turned to Natasha. "Shall we?"

"Damn straight," she said.

We jumped to the spot Vin and Killian landed, but they were nowhere to be found.

The blood pools formed a red skating rink under our feet. The Rogues balance on it not as good as ours. They slipped and crashed against the ice. Cracks webbed across the crimson patches.

The ones still standing on the outside formed a ring around us. *Surrounded.* Adrenaline filled the air and spurred me on. In the center of a group of Rogues meant a death sentence for most, but I saw an opportunity.

My eyes met Natasha's, and I spun my hands in a windmill fashion.

"Hell, yes," she yelled. Her hand flung a sunshine stick out.

My own sizzled at full power as we skated in a circle. Enough speed gained, I reached my free hand out to her.

Natasha's hand grasped my wrist and I hers. I flipped in a cartwheel motion, glimpsing the ground. The weapons dug into Rogues. The burnt flesh odor filled the air. Our enemies burst into piles of ash with each thrust.

A large Rogue lunged at me. I stabbed my stick into his chest and lifted him off the ground. His shattered scream etched a scar inside me. He burned from the inside out into cinders.

I glanced at Natasha. She held her ground. Her powerful strikes yielded piles around her.

Two came after me at once. I yanked the second sunshine stick from my side. My feet pushed from the ground, and they landed one in the chest of each of my assailants. I jammed the sticks into the sides of their necks. Their bodies

SUSAN PERSON

turned to soot and dropped me back to the frozen stained soil.

Natasha twisted and turned with her back to mine. Still no sign of Vin or Killian. I trusted they succeeded as we did.

The dust from the Rogues built up in the path. Icy wind carried the remnants into the air. Debris coated me from the head down. I spat and wiped my hands across my face.

The number of Rogues left on the field a fraction of what started the fight. My army's success coated in the same dust I wiped away.

CHAPTER 29

JOSIE

The skirmish ended in a short amount of time. The created among us returned to the safety of the compound before sunrise. I prayed to Vin's gods, unsure how we lived without divine intervention. *Thank you, gods. Thank you for blessing us today.*

"I'm pleased to find you well, Empress," Killian said. His arm slipped around Natasha's shoulders. A film of ash covered his body. "We have won the day."

"Where's Vin?"

"A handful ran into the woods, and he chased after them."

"We should go help him." I took a step.

Killian's hand clasped my shoulder. "Let him have his moment."

"How many?"

"Only about five. He can take twice that on his own."

My stomach fluttered. I laid my hand over it. "He doesn't like to kill, Killian. A small group is more intimate. It's not in him like it is us." *Why am I worried? He'd already killed many today.*

"His actions today were noble and wise, and he fought as a vampire warrior."

Nausea formed deep in my belly. "How long ago did he follow them?"

"Not much time has passed. He left just before I came to find you," Killian said.

"I need to find him." The pain twisted in my gut. It compelled me forward.

Killian's arm slipped through mine. "You must go to the compound, Empress, where you will be safe. Life changed the moment you seized control."

My gaze locked on his hand. Fire flared hot behind my eyes. Lucky for Killian, the flames weren't real. "Don't push me on this, Killian."

Killian's hand stayed firm in place. "I must do my duty to protect you."

I stepped forward on my left foot and kicked my right leg in the air. My body flipped around to pin his arm behind his back. "Then as your Empress, I command you to stand down."

He bowed his head. "So be it."

My grip released, and I dashed through the woods. I might not be a tracker, but Vin's scent stood out among the others. Another odor tainted the air. *Vampire blood.* Lots of it. Not from the direction of the battle, but from the direction I headed. My feet peddled faster through the dark forest.

A trail of crimson puddles led to a pile of ash. My gut tightened. A loud thump pounded in my ears. I knelt down and inhaled. *Not Vin.* My breath flowed out over a few beats.

Grunts in the distance led me deeper into the darkness. Rogue stench filled the air. They smelled like rot, no matter how young or old. Vin's pure vampire scent clear over the others. *How had I never realized it was such a pure scent before?* Not that it mattered. I would have chosen him anyway.

A scream shattered the night. The kind from pain inflicted by the brutality of a Rogue. Another wail pierced my eardrums. I couldn't tell for sure if it was Vin.

I ground my teeth and pushed my feet faster. *Fuck the path.* Underbrush sliced through my pants. Blood ran down into my boots before the wounds healed. The trees parted and broke into a clearing. Vin stood in the center. Four Rogues surrounded him.

His shirt shredded and soaked in blood and a few scratches, but he looked well otherwise. Magnetic blue eyes linked with mine. He shook his head in a tiny motion from side to side.

A warning I couldn't accept. I shrugged my shoulders and winked at him.

"Hey scumbags. I'm a much better meal than him." The sweetness of my blood drifted up around me. It would drive them crazy. Something in my blood differed in the slightest ways from others. I didn't need to move.

Seven red eyes directed their curiosity at me like a spotlight. The one with the lone eye stood a foot higher than the rest. The missing eye a recent loss by the mangled remnants in the socket. His face no longer included human characteristics. He'd been Rogue for quite some time.

"Josie, what are you doing?"

"I got your invitation for a moonlight stroll." I grinned. "Natasha and I warmed up our dance skills earlier. Think you can hang?"

"There's no way I'm letting Natasha out dance me with my future wife."

Lone Eye led the Rogues as they took cautious steps in my direction.

"Waiting's not an option," I said under my breath. I ran full speed toward them and pushed off in an aerial. I flipped over their heads, and Vin's face came back into view. My ankle, blood covered but healed, twisted away. My back thumped against the hard dirt. "Fuck."

"The Emperor will pay nicely for you." Lone Eye leaned over me. The insanity of the Rogues prevented them from speech, but not this one. He spoke near perfection. Well, caveman style perfection. Saliva trailed from his mouth. A black boot connected to the side of his head, but he didn't budge. Lone Eye looked up at Vin. "He said we can feast on you."

"He's not food, and my father isn't the Emperor anymore." I planted my foot square under his chin. He shot up and back.

Vin grabbed my hand and pulled me up. "It's going to take more than that."

"I figured if it was that easy, you would have been done already."

"Smart ass." He squeezed my hand. "I'm going to outdo Natasha."

I squeezed back. "I'm counting on it."

"I hope you didn't squeeze Natasha's hand like that." He grinned.

"Only when she spun me around."

His fingers wrapped around my forearm. He propelled me around him and into the air past Lone Eye, toward one of the smaller ones.

I landed in front of one on the opposite spectrum of Lone Eye. He wrinkled his nose in a snarl. Broken teeth bared.

Dust stirred up around us. I heard scuffling behind me

from Vin and Lone Eye. I glanced back. Neither had an advantage. I needed to tip the scale.

A hand grabbed my arm. Nails sunk into my flesh and drew my attention.

"Sorry. I don't have time to play today." I withdrew the knife hidden in my jacket. It crunched into his skull and sunk between his eyes. I pulled the last stake from my belt and turned him to ash. Made a quick check of the fight behind me. Vin held his own.

The other two Rogues circled me like stalkers. *Classic predictable Rogues.* Blood stains painted their lips. The ones responsible for the dead vampire.

A low-hanging limb caught my attention. I propelled myself up and snapped it from the tree. The limb broke easily in two. I twisted my wrists around and jammed the stakes straight into their hearts. Both dropped to their knees and crumbled into ash.

Lone Eye's dagger like nails connected to Vin's cheek. Crimson oozed from the lacerations. Vin's fists thudded against Lone Eye's jaw in repetitive succession. The Rogue shuffled backwards but didn't fall. His attention turned to me.

I side-stepped around Lone Eye to Vin's side.

"Get behind me. He's here for you."

"Together. That's how we work best," I said.

"Remember the training exercise we did on the beach last year?"

"How could I forget?" I winked.

"I love you." He hooked his foot behind my ankle.

I knew what to expect this time, and I landed on my ass a little more gracefully than on the beach. My hips pivoted, and my legs swept Lone Eye's feet out from under him. The ground shook around me.

Vin jumped over me and onto the Rogue. The weight of the impact drove Lone Eye down on the fallen branch. Impaled in the exact spot to end him. The evil bastard turned to dust. Vin dropped through the cloud. His feet rested on the ground.

I wrapped my arms around his waist and laid my head on his shoulder blade. "I love you too. That was the perfect move. How did you know?"

He turned and pulled me to his chest. "It was the one and only time I surprised you."

"Not the only time." I tilted my head back. A hollowness filled my chest. "Your face. The scratches are not healing." I reached my hand up to touch his cheek.

Vin grabbed my wrist. "It's poison." He crumpled in my arms.

"Vin?" My heart slowed. Tears filled my eyes. I had to save him. *You will see your ending tonight.* "No, you are not leaving me. Do you hear me?"

The woods blurred around me. Tears. Speed. More tears. Vin's still body in my arms.

Finally. The compound came into view. Killian and Natasha met me near the back door. "He's been poisoned, and we turned the damn vampire who did it to ash, so I don't even know how to treat it."

"Let's get him inside," Natasha said.

Killian's face looked grey as he took Vin from my arms. "The poison didn't touch you, Empress. Did it?"

"No, I'm fine."

Vin's eyes flashed open and faded back out of consciousness. His skin paper white and looked as thin.

Killian placed Vin on a table in the infirmary. Nothing about it said vampire other than the blood.

Natasha squeezed my hand. "He's going to be okay. You will figure it out. What do we need to treat him?"

"We need to identify the origin of the poison." I just wanted to just hold him. Everything jumbled in my head. I couldn't think straight. "But we killed the vampire who did it." I wiped my hands down my face.

"You are a scientist, Josie. This is your world. You will figure this out," she said. "You saved me after all,"

Scientist. A scientist would use deduction and Occam's razor. Focus Josie. "We need to write down the symptoms we can see."

"I'll grab something to write with," Natasha said.

"Unconscious." The scene familiar with Vin on the verge of death and me left wondering if I could save him. For the first time, my mother's garden broke me instead of inspiring me. "Grey skin color. Wound not healing." I finished the list of symptoms.

Natasha tore the paper from the notepad and passed it to me. "Now." She took my free hand. "Go do your magic. We'll stay with him."

My body felt numb. "I can't leave him."

"Tell me what books you need, and I'll have them brought here."

I recited the titles from memory, more like a robot than a vampire.

She and Killian left me alone with Vin.

I slipped on gloves from the tray and cleaned his wounds. The poison leached into his flesh. Deep inside. The lacerations refused to heal. Blood trickled down onto the table. We are immortal, because we heal and heal fast. If we can't heal, we are no longer immortal, and Vin wasn't healing. Nausea rolled in my gut. I pressed my forearm to my mouth. A single sob escaped my lips. *No. Be strong for him.*

SUSAN PERSON

My hip bumped the tray. I kicked the stand with my foot. The relief I wanted didn't happen. My hands reached under the tray and flipped it over. The metal rang like a gong against the wall. "Damn it."

I ripped the gloves off and threw them at the tray contents on the floor. What kind of poison is this? I captured his hand in mine. "I'll figure it out, Vin. We're not going to waste any more time. We're getting married as soon as you wake up. I'll show you every day how much I love you."

Vin's fingers fluttered around mine.

Another sob came I couldn't keep inside. "Vin? Can you hear me?"

Puss oozed from the gashes. His arms twitched.

Seizure. "Vin, if you can hear me, I think you're having a seizure. Just relax and let it pass."

He squeezed tight on my hand.

Unable to get loose without hurting him, I sat on the edge of the bed and watched his face. No signs of pain. His lips formed a circle.

"Are you trying to say something?" I studied the lines creasing his face. "Are you awake? Are you in pain?"

His grip tightened.

I leaned in close to his mouth.

"Pain," he whispered. "Pain not bad."

Tears streamed down my face. My words lodged in my throat.

"You're awake." I squeaked out and kissed his uninjured cheek. My pink tears fell on his face. "And a liar."

More puss discharged from the other side of the gash. The wounds closed and jagged pink lines replaced them. He was healing. His eyes jerked back and forth behind the lids. A sliver of blue peaked out between the narrow slits.

Relief rushed through me. Fresh tears spilled down my face. *Poison is fickle. He needs time.* "Take it easy. There's no rush."

His eyes opened and closed quickly. And again. They opened all the way. The whites red and full of blood.

"Throat." His voice raspy and hoarse.

"You need some blood." I jerked a couple of bags off the other table, the one I hadn't flipped over, and ripped them open.

He raised his head and parted his lips, ready for the crimson liquid. He sucked it down in long swigs. In seconds he had the first bag drank. *Good sign.* He needed it to heal and purge the rest of the poison.

"How am I not a Rogue?"

"He didn't bite you. It was a scratch," I said. "His nails were tainted with poison."

"Did our plan work?"

"We got him. He's ash." *I'd end Lone Eye ten times over for this.*

"Good," he said. "Then kiss me."

I leaned forward, but he hesitated.

"What about the poison?"

"You didn't drink it. It won't be on your lips." I ran my finger over them. "Or in your mouth." I pressed my lips against his.

His fingers slipped in behind my neck and tangled in my hair. He pulled me tight against him. His lips urged mine apart.

"We've got all the books you wanted," Natasha said from behind us. "Ooooh."

"Glad to see you awake," Killian said.

"You two have the worst timing." I laughed. "But I'm glad you are here. Thank you for your help."

"How is he awake?" Natasha checked out the almost gone scars on Vin's cheek. "No offense."

"I don't know," I said. "I don't know of any poison that has a quick recovery after those kind of symptoms."

"Maybe your love did it." Natasha grinned.

My cheeks burned.

"Do you want me to move you to your quarters?" Killian asked.

"Oh hell," Vin said. "You carried me in here?"

"Yes," Killian said.

"That's embarrassing." Vin laughed.

"Better than the alternative."

I glared at Killian. *That might be funny later, but it wasn't right now.*

"I can manage myself to my room," Vin said. He shifted up on one elbow. "My lady said she's going to marry me as soon as I woke up."

Natasha and Killian stared at me.

My body felt loose and wiggly. "I didn't mean the second you woke up. Let's get you up on your feet first."

"No, backing out now. We're going to the chapel." Vin smiled.

"We're born vampires. We don't get married in chapels." *I'd go to a chapel, like a human, for him though.*

"Since when do we do the expected?" Vin slipped his hand in mine.

My fondest wish was for him to be happy. If a chapel commitment was what it took, I could give him that. "Okay. Let's do it." I looked to Natasha. "Will you stand up with me?"

"I had your back on the battlefield. I think I can handle a little wedding," Natasha said.

"And you'll be my best man?" Vin asked Killian.

"I'm always the best man, but I will stand up with you." Killian smiled and tucked Natasha into his side.

"This one thinks he's got jokes," she said.

Vin and I both laughed.

"I know I do." He tickled her.

"Stop," she yelled through her giggles.

Killian relented. "We'll discuss my jokes later."

"Yes, we will," Natasha said. She tore her gaze away from him to look at us. "So, why don't Killian and I go see how soon it would be possible to make this happen?"

"That would be great," I said. "Thank you."

I never pictured myself getting married. My life centered around preparation to lead a nation that no longer existed. We were birthing a new nation, and there were two new vampires on the way. *Was the time right? Committing to Vin would always be right.*

"The sooner the better," Vin added.

Killian gave a thumbs up and closed the door.

"She has really changed him," I said.

Vin raised an eyebrow. "Love will do that. You've really changed me."

"I can't take credit for that. We've both changed a lot through this revolution."

"We have." He took my hands. "We still have to deal with my mother and your father."

"I know," I said. "Ezra escaped, and that is on me. I was too blinded by the goal to see I played into his hand."

I pushed the empty tray away from the bed to give Vin room.

"And Calidora has her own agenda, and I'm worried her agenda and his are linked."

I touched where the wound had been on his face. No trace of it left. "That feels like a safe assumption."

"Will he come for Livia?"

It sickened me what Ezra altered her, maybe without her knowledge. "She's pregnant, which makes her a project. He'll want to know the results of his experiment."

"She and Natasha both pregnant. What a bizarre world."

"Yes, and we don't know what Calidora and Ezra were doing to them." *But we will love the children and keep them safe.*

"One born. One created. They should be sterile."

"Should, but yet they both conceived," I said. "I heard the heartbeat from Natasha's baby earlier." *A baby. Natasha is going to have a baby.* A little sadness crept in that it wouldn't be me, but my happiness for her and Killian pushed it away.

"Throwing us into an ice age wasn't enough? Now, they are playing with genetics." Vin said, his voice loaded with disgust.

"The two events tie together. They wanted control, but the endgame is a mystery."

"Is it?" Vin scooted to the edge of the bed. "They are building an army."

"They have the Rogues," I said. "It doesn't get much more brutal than them."

"It's not cold brutality they are seeking. They are looking for control. If they can give the created vampires something the born vampires no longer can, they have a powerful mechanism to leverage," he said.

"It gives them power. That doesn't sound like something Ezra would relinquish," I said. "Unless he gets to pick and choose who will conceive." *What was Father doing?*

"Like he has decided who lives and dies? There's something in it for him."

"I remember seeing some work in the lab on infertility, but it was all centered on born vampires. He doesn't consider created vampires our equals."

Vin stood up. He didn't sway or shake. His body recovered from the incident. "Maybe he's changed his opinion. Or maybe he's using the created vampires as incubators."

I put one of the gauze pads with puss and blood on it in a bag to analyze for the poison later.

"Holy ..." I paused, absorbing what Vin said. "Do you think he's using them as surrogates to be raised by the elite vampires?"

He nodded. "That's a good possibility, and Calidora is right there in the midst of it with him."

"He's a real bastard." I sank down on the bed, suddenly tired. "But Natasha is a born vampire. It doesn't make sense."

"Natasha and Livia must know something."

"I don't think they know much," I said. "I trust nothing that comes out of Livia's mouth, but Natasha would have said something if she knew."

"I wonder how many more are out there." Vin squeezed my knee.

"That's a good question." I stood up. " Are you up for a walk?"

"Pass me another bag of blood, and I will be."

CHAPTER 30

JOSIE

The next day, I asked our small circle to regroup and walk through what we knew about the pregnancies to see if we could determine Ezra's plan. Natasha perched across from me at the table in the big office. Killian sat next to her. His arm draped lazily around the back of the chair. Vin sat on the other side with me. We tried to understand the experiments she suffered through.

"They gave me shots that were supposed to boost my special skills," Natasha said.

"Did you notice anything when you were given them? Any changes?" Vin asked.

"Not really. I was a little achy after they administered it, but it didn't last long." She rubbed her arm as if ached from the shot still.

"You didn't hear anything or see anything else?"

"No, I was just trying to stay alive. What does Livia say?" She looked from one of us to the other. "You haven't asked her?"

"We don't trust her," I said.

"There was a time you didn't trust me, and I was in a similar situation. Kind of hypocritical to give me a chance and not her."

"It's different, Natasha," I said. "She was my father's spy. He groomed her to be elusive and deceitful, and she admitted to killing Steven Smith."

"And that differs from me how?" She placed her hands on the table and pushed back. The chair scraped the floor. "She's pregnant and alone."

"She's not like you. She still sides with Ezra," I said.

"Geez. Let me at her again. I'll get the answers, and then we know we can trust them. You need to recognize the difference between someone scared versus loyal. Here's a clue. She's not loyal to him." Natasha slammed the door behind her.

I shook my head. *What just happened here? Why was she so upset?* I reached for the doorknob, but a large hand covered it.

"I'll go, Empress."

"Yes, as you should, Killian." I side stepped out of his way.

He closed the door in a softer click than Natasha.

"She's right, you know," Vin said.

I met his eyes. "She is. We're jaded." I crossed my arms. "Or at least I am, but I don't trust Livia."

"I still don't trust her so I guess I'm jaded too."

"But you were willing to give Natasha a chance before I was."

"You came around."

"If I'm going to be the Empress, I have to be open to see all sides. I feel like I have to keep reminding myself of that."

Vin rubbed my arms. His hands slid around my shoulders and pulled me to him. "You grew up differently. Change takes time. The important thing is that you want to lead the world into a new future. A better future."

"I do. I really do, but I can't stop wondering if I am the right person to do it."

His fingertips traced a path up my neck until his thumbs rested on either side of my jaw. "You are exactly the right person, because you understand what is at stake and what can happen."

I looked over his shoulder, unable to agree. "What about the pregnancies? We're going to have to protect Natasha and Livia, and I'm not exactly thrilled about the latter." I bit down on my lip. "What if that thing growing in her belly is my brother or sister?"

He laid a finger against my cheek and turned my face back to his. "That thing is a baby, regardless of how it was created. If it is your brother or sister, wouldn't you rather the child be here where you can influence it?"

A sickening pit formed in my stomach. "There's no telling what my father did to it. It might be pure evil."

"And it might just be an innocent child caught up in a crazed man's world. Not unlike someone else I know."

Was that me? I didn't think of myself as an innocent. I'd done Ezra's bidding for years, so maybe I was. "You're right. It doesn't erase the uneasiness though."

"Why are you so much more accepting of Natasha's pregnancy? My mother had a hand it that, and she's no better than your father."

"I don't know," I said.

"You do."

I did. Natasha is my friend, and I support her. I couldn't fake sympathy for Livia or her pregnancy. I despised Livia, and I needed to figure out how to get past that to make sure she delivers safely.

"I need to be alone if you don't mind." I stepped back out of his arms. "Can we catch up later after Natasha interrogates Livia?"

His eyes narrowed. "Of course," he said. "My Empress." He spun on his heels.

I wasn't trying to dismiss him like that. I seemed to piss everyone off today.

"Vin, don't be like that." The door slammed in my face.

Damn it. The last thing I wanted to do was hurt him.

I dropped down into the big chair. Short of a truth test, which could be risky with the baby, there wasn't anything that could make me trust Livia. Natasha didn't know her like I did, but Vin and Killian did. *Is Natasha's opinion enough for me to give Livia a chance?*

Papers on the desk blurred. My mind drifted to a conversation Ezra and I had. He was adamant I would have children someday.

Bawwnk. Bawwnk. The alarm, hooked up right before we left for the Southern Compound, sounded. *Fuck. This is it. Bawwnk. Bawwnk.* I pushed to my feet and pommeled over the desk. The door slung open, and Vin filled the space.

"You're okay." His eyes closed for a brief moment. "We're being attacked."

"Rogues?"

"None so far."

"Where are they attacking?"

"The far side of the courtyard by the back entrance."

"You warn Natasha and Killian and get them out of the basement. They will be cornered." It hit me he'd be cornered too. "Be safe. Vin. I can't do this without you." I took his hand and placed it over my useless heart.

"Where will you go or do I have to even ask?" He didn't challenge me.

"To our people." I smiled. "I love you, Vin."

He nodded. His hand moved from my chest to my cheek. "I love you too."

We crossed paths and sprinted in opposite directions.

I tried to formulate what I would say to rally my people. Words evaded me like hidden gems in a cave. Every step took me closer, and I prayed my brain would work once I got there.

People gathered. *Correction.* Soldiers gathered at the weak point where what I assumed were Ezra's troops pounded on the other side. No one had noticed me yet. I took a deep breath. The motion relaxed me. I repeated it.

My voice came out like a megaphone. "I want you to know what you are fighting for."

Men, women, children. *Why are there children here?* A tight ball formed in my throat. I swallowed hard against it. They all looked at me.

"My father did unforgivable things to humans and vampires. He needs to pay for his crimes. However, he has enabled a vampire to procreate. For the first time in decades, a vampire is pregnant." No need to tell them one was a created vampire or two vampires were pregnant. "We need him alive until we understand how he solved the infertility issue."

Silence. Everything was silent except for the rhythmic bang on the wall. It beat like a drum that I thought might be a death march tonight.

"Stay strong. Stay alive. I need five volunteers to round up the children and take them out of the fight area." Two male and two female humans stepped forward and one vampire woman followed them. It was Agata, my maid from the Southern Compound.

"Agata." I embraced her quickly.

"Empress." She lowered her eyes. "I'll take care of the children."

"I'd trust very few more than you. Please go now." I motioned for them to go toward the muster point. I'd let her know she could call me Josie instead of Empress later.

"They threaten our safety. They threaten our newfound sovereignty. We will fight. Be mindful of Ezra and take him alive." My urge to throw my hand up for a battle cry thwarted by the vast hole in me from the risk. I laid my arm across my chest and kneeled to my people. Unheard of for an emperor or an empress. My mother, so full of compassion and love for her people, had never done it. I closed my eyes tight, unsure of how it would be received.

A rustle at my feet drew my eyes open. Two women knelt in front of me, and two men on either side of them. My gaze moved out over the crowd to find everyone on their knees. Not the best place for an army about to battle. I stood and thrust my fist into the air.

"Josephine!" A man in the back jutted his fist up.

"Josephine!" One woman in front of me said and repeated his actions.

One by one, the entire group did it. Tears formed in my eyes, but I refused to let the pink liquid run down my cheeks. A lump formed in my throat. "We will have victory!" I yelled through it.

"Take the defensive formation we practiced and take only the lives you must." My voice, forceful and strong, boomed out over the crowd.

Each vampire took their position to cover the area where Ezra's army pounded against the wall. The battering stopped. Silence filled the space all around us. An eerie sensation slivered up my spine. It called me. I turned towards the strange pull.

"I taught you better than this, Josephine." Ezra and his elite guards stood behind me.

The sight of him left enraged me. My assumption proved true. "Father."

Natasha and Livia's hands chained to their waist and shackles on their ankles like prisoners. Vin and Killian, on their knees, beaten to the point the damage would take time to heal. Guards on either side of them with long swords drawn and angled at their necks.

Ezra controlled the existence of my family. My body shook. No way to save all of them without sacrifice, and I wasn't willing to sacrifice any of them. *Bastard. Only one thing would resolve this.*

"Let them go, and I will go with you," I paused. "Father." My voice unrecognizable to me, strong yet full of hate.

CHAPTER 31

JOSIE

The smile on Ezra's face sickened me. It renewed my goals, and a planned formed. Forgiveness for me would have to come later.

"I'll accept your terms," Ezra said. "With an exception." He swept his hand towards Vin and Killian. "These two you can keep if you allow me to leave peacefully with the mares."

Livia gave an almost unnoticeable shake to her head.

Did he say what I think he said? My chin jutted up and eyes narrowed on him. "Did you just refer to them as mares?"

"Broodmares. Yes. They will be used to usher in our new age."

"They are strong vampire women. The fact that you think you can use them and refer to them as livestock proves you are unfit." My fangs sunk into my tongue. Blood and venom pooled in my mouth. "I challenge you to the Vampire Blood Rite to Rule." I smeared the blood on my lips across the palm of my hand and extended it to him.

"You do realize it is a fight to the death, and you will not win."

"You've underestimated me my whole life, so go right ahead and continue." My hand hung in the air. If he refused, the rite would not bind, and we would have no choice but to face them in war. This was the only way to save lives. He had to accept.

Ezra repeated my actions and clasped my hand.

A burn seared my hand where our blood met and sealed the oath we made. To the death. *His death. I spared him once and not again.*

"By full moon night, complete the blood rite," Ezra said.

"One must die or both here will lie," I finished.

"Lucky for us the full moon is tonight."

This did not escape me when I made the challenge. No one had issued the challenge in my lifetime or his, as far as I knew. It was ancient and binding with old magic that was believed to only exists in small doses now. The binding of the rite was the first time I was aware of it. Vampires who saw their family rule entirely too long and become corrupt created the Vampire Blood Rite. Sadly, the corruption did not end until old magic died out among the masses. They prepared for years for the task.

"You have my word and binding oath. Release them until after the rite."

"No, I think you would front an escape attempt even at the expense of your own life."

He's not wrong. I would. "The difference between you and me is that I would not save my own skin at the expense of those I lead."

"Is that what you think?" He shook his head. "It is so much bigger than you or these people. It is our future."

"A future you want to create by culling a group that will bend to you without question."

He took one large stride into my personal space.

I stood resolute and firm.

"No, Josephine. These women carry vampire children who will not require blood. All the strengths of our race and none of the weaknesses."

My stomach flipped. My hands shook. "How can you know that?"

"Have you not heard the strong heartbeats? These children live."

"And are they immortal?"

"Our studies show they are, but we will not know the proper answers until they are born. It will be years before we know if the girls can reproduce."

"Girls? You already know the sex." I peered around him at Natasha and Livia. Both had glazed over looks.

"Yes. We made it so they would only form female embryos."

"How? Sperm determines the sex." I probed on, unsure how much information he would divulge.

"We manipulated the eggs to mutate."

"You genetically engineered a new race of vampires, and they can only be female." I paused. A sour taste formed in my mouth at what he had done. "Because altering the DNA of immortal beings sounds like such a good idea. Do you not even begin to see the flaw in this?"

"There is no flaw. Only new life. Better vampires. Stronger vampires."

"You don't know what you are going to get from these test tube creations."

Natasha made a whimper noise.

I closed my eyes. *That was cold even for me.* "Sorry, Natasha and Livia. I didn't mean it like that." *Except I did, and I hated myself for it.* I couldn't look at Vin. He would no doubt feel shame at my reaction.

"You've put your life on the line for those creations. Too bad you will lose," Ezra said.

"Enough of this dancing around. We will return when the moon is full to finish the rite."

"So eager to try to kill me, or so eager to die?"

"Neither," I said. "Which is the difference between you and me."

"We will wait here for dark."

I gestured to my friends. "The four of them to spend the remaining time with me. You can post men nearby if you don't trust my word."

Ezra nodded. "If you enter the house, they will go with you. The ma..." He stumbled. "Livia and Natasha will not be allowed out of the guard's sight."

I nodded. In no position to negotiate, but I couldn't leave them under his eye. "And your word that no harm will come to the humans or vampires on this compound." I pushed.

"Until midnight."

"That will do."

I SLAMMED my hands down on the desk. Pink tears threatened the brim of my eyes. "I'm sorry. I can't beat him, and this is our best option."

"You shouldn't have challenged him to that ancient rite. It's bound by the old laws. That was stupid," Livia said.

I ignored Livia's pessimism, but it was hard to deny my bold choice might only be a delay to Ezra's plan.

Natasha crossed her arms. "Can we put her and the guards outside?"

"I agreed that both of you would stay in the guards' sight."

"Fine. I'll go out in the hallway with her and the guards. You three need to have a serious strategy convo, and there are too many elephants in the room."

"Take chairs for them. They should not have to stand in the hallway," Killian said. His wounds healed, but his anger remained unquenched.

"We're vampires, dearest. We don't get tired, and our ankles don't swell." Natasha kissed his cheek. She reached a hand out to Livia and pulled her into the hall. The guards followed. Natasha smiled around the door and closed it with a small click.

"You can't match him in a battle of strength, but blood binds this rite. Our ancestors often tried to make it a challenge of brawn. It's not. It is about strategy and magic," Killian said.

"I don't have any magic. Those ways have long been gone from our people." *Who knows if the magic really even existed? It could just be myths and legends, but it certainly felt real when the bond of the rite sealed.*

"We can awaken it in you," Killian said.

"I doubt that. If it were that easy, there would be more than the tiny traces we see, which could be imagination too." I paused. "What if I use poison? That's strategic."

"The binding of the rite will not allow it. It will backfire on you," Vin said.

I turned in his direction. He had dark circles under his eyes. His shoulders slumped forward. "Have you studied this challenge?"

"The library at the Southern Compound had a few books.."

Vin met my eyes. "I don't understand why Ezra would agree to it, though. He knows one of you must die."

"We all, eventually, become expendable to him. Even his own daughter." I closed my eyes for the briefest of moments to push the old hurt back down.

"He's always protected you. Why now?"

"The coup. Pregnant vampires. And I'm standing between him and what he wants. Didn't you hear what he said out there?" I covered my stomach as if it could protect Natasha and Livia's babies. "He's done something to Natasha and Livia's eggs. The babies will not require blood, but they are still vampire. At least that is what he thinks."

"They are the test subjects."

"Yes." Disgust rolled in my stomach. Vomit threatened to barrel up. "I can't let him raise those babies. Promise me you and Killian will get them out of here if he succeeds."

Killian stood near the door. Faint sounds of Natasha's voice drifted into the room.

Vin's face grave. He took my hands in his. "You will be the one who triumphs."

"I am the underdog," I said. "Promise me, Vin."

He dropped his head. Pink glistened in the corner of his eyes. "I promise."

"I want you to know that I loved you even when I was ignorant and stubborn. I never could have really let you go. Not in my heart."

"Stop. That's not you, Josie. You do not give up."

"I'm not." I forced a smile. Father fought many battles, and I'd been raised in a time when warfare had passed. We trained and fought Rogues since the ice age, but nothing compared to full-scale wars father had experienced.

Vin leaned in close. His nose rested against mine. "I love

you, and we will have our own babies someday, whether they are like us or not."

Hope. He'd given me hope so many times. He inspired hope, if only for a moment in me.

His lips pressed against mine. Softer than usual, he caressed in a gentle touch.

I pushed back against his chest. *Love. I want it. I want it from Vin.* "You shouldn't–"

"Stop," he said. Softer this time. "Stop thinking you don't deserve love, because you do."

"Do I? I'm the heir to a horrible history. And I'm going to build on that history by killing my own father."

"You are doing what needs to be done for a better future. That future will be defined by your actions now and not your father's. You are going to be an influential leader."

His confidence in me like a newly created vampire fixated on its first prey. "You need to make a statement and an entrance that shows strength."

"What? Like wear leather?"

Vin's eyebrows shot up and a grin spread across his face. "Exactly."

"It's not going to make much difference with Ezra. His fangs are long, and his strike is swift."

"It's the impression it will give. Look like a warrior."

Vin opened the closet in the adjacent bedroom for the first time. A benzine-like smell similar to mothballs hit my nostrils.

"I'm not sure I'm the leather-clad warrior type." I covered my nose and held my breath. *It's not like I needed it, anyway.*

"Whose room was this?"

"Uncle Jim's. Why?" I peered around him.

Only two garments hung there. A t-shirt brazened with

the slogan *Love Is Love* and a pink and white seersucker romper with Gay Pride flags on it.

I laughed. "Evidently, the romper was too tacky to take. The t-shirt is cute though."

"Why would a man ever wear a..." he held it up "Romper?"

I laughed harder at the terrible garment. "I can't recall that every being in style, but love does strange things to us all."

Vin gave me a little side eye.

"Uncle Jim was in love with a human. It was an important message when the humans were still the majority of the population. Vampires love who they love and don't care about gender. Humans were not so understanding of that with each other." They had beat each other and berated each other over who should love who. Always judging each other. *How we looked at the created vampires wasn't that different.*

"I remember," Vin said. "This isn't what I had in mind for a warrior empress though."

"Probably not going to strike fear in Ezra, but I'm keeping the t-shirt. We need these kinds of reminders." I tugged my shirt off and pulled the gray t-shirt with rainbow lettering over my head.

"Fits you well." Vin's eyes focused on my breasts. "I like how the L wraps around--"

"Before you get any ideas, let's go find that warrior empress armor."

"Too late."

I lifted his chin so his eyes would meet mine. "Armor. Focus."

"Oh, I'm focused." His arms caged me against the wall.

"Vin, this is serious." I could duck under his arm. Could.

"I agree." His head dipped down.

Lips pressed against mine as gentle as a breeze.

He pulled back. His hand pressed against my chest where my heart was. "I'm here. Always, Josie. In the moonlight. In the daylight. In the darkest hours and the best still to come. Always."

"Careful. That might be a very long time."

"I'm counting on it." His lips found mine with hunger this time.

CHAPTER 32

The leather clad warrior garb was not my first choice. Vin insisted on it to convey the strength we bring with us as a group. I resembled an ancient roman soldier only all in leather and minus the headgear and shield. *A human would freeze to death in this outfit.*

The courtyard stood divided. The masses close to equal on either side. My father's army stood stoned face. My own forces lined up against them in somber poses.

Ezra waited in the center. "Since you made the challenge, I choose the form of battle. Sword will be our weapon today." He crooked two fingers at one of his men.

The vampire brought two swords forward.

Ezra selected one.

I waved away the one presented to me.

Vin held the one I brought from the Southern Compound in his palms. It was the one I'd chosen from the armory when we met there before the mission. I grasped the hilt and lifted it in a triumphant gesture. *Vin's idea.* The half of the crowd with us cheered. Vin stepped to the side with the others. His body stiff like mine would be if the situation was reversed.

"Poison?" Ezra inclined his head toward my weapon.

"I remind you so much of my mother. Right?" I hadn't tainted it with poison. Part of the history of the rite said it was not allowed. I might have taken the risk with myself, but not with my family. And that's what they were. Vin. Killian. Natasha. Maybe in time Livia would be too. Doubt it, but maybe.

"You do." He smiled. It wasn't pleasant at all. The iron scent of blood wafted toward me from his way. He'd gorged himself to prepare.

It should probably flatter me he thought he needed to in order to battle me.

Ezra wore no armor. Age and strength were his. Maybe he thought I would be stupid enough to make a mistake like poison.

"Till the end. This is my blood rite." Ezra spoke the words to start the fight. He rolled his neck.

"Till the end. This is my blood rite," I repeated. Old magic zinged through my body. I jerked and rolled my shoulders. *What the Hell? Wasn't old magic dead? Could there be a thread of it left?* I tucked that back to investigate if I survived.

Ezra held the sword in a rigid form.

I raised mine to meet his. *Clank.* They touched. Magic hummed down them. I'd never felt it before. The consequences didn't make magic, whether it was real or not, a viable option most of the time, but this was a desperate stand.

He extended his hand and sword out at his sides.

A trick to get me to strike first. My patience greater than his, I waited.

He dropped the sword at his side. The tip slid into the

ground like a sheath. He took a knee. "Take your victory, Josephine."

I narrowed my eyes at him. "There is no honor in a win without dignity."

"Victory was yours the moment we sealed the challenge."

"What do you mean?"

"I could never kill my own daughter."

"With your own hand, you mean? Killing family seems to be a task you order."

"No, not my daughter, who is with child."

A flutter rippled through my belly. I resisted the urge to touch my mid-section. *He's a liar.* "I'm not pregnant," I said.

"You are."

I swung my sword up to his throat. The tip pierced the skin under his chin. A thin red line leaked down his throat. "You experimented on me, too." *I'd gut him for lying. I might gut him anyway.*

"No."

"Then how am I pregnant?"

His eyes flicked towards Vin. "It's a natural pregnancy. The first in a hundred years."

My eyes met Vin's. My free hand rested on my stomach. *Could it be true?*

Vin's mouth gaped open. He rushed towards me.

I positioned myself between him and Ezra. Whether he spoke the truth or not, irrelevant at this point. I didn't want him to have a shot at Vin.

"Step back." I gazed over my shoulder. "This is still a binding rite, and we must finish."

Vin's face wrinkled. He placed a hand over the one on my belly. "Take care of our child." His voice strained. He backed away.

I drew my sword back from Ezra's neck. "How do you know I'm pregnant?"

"I sensed the child when you were at the Southern Compound. The same thing happened when your mother was pregnant with you."

A coldness settled in me, and I strained against a tired ache. "How do you sense it? And how do I not?"

"Maybe it's my age." He shrugged. "Wisdom beyond your years."

Not sure I believed him. *The chance I could be. Damn it. Is it a mind trick? No way am I pregnant.*

"Take your prize, daughter. It is my gift for our future," he said.

My body frozen in place with indecision. I feared becoming him, but I feared a world with him in it more. *How are either of these a win?* My fingers loosened on the cold metal.

"If you don't, we both die and you take the future of vampires with us."

Vin's voice came from what seemed like a great distance. Muffled and hard to hear. "Josie, you made the challenge. You must kill him."

Suddenly, I didn't want him to die, and I wanted him to live. To see what the world could be without his manipulations and tyranny. To see his grandchild, even if it was from a cage for the rest of his existence. Maybe even to see him change.

"The rite is flawed. We're already dead," I said.

"The rite guarantees an end if one is not given," Ezra said.

"We'll drain your blood," I said. "It would simulate death."

"It won't work," he said.

"You don't know that."

"I do. It is the way."

The sword dropped from my hand and clanked against his. Mine landed flat against his upright one.

"You might think you know I'm pregnant, but my gut says I'm right about this." A zing sizzled through my body. My extremities warmed, but my belly didn't. The strange sensation unnerved me.

Ezra jerked and fell back on his buttocks. His eyes bugged out and rolled back in his head. He slumped off to the side and thudded against the ground.

Did I do the right thing? A chill cooled the warmth, and my body shook. I knelt beside him and reached out.

"Don't touch him." Vin grabbed my hand.

"What just happened?" I looked up at Vin. My eyes burned.

"I think the rite claimed its payment."

"But we didn't battle," I said. A knot cinched up around my throat.

"You did in words." He dropped down. Arms wrapped around me from behind. He sealed me in a protective bubble.

I collapsed back against him. Tears flowed in a wave down my cheeks. Drawn forward, I leaned over Ezra. Pink liquid dripped onto his cheeks, but Vin held me at a distance so I could not touch.

The tears soaked into his skin instead of rolling off. "Did you see that? I've never seen that before."

"What?" Vin asked over my shoulder.

"My tears," I said. "They..." I struggled to find words.

He held tight with one and used the other to wipe some from my cheek. "It's normal to mourn. He was your father."

"No." I shook my head. "His skin absorbed my tears."

He leaned forward and looked at Ezra. His voice soft and barely audible. "I don't see anything, Josie. Maybe you imagined it."

"No, I saw it." I wrestled myself loose from his hold. My teeth ripped into my wrist, and I pressed it to his mouth.

Blood trickled through his lips. Not much made it before my skin healed. I bit down on my wrist and tore the skin open again and repeated it several times.

Vin's fingers covered the raised pink marks. "Stop. He's gone."

I leaned into him.

"Dry your eyes, Josephine."

My eyes sought out Vin's. The voice wasn't right. *Not his.* I looked at Ezra's body. Eyes closed. Red stained lips.

"Yes, it's me." Ezra wiped the blood from his lips on the back of his hand.

My shaky fingers covered my mouth. "Your still..." I placed a hand on his shoulder. "How?"

"I don't know." He propped himself up on an elbow. "But I have one bloody headache."

"You probably need blood," Vin said.

"No, Josephine needs to finish the job."

My conviction strengthened, and my body steadied. "I have no intentions of ending you," I said. "Enough vampires and humans have paid for your atrocities. You will live to see what happens when the world is set right."

Ezra stood up and looked around.

The crowd inched closer. Mouths gaped open.

Vin extended his hand to me and took me with him as he stood.

"The rite has been satisfied. Let's call a truce, Ezra."

Ezra found his footing without aid. "There was a time you called me Father."

"A time that passed in the same manner as my mother." I intended it to be brutal, like her death.

"And no truce can happen here. We are at odds with our beliefs. The people need one voice. Either mine or yours."

"If you do not want to be under my rule, you can take your guards and go north to the unclaimed lands."

"Those are terms for a truce, Josephine. No deals can be stricken."

"Why are you so obstinate?"

He stared at me. It was uncomfortable, like he waited for me to answer the question myself.

If he didn't agree to my terms, I didn't have another move planned. I hadn't thought I would survive the night. Not really. A full moon high in the sky, and we'd both lived. *Why?*

"Take what I am offering," I said. "The position might not present itself again."

"I will take my leave. The regret will be yours when we meet again if you do not end it today."

"The regret will be yours if you come after me, my people, or my family again."

"Your family?" Ezra laughed. "My child, you will only understand what family really is when you face death."

"Your wrong. Family is made up of those truest to you. Those who make you a better person. The ones who stand beside you, not against you."

Ezra took three giant steps and leaped the wall. A show of strength. His men filed out the gate Killian opened.

Ezra's departure left lightness, like a weight was gone, even if it was temporary.

Vin pinned me to his side. "How long do you think we have to prepare?"

"He'll regroup and build up his forces, but he will return. The pregnancies are too important to him." I slipped my arm around his waist. "He's not one to give up, and we need to make sure Livia and Natasha have guards at all times."

"And you," he said.

"We don't even know I'm really pregnant. He could have been playing his usual tricks."

"No, he was willing to sacrifice his life. He wouldn't do that unless he was sure."

I sucked in air into my undead lungs. A tiny heartbeat resonated up from my belly to my ears.

I'm pregnant.

CHAPTER 33

JOSIE

L ivia and Natasha met us in the office after their appointments with the vampire physician.

"The pregnancies are advancing much faster than normal," Killian said. His hand laced with Natasha's.

"Except yours, Josie," Livia said.

"I'm not as far along as you to," I said. At least development wise, I wasn't.

"We need to be prepared for the fact that Ezra and Calidora might have messed up." Natasha didn't meet anyone's eyes as she spoke.

"What do you mean messed up?" Livia took a step in front of her.

"These are not normal vampire babies inside of us. There is no denying it."

"Hers is though." Livia pivoted towards me. "How is it you come up pregnant the traditional way while we end up with Frankenstein babies?"

Vin stepped between us. "Back up, Livia."

They looked almost full term in the matter of a few months,

and I barely looked pregnant. No denying the outer differences, which made it hard to deny there were internal differences, too.

"You think I'd hurt a pregnant woman?" Livia spat at Vin's feet. She stomped out of the room and slammed the door behind her.

Only when Vin stepped aside did I see Killian placed Natasha behind him as well.

"She has no one here," Natasha said.

"That's her own doing," Vin said.

"She doesn't trust any of us, because we don't trust her. We need to try harder." I put my hand on Natasha's belly. "These little miracles need us to be better people for their future."

Natasha smiled. "I've been craving blood more often. I think it will happen soon."

"The birth?"

"Yes, the time is near."

A foot kicked the spot where my hand rested. *Oh!* I smiled. "Someone seems to be ready to meet his or her parents."

"Her. It's a girl," Natasha said, her voice soft. "Just like Ezra said."

"He doesn't know everything."

"He knows enough," she said.

I squeezed her hand. "She will be fine."

She rubbed her round belly. "If something should happen to me, promise me you will help Killian."

"Nothing is going to happen to you," Killian said.

Natasha grimaced at me.

I held her hand. "I promise."

She squeezed my hand back.

"A promise you will not need to keep." Killian's careful eyes on Natasha even as he spoke to me.

"I'm going to check the birthing rooms and make sure they are ready. Come with me?" Natasha hooked her arm through Killian's.

He opened the door and scooped her up in his arms before they crossed the threshold.

Natasha squealed in delight. Her laughter echoed in the hallway.

"No sign of Ezra and his army?" I asked once they were out of earshot.

"No. Not a sign of him since you sent him on his way."

I dropped down into a chair. "Don't you think it's strange that he has just disappeared?"

"He wants those babies, so he will be back. We're ready for him. The training has been solid."

I nodded and relaxed some. "The training has been strong. I have faith in our forces. What about your mother?"

Vin winced. "She's not my mother."

He hated acknowledging she birthed him. "Sorry. Calidora. Have you had any sightings of her?"

"No, none of her either, and that worries me more than Ezra."

"Why?"

"She's even more evil than him."

"I don't think that's possible."

He wiped his hands over his face. "I felt it, Josie. When we were there. And I haven't been able to shake it since then. It's like a piece of it is stuck inside me."

I blinked a few times. He hadn't shared much of his time there. My hand rested against his cheek.

"We'll handle it," I said.

"I want you and the baby safe. Nothing else matters."

"I'm safe. You're safe. The baby is safe," I said, trying to convince myself too.

"Why do I feel like we're not, then?"

I pulled him to me and wrapped his hands around my waist. "Because you have something worth fighting for. We both do," I said. "Natasha and Killian do too."

"And Livia?"

"She may not realize it, but she does too. I'd fight for her and her child as I would for any of you, and I'd expect you to do the same."

"Do you think she would fight for you? For all of us?"

"That doesn't matter. We do what we know is right even when others don't."

He wrapped me up in a hug. Tight against his body, he turned his mouth to my ear. "Don't do anything stupid."

"That goes both ways."

He swept me up into his arms like Killian had Natasha. I laughed all the way to our room.

KNUCKLES RAPPED against the door of our bedroom.

I sat up and pulled the sheet over me.

Vin was on his feet and at the door. He cracked the door open and peered around it.

"Sorry to disturb you, but Natasha is in labor," the guard said.

"Thank you. We'll join them in the infirmary shortly." Vin shut the door.

As soon as the lock clicked, I jumped to my feet and threw on my clothes. I giggled. *Natasha was about to me a mom. I was going to be a mom, too. We are going to be moms.*

"I've never seen a vampire baby born." Vin pulled his shirt over his head.

"Neither have I." My stomach did flip-flops. We weren't going to have just one baby in the compound, but three at some point.

Vin and I ran to the birthing rooms with the same enthusiasm we'd ran to the bedroom with earlier. Natasha had done an excellent job directing the build of the birthing rooms. The sterile scents still surrounded us, but the plain white colors replaced now with the soft warm yellows, blues, and pinks.

The tray of tools needed for a vampire birth, archaic looking instruments, but necessary if the delivery became difficult. Our bodies didn't labor the same as a human. It wasn't uncommon to need a diamond tip saw to cut through the amniotic sac. Vampire women died in childbirth from a distressed fetus when it ripped through the sac and crushed their heart.

"Where's Livia?"

"She wasn't in her room," one of the guards answered.

"Thank you. Can you wait outside the doors, please?" I asked. I leaned over to Vin. "That's concerning."

"She's probably in the garden. She's been spending a lot of time there."

I nodded. *That concerns me more.*

Killian stood on one side of the bed and held Natasha's hand. His brows pinched together, and his face whiter than any vampire I'd ever seen.

I moved to the other side and took her free hand. "Are you ready for this?"

She wrinkled her forehead. "Is it normal I am excited and scared?"

"I imagine it probably is." I smiled at her. "You are going to do great."

Her grip on my hand tightened. She groaned. "Shit. That hurts."

The machine ticked away beside the bed. The monitors had been placed in a storage closet. They were in terrible shape, but we got them working in time.

The doctor walked up to the bed and patted her leg. "It won't be long now." He'd delivered babies before the ice age. *Thank goodness he is here.*

A scream ripped through the air the other side of the wall. I turned in that direction. Another screamed followed. I swallowed hard.

"Livia came in about thirty minutes ago," the doctor said. "She'll deliver first, I believe. I'm going to check on her, and I'll be back soon."

Natasha's eyes were wide. "Did you hear her scream?"

"Everything is going to be fine," I said. My legs weakened, but I forced them into a steady position.

A scream loud enough to deafen a human bounced off the walls. I cringed at the sharpness.

Natasha's nails dug into my hand.

Silence followed.

The doctor came back into the room with a coat covered in blood. He shrugged out of it, and a nurse assisted him into a clean one. He stood stiff backed and no smile or emotion on his face.

Panic gripped me.

"Did Livia have her baby?"

He nodded, but said nothing else.

I wished I hadn't asked. No baby had cried when her

screams went silent. Whatever he wasn't telling us was not good.

The doctor sat on a stool at the end of the bed. "Natasha, when I tell you to push, you will lean forward like in the practice sessions."

"Wh-what happened in Livia's room?" Her voice shook like my legs were.

"Let's focus on you right now," he said.

I couldn't speak. My mind raced through scenarios. *Would Natasha and the baby be okay? Were Livia and her baby okay?*

The nurse's eye was on the machines. She nodded to the doctor.

"Push," he said.

Natasha lifted her back off the bed and leaned forward. A grunt came from her.

"Harder," the doctor said.

"Aaahhhhh!" She let out a gut wrenching scream.

My knees almost gave way. "You can do this, Natasha."

Her eyes widened. "I don't think I can."

"The baby is not moving. We need to get it out," the doctor said.

The nurse slid the tray of tools over to the bedside. She picked up a syringe and measured a liquid into it.

"What are you giving her?"

"It's a poison that will dull the pain for her. She might hallucinate."

I studied the color of the liquid. "Jimsonweed?" They used it in small doses in the past for difficult births.

"Yes." The nurse poised the needle at Natasha's vein in the bend of her arm.

"She had a reaction to jimsonweed a few months ago," I

said. "Through accidental contact. It would have been during the early stages of her pregnancy."

"She'll be fine," the nurse said. "It's diluted with stabilizers."

Stabilizers? How do you stabilize it like that?

"You all need to leave the room." The doctor's face ashened even for a vampire.

"I'm not going anywhere," I said.

Vin took my free hand. "Let the doctor do his job, Josie." I didn't budge.

Natasha squeezed my hand so hard I thought the bones might snap.

"I'm sure as hell not leaving," Killian said.

"Very well." The doctor nodded to the nurse.

She slipped the needle into the vein. The liquid made a slow descent from the syringe.

Natasha leaned her back against the bed. Her eyes rolled back in her head. The grip on my hand loosened. She laid still. *Did they give her too much? It should make her euphoric, not out cold.*

The doctor slid the blade across Natasha's skin. The metallic odor of vampire blood hit my nose. My nostrils flared in revolt. *Baby doesn't like it.* I rubbed my belly. *It's not for us.*

The doctor's slice held open by the nurse while the doctor cut into the protective bubble around the baby. Fluid oozed out of Natasha's belly and onto the bed and all the way to the floor. *Drip. Drip. Drip.*

The baby hung upside-down by the feet in the doctor's hands. Blood and amniotic fluid covered it. No sounds. No movements.

Killian's head dropped. He laid his head on Natasha's shoulder. She was still out.

The poison.

I had an overwhelming sense of dread. "Did the same thing happen to Livia's baby?"

The doctor nodded and handed the tiny, lifeless body to the nurse.

She wrapped it in a towel.

"Stop. Let me see the baby," I said.

The nurse held the baby close. "There is no life."

"Give her to me." I held out my arms.

She put the tiny girl in my hands, and I ran straight to my new poison lab in the same wing. It might be a long shot, but I had to try.

I placed my friend's baby on the table. My fingers worked quickly to mix up the proportions for one so tiny. The stirrer clinked against the glass. I took an eyedropper and filled it. Three drops into the baby's mouth.

Tears threatened my eyes. *This baby will live.*

Tiny fingers and hands twitched. A cry erupted from her. Her scream a sweet sound to my ears.

Heat filled my eyes. Tears spilled over. I scooped up the infant and hurried back to the birthing room with the antidote in my hand.

"Give this to Natasha." I handed the beaker to Vin. "Use the dropper to administer it. A full one."

Killian met me halfway around the bed. "Is she?"

I choked through fresh tears. "Meet your daughter?" She fit in the space between his hand and elbow.

Natasha coughed. Her voice hoarse. "Where's my baby girl?"

Killian placed her in Natasha's arms.

"My little Emilia Josephine," she said.

"It fits her perfectly." Killian pressed his lips to Natasha's forehead, and then Emilia's.

"I'm honored to share a name with your daughter," I said.

I inspected the incision the doctor made. It started to heal. He'd given her too much poison. A vampire healer should've known how much was enough.

"We need to give this to Livia and her baby. Where did the doctor and nurse go?" I looked around for them.

"To Livia's room," Vin said.

I took the antidote from his hand. "Hopefully, it will save her baby, too."

I darted the few steps to the next room to find it empty. Dark red stains on the bed. Crimson puddles on the floor. No Livia. No baby. No staff. They were gone.

"Livia?" I called into the hallway.

Vin joined me. "They're not in the room?"

"They are all gone. Livia, the baby, the doctor, and the nurse. This smells rotten to me."

Vin took a few steps. "They kidnapped them."

"Yes, and I think they would have done the same to Natasha and Emilia if we hadn't been there."

"We'll send the guards after them," Vin said.

"It's bound to be my father." I sighed. "Tell the guards to keep their distance. I don't want to endanger the baby."

"The further they get away, the harder it will be to find them."

"We know where they are going. Straight to my father."

"Or my mother. Maybe spies among us and didn't know it. That sounds more like her."

"It should be me going," I said. "Damn it. We can't leave Natasha."

Vin's hand rested on my lower back. "I'll send our best guards."

"Do it. Tell them not to come back without her."

I entered Natasha's room and found Killian on the bed next to her. One big happy family.

Natasha looked up, and her smile faded. "They took the baby."

"And Livia too it seems."

She shifted to get up.

Killian's hand pressed against her shoulder. Firm but gentle, to push her back against the bed.

"Vin is sending the best guards after them."

"Will it be enough?" She asked.

"I don't know." We had to save them, but it was like hunting for a single drop of blood on a mountain.

"We should go after her and the baby," Natasha said. "You and me. We are the only ones that understand."

Killian's body stiffened next to her.

"We have other obligations." I glanced at baby Emilia in her arms. "If something happened to you, what would become of your daughter."

My hand fell to my belly. Risk was part of vampire life, but the decision on whether or not to take the risk changed when babies came into the picture.

"I don't even know what to feed her," Natasha said. "Will she drink blood or milk? Pretty sure there isn't any milk coming out of me."

"Why don't we focus on figuring that out and let Vin focus on getting Livia back?"

"I'll get some blood from the stores," Killian said.

"While you are out there, ask if the human woman that has the infant if she will be a wet nurse."

SUSAN PERSON

"I will not give her a choice if it comes to that."

"Let's try the blood first," Natasha said. "She is my daughter." She smiled.

Killian's body relaxed.

Natasha's smile the antidote to all his stress.

He stood up from the bed. His lips pressed against her forehead and then Emilia's. The door clicked shut behind him.

"If the guards don't come back by morning, I will go myself," I said.

"Vin will freak if you go. I was stupid to fight pregnant, Josie." Natasha snuggled Emilia closer to her. "Look at this beautiful angel. If I'd caused any harm to her, I wouldn't be able to live with myself, and you will feel the same."

"I can't let them have Livia or her baby. It's my duty."

"And it's your duty to protect the baby inside you."

"Our bodies are fortresses. I believe you said something similar in a battle."

"And I was wrong. It was a stupid risk."

The door creaked open. Killian emerged with enough blood for five vampires.

Natasha's laugh startled me.

My own laughter followed.

"What?"

"That's a lot of blood for a baby," I said.

"We don't know how much she eats. Besides, Natasha will need some for recovery."

"We don't have any bottles," she said.

"I thought of that. I borrowed one from the humans." He produced the bottle from the bend of his arm.

"Let's see what happens then."

Killian held the blood and bottle at arm's length in my direction. His hands shook.

I put my hands up to form a wall between us. "No, sir. This is your child. You need to learn how to take care of your newborn."

He turned to Natasha.

"Just gave birth. Holding the baby. You've got this." She shot him a grin.

Killian tore open the blood bag and filled the glass bottle to the top.

Natasha held the baby out to him.

"You want me to feed her too?"

"She's your daughter," Natasha laughed.

He cradled the baby in his forearm with the head supported at the bend of his elbow.

"Squeeze the tip to get a little blood on it first," Natasha said.

Killian followed her instructions.

The baby drank the blood, but only about four ounces.

"Is she okay?" Killian's eyebrows pursed together.

"She's just sleeping. Look at her eyes." Her little eyeballs moved back and forth under the lids.

"That's the sweetest sight I've ever seen," I said.

"Right. See what you have to look forward to?"

"Yes, I do." I squeezed her hand. "I'm going to find Vin, but I'll check on you later."

I stopped in Livia's room again for a look around. The poison syringe still on the metal table. *Ezra did this. We will find him, and he will pay.*

CHAPTER 34

JOSIE - VIN

I sat on the couch in the apartments she and Killian shared. The baby advanced at a pace quicker than expected. Two months after she was born, she crawled.

"She's just perfect, Natasha," I said.

"If she will slow down..." She didn't finish her thought. "You are glowing."

"It feels so slow compared to you and Livia." I rubbed my hands on my belly. It stuck out enough I looked pregnant.

"Any word on Livia and her baby?"

"No. We pick up a little scent here and there, but nothing substantial." I didn't blame the guards. My father was good at covering his tracks.

"Does your gut say it was Ezra or Calidora?"

"Both."

A soft knock from knuckles on her door drew my attention.

"Come in," she said.

The guard cracked the door. "Vin is requesting you in the main office, Empress."

"Thank you," I said to him. I turned back to Natasha and Emilia. Patted the baby's back. "I'll check on you later."

"We always appreciate your visits, Empress." Natasha drew out the last word.

"Don't you dare start that, too." I smiled and hugged her. In such a short time, we became family. This bond between us held stronger than it ever did with Ezra.

VIN CLOSED the door to the office. "We found something."

"What?" I leaned back in the chair and rested my hands underneath the pooch.

"Signs in the far north, near what was Chicago." He sat on the corner of the desk. His eyes darted to my belly and back to my eyes.

"It's so far away from any human sightings. It must be my father."

"And he has Livia and her baby."

I knew it. I knew he was behind it. The blood I had for lunch threatened to come up. "We need to get them."

"Are you sure they want to be rescued?"

"Who wouldn't want to be rescued from my father?" I rubbed my belly. There wasn't anything I wouldn't do to keep my father from harming a child. *Please don't let him have harmed Livia's baby.* Nausea waved over me.

Vin put his hand on my belly and spread his fingers. "You will be sitting this one out."

"I'm not fragile glass. My body is like Fort Knox was a hundred years ago."

"Sit it out for me then, so I don't have to worry about you and the baby."

I wanted to argue, but one of us needed to stay here. He was right. If it gave him peace of mind, I could do this for him. My thoughts scattered the bigger my stomach got. I'd probably do more good here than there.

"We'll be here waiting for you to return." I put my hand over his. "Words I never thought would come out of my mouth."

"Thank you." He leaned over and pressed his lips to mine. "Thank you for hearing me." He brushed his lips across my cheek. "Thank you for putting our baby first." He kissed my forehead.

"Don't put me on a pedestal. My pregnancy brain makes me a liability or I would probably force the issue more."

He chuckled. "I love you, Josie."

I leaned my forehead against his. "I love you too."

"I still have to get you in a chapel. Hopefully, before this baby arrives."

"That's a human thing. Vampires don't need that. We've already committed to each other." There was so much to do. The new government needed to be formed. I hadn't finished the council selections, and that had to be a priority. After the baby.

"You promised a chapel wedding, and we are having one. Soon." He pressed his lips against mine. If a wedding provided reassurance and stability to him, I'd wear a white dress for him, if we could find one.

A soft knock interrupted our moment like so many times.

"Come in." I sank back in the chair.

"My apologies," the guard said. "Livia is at the gate."

Thank the Gods. I pushed up out of the chair. "What? She's here? Let her in," I said. "The baby?" Vin extended a hand to me, which I accepted.

SUSAN PERSON

The guards' face turned grim. "No, she's alone, and she is very thin."

"Take her to the infirmary and make sure they give her blood," Vin said.

I threw a paperweight at the wall. It sank into the plaster and stuck. "The bastard took her baby."

"Easy. Let's see what she has to say," he said.

"Get Killian and meet me there."

"You might not be who she wants to see." Vin inclined his head towards my belly.

"I'll put a big coat on to cover it." Not that it will help, but I couldn't do anything else.

They met me at the entrance to the infirmary. I grabbed the white lab coat that hung just inside the doors. The guard pointed to the room they had Livia in.

The bed rattled. Livia shook like the cold embraced her. Straps confined her to the bed. The guards used the ones built for vampires despite her weakened state.

I put a hand on her arm. "Livia?"

She jerked it away.

"This looks like a detox."

"P-p-poison," she said.

"Was it the doctor and nurse from here?"

"Y-yes."

"And your baby? Do they have it?"

The palest of pink tears streamed down her face. Her body starved of blood. "Ezra."

"My father has your baby?"

"Took her."

Anger mixed with regret for letting him go. I knew better. "I'm so sorry, Livia. We'll get her back."

Her hand struggled to reach against the straps. "He wants

yours too."

My body twitched against my attempt to not react. "I'm going to give you something to rest."

She jerked against the straps. "He's different. Changing."

I imagined she'd suffered at his hands. "He's always been bad, but you're in excellent hands now. I promise we will not torture you."

I told the nurse what to administer and watched to make sure she followed it.

"Do not go without me." Livia's eyes pinched closed, and the violent shakes stopped. It would take a while to clear her system without draining her blood. She wouldn't be well enough to travel any time soon.

I turned and smacked into Vin's chest.

His hands landed on my shoulder. He pulled me close until my belly pressed against him. "He will not come near our baby, and he will not take you."

I rested my head in the crook of his neck. "I have no intention of letting him anywhere near our little boy."

"Boy? I thought they were all girls." His head leaned over against mine.

My heart warmed at his surprise. "Our little guy was conceived differently, though."

He pushed me back gently. "And you're sure?"

I smiled. "Yes, a vampire knows these things. I've known for a while, but I'm sure now."

"I thought they couldn't confirm it because the sac thing was too thick."

"They can't test through our embryonic sacs. A vampire mother can feel their child."

His confusion turned into a big, broad smile. "We're

having a boy." He wrapped me up in a bear hug and spun me around.

"Easy. You're going to pop him right out."

He set me down in slow motion and checked me over.

I laughed. "I'm fine. He's fine."

"What are we going to name him?"

"Not Ezra." My upper lip curled up in a snarl.

"Definitely not Ezra," he said. "We can't name him after my father, because we have no idea who that is. It wouldn't have any meaning."

His desire to find his birth father never waned. The searches I performed found three possible candidates, but nothing conclusive. I decided to wait to tell him until something substantial materialized.

"We'll figure it out together," I said. "Our little boy's name and your father."

"When Livia wakes up, I'll need to interview her."

"Yes, I need to figure out what they poisoned her with so I can ween her safely off."

"She's gone this long. Why not just let it keep going cold turkey?"

"Poison is different. The withdrawals can be much more severe. Her will to save her child is what has kept her going. Now that she is safe and knows we will fight for her child, her body is going to revolt against the punishment they have dealt it."

"If you want to go work on that, I can stay here with her."

"Thank you." I gave him a small kiss.

I asked the nurse to have blood ready for Livia when she woke and headed to my lab with a sample in hand.

The combination of poisons were rare and elusive. It took time to break them all down. My father had endeavored to keep her alive but compliant in a constant state of euphoria. The trace levels in her blood meant it had been a while since she'd had any. I could mix up some herbs and blood, like I had done for Natasha, and wean Livia off easily.

My new assistant, an old friend, brought my requests from the garden. One of my compromises with Vin. I'd stay away from the dangers of the garden. I thought it was silly, but I wasn't sure what the effects would be on the little guy if I accidentally ingested some. In the lab, the containment practices reduced the risk of exposure.

"This is it," I said.

"You cracked it?" Agata asked. "You know how to treat her?"

"Yes." I mixed up the concoction and put it in the glass bottle. Sweat beaded on my forehead. *Why am I sweating? Vampires don't sweat.* My hand went to my belly.

"Will you take this to the nurse and tell her one tablespoon every time Livia drinks blood?" I handed her the bottle. A rush of wet flooded down my legs and puddled on the floor. "Oh."

"Your water just broke." Agata's hand rested on my arm. "We need to get you to the medical wing."

I looked down at the mess and back up at her. Fear mingled with anticipation. I thought vampires didn't do this."

"You're going to be fine. Let's get you to the room."

"Vin is with Livia. Can you tell him?"

"Of course."

We took a few steps, and pain gripped me. I dug my nails into the wall. Dust shot out towards us. *What the hell is going on? I expected pain, but not like this.*

"Take a deep breath. We can move slowly."

A few more steps. Pain ten times worse than the original ripped through my abdomen. "Aaagh!"

"I think this baby wants to get out. Those contractions are close together."

I muttered. "Contractions..." *Yes, Natasha had them.*

A blur stopped in front of us. *Vin.*

"What happened? Is she okay?"

Livia? Oh. He's asking Agata about me. I'm she.

"Yes, her water broke and the contractions are coming fast." Agata's nails dug in, her grip on my arm the only thing holding me up.

"I've got you." Vin's arms swept me up and carried me down the hall.

"I can walk."

He chuckled against my temple. "I'm sure you can, but just today, let me think you need me."

"I always need you." My voice didn't sound like my own. Quiet. Not mine.

"Good to know." His lips pressed against my forehead.

Pain exploded in my back and stomach. I stiffened in his arms. "Aaayyyyyy."

"It's going to be okay," he reassured. "Do you know what medicines we should give you?"

"None," I said. "No medicine."

He lowered me onto the hospital style bed. "The doctor is on his way. Do you need anything?"

"Just to see my son."

"It looks like you will meet him today." Vin squeezed my hand.

"I've never felt pain like this." I gripped his.

"You are strong. You can handle it."

"You handle it. It fucking hurts." My free hand grabbed the bar on the side of the bed and twisted it.

The door flew open wide. Natasha came to my side with Agata a few steps behind. "Your turn." She took my other hand, just as I had done for her.

"Where's Emilia?"

"No need to worry. She's with her daddy."

"Good." Pain like hot pokers ran through my lower back and to the front. "Aaaaagggh."

"It hurts now, but you will forget about it when the baby is here," Natasha said.

Pain went up my sternum. I gritted my teeth. "Where is the damn doctor?"

"Right here." He stepped out from behind Vin.

"Something's wrong," I gritted out.

Vin and Natasha both snapped their faces towards mine.

"Josie?" Vin's eyebrows pulled as tight together as possible.

"Help," I choked out. "Baby." The word that made it out of my mouth through a gurgle. Everything went dark.

"Josie?" She didn't respond. I screamed at the doctor. Fully aware my voice echoed off the walls. "Get the baby out now."

"Nurse, get the instruments ready." Metal clanked against metal as they moved a cart closer. Scrapes grated in my ears.

"Josie, can you hear us?" Natasha searched her face.

No movement. "Josie, my love, hang in there."

"The baby is killing her." Natasha's eyes dribbled pink.

"Give us some space," the doctor said.

"Work around us," Natasha growled.

I stood frozen. *She did not let me end when Calidora called me. She will not meet her end today.*

"At least move up by her head," the nurse said.

Natasha and I complied.

"We're going to open her up." They prepped her stomach for the incision.

"I've been through it. I know what to expect," Natasha said.

My teeth clenched and ground. "Just save her and save my son."

"We'll do our best."

I grabbed one side of his collar and twisted, winding him closer to me. "You will save them both."

"Vin," Natasha hissed. "Stop." She pulled my hand from the doctor's coat.

I growled, but let go.

He sliced her open from hip to hip. The iron odor of vampire blood assaulted my nostrils. Red liquid ran down her hips and spilled over her sides. The baby wasn't visible. Panic thrummed in my heart.

Josie's head flipped back and forth.

"Should we give her something?" I looked at Natasha, not the doctor.

"No, she said she didn't want the baby to be at risk."

"Your baby is fine, and you were medicated." I pushed.

"We almost died from the poison, and my baby is also genetically engineered." She gave a half smile. The kind someone gives when they're afraid and don't know what else to do. Her smile faded. "And my baby wouldn't be here without Josie."

I nodded. I was being irrational. *Focus on Josie. Focus on your son.*

Josie's face lost color by the second. Her stillness eerie and unnatural. Her hand limp in mine. Dread spiked up my throat as bile. *Don't you dare leave me.*

A cry shattered the surrounding silence.

"You have a son, Vin. Look," Natasha said.

The nurse wrapped him in a blanket and handed him to me. He was perfect and healthy.

"Josie, wake up and meet your son," I said.

Not a muscle moved in her body. Not a twitch. Not a sign of life.

I looked at the incision. No healing. The fibers should have pulled together, or at least started.

"Can we give her the same serum she gave Natasha?"

"That was an antidote to poison," Natasha said.

"What's wrong then?" The baby cried, and I handed him to Natasha. I stepped up close to the doctor.

"A distressed baby can wreck the inside of a vampire mother's body. Her heart could be crushed."

Blood. She gave me hers once to save me. Mine would save her. It must.

I nashed at my wrist until blood seeped from it. I positioned it over her lips and let the blood run into her mouth. It started to heel, and I scratched at the wound to keep it open.

Blood pooled in her mouth.

I laid my head on her chest. "Josie, we need you. Our son and I need you."

Her chest rattled. A cough erupted, and blood spewed on me and the bedding. Another ragged cough sprayed blood on the baby and Natasha. A small amount of relief came to me.

"Josie?"

Her eyes remained closed. She was alive, though. I wanted to hold her, but she looked frail.

Our son's cries grew louder.

"Take him out and clean him up. Give us a few minutes before you bring him back."

Natasha bolted from the room.

"Josie? Can you say something?"

Her eyes moved under the lids.

Relief stilled over me. "Open them. I'm right here."

The separated skin on her belly closed the gaping flesh. *Healing. Thank the Gods.*

"I'm here. You're going to be fine. Our baby is fine."

Her eyes opened wide.

Her voice rough, barely audible but distinct. "Where?"

"Natasha is cleaning him up. She'll bring him back in a minute."

"Hold him."

"You will. Let your body heal, and you'll hold him."

"Now." Her words stronger but raspy.

All I could do was nod.

I looked over my shoulder and yelled at the door. "Natasha. Bring him in."

I grabbed a towel near Josie and wiped blood off of her face and neck.

The door opened in slow motion.

Natasha emerged with our son in her arms.

"Meet your son." I slipped my hands under his neck and bottom and placed him in my love's arms.

She let out a small sob. Pink tears rolled down her cheeks.

"He's perfect," she said. Her voice closer to normal. "No one will ever take you away from me." Her promise written as she spoke.

"Or me. I'll protect you both to my end."

"What do you think of Adam? It could be first or second name," Josie said.

"Seems appropriate for the first baby boy born in a hundred years." I touched his tiny cheek.

"Yes." The smile on her face brought me to my knees every time. She doesn't do it enough. She could have whatever she wanted.

I'm going to make sure she and Adam smile every day.

"Do you want to pick the second name, then?" She had to know I'd give her anything, but she compromised.

"How about Killian?" I asked and turned to Natasha. "Unless you and Killian plan on a junior?"

"Even if we did, we'd be thrilled for them to share a name," she said.

"Adam Killian Cavanaugh, we are so glad you've arrived." Josie traced her finger over his face. "Handsome. Just like your father." She touched his lip with her fingertip.

He bit down.

"Oh," Josie said. "He has fangs already." She held up her finger with two tiny droplets of blood on it.

"I didn't realize they came in that fast," I said.

"Emilia had them. We didn't realize it right away, but I think it's normal," Natasha said.

"Can we get this little guy something to eat?"

"I'll find a bottle and some blood," I said.

"I've got it." Agata placed a hand over my shaky ones. She poured the blood bag into the bottle and handed it to me.

"Do you want to feed him?" Josie asked when I held the bottle out to her.

"You did all the work carrying him. You've more than earned the right to first feeding." I kissed her forehead.

Her face glowed. She took the bottle.

He latched on to it right away and sucked down the blood.

"I was afraid he wouldn't take it, because I had such a reaction to blood in the operating room."

"That was vampire blood," Natasha said. "He obviously likes human blood."

"That is something we are going to have to tackle, but not today," Josie said.

"Not today," I repeated.

"We are going to have to invest in more bottle nipples, though." She held up the bottle with two puncture marks in the rubber tip.

Laughter filled the room. Warm, loving laughter. My heart swelled in my chest. Unneeded but filled with hope for our future built on love.

CHAPTER 35

JOSIE

Love changed with the arrival of children. Vin and I loved our son in a way I didn't understand possible before. The vampires and humans showered the children with love, too. The human children and our vampire children had structured play dates. With watchful eyes and structure, of course.

"He's getting big fast." Vin watched Leslie, the new nanny, carry Adam from the room.

"He's not growing as fast as Emilia," I said. "I worry about her. Still no word on Livia's daughter?"

"No. We're sending another team to the Chicago area, but the last three have found nothing." His eyes met mine and dropped to the floor. He and I both knew the only answer.

"I think it's time for the old team to get together for this one." My voice came out more confident than I felt inside.

"We have children now. The four of us can't all go at once." Vin shook his head and moved the papers around on my desk.

"If it was our child, we would both go, and I'm sure Killian and Natasha would be right there with us."

"You're right." He looked up.

"I'm always right." I smiled.

"That's a bit much." He chuckled. His laughter warmed me.

"Blood stores are running low," I said.

"Our original mission.."

I looked at the door between our room and our son's. "Yes, I don't feel right asking the humans here to donate."

"Some have offered," he said.

"Just not enough, and I can't mandate donations. That would make me everything I despise about my father."

"Not everything, but mandating it will drive many away."

"Exactly. How do we find the middle ground?"

"What about charging rent with blood as the payment?"

"And what? Offer our protection like a bunch of mobsters?" I chuckled. "They do need our protection from Rogues and other predators."

"What about animal blood? The animal populations are growing."

"I'll have to think on it," I said.

"Figure it out before we run out of blood," he said.

"Without a doubt, we will not be doing anything that resembles Ezra's rules."

"Good choice." He kissed the tip of my nose.

"I need to head down to the lab. We are really close to a breakthrough in my Mother's design." I stood and stretched. "If only her notes had survived."

"It's so interesting to me that she worked on it while Ezra worked on the opposite."

"Yes, if she had lived more than a few years into the ice age, we might be in a different place." I followed a trail of sun out the window to the courtyard. Voices drifted up. Peaceful. Happy. Life.

"We are in a different place." Vin slipped his arms around my waist and nuzzled my neck. A familiar warmth spread around me.

"I suppose we are, and we will continue forward." I leaned back in his arms and pressed myself tight against him. This place first bound us together in blood and ice, but it proffered hope for the future. "Our people will know their worth. All of them."

To be continued...

ACKNOWLEDGMENTS

This book started as a little nugget of idea in my head. Many family and friends listened as I rolled the idea around before I ever typed a word. To those who listened, I am grateful!

I was still unsure about the concept, because it was different than other things I had read and written. My fabulous critique group supported me through the dreaded imposter syndrome, and I eventually submitted to contests. It was the contest success and positive feedback that finally made me understand I had something special. To all those who read the manuscript in its early stages, I thank you. Your feedback pushed me to finish this book.

To my unbelievably amazing editor, Dawn Alexander, I literally could not have done it with out you. Thank you for always challenging me to do better and grow in my writing journey.

To my family, you have looked at covers, read blurbs, and given some of the tough love I needed to get this book across the finish line. Thank you for your never ending support. Love you all so much.

ABOUT THE AUTHOR

Susan Person is a multi-contest finalist in the paranormal and dark paranormal categories. Recently, she returned to college to pursue a degree in anthropology and graduated in May. Susan enjoys meeting writers and readers alike at conferences. She knew at an early age she wanted to write powerful heroines and fulfills that dream by writing badass empowered heroines who take charge in their paranormal worlds.

Susan grew up on a thoroughbred horse farm before moving to the big city of Dallas. She considers herself a Texan but is loyal to her home state of Arkansas. A lover of travel, she has visited several countries with many more to go on her list. She particularly loved dowsing at Stonehenge. The outdoors are a place Susan finds inspiration and can often be found in a park, at the lake, or on a road trip. She especially loves the mountains. Furry animals hold a special place in her heart, and dogs tend to seek her out as a friend.

Connect with her at susanperson.com

facebook.com/therealsusanperson
twitter.com/susanwritespnr
instagram.com/susanwritespnr
goodreads.com/susanperson
amazon.com/author/susanperson

QUEEN OF SACRIFICE

THE BLOOD MOON PROPHECY, BOOK 1

Coming in March 2022

Save humankind and make peace with the vampires. Easy enough for a witch, right?

Except for the fact, I'm a vampire hunter in love with a vampire who just happens to be a prince of his kind. Oh and don't forget his vampire father who wants to turn me because of my stellar parentage to create an army of witches under his control.

The prophesied queen who will lead the witches to peace with the vampires while protecting humanity. That's me. Brie Danforth.

The Blood Moon Prophecy says I must make a sacrifice of love, and my choice will determine whether I will fight for light or dark. My ancestors certainly think I'm worthy by blessing me with powers like teleportation which no witch has possessed in centuries.

I'm determined to keep my love, Nick, and choose light even if it costs me my own life. It's taken me a longtime to accept who I am, and I plan to stay this way. My coven will have to learn I will lead us, but it will be my way. They chose to shelter me from the truth, and I am the product of their decision. Now, I am the only one who can save us.

It will all work out. Even if I am permanently marked with this ancient "tattoo" on my arm thanks to The Blood Moon Prophecy.

ALSO BY SUSAN PERSON

www.ingramcontent.com/pod-product-compliance
Lightning Source LLC
Chambersburg PA
CBHW030550020726
47494CB00005B/1558